W9-BRQ-407

celebutantes

celebutantes

Amanda Goldberg

and Ruthanna Khalighi Hopper

St. Martin's Press

New York

www.stmartins.com

LIBRARY OF CONGRESS CATALOGING-IN-PUBLICATION DATA

Goldberg, Amanda.
    Celebutantes / Amanda Goldberg and Ruthanna Khalighi Hopper. – 1st ed.
        p. cm,
    ISBN-13: 978-0-312-36229-4
    ISBN-10: 0-312-36229-3
    1. Hollywood (Los Angeles, Calif.)—Fiction.   I. Hopper, Ruthanna Khalighi.   II. Title.

PS3607.O4375C46   2008
813'.6—dc22

                                                                            2007040440

First Edition: February 2008

10 9 8 7 6 5 4 3 2 1

To Wendy & Leonard and Daria & Khosrow

for everything

celebutantes

vanity unfair

1 hour, 22 minutes, 17 seconds since the last

Oscar was handed out for Best Picture of the Year.

aulie! Blanca! Lola! Christopher! Over here! How about one of the Santisi family all together!" the paparazzi shout as we're bathed in a meteor shower of flashing lights. It's blinding as we make our way down the photo-frenzied Red Carpet for *Vanity Fair*'s annual post-Oscar bash—Hollywood's primo party of the year.

My mother tugs my older brother, Christopher, and me to her and shoots her husband a pleading look. "Please, Paulie, just one of the four of us," her blood red lips purr, her Mediterranean-colored eyes sparkling through the smoky Paris-runway-ready eye shadow that François Nars *himself* applied not five hours ago at Villa Santisi. "We can put it on the Christmas card." Only my crazy Jewish mother would send out Christmas cards—from the *VF* Red Carpet. Even if we're not the perfect Norman

Rockwell family, my mother would like us to pose for the cameras as if we were.

I swear my mother could stand here all night as if she'd won her own Oscar, pirouetting and fanning out the skirt of her shocking pink ruffled satin Chanel gown for the photographers, canting one olive Pilates'd thigh forward ("Slims the profile, Lola, you should try it"). Even the black diamond Neil Lane dragonfly pinning back her shoulder-length platinum hair seems to be begging for a photo. She's acting like she's back in Irving Penn's studio posing for one of the many 1970s *Vogue* covers she graced.

My father rolls his eyes. "Oh, all right, Blanca, just one," he says, and smoothes out the custom-tailored Armani, a gift from one Italian to another—except that my father isn't *really* Italian. He's from Georgia. And Jewish. As for our last name? He changed it from *Sitowitz* when he moved to Hollywood to be more like his idol Marcello Mastroianni, whom he also happened to resemble when he was young—and thin. Papa's tux is camouflaging the 250-pound girth he maintains, thanks to nightly veal parm and spaghetti and meatballs in his corner booth at Dan Tana's. Make that 260 pounds. Poor Papa's been eating for two—his anxiety and his ego—for the two-month countdown to the Academy Awards. He wraps one arm around my mother and gloatingly pumps his little gold statuette in the air as more flashbulbs explode in our faces.

"Smile," I hiss at Christopher as he slumps his lanky 6'1" frame against me. With his mop of mussed dark hair and the green Converse high-tops he's paired with his tux, my brother looks more like a member of the All-American Rejects or Panic! at the Disco than the director of their music videos. "Do it for Mom," I say as the photographers bathe us in another meteor shower.

Freeze frame on the snapshot of my family on the Red Carpet—and where do I fit in? The picture on the late-night WireImage log-on after the after-party tonight is going to reveal: Me, Lola Santisi, a twenty-six-year-old member of Hollywood Royalty without a kingdom—or even a condo—to call my own, who's 5'7½" (in four-inch stilettos), shoved into a last-minute wardrobe emergency—a borrowed size zero beaded garnet dress that's two sizes too small, four inches too short, and makes me feel like the blond Ugly Betty.

"No more pictures," Papa declares. He waves the photographers away while he reaches into the inside pocket of his tux jacket for a celebratory contraband Cohiba Esplendido. He's choking that Best Directing Oscar around the neck like it might disappear if he doesn't hold tight enough.

Getting his second Little Gold Man after eighteen years (and after a string of box office failures and more gray in his beard than brown) is proof of what my father's believed since he was sixteen: He *is* the greatest living director. If tomorrow anyone's forgotten? He'll remind them.

I just wish my father loved *me* as much as that Oscar.

"I've got to get out of here," Christopher whispers. "See you inside." He disappears into the throng.

A photographer suddenly darts up to me in a low crouch after snapping 143 pictures of Jennifer Garner and Ben Affleck in a lip-lock. He must be a newbie if he's training his lens on me. No one's going to want any photo of me without my father. I freeze. Christ, no, not in *this* dress. I didn't have time to Polaroid.

Here it is straight: You never really know how you look until you see yourself in a photograph. That's why you should always Polaroid your party dress *before* you walk out the front door. You're in major denial if you think the mirror tells you the truth. A mirror is like a bad relationship. It reflects what it thinks you want in the moment, only to screw you with the truth later. I know. It hurts. And it never hurts more than on Oscar night.

Truth is, on my better days I'd rate myself at least an eight. Okay, so that would be walking down Main Street in Muskogee, Oklahoma. But we're in Hollywood. Here I'm about a six. Especially standing anywhere near Charlize Theron, who's ten paces ahead of us in a form-fitting ice blue satin organza and silk tulle Christian Dior heart-stopper. The chandelier diamond earrings tickling her bare shoulders are virtual flamethrowers, and the photographers are eating it up. She definitely Polaroided. *And* she gets to go home with Stuart Townsend.

I tug at the hem of my dress, willing it to grow, wishing I were wearing anything but *this*. All the false eyelashes, bronzing powder, and red lipstick in the world couldn't detract from this disaster. *This* makes Janet Jackson's wardrobe malfunction look like a walk on the Alexander McQueen runway. Not even a hot bath with Wayne Dyer on the iPod is going to alleviate the pain when I see those WireImage shots. These hand-sewn ruby beads completely clash with my purple eye shadow and my purple Louboutins, which so perfectly complemented the exquisite gown I was *supposed* to wear.

But nothing about this night—or this week—has turned out the way it was *supposed* to. I was *supposed* to get my Happy Hollywood Ending. My first and only Kate-Winslet-and-Leo-DiCaprio-in-*Titanic* kind of love—was *supposed* to be here with me. I feel like I've been stabbed in the chest with those YSL silver stilettos Nicole Kidman's wearing.

"Angelina! Brad! Angelina! Brad! Look over here! Just one more!" the paparazzi roar. Their booming, stadiumlike chant shifts from my family to the more impressive Mr. and Mrs. Jolie-Pitt, the top of the Hollywood food chain. Graydon Carter used this chain to create his Darwinian theory of staggered invitations for the post-Oscar party. The superior species gets the superior time slot. Angelina and Brad get in at 9:30 P.M., the winner of Best Achievement in Sound Mixing (no "plus one") at 11:30 P.M. and not one second before. At least she and her

Oscar weren't relegated to Elton John's viewing party at the Pacific Design Center with Paula Abdul and John Stamos. The day the invitations go out, everyone in Hollywood obsesses about whether they'll make the list and the most coveted time slots. For the record, my invitation reads 9:30. Okay, so it has nothing to do with my first name and everything to do with my last. But it sure beats watching *Barbara Walters' Oscar Special* in your Wonder Woman pajamas with that pint of freezer-burned Häagen-Dazs. Or does it?

My mouth is throbbing from smiling as we walk through the front door of Morton's. I'm desperate to free my hair from this facelift-tight chignon, grab a glass of bubbly, and find Kate, my BFF. The thought of braving *this* party all alone and without some liquid courage and my best friend is inconceivable. Kate's an 11:00—but surely they'll let her in early. Her red-hot client Will Bailey, a 9:30, just snagged the Best Actor Oscar tonight.

I don't know how I'll ever find Kate; Morton's is a mob scene. Every presenter, winner, and even the losers are here. Even if the fire marshal shuts off the electricity, J-Lo's two hundred carats of borrowed Fred Leighton diamonds will keep the place lit up. I maneuver through the smiling faces of Ang Lee, Al Gore, and Sandra Bullock, who are swarming my father while Mom beams proudly by his side.

Graydon Carter, the *Vanity Fair* man himself, is holding court in the center of the room. G. C.'s winged haircut is so impressive that it looks like Robert Graham sculpted it. "It's not who you say 'yes' to, it's who you say 'no' to," I overhear Graydon Carter say to Kelly Lynch (a card-carrying member of the G. C. Inner Circle). G. C. is *very* good at saying no. *InStyle* may have featured your five-million-dollar wedding at the Cipriani in Venice, but if your megastar other half is on location shooting in Toronto, forget about coming solo to *this* party. Think Russell Crowe's wife. (Don't worry, I don't know her name either.) Fax a headshot and résumé and send a 450-dollar Hermès ashtray and the answer is still no. Nope. No way. Not that it stops people from trying. G. C. reportedly even said no to one desperate wannabe guest who offered him a hundred grand for an 11:30 P.M. invite. The *VF* party is harder to crash than the presidential inauguration—though I don't know why anyone would want to go to *that*.

I squeeze by super-agent Ed Limato chatting up David Beckham and duck past Sir Elton. Guess even E. J. would rather be *here* than at his own party. As I dart by Dominick Dunne and Jessica Simpson deep in conversation, I hear him patiently explaining to her, "No, dear, you won't catch the *Avian* flu by drinking *Evian* water."

"Lola!" I spin around to find a certain Teenage Movie Queen, whose proclivity for hitting the hotspots sans panties has given her a second crown: Queen of the Noonie Moonie. She's placed her chipped Black Satin Chanel fingernails on my naked shoulder. At least she's no longer scarily skeletal after that unfortunate diet Death Spiral. Though she is a radioactive Day-Glo orange, another victim of the spray-on sickness that plagues celebrities during Awards season. "Great dress," she says with an aspartame smile.

"Thanks," I say, feeling a glimmer of prettiness rush through me. Maybe those WireImage photos won't be so bad after all.

"Couldn't they make it in your size?" Don't let it in. Do not let it in. The Teen Queen's flaxen hair extensions flick me in the eye as she barrels toward one of the few people past third grade that this dress would actually fit—her sidekick Nicole Richie—who's thumbing away on her Swarovski'd Motorola Sidekick.

Two piercing wails split the air: Madonna and Gwyneth's shrieks of panic when they see each other in the same shade of red. Stylists' heads *will* roll tomorrow. The screeching nearly makes me crash into Penélope Cruz, who's throwing rapid fire-Spanish in Alejandro González Iñárritu's direction.

Penèlope's face is pure Sophia Loren in *Two Women*. She must have stopped by the Soho House for one of their *free* Diamond Facial Acupuncture Treatments. No one wakes up looking like Sophia Loren. Not even Sophia Loren.

"Lola, get your ass over here!" I'd recognize that gravely voice anywhere. That crazy hair. That grin. Those dark old-school tortoiseshell Ray-Bans. I swear they're the same pair Uncle Jon wore to Passover dinner when I was eight. He's the only man in Hollywood who actually looks cool wearing sunglasses at night. He summons me with a magisterial wave from the prime-positioned booth at the front of the restaurant.

"I hate these fucking things," Uncle J whispers in my ear as he stands up to give me a hug.

"Yeah, unless you have a new gold man to add to the three you already have above the toilet," I whisper back.

"And now your dad has two. I always knew Paulie Santisi would be back on top. Come give your uncle some sugar." Hollywood's most famous satyr pulls me in for a kiss. At least this time Uncle J, who, I need hardly add, is no uncle of mine, keeps his tongue to himself. He makes space for me beside him next to Barry Diller and Diane von Furstenberg, who are on their third order of sticky toffee pudding with vanilla bean ice cream. B. D. and D. V. F. got the next best thing to a little gold statue tonight. They're among the 170 Carterwinian "naturally selected" A+++ specimens who were invited to watch the Awards over dinner at 5:30 P.M. The first and most touted time slot of the evening goes to those alphas not attending the Oscars, like Annette Bening and Sumner Redstone. They get to take home one of the light-up glass dome centerpieces etched with "*Vanity Fair*" to put on top of *their* toilets.

D. V. F. offers me a bite of pudding.

"I'm off refined sugar," I say.

"Aren't we all," she says, putting a heaping spoonful into her mouth. "We are so thrilled for your father, dear," she adds as she pushes the pudding toward me. It's easy to feel like Bill Murray in *Groundhog Day* during Oscar Week. It's the same people, same conversations, only different designer outfits. We were at Barry and Diane's house just yesterday for their annual pre-Oscar brunch, where D. V. F. was dragging my father back and forth like a pull toy across the lawn from Nic Cage's table to Naomi Watts's.

I spot a small gray notebook on the table tucked between an ostrich Judith Leiber pouch and the square sterling silver rose centerpiece. I flip it open. There's a silver pencil tucked inside so each guest can vote for their picks while watching the Awards during dinner. I turn to the "Best Achievement in Directing" page. Someone has passed over my father's name and has checked the small box next to Clint Eastwood's. I tear out the page and shove it into my Bottega python clutch. Can't you just see it in the family scrapbook?

I imagine the primo diners chomping on the ritzy restaurant's popular mache salad—sliced New York steak with French fries, haricots verts, and shiitake risotto—as they placed their wagers. Did *any* of G.C.'s Table One dinner guests lobby for my father? Surely B. D. and D. V. F. did, right? I envision Ronald Perelman lighting Amber Valletta's cigarette with one of the silver *VF*-engraved Dunhill lighters as he brags to Fran Leibowitz that Clint was just at his house in East Hampton. I can hear the sighs of disappointment that came from this booth when Julia Roberts read my father's name.

I contemplate reaching across to the adjacent booth to see if Francis Ford Coppola, Larry David, or Anderson Cooper checked my father's name. It's a good thing the dinner tables are being whisked away or I'd be running from table to table stealing voting books.

There's that waiter with my champagne. I lift the glass to my lips as I glance up at one of the plasma screens televising the arriving celebrity circus outside. My glass shatters on the terracotta tile floor.

SMITH's face accosts me from the big screen. He's flashing the photogs *that* smile that caused *People* magazine to name him their "Sexiest Man in the Hemisphere" (although that's such a mouthful I just call him S.M.I.T.H). He used to train *that* smile on *me*. Before he demolished my heart and gave the tabloids their heartiest meal since poor Britney's razor rash.

Oh God. Oh no. He's with HER. And they're—KISSING. I can't breathe. I'm going to be sick. After what happened four hours ago, I thought I'd be ready, but I'm *not*. I contemplate licking the champagne off the floor near Rachel Weisz's beaded Blahniks, but don't want to look too needy. SMITH and HER are everywhere. No matter which direction I turn, there's another plasma screen projecting their nauseatingly famous faces. I'm Alice riding the spinning teacups, and the ride is spinning faster and faster.

I feel the full frontal humiliation of an attack of the Unworthies coming on. You know, that horrible, sickening, sinking feeling that everyone on the planet is prettier, smarter, sexier, funnier, and better dressed than you. The Unworthies go into overdrive during public breakups (and with TMZ.com, is any breakup not public in Hollywood? Including my own?), box office duds, and birthdays, and they're positively rampant during Oscar Week. Symptoms include overdoses of Botox, Kabbalah, photo ops, couture, and Ativan, but I prefer the good old-fashioned assumption of the fetal position. I cast about wildly for something to keep me off that cold floor; my gown would clash terribly with the burnt orange tiles. I down Uncle J's scotch and water to stem the tide.

"Honey, you okay?" Uncle J covers my hand with his own. "You look kinda pale."

"I'm fine, Uncle J," I stammer. "I'm just going to make the rounds and get some air, you know?"

Uncle J glances up at the plasma screen, looks back at me, then arches that famous eyebrow and grins. "Lola, the only people you should ever lie to are the cops and your boyfriend," he tells me. "Take care of yourself, honey, and tell your father I love him." An unidentified brunette sidles up to him as I make my getaway.

THEY'RE walking through the front door. I've got to get out of here before there's a run-in. SMITH can*not* see me looking like *this*. And all *alone*. I spy Daniel Craig and wish he would helicopter me the hell out of Morton's and straight to Monte Carlo.

Where's Kate? I've got to find her.

Om, shit, ram . . . um . . . *shit*. I try to remember my equilibrium mantra to keep me grounded. Especially when I'm teetering on four-inch stiletto Louboutins and Natalie Portman's tiara is flashing in my eyes. Thank God I didn't borrow that Winston diamond tiara. Who can compete with Natalie Portman in the tiara department?

The mantra's not working. SMITH, Uncle J's scotch and water, and blinding tiara gems have me totally off balance.

I've got to get to that back room. I wobble my way through all the distorted faces. George Lucas and Arianna Huffington, Jack Black and Stephen Colbert, Carrie Fisher and Meryl Streep—all whirl in and out of focus. We're pressed so closely together it's difficult to move forward. I feel my throat chakra being cut off by the perpetual motion of checking over my shoulder for SMITH. I'm so focused on looking behind me I don't realize I'm stepping on Kate Bosworth's dress.

"Um, excuse me? Do you mind? You're on my Balenciaga," Kate trills, switching the ivory chiffon train out from under my stiletto with a spectral arm. I murmur an apology, but she's already training her full-wattage smile at someone behind my right shoulder, someone not Unworthy. I swerve around Adrien Brody, who's busy putting Donald Trump's number into his cell.

I step inside the all-white room. At last. It's how I imagine heaven. Especially since the Devil's in the other room. Every year Graydon Carter flies in an architect to yank down the back wall of Morton's and transform seven thousand square feet of dingy parking lot into an Ian Schrager monochromatic dream that makes the Coco Chanel suite at the Ritz in Paris look like a Motel 6. The warm, pale pink lighting is so supremely flattering that it looks like Annie Leibovitz lit the place herself. I'd love to flop down onto one of the coveted Mies van der Rohe white couches lining the perimeter of the room, but those lucky dinner guests snuck in here during dessert to stake their claim.

"Something sweet, miss?" The waiter holds out a silver tray laden with sugar cookies and fruit-flavored lollies with all the flawless faces of the A-list celebs airbrushed on them. Nice as it'd be to suck on Orlando, I gag at the sight of HER on one of the lollipops. I feel my blood sugar plunging. I bolt for the In-N-Out cheeseburgers piled on platters in the far right corner of the room. Kanye West lifts his candy apple red fur out of the way as we bite into our cheeseburgers, which somehow taste even better when you're wearing couture. Even couture that's the wrong size and color.

A man in head-to-toe black Ducati leathers and helmet ducks through the emergency exit next to me. I freeze; it's a member of a terrorist cell sent to wipe out all of Hollywood. My first instinct is to hit the floor. Since that's not an option in this dress, I instantly take cover behind Kanye West's lime green plaid tux. As I brace myself for the impact of a deadly explosion, the helmet flies off à la Lucy Liu in *Charlie's Angels* and inches in front of me stands Tom Cruise. Guess Katie's on Suri duty or maybe baking up a new addition. Is T. C. here to wipe us all out for having our shrinks on retainer and our pharmacists on speed-dial? On second thought, full protective gear isn't a bad option for a night like tonight. Especially if the only thing you're taking are vitamins. T. C. may have made the most daring fashion choice of the night. I wonder if he'd let me borrow that helmet.

A petite brunette waitress walks by carrying a tray of rainbow-colored cigarettes. What the hell; I grab one. I only smoke when I'm drunk. Or when I feel like killing myself, anyway. Tonight it's both. It feels so rebellious lighting up *inside*. Thank you, Graydon, for being a chain smoker. I blissfully exhale and watch my cloud of smoke mingle with Benicio Del Toro's—doubtless the only thing of mine that will ever mingle with the sexiest mumbler this side of San Juan. He gives me a heavy-lidded wink as SMITH and HER pulverize the only pleasure I've known all night by invading *my* back room. Suddenly I can't exhale. Stars swim before my eyes—not the celebrity kind, the I'm-about-to-asphyxiate-and-die-and-ruin-Ian's-décor kind. Please God, don't let THEM see me. Thankfully I spy Will Bailey, Best Actor Oscar in hand, clad in Prada down to his underwear. His shaggy hair and attitude is a flashback to De Niro in *Mean Streets*.

"Will, thank heavens," I tell him, grabbing the cuff of his tux. "I need you to shield me. THEY'RE here, and SHE should be Roman Polanski'd to a barren desert with no water and lots of land mines."

"Lola, hi." Will spins me in place and kisses me on both cheeks. "Guess what? Pacino just told me he's dying to work with me. So did Oliver Stone. And your father gave Christian Bale the part he promised me. I bet he's regretting that now. When do they start shooting?"

"I don't know, Will. By the way, congratulations," I say, nodding at the gold statuette he's clutching by the throat, wishing someone would just wring *me* around the neck and put me out of my misery. "I knew you were gonna win."

"That's what Kate kept telling me, too. Hey, do you know if Reese Witherspoon is here with anyone?" Will is scanning the crowd wildly. "Where *is* Kate? I have a buddy I need her to get into the party."

"What do you mean? I thought she was with you," I say, devastated by the possibility that my best friend might not be here. She *has* to be here.

"There wasn't enough room in the limo."

"So you just *left* her?" I say, panic rising.

"Well, it was my mother, my brother, my cousin, my buddies from Jersey. I would have put her in the trunk if I'd known it would take her this long. She should be here, for fuck's sake. I just won an Oscar. I shouldn't have to worry about this. She's my agent. I'm paying *her* to do the worrying."

"Kate will be here any second," I say, patting his arm. "I'll go call her for you, okay?"

"Thanks, Lola," Will says. "At least *you're* not letting me down." Christ. Actors. Will was serving pizza at zpizza before he met Kate! "Plain or pepperoni?" was the extent of dialogue he had in those days. Kate's the one who's championed his career. Scorsese was thisclose to casting Mark Wahlberg as the lead for *The Day Before Today Is Yesterday* before Kate waged her relentless—and successful—campaign to win her client the part. Will wouldn't *have* an Oscar if it weren't for her— and now he's mad that she's not here after he tossed her out of the limo!

I race toward the front door and speed-dial Kate, who's in full Vesuvius mode.

"It's ten fifty-five! The door bitch just told me to drive around the block for five minutes because my invitation isn't until eleven!"

"Kate—" I try to interrupt.

"My client just won an Academy Award! Will thanked me on national television!"

"Kate—" I try to interrupt again.

"Now I'm supposed to circle the *block?!* It took me a pink parking pass, twenty minutes, and two checkpoints just to make it *one block* down Robertson from Beverly. Bush should make Graydon Carter head of Homeland Security."

"Kate!" I finally scream.

"What!" she screams back.

"Will's tantrumming. And I'm teetering on *Girl, Interrupted.* Please, SMITH's here. Could you just ditch the car and walk?"

"Tried that. A cop shoved me back in the car. It's like Abu Ghraib out here. I'll figure something out. Tell Will I'll be there in five minutes."

Click.

My best friend just hung up on me, I'm drunk, I'm queasy from that In-N-Out cheeseburger, and from that seasick feeling a broken heart induces, and the bobby pins in this chignon are causing pinpoint hemorrhages in my scalp. I debate dialing Cricket, my BAF (Best Actress Forever). But how can I be feeling sorry for myself when my beautiful, talented friend is in her shoe box off Abbott Kinney in Venice having her own attack of the Unworthies, eating tofu out of the plastic container and obsessing about the latest audition she bombed?

Time to go to Plan B: an aura-cleansing minimeditation in the bathroom stall, regloss, and quick pee so I can get the hell out of here and over to Patrick Whitesell and Rick Yorn's after-after-party featuring the Leo crowd. At least THEY won't be there. Maybe I'll recover my appetite in time for that 1 A.M. Four Seasons catered breakfast buffet.

I open the bathroom door expecting my own private runway show. Or at least some starlet power-puking. Instead the only thing I find are a pair of scrumptious, strappy, four-inch silver Manolos peeking out from under the bathroom stall. I move in for a closer look to find the Blahniks cozying up to a second pair of shoes: black, patent, of the male variety, accompanied by what is now becoming audible moaning and groaning. I take a step back.

I am not at all morally opposed to a little canoodling in the commode. It is of immense cachet to have gotten it on in the bathroom of Morton's at the *VF* party. After all, the bathroom walls are teeming with the simple wood-framed party pics from Graydon's first fête in 1994. The photos are practically all that's left of some of the famous relationships. Remember Nicole and Tom, Bruce and Demi, Ellen and Anne? Of even greater cachet than doing the deed is to be the first to know who's canoodling whom *before* it lands on the cover of *Us Weekly*. I quietly kick the toilet seat down in the next stall and climb up for a better view. Our lucky guy's scored twice tonight. He's got a shimmering gold Oscar clutched tightly in one hand and a Mystic Tanned ass in the other.

Wait a second. Oh God, I recognize the Hawaiian Orchid polish on those toes. And that dress. Even if it's a tad hard to make out yanked up so high. And I *definitely* recognize the top of that man's head.

"Papa?"

My father cranes his neck around and blanches. "Lola, it's not what it looks like."

"It's not?" I say. "I think Mom would beg to differ."

"Lo-la," her glossless mouth sing-songs as her intoxicated brain struggles for what to say next. "Wow," is all she comes up with as she flashes me her brightest, widest, twenty-million-dollar smile. Wow.

My head is spinning. I feel faint. All I can picture is my mother's hand squeezing my father's—hard—the moment before Julia Roberts tore open that envelope. "It's going to be your night, darling," she'd whispered.

I stumble down from my perch and sit with my head between my legs. A loud rap on the stall door makes me slam my head up into the toilet roll dispenser.

"I can explain—" my father pleads. I can't listen to this for one more second. I've got to get out of here. I've got to find Kate. The bathroom door slams behind me.

Thank heavens, there's Kate rushing through the crowd toward me. But her face is drained of all color and her blue eyes look gray. Her dark chocolate hair flies wildly around her head. Her Marc Jacobs chiffon dress hangs limply, a feat on such a perfectly sculpted figure. She isn't teetering on *Girl, Interrupted*. She's full throttle. This is only the third time in the eleven years she's been my best friend that I've witnessed her G.I. Jane steely exterior crack. I grab her shoulders to steady her.

"You first," I say.

"My life is over," she exclaims.

my life in little gold men

was born the night of legendary agent Swifty Lazar's Oscar party at the original Spago on Sunset Boulevard—*the* Oscar fête before Graydon Carter grabbed the torch for *Vanity Fair*. My mother was mid-bite into Wolfgang Puck's not-yet-famous smoked salmon pizza and mid-reach for Dustin Hoffman's Best Actor Oscar when her water broke. My father was furious. "Jesus, Blanca, couldn't you hold it for a few more hours? I haven't even had a chance to congratulate Jodie Foster!" Mom was still in her Thierry Mugler one-shoulder black-and-silver sequined minidress when Papa took the first photo of us in the delivery room at Cedars. I'm sucking on my mother's boob and she's sucking on a Camel Light.

Being born on Oscar night is like being born on New Year's Eve.

Everyone has a party to go to, but none of them are for you. In fact, it feels like I've spent my whole life with that little gold man as the life of the party instead of me.

While my friends were celebrating their eighth birthdays at Chuck E. Cheese over foosball and pepperoni pizza, I was celebrating mine at the Oscars, sitting beneath glaring lights for three and a half hours straight, sandwiched between Nanny No. 5 and the seat-filler for Martin Landau, who never showed. I would rather have been with my friends at Chuck E. Cheese—but my father was nominated for his first Best Director Oscar for *The Assassination*. And at least I had on a great outfit.

I'd lobbied my mother for months for the short white taffeta Lacroix pouf I paired with a black silk camisole with white polka dots from Pixie Town and black patent Mary Janes from Harry Harris. I looked smashing. Ten minutes before we were supposed to leave for the Awards, however, Mom was still padding around beneath the Warhol portrait of herself in her vast walk-in closet, naked except for a glass of Dom in one hand and a Camel Light in the other. "Darling, Issey Miyake or Hervé Léger?" she asked me, oblivious to my father's screams for us to get into the limo.

"I love the molded red fiberglass Miyake bustier, but you'll never be able to sit in it, and you'll look more like a mummy than my mommy in that cream Léger," I said from my perch on the champagne-colored settee. Even though I was only eight, I had the inner fashion voice of Diana Vreeland. Either you're born with it or you're not. And I was born in Thierry Mugler. "Why don't you wear something of Karl's?" My mother had worn a see-through Karl Lagerfeld blouse with a plunging neckline and cream hot pants when she'd married my father in St. Tropez two months after they'd met at the now-defunct Yugoslavian Film Festival. She'd always done well in Karl. As for my father, the Italian Jew from Georgia, it took him going all the way to Yugoslavia to meet a nice Jewish girl.

"Perfecto," she purred. "Chanel. You're a genius," she said as she spritzed herself with her signature Yves Saint Laurent Opium perfume. I left her to finish dressing and dashed to my bedroom to grab my sketch pad so I could draw my favorite gowns at the Awards.

My father ended up winning his first Oscar that night, and I bestowed my own private Oscar for Best Costume to Cher, who wore a stunning Art Deco-inspired nude beaded Bob Mackie. My mother got an award too: a spot on Mr. Blackwell's Worst Dressed list. Even now, I cringe thinking about the close-up on her backless bright yellow Versace gown with one butt cheek peeking out. If only she'd listened to me.

Fast-forward eight years, and Papa's gone from Oscar gold to sour grapes after a string of box-office bombs. Our personal box office tally: My father was millions of dollars in debt, forty pounds heavier, and looked twenty years older. His iconic standing was in the Hollywood toilet and he'd been forced to take a big studio film, *Bradley Berry*—a major demotion in prestige—to pay the bills.

Mom, mortified by the loss of the best table at Chasen's and my father's drop below Michael Bay on *Vanity Fair*'s Hollywood power list, had taken to consulting a shaman to yank Papa's career out of the shitter—when she wasn't galloping off in her champagne-colored G-wagon with the personalized "om" license plate to the office of Brian Novak, cosmetic reupholsterer to the stars. She told everyone she was taking off for a spiritual uplift, which was, strictly speaking, true if by "spiritual" you mean "eye," "boob," or "ass." Christopher was skulking around Papa's Texas set with his super-8, chronicling our father's humiliation for his application to USC Film School. And me, I was about to date my first actor.

Papa might have been mortified to direct *Bradley Berry,* but I was thrilled to be spending the summer living on the movie set because my *Tiger Beat* cover-boy crush (who's now a star of *Titanic* proportions) was playing Bradley. I'd heard that Alyssa Milano had dumped Bradley for Justin Timberlake, and I decided to console him with the gift of my cherry. Sure, I'd played plenty of spin the bottle with Lukas Haas at home in L.A., but after where his career went post *Witness*—I mean, *Solarbabies? please*—I knew he wasn't cherry-worthy.

I met the Boy-Man Who Would Be Actor Boyfriend No. 1 at Aunt Tilly's Rib House at the production kick-off party where the cast and crew are supposed to "get to know one another" over free beer and ribs. That's code for scoping potential on-set romances. Who was I to break the tradition? I sent word of my interest through the time-honored chain: I told the costume designer I liked him, who told his on-set dresser, who told his hairdresser, who told his makeup artist, who told him. Two weeks later—which is like three months in the real world— while the crew snacked at the Craft Service table during the usual hurry-up-and-wait rhythm of a movie set, we were sneaking off to his trailer to rip our clothes off between scenes. "Hurry, Lola, I'm cumming. . . ." "No, wait, wait, wait, wait—"

Actor Boyfriend No. 1 gave me my first flannel shirt, my first Nirvana album, my first Marlboro Red cigarette, and my first sex. I wish I could say my first orgasm.

He also gave me another first—jail. I called Christopher frantically to come bail me out, but since he didn't pick up his cell, my parents had to get me and Actor Boyfriend No. 1 out of the Big House for underage drinking and "public lewdness," which I guess is what they call it when you're caught with your Hanros around your ankles in a bathroom stall at 4 A.M. After Actor Boyfriend No. 1 dared me to split the worm with him at the bottom of the Tequila bottle at the Hawg Stop, what'd you expect?

"Sorry, Paulie." Actor Boyfriend No. 1 hung his head sheepishly. "It was all Lola's idea." What?! How could he lie like that? He told me that he loved me! In the movie of my life, that was Narcissistic Actor Bullshit take one. (Since then there have been countless takes. Actually, I'm still waiting for the director to yell, "Cut!")

"Papa," I protested, "that's just not tr—"

"Lola! This is all your fault!" My father was livid. "My sunrise shot is in one hour. It's the most crucial shot of the movie." He shook his fist in my face. "If he screws up the scene this morning, it's on your head. I can't believe you would do this to me. You *know* how important the early morning light is to me." How could Papa believe his lead actor over me, his own daughter?

The moment I arrived at our Texas rental after being sprung from jail, I stormed into my brother's room to find out why the hell he hadn't picked up his cell. I found it buried beneath Kate Woods's pert ass—the bitch who'd been driving me nuts all summer and was at this very moment screwing my brother. I cursed my father for letting his bank loan officer's daughter intern on the movie as part of the deal for getting an extension on his defaulting second mortgage payments.

Kate and I had as much in common as Lindsay Lohan and Rachel McAdams in *Mean Girls*. She was a chocolate-haired, blue-eyed, lacrosse-playing, straight-A Preppie who took notes furiously on a steno pad wherever she went. And I was a fishnet stocking, Converse All-Star, and black eyeliner-wearing, PE-failing, straight-B-minus Preppie-hater, who was perpetually serving detention at Crossroads, my high school, for tardiness. And the only notes I was taking were in the margins of *Teen Vogue*. As I stood in Christopher's doorway, I had a strong urge to grab Kate by that long ponytail and yank her away from my brother, but an even stronger urge took over.

I stumbled to the bathroom and puked. I totally identified with the worm spinning down the toilet bowl, thinking about how Actor Boyfriend No. 1 had sold me down the river.

As I splayed out on the cold linoleum floor, Kate barged through the bathroom door, pulling on her kelly green Polo shirt and her matching Polo panties. The sight of her made me gag again.

"Your brother said to give you some of this," Kate said, rifling through the medicine cabinet and shoving a bottle of Pepto-Bismol in my face.

"Get it the hell away from me. I can't believe my brother screws someone who turns up her collar."

"Believe it. And the head's even better than the sex."

"What?"

"Oh I'm sorry, your boyfriend doesn't go down there?"

"Down where?"

"You're kidding me, right?"

"Wait—my noonie?" I exclaimed. I'll admit I was curious—when I gave Actor Boyfriend No. 1 my cherry, I assumed I'd get some of the sundae back—but now I was too pissed off to better my education. "You're such a fraud with the whole preppy, straight-A, president-of-the-debate-team thing going on. Truth is you're just the next Traci Lords," I said.

"Please, give me a break with your whole Marlboro Red, flannel shirt, Doc Martens, faux-rebel act. You're a spoiled prima donna from Bel Air." Kate folded her arms smugly across her chest. "And FYI, no one in Seattle in the real grunge scene would wear a Marc Jacobs dress from his quote-unquote grunge collection."

The assault against my beloved MJ dress was my breaking point. I burst into tears, black rivers of mascara running down my cheeks.

"I gave my cherry to Bradley Berry and he just tried to save his own ass by telling my dad it was *my* fault we got thrown into jail," I said.

"He's an actor. What'd you expect?"

"Him to love me. Like he said he did."

"Haven't you learned by now that the only people actors love are themselves?" Kate said, handing me a box of Kleenex from the counter.

"But I really *love* him," I sobbed.

Kate threw up her hands in frustration. "Please, stop crying," she said, climbing into the empty bathtub. "Really, I can't handle it. I'm just not very good with the whole emotional thing. Look, I'm a WASP. We just don't do feelings. My parents have been divorced for three years and still haven't told anyone because they're worried about how it will look." I continued sobbing. Kate pulled herself upright in the tub. "Okay, look. Your brother was my first. Don't you ever repeat that to anyone."

"I hate Nirvana. Don't you ever repeat that to anyone," I confessed.

"I once got a B in Latin," Kate said.

"I've never had an orgasm," I said.

"Neither have I," she said.

"Really?" I said.

"No, not really. I was trying to make you feel better," Kate said.

"I'll *never* feel better. He dumped me!"

"Lola, we're sixteen. It'll pass. And besides, you're too good for him," Kate said.

"Are you sure?" I asked.

"Positive."

"Thanks, Kate," I said, still sniffling.

Kate peered at me carefully as my shoulders heaved. "All right, come here," she said, pulling me into the bathtub next to her. "I guess you need a hug. And don't tell anyone about this either." Even though I knew it made her uncomfortable, she let me cry in her arms for twenty minutes. She finally pushed me away gently. "You're going to be okay," she said. And she made me believe she was right.

"Look, Kate, you and Christopher. It's totally cool if you—"

"Don't even worry about it. The only thing he's really into is his goddamn Super-8." I noticed that Kate was suddenly having her own mascara issues.

"You okay? I thought WASPS didn't do feelings."

"Screw you," Kate said.

"Screw you too," I said, smiling right back. "And you are totally wrong about Marc Jacobs."

We became best friends forever right then and there in that bathtub. Kate in her Polo shirt and me holding a bottle of Pepto—in a reeking bathroom in the middle of Nowhere, Texas.

I didn't see Actor Boyfriend No. 1 again until the Oscars the next year. He was nominated for Best Actor for *Bradley Berry*. The Academy decided what I already knew; he was a loser. But I was a winner in a black leather-and-lace strapless Chanel I borrowed from my mother for *Vanity Fair*'s first Oscar Party at the original Morton's. Kate, who was my date, was right about the whole grunge thing. Couture is clearly the only way to go. If only I'd listened to her about actors as well. Against Kate's sound advice and my better judgment, that night I locked lips with Adrian Grenier—before he was *Adrian Grenier*.

A couple weeks after the *VF* party, Adrian became Actor Boyfriend No. 2. Things were going so well two months after that, that he agreed to come with me to my senior prom—and was even endearingly enthusiastic about thumbing through my dearly loved fashion magazines in search of the perfect dress. (In the end, I just borrowed another Chanel from Mom.) I guess it was naïve to think he was actually looking at the dresses, though, because a week after the prom he dumped me for an Amazonian six-footer. The very same supermodel, I noted, that he'd found while trolling through my *Vogue*.

I'd dreamed of working at *Vogue* after high school, but after being dumped for a supermodel I couldn't bear the thought of having to face those living Barbies on a daily basis. My mother, who'd done her time with Warren (Beatty), Mick (Jagger), and Richard (Gere), found me sulking around my room and immediately packed me off to a therapist. "Lola, darling, take it from me, we must nip this actor thing in the bud."

Dr. Gilmore's office on Ocean Avenue in Santa Monica was a virtual duplicate of the Ivy At The Shore because Lynn von Kersting, who owns the Ivy, designed it. I poured out my heart to her from her petal pink chintz sofa. As Dr. Gilmore stared at me gravely from her beat-up 1920's French leather armchair, I found myself wishing she'd consider serving those Ivy gimlets.

After watching me doodling furiously in my sketchbook during our sessions, Dr. Gilmore browbeat me into applying to Otis College of Art and Design: "I want you to take those negative self-image issues and channel them onto the canvas."

Thirteen weeks and eight canvases later, I'd so successfully exorcised my supreme supermodel envy that I found I'd channeled Frida Kahlo in her most self-mutilating, self-loathing, self-portraits in my "Gnomic Mirrors: Inflections and Resurrections of the Self" class at Otis. Despite my mother's pleas, I'd stopped letting Anastasia wax my eyebrows and had dyed my hair jet black with Clairol Nice 'n Easy No. 122. Blondes have way too much fun to feel Frida's kind of pain.

My father thought Otis was a complete waste of time. "Why am I paying all this money so you can make ugly paintings like these?" he demanded, pointing at the portrait I'd ripped out of my own heart: "Broken Column," an image of me naked and crying (Adrian Grenier pain/Amazonian envy), bound by a Vivienne Westwood corset (distorted body image sprinkled with haute couture pain). "You should make pretty landscape paintings. This is a waste of your talent."

"I don't know what my talent *is*. I just want to find something I'm good at. And I think I might be good at this."

"Fine. You want to make art? Just make the kind of art that people give a shit about." A quick call from my father to his buddy Scott Rudin, and suddenly I was spending my summer break after freshman year at Otis as a Production Assistant on *The Red Tent*. Fresh off the box office triumph of *Charlie's Angels: Full Throttle,* Cameron, Drew, and Lucy were re-teaming in the feminist retelling of Genesis. "Do this and I'll keep signing those tuition checks," Papa ordered.

You'd think I'd have learned, but from the moment Actor Boyfriend No. 3 walked onto the set, I was a goner. I don't know whether it was the biceps flashing from beneath his flowing Old Testament robes (he was Levi), or the chestnut streaks in his beard and chest hair, but it wasn't long before we were knowing each other biblically.

Actor Boyfriend No. 3 made me forget that P. A. really stands for: *Please Abuse.* I had to get to the set every morning between 3:00 and 5:00 A.M., hours before call time, to make sure the thermostat in the director's trailer was set perfectly at 72 degrees. The director, who was only to be referred to as Captain, made me patrol the perimeter of his trailer daily, ready to beep him if his boyfriend approached while he was inside drooling over Rupert Everett's interpretation of Jacob. I had to make sure Craft Service had the glazed Krispy Kremes Captain craved after the delivery of Captain's pot, which the First Assistant Director had couriered to the set every Monday, and which they made *me* sign for.

Getting arrested would have been a relief. Each day brought fresh humiliations. Captain tore me a new one in front of the entire crew because I'd walked his teacup poodle on the asphalt instead of the golf course. "You know Cleopatra has sensitive paw pads!" That was nothing compared to the one Rupert's assistant ripped me.

Sonia held out the roll of toilet paper in disgust, as if it were a dead rat or Rite Aid moisturizer. "This is completely unacceptable. This cheapy Charmin imitation totally offended Rupert's ass."

I took a break from licking my new orifices to make Captain's Krispy Kreme run and pick up Kate from LAX. She'd flown back from Harvard for her summer internship at the William Morris Agency after finishing a summer session. (She planned to graduate in three years and be an agent at uber-agency CAA in four.) "You look like Morticia," Kate said, throwing her arms around me outside of baggage claim. "Are those huaraches? I'm surprised any guy would want to screw you looking like that," she said, taking a step back from our embrace. My BFF looked positively dewy, glossy hair pushed back with her tortoiseshell aviators, faded Levi's molded to her perfect ass. "What's going on with you, anyway?"

"This is what suffering looks like, Kate. I'm completely exhausted, Actor Boyfriend No. Three can't get it up half the time, everyone at Otis hates everything I do—and look," I said, pulling out a plastic bag from every pocket on my body. "For picking up the director's dog's shit. I resent your disgusting, rosy glow. What are they putting in your Cheerios at Harvard?"

"I'm working my way through the rowing team."

"I've missed you, you bitch," I said, squeezing her.

"No honey, you've missed yourself. The Lola I know is buried beneath this whole get-up you've got going. I want her back. Now."

Kate's always known how to cut through my crap. Just the sight of her was making me homesick for myself. I sucked as a P. A. and I wanted to be blond again. Kate got us to Frédéric Fekkai on Rodeo Drive in a record twenty minutes.

"*Mon dieu,*" Frédéric gasped, dropping his scissors to the floor.

Eight hours in the chair later, I couldn't wait to show Actor Boyfriend No. 3 my new sun-kissed tresses. Now that I was a California Girl again, I was humming David Lee Roth's song as I took the steps two by two up to Actor Boyfriend No. 3's apartment. Where I found him in bed—with Captain. Apparently Actor Boyfriend No. 3 wished they all could be California boys.

"Wait, you're gay?!" I gasped.

"Wait, you're blond?!" Actor Boyfriend No. 3 struggled to sit upright in the futon, knocking over a bong in the process. "Does this mean you're not gonna give your dad my résumé?"

"Hey, Lola," Captain said lazily from the other side of the mattress. "Got any Krispy Kremes with you?"

I never went back to the set. Or to Otis. I ate the Krispy Kremes.

Dr. Gilmore peered at me gravely over her Oliver Peoples tortoiseshell-framed glasses. "Lola, I'm afraid you're an Actorholic."

"A what?"

"An Actorholic," she repeated. "You're addicted to dating narcissistic actors because you're trying to work out a relationship with a narcissistic father who's incapable of loving anyone other than himself. As long as you continue to date actors, you're perpetuating a fantasy life that is blocking your chance at a real one."

"But that's exactly the problem." I shredded the Kleenex in my hands. "I don't know what to *do* with my real life!"

"Ah, yes. Career Deficit Disorder. It's very common with *Adult Chil-*

dren Of's in Hollywood." Dr. Gilmore leaned forward and tugged my sketchbook gently out from under my arm. "But, Lola, I think you *do* know what to do with your life," she said, flipping page after page of drawings. "I think it's time you pursued your real passion. I don't think you're a painter. I think you're a *designer*."

Dr. Gilmore was right—I wasn't cut out for the whole suffering artist thing. I'd leave that to Christopher. I begged my mother to get me a shot at her dear friend Karl Lagerfeld's coveted design team in Paris. I disembodied Frida and fantasized about embodying Coco. I mean, Karl—the man's such a genius that Kim Jong-il would look good in Chanel. There was just one little problem: There was one internship, and three of us wanted it.

My BGF (Best Gay Forever), Julian Tennant, had also begged my mother to recommend him for the position. He'd been my BGF since we were ten and collided while reaching for the last Rifat Ozbek studded belt at Neiman's. Julian and his mom were in L.A. for the Judy Chicago show "The Dinner Party" at the Hammer Museum. It was the closest Julian would ever get to eating pussy.

After our mothers separated us (Julian got the belt), Julian tugged at the sketchbook I carried with me everywhere. "Can I see that?" He flipped the pages and his raven Farrah Fawcett-feathered tresses in chorus. "This one's good—I like it." He pointed to my *Working Girl*–inspired suit. "But you'll get more movement if you cut the skirt on the bias. And lose the shoulder pads." He snatched up my pencil and made some quick movements across the page. "See?" Even though Julian was only ten, he was a maestro.

From that moment on, Julian was as constant a companion as a bi-coastal relationship would allow. Magnolia Bakery, the Met, Bungalow

8, and Julian's fabulous sketches from Fashion Week in New York. The Chateau, Fred Segal, Mann's Chinese, and my doodles from Oscar Night in Los Angeles. Hours-long phone calls debating the merits of YSL pre- and post-Tom Ford, colonics, and J.Crew cashmere. If I had to fight someone for the position with Karl, I was glad it was Julian.

We flew out to Paris together and met the third intern wannabe at Karl's atelier on Rue Cambon, which was as pristine as an operating room, with more interlocking Cs than at *Premiere* magazine's "Most Powerful Women in Hollywood" luncheon. Adrienne Hunt was five foot three and a size zero with a razor-sharp black bob. I fully envied her London accent and the way she smoked Gitanes as though she'd been clutching one in utero. The love affair ended there—full stop.

"Let's not do the fake friend thing," she'd said flatly, waving my hand away when I'd tried to introduce myself. "I earned my way here. You're only here because your mother called in a chit. You won't last a week."

I was determined to prove Adrienne wrong. Simply breathing the Parisian air filled me with inspiration, and my sketchbook was soon bulging with ideas. I was particularly enamored of a doll-size quilted shoulder bag I dreamt up while visiting one of Degas's paintings at the Louvre. That ballerina totally needed a tiny lavender Chanel hanging from her slender wrist. Adrienne smirked as she peered over my shoulder. "Designing for Mattel now, are we?"

"Forget her; she's completely wrong," Julian said. "That bag is *très jolie.*" Julian had been walking through the Tuilleries and was madly sketching a series of gowns he called his "Le Cabaret" collection.

Any visions we had of Karl transforming our copious batches of sketches into runway fare was quickly extinguished by Mademoiselle *tout en noir,* Yvette de Taillac, who'd been Karl's right-hand woman at Chanel since before I was born. We would not be speaking to the great

Ponytailed One himself. "Do not even look at Monsieur Lagerfeld," Madame Yvette warned us sternly.

Our job was to catalogue Karl's fabric swatches, clean out the sample closet, and rise at the crack of dawn to be the first ones at the Clignancourt to search for flea-market inspiration for the Oscar gown Monsieur Karl and his intimates would be designing for Marisa Tomei (so adorably tear-stained in *In the Bedroom*).

As the Oscar date bore down on us and Marisa rejected one sketch after another, we all developed migraines from the sound of Madame Yvette's heels pacing through the atelier, which reeked of fumes from the Gauloises the designers smoked nonstop when they weren't gnawing their fingertips to nubs.

"If only I could get Madame Yvette to look at this one," Julian sighed, pushing his sketch pad toward me. "This would be so perfect for Marisa, I know it."

I bent over the pad to find a rose-colored Folies Bergère ooh-la-la satin gown.

"Julian," I breathed. "It's exquisite. You have to show it to Madame Yvette."

"Do I dare? You know how she feels about the interns."

"Julian, this is *the* dress. Go, go, go!" I shooed him out the door and down the hall toward Madame's office.

An hour later, a dazed Julian returned, a trembling smile on his lips. "Madame said it was '*absolument magnifique*.'" Julian sat down on the ottoman in a daze. "It's a dream come true."

I squeezed Julian's hand tightly the next week as Marisa pirouetted in a slow turn before the triptych mirror, the skirt of the billowy rose gown lofting gently.

"Madame, I simply adore it. I knew Karl would come through. This is *the* dress." Marisa stretched out her arms and drew Madame Yvette into a double-cheek kiss. Madame cupped Marisa's face for a final lip-lock.

"We knew Mademoiselle would love it," Madame Yvette said serenely. "And now for the accessories." She clapped her hands briskly, and an assistant strode into the room with a velvet-lined tray. In the center was a pale lavender doll-size quilted shoulder bag. My bag.

"This was designed by one of our most promising interns . . . Adrienne Hunt," cooed Madame Yvette, sliding it delicately over the actress's arm. "You will agree that it is a very witty bag."

Marisa nodded approvingly. "It's genius, Madame, sheer genius."

I stepped forward. "Madame, that's my—"

Madame silenced me with a slicing look.

I flew down the atelier's stairs and ran back to the apartment, where I found Adrienne smoking a Gitane and turning the pages of a sketchbook. My sketchbook.

"Looking for this?" She exhaled a plume of smoke in my face.

I grabbed it away from her. "Adrienne, what the hell do you think you're doing? You stole my design!"

Adrienne exhaled a smoke ring expertly. "Please grow up, Lola. Nothing's original anymore. I'll admit I did get some inspiration from your little scribble, but of course I made the design mine before I gave it to Yvette."

"All you did was add the interlocking Cs to the front!"

I tried to enlighten Madame Yvette later. But she said she didn't believe me. I should have figured out earlier that Adrienne Hunt had been literally kissing Madame's ass. (While I'd been squandering my nights dancing at Club Les Bain Douches, Adrienne had been far more productively occupied at Madame's Right Bank apartment.) But our little *Dynasty* moment didn't matter anyway because Julian got the internship. I was crushed to have my fashion dream stunted, but Julian totally deserved it. And I flew out to New York to hold his hand when Marisa Tomei triumphantly posed backstage with her Oscar after the ceremony—unfortunately in a gold sequined Elie Saab with a shearling pouchette dangling from her dainty wrist.

Après Paris, I got a job as third assistant to the costume designer for the *Crash* sequel but got canned along with the rest of the staff when the director decided to do virtual wardrobes with a green screen. My line of reclaimed bamboo maillots with switchgrass appliqués turned out to be a little too biodegradable. I worried that even if fashion was my real love, maybe I was better at buying clothes than designing them. I enrolled in Scripps College, an all-women's (read: no actors) liberal arts school to study psychology because I determined I really needed to understand myself—and work through the crisis I was having with my inner Diana Vreeland. By my second semester I'd diagnosed myself as a Paranoid Dependent with Narcissistic and Avoidant tendencies. After that I transferred to Pepperdine because, well, the location was a convenient Malibu bluff overlooking the Pacific. I was going to major in Oceanography—I couldn't wait to update the look on those tired black wetsuits—but I was bummed to find they didn't give out credits for lounging on Carbon Beach or roasting s'mores at Courteney Cox Arquette's barbeques. The only class I found myself going to was Shiva Rea's at Yoga Works in Venice Beach.

Cricket Curtis, My BAF, and I met in Downward Dog at my first Bikram Choudhury yoga class. Even in the sea of unjustly stunning actresses in class, Cricket, with her pale green eyes, her poreless milky skin, and her unextensioned, *naturally* blond Rapunzel-like locks, was a standout: one part other worldly, one part girl-next-door. She managed to look radiant even as we dripped sweat onto our sticky mats in the one-hundred-degree heat.

"So what brought you here?" I asked when we ran into each other at the raw juice bar after class.

"I'm majorly blocked in my career corner, and I figured Bikram would really get all the toxins out and free me up," Cricket said, then leaned forward to whisper in my ear. "In all honesty, I'm also here 'cause I heard Brian Grazer was coming."

"What were you planning on doing, cornering him in the showers?"

Cricket smiled sheepishly. "Well, I guess I really didn't think it through. But I'm desperate. I moved here from Ohio to be the next Cameron Diaz and instead I'm parking her Prius at Spike Jonze's birthday party. I'm a freaking Valet of the Dolls. It doesn't get much worse than this."

"Look on the bright side: That black miniskirt tuxedo uniform with the pink bowtie is a real stunner," I said. "And it *does* get worse than that: Try having every Hollywood connection in the world and *still* being a total failure."

I finished giving her Lola 101 as we sipped our wheatgrass smoothies. When it was her turn for Cricket 101, we discovered we had a lot in common: absolute devotion to yoga (I'm totally devoted to those Hard Tail Rollover pants), a failed flirtation with macrobiotics (I couldn't quit the steak from Dan Tana's, but I still love the grilled seitan from M Café de Chaya), and an obsession with the Rose Bowl Flea Market. She'd been the face of Abercrombie & Fitch's print campaign, and I'd shopped there. But there was one thing Cricket had that I didn't: the most endearing, genuine sense of optimism and generosity I'd ever seen.

Cricket gave me a searching look. "You know what, Lola? I don't think you're a failure. I see someone who's creative and caring and who keeps putting herself out there and who doesn't give up. You're going to make it, Lola. I really believe that."

Looking into those pale green, guileless eyes, I really did believe that

Cricket really did believe in me. "Thanks, Cricket. You know what? I think you're going to make it too." As I said the words, I was shocked to find that I actually believed them.

The whole Bikram thing was totally worth having Anastasia's $150 Brazilian wax chafe murderously with heat rash for a week, because I met Cricket and she became my BAF (Best Actress Forever).

While I was shuffling majors at Pepperdine, Kate was now officially an agent at the Douglas Reed Agency. The boutique agency had wooed her away from Jim Wiatt's desk at the mega agency William Morris. She'd clawed her way out of the William Morris mailroom faster than Adam Sandler can get a movie green-lit, but the Douglas Reed Agency offered to get her out of assistantdom and make her a full-fledged agent—with her *own* assistant. Julian had gone from the internship at Chanel to becoming a design assistant for Oscar de la Renta in NYC to winning a spot in Gen Arts Fresh Faces in Fashion. His delectable ruffled satin draping and fishtail hems put him on the bullet train to his first major runway show. And Cricket had finally snagged her SAG card with one line in *American Pie 2* as Courtney, the Random Cute Girl.

And where did I end up? With a very belated B.A. in English Lit and a string of failed jobs on my résumé. My graduation present—make that a command performance—was as yet another third assistant to the costume designer, this time on my father's *Zorba the Greek* remake, a job he'd taken once again only to pay the bills.

When I arrived in Santorini, Papa was beside himself. He'd humbled himself for years in the commercial trenches (*I Know What You Did to the Babysitter's Pie Last Night*) to pull himself back into the black and then some. Papa had used up all the "some" to self-finance *Whispered Screams,* an art-house gem starring Maggie Gyllenhaal as the widow with scleroderma and David Strathairn as the mute gardener. Papa felt it was his best work in ages, but it'd put him back into the red and once again he had to take a big studio film to pay the bills. Universal had forced him to cast *People*'s "Sexiest Man In The Hemisphere" as his leading man—"a talentless hack who isn't fit to kiss De Niro's dick," Papa called him. And his leading lady Charlotte Martin, the Georgia peach prom queen turned Revlon spokeswoman, was still in Toronto filming her Farrelly brothers movie with only two weeks to go before principal shooting began.

I was scrubbing one of the extra's underwear in the costume trailer, dreaming of sunning myself poolside in the Missoni bikini I nicked from Mom, when Papa stalked up to me.

"Lola, I need you," my father said, tossing a script at me. "Charlotte is out of town until next week, and I can't hold off rehearsals any longer. You've got to do her part at the table reads."

"Papa, what do you mean? I can't act! The only thing I've ever played is an extra in one of Christopher's USC films." Of course, my father hadn't seen my turn as the Bearded Lady in *Zampano Redux*. He never watched any of Christopher's films, even though he has a screening room right at home with its own reclining red velvet seats and popcorn machine.

"Lola, *finito*. Just be there tomorrow at nine sharp." Great. I couldn't decide which was worse, being stuck scrubbing dirty panties in a hot, windowless trailer or spending twelve hours a day in a rehearsal room with Papa—Il Duce.

In my final hours before I had to walk the plank to rehearsal, the doorbell of my white and turquoise hotel room rang. I rolled out of bed and flung open the door.

It was *People* magazine's "Sexiest Man In The Hemisphere." Known to me from that day forward as SMITH. He was Steve McQueen in *Bullitt* sexy. Oh no. I was wearing my Wonder Woman pajamas and had

Sonya Dakar's Emergency Drying Potion all over my face. Uh-oh. I was in trouble.

I slammed the door shut and ran to the bathroom to rinse off my face. When I opened it again, I was wearing a lavender and white sarong and a white tank.

"Hi," I said, out of breath.

"You look gorgeous, but I liked the pajamas better. I have a pair of Superman Underoos myself," SMITH said. "I'd like to show them to you, but I'm really here because I thought it would be more comfortable for you if we met before rehearsal. I'm sure you'd rather be working your way through *The Lonely Planet Guide to Santorini*." His grin went straight to my groin.

Rehearsal was a total blur. The rest of the world disappeared. Even my father's directorial barks were muted. SMITH's was the only voice I could hear, the only face I could see. So this was what that D. H. Lawrence guy in my lit class meant when he said, "What the blood feels, and believes, and says, is always true."

That night I stumbled back to my hotel room, exhausted from twelve hours of rehearsal. When I stepped out onto my small terrace, I was shocked to find a table set for two with an extraordinary feast of warm pita with tzatziki, fresh Greek salad with kalamata olives, dolmades, moussaka, grilled lamb and vegetable skewers. A small white envelope rested on a plate of baklava. I tore it open. "May I join you?" I dove for the phone and dialed SMITH's room.

We had dinner overlooking the sea every night for the next two weeks of rehearsal. Occasionally we'd have our grilled salmon and dolmades in our pajamas. Sometimes we wouldn't even bother eating.

"Your face," SMITH said, tenderly cradling my cheeks on one of the nights we didn't get to the food.

"What's wrong with it?" I asked.

"It's perfect," he said. Who cared that he was ripping off Cary Grant in *Charade*? It was incredibly romantic. SMITH didn't need to steal anything from anyone in the sack. Okay, maybe he borrowed a little bit from Mickey Rourke in 9½ *Weeks*.

When SMITH took me to the moon for the first time, I called Kate.

"You're not Neil Armstrong. Please don't ever call it that again," Kate said.

"That's all I get? I came!" I said.

"It's about time. If you want more, call Cricket. I've got Sofia Coppola on the other line and it's almost seven-thirty. I'm gonna be late to meet Jeffrey Katzenberg for his second breakfast meeting at the Four Seasons. He wants Will to be the voice of Mohammad in his animated Koran project." Will Bailey had only been Kate's client for a few months, but she'd already rescued him from a sitcom opposite Adam Carolla and positioned him as the next Russell Crowe.

Cricket spent hours on the phone with me paging through *Sex Signs: Every Woman's Astrological Guide to Love*. "It says here that Leo provides the sexual stimulation Pisces has been seeking." Between rehearsals, I was logging frequent-NASA-flyer miles. In all honesty, all those lunar excursions were making me more than a little sore.

A week before shooting, Papa got the call from Charlotte's agent; she'd checked herself into Promises for "exhaustion," which nearly made my father check himself into Bellevue. We all know what brings on Hollywood "exhaustion": The inevitable disclosure to the *Star* by a "dear friend" that you were seen snorting blow like a truffle pig backstage at the Actors' Fund Nursing Home fundraiser. Followed by the embarrassing videotape of you behind the wheel of your Bentley, with your Venti Starbucks in hand, running down a photog staked outside The Ivy, then making a getaway in your bodyguard's Escalade.

In my father's depressive collapse over losing Charlotte, he mistook my red-hot chemistry with SMITH during rehearsal for an ability to act. My father figured he was such a brilliant director that he could even unearth some hidden acting talent in *me*. I had no aspirations of becoming an actress, only aspirations for SMITH. But the cold hard truth was that this was the most attention I'd ever gotten from my father. And I liked it. (Well, except for that moment during my first love scene with SMITH, when Papa yelled from behind a camera with lights glaring down on my naked body, "Lola, move your ass two inches camera right.")

When we got back to L.A. after the movie wrapped, SMITH had three months off before his next film, so I got his undivided attention. We spent every blissful second together. It wasn't about the Grilled Vegetable Salad at the Ivy (with the side of paparazzi) or the floor seats at the Lakers games at Staples Center with Tobey Maguire and Dyan Cannon. It was all about how SMITH made me feel like I was the only girl on the No-Longer-Lonely Planet. We'd have really intense conversations about how much he adored me, global warming, and his Chris McMillan haircut. He'd read me *People* magazine in the bathtub before bed. And we'd rarely leave the moon before noon. "Lola, you complete me," he told me tenderly. Who cared that he was ripping off *Jerry Maguire?*

I was Ali McGraw in *Love Story,* thank God without the terminal illness. Then the reviews for our movie hit the newsstands and terminal illness seemed like a fabulous idea. Instant death? Even better. *The Hollywood Reporter* proclaimed, "Lola Santisi swallows her words, and maybe that's a good thing." *Variety* screamed, "Just Say No to Lo!" *People* magazine devoted five pages to the evils of nepotism, with me as Exhibit A: "When Bad Daughter Actresses Happen to Good Daddy Directors."

I longed for SMITH to hug me and tell me those stupid reviews were meaningless and that what really mattered was us. But he was in Toronto filming a cameo for a Doug Liman film. When his assistant, Kevin, called to say he had something he needed to drop by for me, I envisioned the pavé pink, yellow, and white diamond Cartier trinity ring SMITH and I had window-shopped, or maybe a box of marshmallow cream-filled chocolate cupcakes from Joan's on Third.

When Kevin showed up with only a small white envelope, I revised my wish list. A massage at The Peninsula? A gift certificate to Maxfield? No, of course: a plane ticket to fly to SMITH pronto. I ripped it open.

> *Dear Lola,*
> *I know you'll understand that at this point in my career, I*
> *can't be associated with the bad press surrounding you.*
> *We'll always have Greece.*
> *Fondly,*
> *Me*

I fell to the floor. It felt like every bone in my body was breaking. I crawled to the phone and dialed SMITH's number, then pressed the receiver to my ear. When the line started ringing, I heard the chirp of a nearby cell phone ring too.

"It's me, Lola. He had all his calls forwarded to my cell phone," Kevin said, looking at me pitifully from my doorway where he was still standing with his cell to his ear. "He doesn't want me to leave without packing up his stuff."

It hit me like a level five hurricane. SMITH was dumping me because of bad press? How was this possible? No! How would I *ever* get over him? And this time I *did* care that he was ripping off Bogart in *Casablanca*.

I unplugged my phone, tossed my cell in the hamper, and took to my bed for days, emerging only for the occasional sip of water. I refused all visitors. It was a toss-up: strangle myself with my hot pink lace Cosabella undies or do a Virginia Woolf by loading my pockets with rocks and drowning myself. Maybe the pond at the Hotel Bel Air with the swans? Or the Roosevelt Hotel's Hockney-painted swimming pool?

After several days—I lost track of how many—I was abruptly disturbed from my deep depression by the overwhelming smell of smoke. What a relief it would be to go up in flames. Then came hushed voices in a foreign tongue. Perhaps I'd already died and was entering a strange land of mystics.

"Darling," my mother whispered in her most soothing voice.

I blearily focused my eyes on the alarmed faces of my mother, my father, Christopher, a mysterious man in pristine white kutras and turban, and a few others I couldn't quite make out. They all huddled over me with auras of bright white light glowing above their heads.

"Am I dead?"

"No, sweetie, you're not dead." Kate's face appeared from behind Christopher. "Can we hurry this thing along? I have a signing meeting in an hour."

"Is my apartment on fire?"

"No, we're eradicating the negativity created by your experience on Papa's film," my mother, in her red-for-empowerment vintage Zandra Rhodes caftan, said in her I-haven't-meditated-in-days-because-of-all-the-stress voice. "Isn't that right, Doctor Freedman?"

"Doctor Freedman?" I said weakly. "The Dalai Lama's a Jew?"

"You can call me by my spiritual name, Doctor Singh," said Dr. Freedman.

"He's from Brooklyn," Cricket said as she peered over Papa's shoulder. "We're here for you."

Dr. Freedman took my right hand in his, placed his other hand over my heart, and closed his eyes. "I want everyone to close his or her eyes now. Breathe."

"Yes, breathe," my mother said, squeezing my other hand.

"Feel the love and support of the room and take that love and let it into your heart," Dr. Freedman said. I peeked one eye open, taking in my mother, brother, and father holding hands with their eyes closed, earnestly trying to project love and healing on my behalf. A tear of gratitude rolled down my cheek. It was actually working. I was beginning to feel transformed. I was about to close my eyes again and drop into the tender feeling of this perfect love when the serenity of the moment was broken by a familiar sound.

"Kate!" The human chain of love was instantly broken by the sound of her unabashedly thumbing away on her BlackBerry.

"Look, Lola, they're burning all your bad reviews and all your photos of SMITH, okay? It's time to move on." Dr. Singh had his turbaned assistants feeding every last memento of SMITH into my fireplace.

"Stop them! Those photos are all I have left!" I shrieked, lunging toward the fireplace as Christopher leapt to restrain me.

"Well, obviously A. O. Scott was wrong about your emotional range." Kate had finally lost her patience with me.

Papa leaned in toward me. "Lola, why don't you think about me for a second here? You ruined my movie."

Christopher threw up his hands in disgust. "This isn't about you, Papa! We're here for Lola."

"I hate Hollywood. I don't want to hear about one more movie or one more actor for as long as I live. I want to get out of here," I wept.

Which is how I found myself on a two-day trek on Air India to Indira Gandhi International Airport in Delhi. I felt lighter the moment the plane began its ascent, mostly because in an attempt to leave the material world behind, I'd adamantly refused the Vuitton suitcase my mother had packed for me. Just the thought of walking the land of Gandhi put me into a still reverie.

Three weeks—or was it three months? Time had lost all meaning here—into the trip, I found myself in a vibrant purple cotton sari, covered in puzzling bug bites, drowning in the stink of unwashed feet and patchouli, and lying on some strange ashram floor surrounded by dozens of other purple-clad, chanting strangers. As my body dripped with sweat and clenched from dysentery, I wondered if this was how you got to nirvana, and if they'd have Kiehl's Facial Fuel there. I wanted to grab Sai Baba by his dingy dhoti and beg him to send me home, but I was too weak to crawl across the reeking mats. By some celestial miracle, a beautiful man in an orange sari appeared, presenting me with a portable telephone.

"It's Julian Tennant for Lola Santisi," he said in perfect English.

"Hello," I croaked into the receiver in disbelief.

"You can come home now. You're yesterday's headlines."

"Have you heard anything about SMITH?" His well-being suddenly seemed more important than my own.

Julian's sigh of disapproval hissed over the crackling connection. My poor BGF had called me nightly and borne God knows how many hours of my heartbroken rants, running up a phone bill comparable to the rent on his SoHo loft. "I was about to rescue you from the murky obscurity and dreadful thread counts of your dingy little ashram, but I might have to rethink that now."

"I've been engulfed in mantras of love and compassion here. Now I can't take one more second of it. I can't eat one more bite of chana masala. I miss my bathtub, my bed, and the chopped salad from La Scala. I can't have one more deep thought. It's exhausting," I wailed.

"Well, Lo, I may have the perfect dose of superficiality for you. Do you know about these Hollywood Ambassadors?"

"If Hollywood does have an ambassador, they should be fired because it's the most unfriendly, merciless city in the world," I said through my tears. Self-pity has always been my forte.

"Apparently it's not enough *The Times* and *Women's Wear Daily* gave my last collection rave reviews or that I won the Council of Fashion Designers of America Perry Ellis Award for best new designer for ready-to-wear. All that matters to my investor is which celebrities will be wearing my designs during Oscar Week. No one, not even in Hollywood, can remember who won Best Supporting Actress a day later. But everyone remembers Gwyneth Paltrow in her bubblegum pink Ralph Lauren ballerina dress. And Hilary Swank's Million Dollar back in that backless sapphire Guy Laroche. Which means I have to get myself a quote-unquote ambassador who will get these Hollywood divas in my clothes for the Oscars."

"Julian—" I tried to interrupt.

"The free Oscar press in every magazine from *InStyle* to *Time* to *Hello!* is totally invaluable. And it seems like every designer from Cavalli to Valentino has an ambassador." Julian's voice had become a tight-throated keen. "I want you to be mine. It's time for you to get back into fashion. You're wasting away your talent in India."

"Oh God, Julian, I don't think so. It sounds awful. No." I sniffled.

Silence.

"Julian?"

I could hear his breaths getting deeper—or was he hyperventilating?

"I'm going to say it: I need you, okay? I'd rather give up my limited edition signed Murakami Vuitton sneakers than have to admit it, but you are the only one who can help me. You know what looks good on people and you've spent your whole life surrounded by actresses, you know how to talk to them. And you'll be able to convince them to wear me. If I can break onto the Red Carpet, I can break into the big time.

Now hurry up and say you'll help me. We only have six weeks before the Oscars."

Become a Hollywood Ambassador? Convincing celebrities to do *anything* is a nightmare—especially to wear the designer you're peddling on Hollywood's most significant night of the year. But at least I'd be back in fashion. Maybe I wasn't cut out to design clothes, but Julian was right: I've always known what looks good on people. And being a Hollywood Ambassador was a start. Especially if I was going to conquer my Career Deficit Disorder.

Besides, I was broke. Selling-my-mother's-last-season's-hand-me-down-Chanel-on-eBay-to-pay-the-rent broke. And there was no way I'd ever ask my parents for money. It was time to grow up.

Also, how could I say no to my BGF? He needed me.

"I'll be on the next flight out."

"Are you in costume for your next film?"

I was face-to-face with a pair of five-inch black stilettos at the British Airways gate at Heathrow Airport. I was lying on top of my carry-on in the crowded terminal for the three-hour layover for the flight home from India. I panned up those bird legs. Of course *Adrienne Hunt* had on the *perfect* little black dress. I was so behind on my fashion magazines I couldn't immediately decipher the designer. Just the sight of her was enough to vaporize all those mantras of love and compassion. I leapt to my feet. She may have had the outfit advantage, but I was taller—in *flats*.

I willed myself not to look down at the sweat-drenched two-dollar sari I'd been wearing for weeks. "Actually it's a Commes Des Garçons number I picked up at Colette in Paris," I said.

Adrienne raised an eyebrow. "Really? So what's on your agenda? When *can* we expect you on the big screen again?"

"I'm finished with acting," I said.

"What a shame. I'm sure Hollywood's weeping at the loss," she said, exhaling one of her perfect smoke rings. I wanted to rip that damn Gitane out of her red-painted lips and light her flat ass on fire.

"What are you doing on this flight?" I asked. "I thought you said you'd never step foot in the silicone city."

"I'm making an exception—for *Miuccia*," Adrienne said. "She was practically on her hands and knees begging me to help her dress people for the Oscars, how could I say no? Plus it sure beats that pauper's pay at *British Vogue,* and Miuccia's arranged for me to stay at Madonna's house while she's in London."

Of *course.* Her little black dress. Pure *Prada.* Lord only knows who that talentless bitch stabbed or stole from to get that gig. What was I thinking, agreeing to be Julian's Hollywood Ambassador? Go head-to-head with Adrienne Hunt?

Wait. Maybe this was my chance for revenge—*at last.* "How lovely for you, Adrienne," I smiled serenely. "Actually, I'm doing the same thing as you for Julian Tennant."

"Julian? Oh, that's so *cute!* I'll give you a tip for old time's sake: I hear Denise Richards doesn't know who she's wearing yet," she said, practically slicing me with her razor sharp bob as she turned to board. "I'll try and send you back a warm cookie from first class. I assume you're flying coach."

Did those stilettos wobble just a little bit as Adrienne headed down the gangway? *Girl,* I thought, *it is so on.*

The second we landed at LAX, I drove straight to Dr. Gilmore's office.

"So what if Adrienne Hunt has a B.A. in bitchiness, a Masters in manipulation, *and* a Ph.D. in backstabbing?" I said, looking searchingly at

Dr. Gilmore for reassurance. "We're not in Paris anymore. This is *my* town. I'm not going to let *her* stop me from conquering my CDD. No way. I *need* this job. I can totally *do* this job." I dropped my face into my hands. "I *can* do this job, right? Oh God. I don't think I can do this. I'll have Kate call Julian and tell him that I went into anaphylactic shock from the chicken cacciatore on the plane and died."

"That's very creative, Lola. But you know I don't condone your lying."

"Doctor Gilmore, if you met Adrienne, you might feel differently. You'd probably drive me straight back to the airport *yourself*."

"Lola, your issues will stay with you wherever you go—even in India. It's important for you to face your life. And as you pointed out, this is a good opportunity for you to work on conquering your CDD. And I'm glad to hear you're getting back into fashion. You've got the talent. Now you just have to make it work. And I just have to ask, how's your Actorholism going?"

"I'm 151 days sober," I said. "Of course, they weren't filming any Bollywood movies at Sai Baba's ashram."

"I'm proud of you, Lola. You're doing great, kiddo," she said, standing up.

"Promise?"

"Lola, I have confidence in you and so does Julian. We need to keep working on your not believing in yourself because that's what keeps you stuck in your CDD and your Actorholism."

"So I can do this, Dr. Gilmore?"

"Lola, life's hard. Get a helmet."

"Didn't Jennifer Aniston say that?"

"She must have a good therapist," Dr. Gilmore said, smiling. "Now go get some sleep. You've got a lot of work ahead of you."

Dr. Gilmore held the door open for her next client, some guy who was kind of cute in that Paul Rudd way. He gave me that therapy comrade smile—he was going in to battle his issues and I'd just come back from the war. Jeans—*unidentifiable*—not Seven, Paper Denim, *or* Blue Cult. Sneakers—*unidentifiable*—not All-Stars, adidas, *or* Puma. I don't think he even had any product in his hair. What was a guy like that doing *here?* He looked so *normal*.

I suddenly caught myself staring at Therapy Guy and quickly averted my eyes. As he walked inside Dr. Gilmore's office, I realized I wasn't sure I was ready to leave the safe arms of her office and re-enter Planet Hollywood. Was I going to be able to get anyone to wear Julian Tennant down that Oscar Red Carpet in six weeks? Was I really finally ready to conquer my Career Deficit Disorder and my Actorholism *for good?*

Yes. I took a deep breath, opened Dr. Gilmore's office door, and walked out.

sunday

176 hours, 12 minutes, 48 seconds until

the Oscar for Best Supporting Actor is handed out.

t's 8 A.M. on Sunday morning. It's 80 degrees and sunny. Of *course* it's 80 degrees and sunny—just like every other day in Hollywood. Even in the middle of February. I'd normally be deep in REM, but the Oscars are in seven days. So instead I'm on my hands and knees on a white shag carpet in the master bedroom of a Malibu mansion on Carbon Beach. I wish I could say Jake Gyllenhaal was behind me. My fingers are bloody from pinning the hem of a duchess satin silver strapless floor-length Julian Tennant gown on Candy Cummings. The looped-out, electric blue-haired, loud-mouthed British rock star is nominated for an Oscar for Best Song for Quentin Tarantino's *Kill Bill Volume 6*.

It's come down to this: I've spent more than a month banging my fists and head on stars' doors, trying to get them to wear one of Julian's gorgeous gowns down the Oscar Red Carpet. Julian's been defaulting sleep, health, and hygiene, working his fingers to the nub while I've been squaring off against countless other fashion ambassadors who are begging, bribing, and blackmailing the celebs to wear *their* designers. I got thisclose to Kirsten Dunst, Salma Hayek, and Emily Blunt. Got the bum's rush from Jennifer Connelly, Helen Mirren, and Beyoncé. I even begged and pleaded with my mother to wear Julian, but she refused: "Darling, you know how much I'd love to help, but Karl's my oldest, dearest friend. You know I have to wear Chanel." My last three hopefuls are:

1. Candy Cummings, who makes Britney Spears look like a NAMI poster child.
2. Scarlett Johansson, who just rescheduled, for the twelfth time, the final fitting we were supposed to have this afternoon. Julian practically took plaster casts of Scarlett's famous boobs to dream up the exquisite red ruffled lace gown that serves up her exquisite orbs like bonbons from Edelweiss Chocolates.
3. Olivia Cutter, the uncommitted grand prize Best Actress Nominee, who *all* the designers are stabbing each other's eyes out with their shears to dress.

And as if *that* wasn't enough to give me an ulcer, I'm also dressing Jake Jones—the pot-smoking, Forty Deuce dancer-dating, Celebrity Poker Showdown-playing *actor*—for the annual General Motors Ten fashion show and Pre-Oscar party. Jake's canceled, six times, the fitting we were supposed to have a week ago, and the GM show is in *two* days. God knows the last thing I want to do is dress an *actor,* but it's a great opportunity for Julian.

Candy insisted our fifth fitting take place at this ungodly hour on my brother's music video set for her latest single, "Bleep Off Mother F***er," because Christopher helped me to convince her to wear Julian Tennant for her performance at the Oscars. That is, if I can survive this hell.

"Isn't this glitter a-*maz*-ing? Look at all these pre-tty co-lors," Candy Cummings slurs as her attention shifts from the hand-sewn bugle beads around her bust to the rainbow assortment of fifty MAC micro-fine "Lust Dust" vials on the makeup table. She begins to pour the vials onto the white shag one by one. I watch in complete torment as the glitter forms a glistening mound of thousands of dollars' worth of makeup on the floor. Celery, her makeup artist, looks unfazed. I guess this is just another normal day at the office.

"Don't worry, we'll pay for it," her manager whispers from the corner of the room.

Before I can stop her, Candy splatters "Pinklette" glitter down the front of Julian's gown, turning a dress worthy of a sultry Marlene Dietrich into a kindergartner's splatter painting.

"Oh shit!" I gasp.

"You're paying triple for that one," Celery tells the manager. "It's discontinued, and I had to pay through the nose on eBay to get it."

I dab frantically at the glitter, which simply adheres more tenaciously to the satin bodice. "How am I going to get this out?" I ask no one in particular.

"It was too long anyway," Candy snaps as she grabs a pair of scissors from the makeup table. Before I can stop her, she's hacked the floor-length gown up to crotch level. It's safe to assume that ABS won't be peddling their knock-off of *this* dress along with Ashley Judd's $10,000 J. Mendel on *The View* the Monday morning after the Oscars. So what if the cheap copy will disintegrate the second you bend over to eat that extra leaf of arugula? You'll be saving yourself at least 9,800 dollars, or 9,700—I don't know, I was never very good at math.

"I l-u-u-u-v-e it," the dazed punk rocker slurs and then plummets face forward into the shimmering Pollock of glitter on the floor. Her Frederick's of Hollywood turquoise patent stripper pumps hang off her ankles by the studded straps.

"Oh my God!" I scream. "Someone call 911!" Neither the manager, Celery, nor Candy Cummings's assistant moves a muscle. Apparently these swan dives are a regular occurrence.

Christopher comes tearing into the room like Jack Nicholson in *One Flew Over the Cuckoo's Nest*, dark hair ruffled, eyes glazed, and the faint gleam of sweat above his lip and brow. "Is she dead?"

"She better be. If she's not, I'll stab her with those scissors for butchering Julian's dress," I say.

"She's not dead," a defeated Celery mutters, trying in vain to rescue the $100-a-pot glitter from beneath Candy's prostrate form. "This is the third time this has happened in the past two hours, but she just outdid herself. This stuff sticks like crazy. It's going to take me an hour just to get it off her face." So *this* is why Celery gets $10,000 a day. I should call Julian ASAP and tell him he's underpaying me by 100 percent.

Christopher leads me off to a corner for a hushed powwow. "I'm totally screwed, La-la," he says in a strained voice.

"Me too."

"How screwed are you? Distract me from how screwed I am," Christopher says.

"Look at what she's done to the dress. How am I going to explain this to Julian?"

"Okay, enough about you," Christopher says, gnawing his index fingernail. He rubs his hand over his eyes. "I've got an entire crew out here ready to go. They've been standing around with their thumbs up their asses since five a.m. I'm gonna lose my morning light *and* my elephants. Dumbo and his brother Bam Bam have to be at Joel Silver's kid's third birthday party by noon," he says. "Lo, what am I gonna do?"

"Let's move her into the middle of the room," Candy's manager suggests from across the room, nodding at Celery. "I'll hold her head up so you can clean her up while she rests."

"Rests?" a fed-up Celery mumbles under her breath. "Yeah, great. Here we go again."

I recognize the glint in Christopher's eye and decide it's unsafe to keep him in a room with floor-to-ceiling windows. I pull him out of the room before he starts breaking things.

"Let's get some air, Christopher," I say, holding his hand tightly as I drag him out the front door of the house.

"There's no time. I've gotta meet with the flame throwers. I've gotta talk to the clowns. We have to move the big top at least a quarter of a mile down the beach for the light. The last I heard, the smoke machines were broken. I have to re-think the crane shot. But right now I have to go find the elephant wrangler," Christopher says, glassy-eyed and frantic as we walk down the Pacific Coast Highway to his trailer. "Put me in a full nelson the next time I tell you I'm thinking of doing another music video. From this day forward, I focus exclusively on finishing my Burning Man documentary."

"Christopher, you've been saying that for the past five years after *every* video shoot. You're way too talented for this kind of stuff. When are you going to get back to the stuff you were meant to do? You always get sucked back in by the big paychecks."

"Why do you have to remind me of what a sellout I am? I hate myself," he says, flinging open his trailer door.

"I hate you too right now. I have to call Julian and tell him about the hack job Candy did on that dress." I plop down onto Christopher's pea green trailer couch as he paces madly. "Julian's still taking Vicodin for the first-degree burns on his hands from the acid in the dye he used on that fabric. He's going to impale himself with a Nobu chopstick when he hears that she's turned the haute in his couture to hooker-on-Hollywood-Boulevard."

"A chopstick? David Fincher's gonna shove a fire poker up my ass. I was $100,000 over budget on the last video I shot for Anonymous Content and they threatened to give the Pepsi commercial to Mark Romanek." Christopher rakes his nail-bitten fingers through his thick, dark hair. "There's no way I'm going to finish all these shots today. I should have known better than to try to re-create a circus on the beach. In three hours I'm officially screwed. My entire concept is ruined. They say never work with children or animals. How did I end up with both?" He pulls out his rolling papers from the back pocket of his faded Levi's. "What am I gonna do, La-la?"

I gaze out the window at the heavy, purple-gray clouds moving over the water and heading our way. Then it comes to me.

"Christopher! *The Garden of the Finzi-Continis, Yesterday, Today and Tomorrow, Shoeshine, Vittorio De Sica!*" If I can't help it that the dress Julian made for Candy is now in worse shape than the ozone layer, I may as well help my brother.

"Huh?" he says through the billow of thick smoke coming from his joint. He looks like he's been plucked out of a George Romero zombie flick.

"You've got to let this Fellini circus thing go. It should be about a stripped-down, bare-bones De Sica-esque simplicity. Remember what you did in that *Bicycle Thieves* remake at USC after you came back from

Naples, that time you were researching De Sica's family tree? That grainy black and white footage when Bruno finds his lost father was so simple, so moving. It took me three therapy sessions to work through it."

"La-la," Christopher whispers in disbelief from behind his hands, which have become a permanent resting place for his far too heavy head. "You're a genius. How could I have gotten so carried away with these commercial gimmicks? De Sica would never depend on a fucking elephant! It's just about me, the camera, and the junkie now." He bolts out of the trailer door as I dart after him.

"It's a wrap. Everyone go home," Christopher shouts over his shoulder at the crew as we rush through the front door of the Malibu mansion. He crashes up the stairs to the master bedroom and busts open the bedroom door.

"You. On the bed. Now." Christopher points at a bewildered Candy Cummings, who's now slumped over in a Lucite chair getting her fake eyelashes glued on for the fifth time today. She's wearing a man's white Oxford button-down that has shifted to expose the nipple of an oddly disfigured breast implant. Julian's mutilated gown is in a crumpled ball at her feet looking like a used piece of sparkly Kleenex.

"But my face," Candy whines.

"Screw the makeup!" Christopher roars. Candy raises a single manicured eyebrow and begins to pack up her valises. "Raw. I want raw. No more of this smoke and mirrors. It's you and me, babe. *You and me.* On the bed. *Now.*"

"I love it when you talk dirty to me, Christopher," Candy purrs groggily. "Can someone get me a razor," she demands, taking a drag off her Marlboro Red with her chipped electric blue nails.

"A razor?" Christopher asks, dumbfounded. The manager and assistant shift uneasily as Candy struggles to her feet.

"If we're getting into bed, I have to shave. I haven't had a bikini wax in three years. I have enough pain in my life without having some Russian cow ripping away at my vagina."

"This isn't a porno," I protest.

"Just get me a razor," Candy insists as she taps the ash from her cigarette onto the carpet.

"Look, it's unnecessary," Christopher pleads. "This is about truth, about honesty, about authenticity. Plus, it's a close-up on your face."

"Is this the hyperrealism you're looking for?" the rock star says coyly as she spreads her legs.

"I'll be back in five," Christopher says as he shields his eyes from the *Basic Instinct* remake. The rock star's assistant hurriedly scrounges through some bags and unearths a plastic Bic razor.

"I'm sorry, but we don't have any shaving cream," the assistant says timidly. "Let me check the shower for some soap."

"Just hand me that Diet Coke," Candy says, pointing to a stray cup on the bedside table. She props a scrawny leg on the bed and dips the razor into the plastic cup of soda. Horror-struck, I turn to leave.

"Where are you going, Lola? Stay here and talk to me," Candy wheedles in her best little-girl voice. "What are we doing about that dress?" I do my best to keep my eyes locked on her face—do not look down, do not look down, do not look down—as she says, "Where the hell is Julian? The whole gown thing is totally tired. I want to shake things up on Sunday. I want a black leather cat-suit with a tail I can use to whip Dakota Fanning's bony ass." Candy props her foot on my thigh to get a better angle for the Bic.

Could it get any worse than this? I thought we'd hit our limit at the third fitting when Candy had me meet her at her dermatologist's office and she flipped through Julian's sketches while the good doctor injected her with Botox. Or, at our fourth fitting, when she summoned

Flea's tattoo artist to her Silverlake estate to finish inking in Eve biting into the apple on her left shoulder while I showed her fabric swatches.

"Lola, you're the only one who understands me," Candy slurs. Oh God, could that possibly be true? How screwed up must *I* be to have Candy Cummings consider me her psychic twin? She launches into an incomprehensible diatribe about her custody battles with her ex-girlfriend over their Siamese cats, loss of her Porsche Cayenne to the IRS, recording misfires, suicide bids, most recent court appearances, and the agonies of enduring the paparazzi.

When Candy invites me to make a full frontal inspection "in case I missed a spot," I make a mental note to phone Dr. Gilmore later and request a double session for tomorrow. This is why during Oscar Week it's mandatory to see your therapist at least once a day between sessions with personal trainers, stylists, acupuncturists, massage therapists, astrologists, and spiritual guides. Maybe I *am* Candy's psychic twin, I reflect as I lean in for a closer look, since I seem to have convinced myself that this is a perfectly legitimate activity if this is what it takes to put Candy in Julian Tennant for the Oscars.

I drag myself out to my black Prius and play back my messages via Bluetooth loudspeaker as I focus my bloodshot eyes on the Pacific Coast Highway, suppressing the urge to floor it straight into the polluted ocean. The first message is from my father's assistant:

"This is Abby calling from Paul Santisi's office to invite you to his abundance ritual to ensure his success at the Oscars. It will be held at Barbra Streisand's house in Malibu at eleven a.m. sharp on Saturday. The Santisis are asking that everyone wear orange for opulence, abundance, and Oscar. Please RSVP by Wednesday and let us know if you're going to bring a plus-one."

Then she leaves my parents' home phone number as if it's changed since the day I was born. Since Papa never calls me directly, I do worry that if Abby were swept out to sea, my father and I might never have any contact again. Although I guess I'll always have Mary Hart to keep me apprised of the significant moments in his life on *Entertainment To-night,* which is how I found out he was nominated for his second Best Directing Oscar for *Whispered Screams.* I wonder if my father's ever going to make me feel like his daughter and not some alien who just landed from Pluto. And if Pluto can get demoted from Planethood, then my father should be demoted from Fatherhood pronto.

I take a deep breath to prepare myself for the next message from Planet Hollywood. It's from Jake Jones's publicist.

"So sorry, but I've got to cancel Jake's fitting tomorrow; he's had re-shoots for *The Ten Commandments: The Musical* with Val Kilmer all weekend and he's feeling spiritually depleted."

Spiritually depleted? Please. Try spending the day with Candy Cummings.

I brace myself, punch Julian's number into the cell, and blurt out the morning's events before he can stop me.

"Our line must have gotten crossed with a phone sex operator, or did you just demand that I make a black patent-leather cat-suit for Candy Cummings," Julian screeches in a panicked cry. "I did *not* get Cindy Crawford, Christy Turlington, *and* Naomi Campbell out of retirement to model in my senior fashion show at Central Saint Martins so that I could make my Oscar Red Carpet debut with a freaking Halloween costume."

"And I did not spend the last six weeks compromising my mental and physical well-being by catering to Candy Cummings's every psychotic whim, demeaning myself twenty-four hours a day, culminating in just inspecting her freshly shaven *crotch* so that she could wear *another* designer," I say.

"*E-e-w,*" Julian shrieks. "Oh my God, Lola. You should drive straight to the gynecologist and make sure you didn't catch anything."

"I didn't have sex with her, Julian," I snap. "I'm just telling you the lengths to which I've gone to make sure Candy wears you on the Red Carpet," I say. "Now focus. The Oscars are in—"

"—Seven days," he says, panicked. I can virtually see through the phone line as Julian's Saville Row seersucker pant leg crosses in consternation, his long, nervous fingers gripping his perfectly messy dark shag, an ode to Warren Beatty in *Shampoo,* his Aeron desk chair seesawing anxiously beneath him.

"Candy's going to win the Oscar for Best Song on Sunday," I say. "And it can either be in a Julian Tennant cat-suit or a Gaultier cat-suit. Take your pick."

Silence. Except for the distinct sound of Julian's John Lobb loafers pacing on the concrete floors of his SoHo loft.

"Julian?"

"I'm thinking."

"Don't think. Just start sewing," I insist.

More silence and pacing.

"I'm sorry, Lola. I can't do it," Julian finally says, resolutely.

"What do you mean *can't,* Julian? I just told you everything I've been through for *you.*"

"And I will totally cover your next session with Dr. Gilmore to work through the whole crotch thing, but I can't make the cat-suit," he says.

"Julian, I don't need you to cover my next session, I *need* you to make the cat-suit. You *have* to do this. You hired me to put your name on the map. Let me do *my* job by doing *your* job."

"Lola, I just can't," he says.

I can't fail at one more career. I take a deep breath. "*Please,* Julian," I beg. "Do it for me. Do it for us."

"That cat-suit would be the end of my career," Julian says matter-of-factly.

A lightbulb flashes over my head. "Okay, look, Julian, make the cat-suit and I'll get you a date with Tom Ford," I say.

"Deal," Julian says instantaneously. "But I'm making it in topaz silk charmeuse."

"No deal. She wants black patent. End of discussion," I say.

"Fine. But when I land tomorrow, Tom Ford better be waiting in my room at the Chateau in a thong with my name scrawled across it in red rhinestones."

Click.

"Sorry, sorry, sorry I'm so late," I call out breathlessly to Kate and Cricket as I pull up in front of my tiny rented Spanish bungalow across the street from the Chateau Marmont. As I rush toward Kate's black Porsche 911 I try not to tumble over the five garment bags full of sundry gowns for Scarlett and Olivia I'm lugging. Kate's behind the wheel with her cell pressed to her ear and an open script in her lap while Cricket sits in full lotus in the passenger seat, poring over the *LA Times*. My poor BFF and BAF have been waiting for me for over forty-five minutes to start our fourth annual Oscar Movie Marathon. And after *this* day I could really use my two best girlfriends, some take-out, and the gangload of the Academy screeners I pilfered from my father. Thanks to screeners, Academy members can judge Oscar contenders in the comfort of their own homes; heaven forbid they should have to set foot in the hexy-dexy-sexy-plexes like the rest of the hoi polloi. "You can't imagine the day I've had with Candy Cummings."

"That bad?" Cricket asks, turning her bright, freshly scrubbed face toward me, fidgeting with the messy knot of tow-colored hair atop her head as she climbs out of Kate's car. Even in a gray T-shirt and a pair of cargos, Cricket glows.

"*Worse*," I say. "If Candy Cummings weren't famous, Nurse Ratched would have her in solitary confinement in a straitjacket."

"Try being an agent. I don't have one client who wouldn't benefit from a month at Bellevue," Kate says, pushing her car door open with a cherry patent pump as Cricket wraps me in a hug. Kate grabs a black cardigan from the backseat and swathes herself in it. Not even the plush four-ply cashmere is enough to disguise her *Sports Illustrated*-swimsuit-edition-worthy body. She adjusts the collar on her crisp white Oxford and tugs on the waistband of her black skinny jeans. Even on Sunday at 7 P.M., Kate looks like she's ready for dinner with Jude Law. "You're lucky I had my script bag with me or we would have left," Kate says.

"I highly doubt that she even remembers a thing she read; she was making a call every other word," Cricket says, carefully folding up the paper and tucking it beneath her willowy arm. "I could barely focus on the real estate section."

"When did you start reading the real estate section?" I ask. Cricket's been renting a teeny 125-square-foot studio guesthouse on Viggo Mortensen's property in Venice for the last two years. He only charges her $400 a month since she feeds his Amazon Homing Parrots when he's on location filming.

"Well," Cricket says, standing very still all of a sudden. "I wasn't going to say anything because I don't want to jinx things, but I *really* want to tell you, you're my best friends. And I have some big news," Cricket says quickly, grabbing Kate and me by the hand. "Lola, take Kate's hand. I want a circle for this," she instructs.

"Cricket, I refused to do the whole 'Kumbaya' thing when I went to sleepaway camp when I was *ten,* I'm not starting now, just tell us the news," Kate demands.

"Come on, Kate," I say, waving my open palm at her.

"Oh fine," Kate says, stuffing the BlackBerry permanently occupying her right hand into her vanilla leather hobo bag. Cricket looks down at the ground haltingly and takes a deep breath.

"You know that *Baywatch* series remake I've gotten all those callbacks on? Well, the producers narrowed it down to me and the Next Cameron Diaz and they sent us both in to read for the network today," she says.

"I thought *you* were the Next Cameron Diaz," I interrupt.

"No, I'm too fair-skinned. The producers told my agent they think I'm the Next Kirsten Dunst," Cricket says.

"Oh my God, Cricket, that's so great," I say.

"When do you think you'll hear back from the network?" Kate asks.

"Well," Cricket pauses, barely able to contain her excitement. "After my audition today, the producers pulled me aside and told me that the network hated the Next Cameron Diaz but they *loved* me and it's looking like a done deal!" Cricket squeals as we start jumping up and down on the street outside my house. Even Kate in her three-inch heels can't help herself. "Oh my God, Cricket," I shriek. "This is amazing!"

"They'd be crazy not to cast you. You're a much better actress than Pam Anderson," Kate says, giving Cricket's hand an extra-tight squeeze.

"Can you believe it? The network already ordered thirteen episodes. I'll be a series regular on a TV show if I get the part."

"*When* you get the part," I correct her.

"I'll finally be able to pay off my student loans and get my own place," Cricket says ecstatically.

"Cricket, this is going to be huge," I say, giving her a hug. "If anyone deserves this, it's you. I have a really good feeling about this."

"So do I! According to the *LA Yoga Journal* astrology chart, it's a time of deep inner alignment for me," Cricket says, heaving a wheelie suitcase out of Kate's trunk as Kate pulls her mountainous bag full of scripts over her shoulder.

"How long are you planning on staying?" I ask Cricket.

"I was hoping I could take a bath later and it's not as much as it looks like. My bathrobe and bath salts take up a lot of space," she says. Since Viggo's tiny studio guesthouse is tubless, Cricket frequents my bathroom armed with her own lavender-scented soy candles and organic bath salts. I worry that when she gets her own place with a tub, she'll go full throttle Margot Tenenbaum on me. Although she may be so waterlogged from *Baywatch* she'll get over the bathing obsession entirely. "This could be my last bath at your place. I saw a great two-bedroom on Ocean Avenue in the paper."

"I think I still have a bottle of champagne in the fridge from New Year's. Let's go crack it open and celebrate," I say.

"I surprised you and got us chicken imperial rolls from Gingergrass, but I might have eaten most of them while we were waiting for you," Kate says. "I had to drive all the way out to Silverlake and I'm starving."

"That's okay, Kate," I say as we make our way up the brick path toward my house. "What were you doing in Silverlake?"

Kate rolls her eyes. "Visiting Will. He wanted me to come over to his house to look for places to keep his Oscar."

"You mean the Oscar Will hasn't even *won* yet," I point out as I unlock my front door and throw the garment bags over the Louis XIV leopard-print chair my mother gave to me when she was doing an "energy clearing" in Villa Santisi last year. I wish I could afford to have it reupholstered.

"Will's *gonna* win," Kate says. "I'm surprised there hasn't been a San-tisi family gathering with the Dalai Lama to clear out space in your par-ents' house for your father's second statuette."

"Actually, my parents are having an abundance ritual to ensure my father's success on Sunday," I say, trying to keep a straight face. "It's at Barbra Streisand's house on Saturday morning and Abby said I could bring a plus-one, so which one of you is going to be my date?"

"Shoot, I can't. And I hear Streisand's house is amazing," Kate says.

"Me neither. Sorry. I told S. D. I'd teach his yoga class Saturday morning since he's doing a private with Elijah Wood," Cricket says. S.D. Rail is the white-hot yogi of the moment with enough magnetism to rival Bowie in his heyday.

"You won't have to sub at Yoga Works for much longer, now that you're going to be the star of *Baywatch*," I say.

"It beats shampooing dogs at Chateau Marmutt. If you need me to come with you to the abundance ritual, I can see if someone else can teach the class," Cricket says as I unload the contents of Kate's takeout bag onto my kitchen counter. "Hey, none of that for me. I've gone raw."

Kate and I look at her in disbelief. "Since when?" Kate asks.

"For a few weeks now. It's hugely energizing. Going raw has made me unbelievably in tune with my body." Cricket's skin does look partic-ularly glowy. "Besides, I've heard that Ashton and Demi shop at Erewhon. I really feel it's going to give me a competitive edge over all the lifeless-food-eating actresses. I mean, look at what's already hap-pened with *Baywatch*."

"Yeah, 'cause I bet it could have gone the other way if the Next Cameron Diaz was only eating *raw* food," Kate says dryly. "Come on, this must be about a guy, Cricket. Did you meet someone on that yoga retreat?"

"No, Kate, why does it always have to be about men for you? This is about my own personal well-being," Cricket says. "Now can we start the movies?"

"Did you get *Lawrence of Arabia?*" Kate asks, gesturing toward the stack of screeners on my kitchen table.

"I'm morally opposed to seeing that. Brett Ratner thinking he can remake it and replace Peter O'Toole with Wentworth Miller is a joke. Wouldn't you rather watch the Woody Allen movie?" I ask.

"I've already seen it," Kate says. "I'm surprised your father loaned you those movies—the Academy is so paranoid about bootlegging. They could throw him out of the Academy if they found out."

"Actually, he didn't officially *loan* them to me—I stole them from his screening room," I say. "I also broke into his Official Academy Award Nominee Gift Basket. I snagged the new Nokia, a year's supply of Sprint broadband phone service *and* a Krups kitchen set, including a toaster, electric kettle, and a lifetime supply of coffee and tea."

Cricket frowns. "If your father auctioned that off on eBay, he could build an ozone water filtration system for all of Malawi," she says.

"Good thing Madonna and Angelina are on that, because the only cause my father cares about is himself. Besides, after all those birthdays and ballet recitals my father missed, I figure he owes me," I say. "Besides, you know he'll get at least thirty other *unofficial* baskets of loot. CAA already sent him one with ten pairs of those Ice Cream sneakers he loves so much. Universal sent an engraved sterling silver razor *and* Peter Luger steaks. Vespa delivered a scooter with his initials airbrushed on the side, for crying out loud. It's not like he'll ever notice that I took that weekend getaway to the San Ysidro Ranch, which I'm saving for my future non-actor boyfriend." Kate and Cricket both raise their eyebrows at me. "Okay, who am I kidding, the trip will expire before I ever meet him. The three of us should go after Oscar Week is over."

"Really?" Cricket squeals. "Ever since I saw those pictures in *People* of Gwyneth eloping there I've dreamt of going. This is so exciting."

"I also snagged a free five-year bicoastal membership at The Sports Club/LA for you, Kate," I say to my BFF. "And TSE cashmere pajamas and a bathrobe for you, Cricket. My father's going to have to foot the bill for the tax since the IRS decided they were tired of celebs getting everything for free."

"Thanks so much, Lo. You're the best," Cricket says.

"Thanks, Lo," Kate says. "The only thing Will gave me from *his* nominee gift basket was the cellophane wrapping. Hey, did I tell you that Bryan Lourd waved to me from his booth at the Grill on Friday?" B. L.'s uber agency, CAA, is Kate's intended final pit stop on the path to world domination.

"Your obsession with Bryan Lourd is even creepier than Lisa Nowak and her astronaut diapers," I say.

"If I'd been with Will, he would have come over to the table. At least I was having a signing meeting with Ellen Pompeo. Doesn't Will look hot on this cover?" Kate picks up the weighty *Vanity Fair* Hollywood Issue from my kitchen table. The gatefold cover of "Hollywood's Sexiest Leading Men" is a signature Annie Leibovitz ratfuck starring Will Bailey, Ryan Gosling, Orlando Bloom, Johnny Depp, Jamie Foxx, Heath Ledger, Josh Hartnett, and Jake Gyllenhaal. Poor Peter Sarsgaard, Zach Braff, and Jake Jones only made the in-fold.

"I can't look at that right now," I say. "It's too depressing, all those rich, successful actors looking happy and sexy. It's disgusting," I protest as Kate pets the image of her Best Actor nominee client like a proud parent. "And Julian asking me to dress Jake Jones is like asking an alcoholic to bartend. The GM Show is in two days, and Jake still hasn't been fitted for his suit. His publicist canceled his fitting tomorrow morning *again*."

"Hey, do you guys want to come with me to the *Premiere* magazine party at The Skybar tomorrow night?" Kate asks.

"Kate, did you not hear anything I just said? There's no way. It's gonna be an actor hotbed," I say. "I just want to survive this week without going within thirty feet of an actor—unless, of course, I have to dress them. I can't let them distract me anymore from conquering this damn Career Deficit Disorder," I say. "I'm twenty-six years old. It's about time I succeeded at something."

"You *are*, Lola," Cricket says. "You're getting Candy Cummings, Scarlett Johansson, *and* Olivia Cutter to walk down the Oscar Red Carpet in Julian Tennant."

"Candy and Scarlett, okay. Olivia, I don't know," Kate interjects. "I don't mean to be a downer, Lo, but why would Olivia Cutter wear Julian Tennant to the Oscars when she looks this good in Givenchy?" She holds up a double-page *VF* spread of the actress looking ravishing in a twenties-inspired frock that matches her icy blue eyes. "She's a real long shot, Lo."

"Don't remind me," I say. "God knows how many gowns Carolina Herrera, Vera Wang, and Badgley Mischka have whipped up for her on spec. And those are just the designers I know about from Doctor Lee." My acupuncturist also treats Olivia's manager's assistant's sister. "Plus Adrienne Hunt's on the prowl for Prada."

I keep an even darker thought to myself: Even if Olivia *agrees* to parade herself in one of Julian's dresses, there's no saying after umpteen fittings that she won't pull a Sharon Stone and wear a fifteen-dollar black Gap T-shirt or Monique Lhuillier at the last nanosecond. The Maldon sea salt in the wound is that even when the prima divas reject the designer's jaw-droppers, they still get to *keep* them. What am I going to do, crawl through Olivia's window to get a reject gown back? Do you think Renée Zellweger is FedExing the perfectly altered Calvin Klein castoffs back to his showroom in New York?

"I have complete faith in you, Lo," Cricket says. "Olivia's going to wear Julian Tennant because you're going to convince her she has to. You've got an incredible eye for fashion. And you know what looks good on people. It's a gift. You just need to work on visualizing it all coming together."

"Well, André Leon Talley did tell me that Olivia was drooling from the front row of Julian's show during Fashion Week last month," I say. "And she sent a huge bouquet of Casablanca lilies to Julian saying his show was her absolute favorite collection."

"And you believed her?" Kate says. "She's just angling for more free loot. She spends fifty bucks on some flowers and gets thousands of dollars' worth of dresses. Maybe she's not as stupid as I've heard. Or at least her agent isn't. She's going to milk the nomination for all she can. That's what I would do. I hear she isn't happy with William Morris—do you think that's true?"

"Kate, could we just let this be about me for ten more seconds? I have an ulcer the size of my father's ego right now," I say. "Thank God Scarlett's wearing Julian. If I didn't have her in the Julian Tennant garment bag, I'd be in a fashion coma right now."

"I just know Olivia's going to fall in love with one of those dresses Julian's bringing tomorrow," Cricket says. "You're going to have an Oscar winner wearing Julian Tennant. Olivia's a shoo-in to win. She gained thirty pounds, wore prosthetic teeth, and played a drug addict."—the Hollywood trifecta virtually guaranteed to garner Oscar gold.

"Exactly. Where's the suspense? America would eat Olivia for breakfast, lunch, and dinner if they could," Kate says. "Anyway, you're going to have *two* winners, Lo. Candy's sure to beat out Phil Collins for the 'In the Air Tonight Remix.' *Extra*'s practically running a loop of Candy singing her hit from *Kill Bill Volume 6*."

"That's only if I can convince Julian to make that black cat-suit for Candy," I say. "I had to promise him I'd get him a date with Tom Ford."

"Lo, you don't even *know* Tom Ford," Kate says.

"Julian doesn't know that," I reply. "This is for his own good. And mine," I say, kicking off my high-heeled Mary Janes, which land on top of Kate's script bag.

"Hey! I've got Alexander Payne's new spec in there!" Kate shrieks.

I nudge my shoes aside with my toe. "What's *this*?" I ask, lifting the black nylon bag with the familiar triangular logo off the floor. "Now my best friend is consorting with Satan's henchbitch?" I sort of understand why Kate let Prada beat out Julian to dress Will, but it still stings.

Kate doesn't even have the good grace to look guilty. "What? I was supposed to send back a free $1,200 Prada bag?"

"Watch your back, Kate, it's just a matter of time before Adrienne Hunt stabs you with her five-inch Prada stilettos," I say.

"Have you driven down Sunset Boulevard lately and seen how good Will looks twenty feet by twenty feet in that Prada campaign? I'd tell Will to fuck Adrienne if I thought it'd be good for his career. Hell, *I'd* fuck her. I don't care that she's a repulsive human being. You know that."

"I can't believe I'm facing off against that woman to get Olivia. It's not that I hate Prada. I love what Miuccia's done for nylon. I have total respect that she can slap one of her cute little logos on a thirty-dollar LeSportsac and charge $1,200 for it. It's that damn Adrienne. She makes Anna Wintour look like a dove," I say. "I heard the day the nominations came out, she tried to bribe Olivia with a hot pink Prada python mini-clutch. We're talking, Kate Moss is number twelve on the wait-list for one. Adrienne grabbed it out of Giselle's hand the minute she stepped off the catwalk in Milan. The cherry on top is she had a

Prada cashmere sweater with fur trim made for Olivia's dog. How can I compete with that?"

"She had fur made for a dog?" Cricket cries. "That's so twisted. That's like throwing my dead Aunt Martha over my neck and calling her a scarf. We should report her to PETA," she exclaims as the sound of a chirping cell phone fills the room. "Oh my gosh, I bet that's my agent," she yelps, diving headfirst for her organic cotton tote.

"Sorry, Cricket, that's me," Kate says. As Kate calmly clicks on the loudspeaker of her Nokia, Cricket collapses in a disappointed heap on top of the contents of her bag, strewing the *Autobiography of a Yogi*, *Baywatch* script, and gray sweats all over the floor.

"This better be good, Adam. It's Sunday," Kate barks at her much-abused assistant, the latest in a long line of overqualified, overly ambitious N.Y.U. Film School grads. Kate seems to have forgotten that the last time Adam took a weekend off, she punished him by not allowing him to drive her Porsche to Santa Palm Carwash for a week.

Adam's meek voice barely registers. "Your sister would really like you to reconsider coming to her rehearsal dinner Friday night."

"Adam, we've been through this. I thought you explained to Sarah that there's no way I can miss Bryan Lourd's Oscar party Friday night. As it is, I'm flying up to Marin for the wedding Saturday afternoon right after the Spirit Awards and missing the Weinsteins' party."

"Are you sure you don't want to call her yourself? She sounded really upset," Adam suggests timidly.

"Good idea. Put her on my call sheet for tomorrow," Kate instructs Adam as she clicks off her cell.

"What?" Kate says, taking in our disapproving looks.

"How can you miss your sister's rehearsal dinner?" Cricket asks. "You're becoming so one of them, a Hollywood sicko. I can't take it."

"Are you even invited to Bryan Lourd's party, Kate?" I ask.

"No. You're taking me," Kate says. "And please, it's not like I'm missing the 'I do's.' Plus, I'm paying for their honeymoon."

"I don't think I'm invited to Bryan's," I say. I haven't been able to bring myself to go through that giant stack of pre-Oscar party invitations that have taken up residence teetering on my bedside table. They're another reminder that I may be Hollywood Royalty, but the only thing that needs homeowner's insurance is my invites.

"Yeah, you are," Kate says.

"What'd you do, go through my mail?"

"Yeah. And can you believe my invitation to the *Vanity Fair* party is for eleven p.m.? I got Graydon the exclusive interview with Will the second we found out he was nominated, and he couldn't even swing a ten-thirty invite?"

"At least you get to go," Cricket says sulkily.

"You'll be invited next year when you're a series regular on *Baywatch*," I say.

"And I'll be living in a house with a bathtub," Cricket adds.

"Should we start the movies?" Kate asks.

"Oh wait—just let me check my e-mail." Cricket scampers toward my black MacBook on the counter. She hasn't owned a computer since she graduated as a Dramatic Arts major from Northwestern.

"I may be able to get you a prop laptop from the Spider-Man 4 set. Will's doing a cameo," Kate offers. "They have a tie-in with Apple so it will be super-cheap and they barely turn them on." Cricket doesn't respond. "Cricket, did you hear me?" Kate says.

"Oh my God. Oh my God, oh my God, oh my God," Cricket says, making gasping noises from behind my laptop.

"Oh my God!" I join in. "Cricket, congratulations!" I scream, racing toward her, ready to resume the jumping up and down position. But then I stop myself. Cricket's milky skin is suddenly translucent against the black night sky creeping through the kitchen window. Her usually crystal-clear ocean green eyes look like they've been doused by the Exxon Valdez oil spill. She pulls herself up into the lotus position and takes a deep, forceful breath.

"I didn't get the part," Cricket says dully, without turning toward us, her eyes glazed over, transfixed by the computer screen.

"*What?*" Kate and I demand in unison.

"They said I was—too tall," Cricket whispers. "They gave it to the Next Kate Bosworth. And there's more."

" '*We are dropping you as a client of The Dorff Agency. Warmest Personal Regards, Greg,*' " Kate reads out loud over Cricket's sunken shoulder. "Fuck that fat queen Greg Dorff and his pathetic little agency. He was doing as much for your career as Michael Brown did for New Orleans. You're better off," Kate says.

"Oh God, Cricket," I say in shock. "I'm so sorry."

"Too tall," Cricket groans. "Too tall!? The casting director didn't tell me I was too tall on my first, second, or *third* audition. The producers never told me I was too tall when they called me back *five* times. When did they decide I was too tall? Was it today when the network execs had me twirl around in that skimpy red bathing suit, lie down and roll over like I was a dog in front of the entire network? Those execs looked me in the eye and said I was good. They said I was *good!*" Cricket wails.

"You *are* good, Cricket," I say.

"This is just *one* TV series, there'll be others," Kate says softly. "Cameron Crowe told Will he was too short, and now he's nominated for an Academy Award."

"You've just got to keep at it," I say, pushing behind her ears the stray pieces of long blond hair that have fallen around Cricket's angelic face.

"Why? So the next casting director can tell me I'm too tall or too blond or too old or too young or too—white. I give up! I quit! Talent's got nothing to do with it," Cricket says, tears streaming down her face.

"You're way too good to give up. Come on, maybe we should go sit in the living room," I say, taking her by the hand and leading her into the other room. "The feng shui guy my mother sent over after my breakup with SMITH said the best energy in the house is in there." I sit her down in the overstuffed linen armchair in the corner, swaddling her fragile body tightly in the orange cashmere blanket the feng shui guy recommended for vitality and shielding. Her small, diaphanous face looks like it might fade away next to the shock of orange fabric engulfing her.

"Do I have your permission to hawk those TSE cashmere pajamas you just gave me so I can buy a plane ticket back to Ohio? I emptied my bank account on full body waxes for the last month for that dumb series," Cricket says, blotting at her tears with her palms.

"Cricket, there *will be* another part," I say, sitting down next to her.

"An even better part," Kate adds, sitting down on Cricket's other side.

"I can't do this anymore. I'm going home. I'm going back to Ohio," Cricket says resolutely.

"No way. We're not letting you give up based on some stupid network exec with a Napoleon Complex," I say. "Besides, what would we do without you?"

"Cricket, do you think Jennifer Lopez thought about giving up and moving back to the Bronx every time some schmuck casting director, or producer, or director told her that her ass was too big? No. She kept going and that's what you have to do," Kate says.

"Kate's right, Cricket," I say. "You can't give up. This is all you've ever wanted. And you were so good on *Law & Order: Special Victims Unit* last month. I thought you were really convincing."

"I played a *corpse,* Lola. I had like five seconds of a five-shot of me and four other girls protesting in a Greenpeace rally before a Hummer ran me over." Cricket swipes her arm quickly across her nose and lets out an unsteady sigh.

"And your guest spot on *Grey's Anatomy* was brilliant," says Kate, who seldom hands out such compliments.

"Kate, I was a crash victim in a coma."

"Yeah, but it was really compelling. You *became* the coma. I believed in the coma," Kate says.

"Listen to what you guys are saying—that I'm good at playing incapacitated," Cricket says. "Remember that audition for that reality show *The Ingenue?* Faye Dunaway said I have the emotional range of Karl Rove. She told me to stick to posing with my mouth shut in the Nordstrom catalog."

"Eew, oh sweetie, sorry," Kate says. "Forget about her, Cricket. You are *way* too good for *The Ingenue.*"

"But the prize on *The Ingenue* is a part on *Lost.* And I totally blew it," Cricket says. "I've made up my mind; I'm packing it in and going back to Ohio. The universe is trying to tell me something."

"We're not letting you. We'd be lost here without you. We're finding you a new agent, someone much better," I say.

"I'll have Adam call David Feldman in our TV department tomorrow to make sure you get out for pilot season," offers Kate. I throw her an are-you-for-real look. "Okay, I'll call David myself first thing in the morning," Kate says.

"Really? You'd do that for me, Kate?" Cricket asks.

"Really, Cricket. You can do this," Kate says unwaveringly. "Now stand up," she instructs, pulling her up off the couch and unwrapping Cricket from the blanket. "And forget about those idiot network execs,"

Kate says, shielding Cricket in her strong arms. I engulf her from the other side.

"You're gonna make it," I whisper into the back of Cricket's neck.

"*We're* gonna make it," she whispers back.

"Okay, okay," Kate says, "we don't need to do the whole hug-it-out thing," but she gives Cricket and me an extra-tight embrace anyway before she breaks away.

"Come on, Cricket, let's watch *The Violinist*. Ryan Phillippe's biceps will take your mind off Greg Dorff and those stupid network execs," I suggest.

"It's about the Armenian genocide, Lola," answers Cricket, disturbed. "Let's watch *Old School 2*. Will Ferrell always makes me feel better."

"That's CAA's movie. They made a bloody fortune on it," says Kate. "Lola, do me a favor. At the fitting tomorrow, could you just ask Olivia whether she's happy at William Morris?"

"Kate, please, could we just focus on Cricket for ten more seconds?" I say, pulling myself up off the couch and heading toward the fridge to confirm how empty it is and how starving I am.

"Okay, I think that was ten seconds. Be sure to ask Scarlett too." I throw Kate an imploring look as I head back into the living room. "All right, sorry," she mutters.

As I reach for a movie, Kate can't resist the urge to say, "Just let me know if Olivia's agent's with her."

"Seriously, Kate," I sigh.

"I'd be up her ass if it was me," Kate says.

Five hours, one cold, soggy imperial role, two windswept Kate Winslet close-ups, one cracking of *The Giotto Code,* and one wicked case of ass paralysis later, I close the door behind Kate and Cricket. All I want is to get into bed and wake up when the scary part's over. When we've all landed exactly where we want to be: career, check; love life, check; cure for cancer, check—the new Chanel patent-toed over-the-knee alligator boots, check, check.

My cell phone rings. Who the heck is calling this late?

"Hi, Angela," I say. Scarlett Johansson's cousin-slash-third-assistant's cell phone number has been branded into my brain.

"Scarlett asked me to call you to cancel the fitting tomorrow," she says.

What's it going to be this time? Pilates? Reiki treatment? Psychic reading with Suzannah Galland? "I understand how busy Scarlett is. Just let me know when she would like to re-schedule," I say, wondering when my mouth will go into paralysis from how far it's shoved up her ass. "We're so looking forward to her final fitting and we feel so honored that Scarlett's going to wear Julian to the Oscars."

"Actually she's not. She's wearing Narciso Rodriguez."

All oxygen is immediately sucked out of the room. "What do you mean, she's wearing Narciso Rodriguez," I say slowly.

"She changed her mind. I don't know what else to say. I have to get the other phone."

"What do you mean, the other phone? She's not wearing Julian Tennant?"

"Lola, it's Nicole from Terminex Pest Control calling and I've been trying to get through for days to schedule our yearly maintenance appointment. I have to go."

"Wait," I implore her. "Pest control? It's midnight, for crying out loud."

"Lola, I have to take this call. I'm sure you understand."

"But—"

Click.

Yeah, I *understand,* all right. On the scale of what's important, scheduling Scarlett's yearly pest control appointment outranks the fact that she's not wearing Julian to the *Oscars.* I'm down to the prostrate Candy Cummings. And I have a better chance of getting a wait-listed alligator Birkin than getting Olivia Cutter into Julian for the Oscars.

I'm Paris Hilton screwed.

monday

149 hours, 13 minutes, 7 seconds until

the Oscar is handed out for Best Art Direction.

please proceed to the highlighted route," requests the female voice on my Prius navigation system as I drive down Marmont Lane. I rely on my navigation system to get me everywhere. Los Angeles natives take pride in not having a clue about getting around in our own city.

"Left turn in one . . ." All of a sudden the navigation screen starts flashing INCOMING CALL. I used to think that one of the absolute best features of my Prius was the Bluetooth integrated phone system. It automatically connects my cell phone to the speaker system in the car so I can talk hands free while negotiating the treacherous streets of L.A. and my large English Breakfast whole milk latte. The only problem is the navigation system goes into "suspend" mode when someone calls.

It's entirely unfair to force a girl to choose between missing a phone call or getting lost on the Howard Hughes Parkway.

"Hello," I say.

"I'm on my way to pick up Will to take him to see a four-million-dollar Lautner house," Kate says. "It's next door to Heidi Klum and Seal's house in the Hollywood Hills. Will's decided, now that he's nominated, he's too big a star for Silverlake. Then I have to take him to the 'Extra' Oscar suite at The Peninsula so he can get a free facial and play virtual golf with the new set of Callaway clubs they're giving him. Then we're going to pick up the Cadillac Escalade the GM people are giving him. Then I have to take him to *The Tonight Show* taping."

"Kate—" I try to interrupt.

"That was the good news. I had to fire the housekeeper I hired for him. Maria asked him for money for a boob job, can you believe it? Now *I'm* the housekeeper. I've already been to Bristol Farms and Gelson's for Dreft because suddenly Will's decided that his skin is too sensitive for Tide, *please,* and I can't find any. Of course, I'd send Adam out to do all this crap, but Will says that *I'm* the one who—"

"Kate—" I try again.

"Plus his egg-white omelet from Doughboys is getting cold and his strawberry smoothie is dripping all over his dry cleaning. Does he even remember that I'm the one who signed him when his greatest accomplishment was that Trojan Twisted Pleasure commercial?" The proud-parent Kate of yesterday has vanished in a puff of Escalade exhaust. Oscar Week does that to you.

"Kate!" I plead. "I need my navigation system. I have to pick up Julian at LAX for our fitting with Olivia."

"Remember, you promised you'd let me know if Olivia's agent's with her."

"Jesus, Kate. I think I missed my turn," I say.

"You've lived in L.A. your entire life, Lola. Learn the roads!" Kate says. *Click.*

"Make a U-turn." My navigation system chirps back to life.

Two plays of Led Zeppelin's "In Through the Out Door" and I finally arrive at the American Airlines terminal at LAX. I'm set to meet Steven from Special Services, who's "meet-ed and greet-ed" my parents since my father won his first Oscar. SS is a brilliant service for VIPs felled by Celebrity Influenza who might otherwise never navigate the treacherous shoals of curbside, security, first-class lounge, and gate. The dreaded Celebrity Flu generally strikes the moment you grace the cover of your first tabloid. Symptoms include loss of ability to do your own supermarket shopping or laundry, cook, screw in a lightbulb, or most definitely board a commercial 767 with the masses instead of the corporate G550. Celebrity Flu is sadly genetic, manifesting in neglected, Fred Segal-clad *Children Of* who require copious amounts of therapy to work through the fact that their parents' idea of a family dinner is midnight at Spago—on a school night—and their idea of a sixteenth birthday present is a trip to the cosmetic reupholsterer.

"I'm sorry I'm late," I call out to Steven, smart in soothing brown tweed. Steven is a total doll. He always upgrades me last minute and sneaks me into the first class lounge so I can stuff my black quilted leather Chanel bag—another Mom manicured-hand-me-down—with free chocolate chip cookies and Fiji water for my flights. He's hand-cutting spools of security red tape for me today so that I can meet Julian at the gate. Julian could no more find his way from the gate to baggage claim than Mel Gibson would convert to Judaism.

"We've got to hustle. The plane is taxiing in," Steven shrieks at me. "Run!"

I give Franka Potente a *Run, Lola, Run* for her money. I'm normally opposed to running. I prefer to save up all that energy for really important things, like the Fred Segal private sale and sex.

"Oh shoot!" I look down to find the turquoise strap on my beloved gladiator sandal has snapped.

"Hurry up!" Steven yells from yards ahead of me.

"Go ahead without me! I'll catch up!" When I finally hobble to the gate minutes later, I've lost track of Steven and the gate is completely deserted.

"Where is everybody?" I wonder aloud. I spot the flight crew in the distance and run toward them.

"Where's Flight 201 from JFK?" I ask a flight attendant.

"It's disembarked," he answers.

"No! Steven!" I call out. He's nowhere in sight. I've blown it. Where the hell is Julian? Suddenly I notice a young flight attendant lugging three of Julian's unmistakable signature white garment bags with his name inscribed in hot pink letters. I limp up to her.

"Where's the man who belongs to those bags?" I beg.

"Are you Lola?" she asks. There's my name scrawled in large letters at the very bottom of one of the bags in black Sharpie ink, Julian's pen of choice. "I feel terrible for Julian. He wanted to get on the plane desperately but he had a terrible case of poison ivy and didn't want to contaminate the other passengers. He asked me to get these dresses to you. As you can imagine, it's against security procedures, but I am *such* a big fan of Olivia Cutter's, I was absolutely honored." The sweet stewardess oozes sympathy as she hands over the bags.

"Thank you so much," I say, knowing full well the chances of Julian Tennant catching poison ivy in Manhattan are as high as Mary-Kate Olsen and Nicole Richie ordering double-double cheeseburgers, fries, and strawberry shakes at In-N-Out Burger. I heft the bags over my shoulder as she heads down the hallway. Steven trots up behind me.

"I'm so sorry, Lola. I didn't confirm that Julian actually boarded the plane in NYC. I've had such a crazy morning dealing with Susan Sarandon and Tim Robbins flying in. You know what Oscar Week is like," he pants.

I collapse onto a bank of gray chairs by the window, laying the garment bags carefully beside me, and start dialing Julian. The phone rings. And rings. And rings. No answer. Oh, of course. I hit *67 to block my number so he can't see it's me calling and dial one more time.

"Hello," Julian chirps, sounding a little too perky for such an ill man with such a dreadful case of poison ivy.

"What the hell happened, Julian? You promised me you had this whole flying phobia thing under control. I FedExed Katya Ambien *and* Ativan and made certain she picked you up at your loft and told her not to take her eyes off you until you were buckled into that airplane seat! We have a meeting with Olivia Cutter in T minus five hours! I need you here! And look, I wanted to tell you in person. Scarlett's out. She's wearing Narciso Rodriguez."

Julian releases a low, tortured moan. "Oh that's just fantastic. I already had one foot in the grave, why don't you just push me all the way in and start shoveling."

"Julian, I thought all of those sessions with Gonzalo and Doctor Friedlander had gotten this flying fear handled."

"I had every intention of getting on that plane, Lola. I took an Ativan and was at the airport with Katya when a taxi got rear-ended right in front of the American terminal. That was it. I saw my life flash before my eyes. It was a sign the plane was going to crash."

"Julian, news flash, the plane *did not* crash! If I delay the meeting an hour and you get on the next plane, we can make this work. What do I have to do to get you to do that?"

"I can't," Julian protests. "I just can't do it, Lola. Besides, I can't meet Olivia Cutter covered in these hives. She'll think I'm a monster. I have these dark circles under my eyes. I can't be seen like this. I look frightful."

"You're not asking her to sleep with you, you're asking her to *wear your dress* to the Oscars!"

A weary sigh exhales into my ear bud. "Do you think Donatella would be spoken to like this? Would *she* fly to L.A. for a fitting? I'm an artist. I'm fragile."

"Julian, first of all, Donatella would take a dog sled to Antarctica to wipe Olivia Cutter's ass if she'd wear Versace. Second, I'm sorry, honey, but the point is, you're no Versace. I'm trying as hard as I can to get you there. And Olivia Cutter hasn't committed to wearing your dress yet."

"You are so cold."

"Julian, what about 'I need you here for this Olivia Cutter meeting' do you not understand?"

"Lola, I hired you to get these fussy Hollywood people in my clothes for the Oscars. Deal with it. And how can you be so cruel to a dying man?"

"What are you talking about, Julian?"

"I'm as good as dead if I get on that aluminum death machine."

"Julian, you're more likely to be struck by lightning than die in a plane crash."

"Don't yell at me. I can't take it right now. I didn't sleep a wink all night and I'm feeling *very* fragile. Creating another gown for Candy Cummings under this kind of pressure is like telling Michelangelo he had twenty-four hours to paint the Sistine Chapel."

"What do you mean, *gown*, Julian? You told me you were making her that black cat-suit!"

"It's the Oscars, not Halloween. Even Halle Berry looked like she belonged on cable access in that dominatrix-gone-wrong Catwoman costume. Forget the cat-suit. Christian Dior came down from haute couture heaven and possessed my body at 3:30 a.m. It's the best work I've ever done. Open the bag with Candy's name on it, Lola."

"Julian, Korean Air is disembarking around me and I'm being swallowed by a sea of tourists. I'm not in the mood for this. Where's the cat-suit?"

"Just open the bag, Lola."

As I fight with the temperamental zipper on the garment bag, a lone peacock feather pops out. Two more inches south reveals a trio of luminescent peacock feathers nesting on a peacock blue satin shoulder strap. Another four inches exposes the delicately nipped-in waist of the one-shoulder bodice. When I finally inch out the entire gown, my heart skips a beat as the hand-painted plume of peacock feathers fans out like a rainbow on the two-foot-long train.

"Julian, this is the most beautiful dress I have ever seen," I say as tears well in my eyes.

"Really?" Julian's voice cracks.

"If Candy Cummings so much as sneezes on it, I'll kill her." I make a mental note to hide all scissors at our next fitting.

"What if she hates it?" Julian whispers, breaking into uncontrollable sobs.

"Julian, hating this dress would be like hating *Citizen Kane*. It's illegal."

"I haven't slept. I haven't eaten. I've had four lattes. And I've taken three Ativan. I'm about to shit my pants. I'm hanging up now. And then I'm taking an Imodium." *Click.*

"Julian! Julian!" Oh dear. He hasn't had a breakdown this bad since Anna Wintour served steak—an offense worse than wearing white after Labor Day to my darling PETA poster boy—at the dinner party she hosted for him last year after he won the CFDA Award for Best New Designer. Steven coughs discreetly behind my back.

I whirl around and give Steven an apologetic smile. "I'm so sorry." I'd forgotten about Steven entirely.

"Just between you and me, Jennifer Aniston has a flying phobia as well," he whispers. "It's really more of an epidemic than people realize. Just let me know if you need me to re-book him." I smile gratefully as he heads back to the first class lounge.

My ringing phone abruptly startles me out of my reverie. What now?

"Look, Julian," I say.

"Darling."

"Oh, hi, Mom."

"What is it, darling? You sound awfully defeated."

"It's Julian. He's not coming. He couldn't get on the plane."

"Really? That's odd. I lit a bravery candle for him last night. Did Gonzalo work on his chakra alignment?"

"He said he couldn't understand a word he said, Mom."

"He doesn't need to understand what he's saying. He just needs him to align his chakras. I'm concerned about Julian's solar plexus and root chakras. I'll call Gonzalo right now and get him over to Julian's right away."

"Forget it, Mom, there's no getting through to him. Besides, those tapered jeans Gonzalo wears are enough to send Julian over the edge."

"Well, in that case, I sent your father to play golf with Uncle J at Riviera and I'm starving. Let's meet for crab cakes at the Ivy."

"Mom, I still have to pull off this meeting with Olivia Cutter this afternoon. Hang on. My other line is ringing." I click over to the other call.

"My rock star's M.I.A. and I need her for some pick-up shots today," Christopher wails.

"Well, my designer's gone AWOL."

"I need a Xanax. Do you still have that prescription from Doctor Gilmore?"

"Christopher, that was for emergency use only after my breakup with SMITH. I'm sure Doctor Gilmore would be strongly opposed to my sharing that prescription with family members."

"You're such a hypocrite. Who drove to the airport to hand-deliver you Ambien for your twenty-thousand-hour flight to India when you were so screwed up over SMITH? Against Doctor Singh's orders, I might add."

"You're shaming me into this," I say. "My bedroom window's open. There's a ladder by the garage. The Xanax is in my underwear drawer. I can't promise it's not expired. I gotta go. Mom's holding on the other line." I click back over to her. "Mom, you wouldn't believe what Christopher's been through with this music video shoot," I say.

My mother gives a rueful chuckle. "I know all about rock stars. I was with Mick and Keith at the Redlands during the February 1967 raid. Marianne Faithfull and I hid in Keith's closet while the pigs tore the house apart. I nearly had a nervous breakdown. Of course I was on acid, so that may have added to my paranoia—"

"Mom, I'm sorry, but I don't have time for this. I've got Julian's dresses here at LAX and a meeting with Olivia Cutter in a few hours. Since Scarlett dropped out I've *got* to make Olivia love Julian's dresses."

"Then you must let me perform a saging ritual on them to remove the fearful energy Julian put on them. You don't want that negativity vibrating off those dresses when Olivia puts them on."

"Mom, there isn't enough time in the day. I am in total crisis mode."

"You're in crisis mode because you don't tend to these necessary rit-uals. Those dresses have been through a lot. It is very important to rid them of any negativity that has penetrated the threads. Fabric is highly absorbent. The toxicity they're holding is very dark."

I suddenly freeze in front of the wall of television screens in the Home Turf Sports Bar. Footage of Candy Cummings flashes across each screen. She's surrounded by cops, handcuffed on Sunset Boulevard, mascara running down her face, hair looking like she's just come from electric shock treatment.

"Mom, I have to go," I say, hanging up and running toward the bar.

"Rock star Candy Cummings was arrested last night during her impromptu performance at the Viper Room," intones a furrowed-brow Sam Reuben from the KTLA news desk. "She allegedly threw her Fender guitar at a fan after repeatedly flashing the crowd with her breasts. The police also found that she was in possession of illegal phar-maceuticals. The Academy of Motion Pictures has just released the fol-lowing statement: 'In light of Ms. Cummings's arrest, Mary J. Blige will be performing in her place at the Oscars.'" More footage of the cops es-corting Candy into the back of a waiting squad car, red lights pulsing in time to the flash blasts of paparazzi cameras. Surreally, she's wearing the violet cashmere Julian Tennant sweater with the silver-beaded phoenix on the front that I gave her. Not exactly the kind of exposure we had in mind. Oh my God, I feel like I've just been hit in the throat with Candy Cummings's mic stand. I take a seat right there in the middle of the ter-minal. I don't care that I can practically feel my ass contracting foot-and-mouth disease on this filthy carpet. I'd gladly take it over the reality that with Candy out of the Oscars, it's Olivia Cutter or bust. My phone trills and I weakly hold it to my ear.

"Darling, are you listening to me? We must help those dresses to free themselves from any fear-based energy." I can barely hear my mother's voice over the roar from my own fresh batch of fear-based energy. "I will simply not allow you to go into a meeting without my protection. It wouldn't be maternal at all."

"You have five minutes with the dresses. I'll be there in twenty," I spit out as I click off my cell and pull myself up off the floor.

"Om ah-pa-sahr-pahn-too teh boota yea boota boo-vee sahm-stee-tah-ha yea bootah vig-nah kahr-tah-rah stea gah-chahn-too shee-vah ahj-nah-yah," my mother chants. Her frizzy, sandy-blond hair tickles the shoulders of her pure white tunic. It looks practically identical to the ones I've picked up at the Hare Krishna store on Venice Boulevard for twenty dollars, but because my mother only wears couture, it's actually a $2,000 Gaultier. "May the spirits that are haunting this area leave and never return, by the order of Shiva," Mom translates as she moves her hands in a swooping motion over the dresses, a smoking bundle of sage clutched in her right hand. Her hundreds of gold bangles clang against one another.

"Mom, I'm concerned the dresses are going to smell like the inside of Woody Harrelson's closet," I say, wincing as the sage suddenly singes my nostril hairs.

My mother is so deep in trance she doesn't respond. Her body gyrates to the African bongos blaring in surround-sound in the middle of the living room. She finally collapses to the ground in a heap of imported silk chiffon, tulle, lamé, and organza.

"I take it you're done," I say, untangling the dresses from her arms.

"Darling, you really need to start chanting with me. I'm absolutely euphoric. My conduit is totally cleared out. You would be so much better off if you joined me in ritual," she says from the floor, her blue eyes glassy.

"I have to go, Mom," I say, kissing the top of her head as I zip the dresses back into garment bags. I'll air them out in the car on the way to Olivia's.

"Don't forget the family Oscar ritual on Saturday," Mom calls out after me. "We're casting the negativity of your father's career into the ocean and ushering in a new chapter."

"I know, I know, Mom, Abby already called me," I tell her. Maybe my mother's onto something with all this ritual. Maybe I need to cast my own negativity into the sea. That, or Adrienne Hunt.

"Be sure to bring that Ganesh you brought back from Sai Baba's ashram in Puttaparthi." Mom blows me a kiss from her puddle of couture on the floor as I heave the garment bags out the door.

"Olivia's had a catastrophe at Sally Hershberger," the twenty-one-year-old ingénue howls, storming through her robin's egg blue den. Above the threshold is a framed, bold-faced mission statement to her staff: TO ENSURE OLIVIA CUTTER'S DOMESTIC TRANQUILITY AND PROVIDE FOR HER AT ALL TIMES.

I have been waiting in this room, squished between racks upon racks of designer duds and sketches of Oscar night hopefuls, for the past two-and-a-half-hours, with Olivia's Dream Team: Her Wonder Twin stylists, a couple of Twiggy look-alikes with tow-colored Pixie cuts and mod-minidresses. Her agent, the female Ari Gold on the inside, pure Jennifer Beals in *The L Word* on the outside—the "L" in this case stands for Lesbian Hollywood Mafia. Her manager, who's got more highlights in his hair—chest included—than Olivia, and teeth as white as Chiclets. Her publicist, who could use a few highlights—her anemic white hair and face look as though she's never seen the sun, unless you count the rays coming off of that four-carat canary rock on her left hand from her studio president husband who has no idea she's having an affair with Olivia's agent. Her assistant, a petite Japanese anime character—think one of Gwen Stefani's Harajuku Girls.

Her agent, sheathed in a pale gray Gucci men's suit and a pair of killer Jimmy Choos, rolled calls. "Jesus, Jesse, how do you expect me to keep this whole hetero act under wraps when *The Enquirer* said they saw you kissing Lance Bass at the top of Runyon Canyon?" (As if anyone with eyebrows that Desperately manicured could pass for hetero, or even metro.) Her publicist scoured the tabs for photos of the Best Actress Nominee, taking notes on which companies she can squeeze for freebies. *Us Weekly* has Olivia in a bikini poolside at the Hollywood Roosevelt, playing tonsil hockey with Owen Wilson—"Has the Butterscotch Stallion Snared Another Mare?"—that's gotta be good for a Presidential Suite upgrade at a minimum. She'll probably score a Swarovski crystal faceplate out of the shot in the *Star* of Olivia tapping on her T-Mobile Sidekick at the *Glamour "Don'ts"* Party. *OK! Magazine* snapped Olivia sucking sulkily on a Parliament Light—the only freebie Olivia can cop from that is lung cancer.

I spent the whole time staring racks upon racks of my fierce competition straight in the eye. The Americans: Ralph, Donna, Calvin, Carolina, Marc, Vera. The Brits: McQueen, Stella, Vivienne Westwood. The French: Gaultier, Galliano, Lacroix, Lanvin, Roland Mouret. The Italians: Dolce & Gabbana, Armani, Valentino. How could I have let Julian send me here alone? The good news: I didn't see any *Prada*.

"Olivia had to stop at Fred Segal to buy a hat to cover this disaster," the actress announces. Her head is camouflaged in a purple fedora and gunmetal gray Christian Dior wraparound sunglasses with mirrored lenses that dwarf her petite face. "Sally wanted to cut Olivia's hair *desperately* and now she's *ruined* Olivia for the Oscars."

I wonder if the shot of tequila I drank at LAX is impairing my hearing. I rapidly surmise that it's more than just a vicious tabloid rumor: Olivia Cutter actually refers to herself in third person. Really.

"Take off the hat, Olivia," her twin stylists say in syrupy stereo, gently placing their hands on Olivia's shoulders. Like heart surgeons about to make the first incision, the Wonder Twins move toward the fedora ever so delicately.

"No! Olivia won't let you see Olivia like this," Olivia squeals, jerking away from them.

"Come on, lovey, you're so perfect, a Sally Hershberger catastrophe couldn't change that," the Twins coo.

Really? That's funny. That certainly wasn't the song the Twins were singing in the two and a half hours we waited for Olivia. Their anthem went a little something like this: "Too short. No tits. Big ass. Pain in the ass. Colossal brat. IQ of a two-year-old. Bad actress (even though she's nominated). Poor hygiene. Bad skin that even famed facialist Sonya Dakar's $500-a-pop facial couldn't fix. Still flabby after all that weight she gained for the part." And the chorus went something like this: "A Big Mac has more taste."

The Twins shoot a warning look at the others cowering on the shabby chic couch. Immediately all of Olivia Cutter's Dream Team coos in chorus, "You're perfect, a Sally Hershberger catastrophe couldn't change that."

"She'd be nowhere without me," I believe were the exact words her manager used to describe her earlier, stroking the $3,500 Paul Smith suit paid for by his hefty 10 percent commission.

"I'm the one who found her at that bus stop," her agent had added.

"Does she really expect me to keep up this act that she's a virgin when she's screwing everything in town?" her publicist laid in.

"She's an absolutely vile diva. She abuses me," were the assistant's words.

"You're perfect, a Sally Hershberger catastrophe couldn't change that," the Dream Team sings again.

The Twins gingerly move closer to Olivia. Ever so nimbly, they lift off the purple fedora to reveal the exact same enviable long blond hair I remember seeing in *People* magazine yesterday. Bearing in mind the celebrity hair guru's legendary Meg Ryan shag and her standard $1,000-a-cut fee, I frankly can't tell that Sally's scissors have even graced Olivia's head.

"Isn't it dreadful? Olivia's so ashamed. Olivia looks like a monster," the actress wails, gazing into the full-length mirror the Wonder Twins have carried over from the other side of the room. "Get it away, Olivia can't bear to look in the mirror." As they edge the mirror away, Olivia shrieks, "Bring it back! Olivia needs to see herself!" The Twins begin a demented dance of moving the mirror back and forth. "Oh no, get it away, Olivia can't look at herself. Don't take it away. Bring it back. Take it away. Wait. Olivia wants to see herself."

In a moment of divine inspiration, Olivia's manager leaps to his feet and shouts, "You're so fucking hot, I'd fucking fuck you." Funny, I thought he was fucking the pool boy at the Chateau.

"I'd fuck you too," her agent says.

"I'd fuck you too," her publicist agrees.

"I'd fuck you too," her maid says as she turns off the $600 Dyson DC14 Animal vacuum cleaner made specifically for pet hair.

All sound suddenly stops. You can hear a pin drop as Olivia Cutter slowly turns toward me, still seated in the corner. "Would you fuck Olivia?" she demands.

"On a private jet from here to Egypt. Hopefully with no tail wind." I watch in astonishment as I somehow vault over this Everest of ass-kissing. It's official: I have just crossed over to the Dark Side with a VIP pass.

"Who *are* you?" Olivia asks in her first moment not about herself.

"Oh hi," I say. "I'm Lola Santisi. I work with Julian Tennant." As I reach out to shake her hand, Olivia's tiny, fluffy white Malte-Doodle (the latest hybrid), Thor, comes running in from another room and begins yapping protectively.

Olivia recoils from my outstretched hand in horror. "Olivia has a germ issue. Olivia does not shake hands. Where's Julian? Olivia thought she was meeting the designer. Ralph visited yesterday." Olivia pauses and I watch the gears turn lazily in her head. "Wait—aren't you Paul Santisi's daughter? Olivia thought you were trying to be an actress."

My hands become instantly clammy, my throat starts to close, and the room starts to spin. It was so much easier when Olivia was all about Olivia. I'm able to compose myself enough to say, "With actresses out there like you, Olivia, there's no chance for me." Wow, I did it again; maybe I have a gift.

Thor has left Olivia's side to sniff gingerly around my ankles. He's wearing an adorable cloud blue sweater with a chinchilla collar. I reach down to pet the little guy, not sure whether I'm sucking up to Olivia or trying to dull the onset of a horrendous panic attack. Is that real cashmere? I sneak a peak at the label on the sweater. Revenge fuels me right out of full-throttle anxiety mode and back to the task at hand. Thor is wearing that custom-made Prada. That damn Adrienne Hunt. I straighten up and smile sweetly at Olivia.

"Julian so, so wanted to be here to present you with the dresses himself. But he's been fighting a terrible flu, and because he's especially sensitive to your delicate constitution, he didn't want to do anything to jeopardize your well-being—especially when you're about to win your first Oscar. The doctor told him he really shouldn't travel. Hopefully he'll be here for your next fitting," I say. Yep, definitely: a gift.

Olivia frowns in unfamiliar concentration. "Do you think he contaminated the dresses?"

I contemplate telling Olivia Cutter that they've been spiritually cleansed just to see the blank look that would befall her face from such a deep thought.

"Absolutely not. But in any case, I had them dry-cleaned," I tell her.

The air is thick with anticipation, maybe because we're all dying for an IV drip of a Marix margarita, the fetal position, a muzzle for Olivia's mouth, or all three. After what feels like an eternity, Olivia finally says, "Olivia will try them on then." She unceremoniously begins to disrobe in front of the entire room. First off is her MY BOYFRIEND'S OUT OF TOWN T-shirt. She flings off her purple satin Victoria's Secret cleavage-creating Miracle Bra, which garners some respect from me. Unlike Pam Anderson and Carmen Electra, this one kept her A-cup breasts intact. She then removes next season's scrumptious Rock & Republic ostrich knee-high wedge boots, followed by her skin-tight jeans. At last Olivia Cutter stands commando in the middle of the room with nothing more than a tiny strip of hair covering her Netherlands. I'd say the tanorexic actress is in dire need of more time on her shrink's couch and fewer hours on the Pacific Sun tanning bed. Although who am I to talk, since I'm desperate for Dr. Gilmore's couch right now and the solitude of a tanning bed sounds incredibly inviting.

I quickly push aside the countless other designer dresses hanging on the stylists' racks to make room for Julian's four dresses. The first one is a stunning, frothy, sapphire blue organza gown with a tiny halter turtleneck.

"Ugh, put this back in the bag. This is awful, not sexy enough. It looks like a nun's habit. Olivia will leave the turtlenecks to Diane

Keaton," Olivia orders me, oblivious to the fact that the delicate dress is utterly backless and oozes tasteful sexiness. Evidently Olivia Cutter has even less taste than Lil' Kim.

"What's this?" asks Olivia as she examines the next gown I hold out to her, an outrageously ornate, hourglass-shaped cream gown with a delicate corset and massive outcrop of gold Edwardian swag. The skirt flounce eats up almost half the floor space. "This is very Napoleon and Josephine. Olivia likes it," Olivia purrs. "Help Olivia get this on," she commands the Twins, who rush over.

She's off by one hundred years and the wrong country, but who cares? Vienna, Egon Schiele, and Empress Sisi inspired Julian's gown. You'd think Olivia would know that. She's set to play Empress Sisi in a John Madden film in the fall, for crying out loud.

"I'm imagining a pale powdered face . . ." excitedly announces one Twin.

"And fuchsia lips, maybe a faux black birthmark above your lip," croons the other Twin.

"Lots of your delicious cleavage spilling out, like Uma Thurman in *Dangerous Liaisons,*" the Twins finish in unison.

Big mistake. "Yuck, get this thing off. Olivia will never compete with Uma Thurman. Olivia will never be six feet tall with spectacular breasts. Olivia will always be five feet tall with tiny titties. Get this off *now!*"

"Get it off her. Hurry," her publicist barks at the Twins.

"Faster," her agent demands.

The Twins scurry over to remove the gown as Olivia falls to the ground in a vulnerable, sobbing, naked heap. Thor starts barking protectively, running in circles around her. He finally settles on top of the sumptuous gown she's cast aside. I wince at the thought of his toenails scraping against the raw silk, but it somehow doesn't seem appropriate to attempt to move him while Olivia is in full breakdown.

"You are so much more than Uma Thurman. She can't compete with *you*," one Twin exclaims, getting on the floor with Olivia and stroking her hair.

"You are far more beautiful," states the other Twin.

"And a far superior actress," Olivia's manager pipes up.

"A far superior actress," the entire staff choruses.

Olivia slowly begins to peek one eye out from beneath her mess of golden hair.

"Uma Thurman has never won an Academy Award. The only thing she's ever won is an MTV Movie Award," pronounces Olivia's manager. Oops, bad move.

"*Olivia's* never won an Academy Award *or* an MTV Movie Award. *Why* hasn't Olivia won an MTV Movie Award?" Olivia yells. "That's your fault!" Olivia screams, pointing at her manager.

"You were nominated for Best Kiss last year," her manager appeals.

"So what, Olivia didn't win," Olivia shouts.

"You'll be a shoo-in next year with the *Grease* remake and it's an honor just to be nominated, honey," reminds her manager.

"It's only an honor to be nominated *and* win. And you *still* haven't even *found* Olivia's perfect Danny Zuko for *Grease*. Get out! Olivia wants you to get out!" Olivia barks as her manager gets up to leave.

No! Pick me! I want to be voted out of the asylum. I'll leave! I want to shout, but then find my lips have not parted and my feet remain firmly planted in place.

As her manager reaches for the door, Olivia yells, "How *dare* you leave Olivia! Where do you think you're going? You're just like every other man in Olivia's life—always walking out the door. You of all people should understand Olivia. You *know* Olivia has abandonment issues! When Olivia tells you to leave, it means stay. Thor would never leave Olivia," she says, reaching for the dog. I breathe a huge sigh of relief as she removes him from the discarded dress and nuzzles her head in his fur. I quickly return the gown to its garment bag.

"I'm sorry, honey," the manager says contritely. "I won't ever leave you. You know I'm always here for you." He walks toward her naked body.

"Really?" Olivia whines, beginning to crack a little smile.

"Really, honey," her manager says.

Sensing her spirits have been adequately lifted for the moment, I bring out the next dress.

"Oh this is it. This is it! This is a gem. It's a gem," one of the Twins cries exuberantly as she grabs the dazzling off-the-shoulder tiered ombré hand-beaded dress out of my hands. The other Twin helps Olivia up off the floor as both Twins expertly slip her into the sparkling tulle confection.

The Twins take in dramatic, gargantuan breaths and place their hands over their mouths. Finally one Twin giddily coos, "Olivia you're gorgeous. You look like a perfect ruby. You're a glistening jewel."

"You're an absolute jewel," praises the other Twin as Olivia moves closer to the mirror.

"I love it," her publicist professes.

Olivia investigates herself intently, like a scientist inspecting a cell through a microscope. She takes herself in from every angle, running her hands gingerly over the garnet satin ribbon tied in a bow at her waist and the same ribbon detail above each elbow of her long beaded, tiered sleeves. The room is swallowed by nail-biting silence as we all hold our breath for Olivia's reaction.

"Olivia absolutely, positively hates it!"

"Hate it," flies out of her publicist's mouth.

"Olivia looks like a shrimp in a sack. Olivia's no Sarah Jessica Parker. Olivia doesn't wear these short funky thingies. And Olivia's no

Nicole Kidman. You know Olivia doesn't have those gazelle legs. Why are you trying to make Olivia feel badly about Olivia's legs? You are *trying* to make Olivia feel short!" Olivia shouts in my direction.

"Honey, it's not you. It's the dress. It's all wrong," her manager says as he solemnly shakes his head. The entire Dream Team looks at me somberly.

I want to tell Olivia she feels short because she *is* short. Sarah Jessica Parker has more style in her left pinky toe than Olivia will ever have. Three very kind women jeopardized their eyesight hand-beading the scrumptious piece of couture she's carelessly casting aside. Instead I say, "Can I use your bathroom?" I don't wait for an answer as I rush out the door.

It's a lie. I don't need the bathroom. I need to walk straight out the front door, get into my car, drive straight home, draw the shades, disconnect the telephone, curl into bed, and lie there for the next forever, never to be heard from again. Surely by the time the police knock down my door to discover my decomposing form, Julian will feel so sorry for me he'll forgive me for throwing in the towel so quickly.

I fling open that front door like Julie Andrews in *The Sound of Music.* As soon as my feet hit the welcome mat I twirl right into an enormous dreadlocked messenger struggling beneath five bulky garment bags.

"Can you sign for these?" the messenger asks, shifting his burden so he can hold out a clipboard.

I glance at the sender's name on the delivery slip: "A. Hunt."

The purity of Julie Andrews drains out of my soul. I thought I'd worked through it in therapy, but I'm suddenly back in Paris, watching Adrienne steal my design and my credit. That job would have changed my life. Okay, I know, Julian deserved that gig the most. But I wouldn't be standing here, in Olivia Cutter's doorway, on the brink of yet another failure unless I suck up to a psychopathic midget and her Greek chorus of toadies. Under the circumstances, I think a soupçon of revenge is in order, don't you?

"Sure I'll sign," I say, as the messenger hands me a pen.

"Number nine," he says.

"Oh, wait a sec. Actually, this delivery was sent to the wrong address. These bags need to go to ICM—for Kathy Griffin," I tell him. I know Kathy would stab herself in the eye with a hanger to get herself off the "Worst Dressed List" care of Adrienne Hunt and Prada. Let's see Adrienne wrestle these clothes back from the D-List. Good luck.

Moving from channeling Julie Andrews to Robert De Niro in *Raging Bull*, I storm back through Olivia Cutter's doorway and head straight into that room full of phonies with a newfound spring in my step.

"You know, Olivia, you're right about all those other dresses. *This* is the dress you should be wearing down the Red Carpet on Sunday," I say, pulling out the magnum opus Julian made for Candy Cummings. "And I know this is the dress Julian envisioned for you as well. This dress was inspired by Olivia de Havilland," I say, as inspiration strikes.

"Olivia thought Olivia was the only Olivia going to the Oscars," Olivia says in a panic.

Deep cleansing breath. "No, no, quite like yourself, Olivia de Havilland was another great actress. *And* she won two Oscars," I say, feeling my enthusiasm infecting the room.

"For Best Actress?" Olivia says, intrigued, moving quickly to put on the enchanting gown that is the same shade as her eyes.

"Yes, for Best Actress," I say, noticing the brand-new twinkle in Olivia's eye as she moves closer to the mirror to take herself in.

"What movies was she in?" Olivia asks, her interest clearly piqued. She examines herself in the mirror, spinning around and around as the plume of peacock feathers dance behind her.

Jesus, is she kidding me? Oh God, she's not kidding. "She was in *Gone with the Wind*," I say, suppressing a sigh.

"Oh, Olivia's heard of that movie. Olivia likes it. Olivia likes this idea. Olivia likes this dress," she says. I must admit she looks spectacularly luscious in the gown, which accentuates her teeny waist.

"You are gorgeous. You're gorgeous. This is it! This is it!" The Twins shriek, grabbing Olivia's hands and jumping up and down. "You are so perfect! Everything about you is perfect! Everything!"

"Even your feet are perfect, honey," her manager trills in rapture.

"Oh my Gawd. Olivia's perfect. Olivia's just perfect. Everything about Olivia is perfect. Even Olivia's feet are perfect," Olivia chants, bouncing up and down with the Twins, Thor yapping joyously. Then she abruptly stops bouncing, raising a scolding finger at the Twins. Oh no. Now what is it?

"Get the Polaroid. Take a picture of Olivia in the dress. It doesn't matter what the dress looks like in real life. Olivia needs to photograph well in the dress. It's all about what Olivia looks like in pictures. It's all about how Olivia photographs on the Oscar Red Carpet."

Well, she's right. Can't argue with that. Please God let her Polaroid well. As the Twins race away to find their cameras, I feel the obscene chinchilla collar of Thor's Prada sweater rubbing vigorously against my foot. I swiftly bend down to swat him away.

The Twins begin snapping Olivia from various angles. "Seeing Olivia like this makes Olivia think Sally Hershberger may be a genius after all," Olivia says as she tousles her blond mane in front of the mirror.

"Oh no!" I yelp as something warm trickles onto my foot. I look down at a yellow puddle forming around my brand-spanking-new silver Stella McCartney sandals. As I search in vain for something to wipe myself off on, it's clear that Olivia and the rest of the Dream Team are ignoring the small, white, irritating elephant in this room. The dog just cocked his leg and peed on me, for Christ's sake! And these people are pretending not to notice! This is the perfect ending to a totally preposterous day. Who *hasn't* peed on me today? At least the dog's straightforward.

"Olivia wants you to come back tomorrow so we can do a full hair and makeup test with the dress," Olivia says, throwing a down-to-business look in my direction. "You, get Jeff Vespa from WireImage here to take pictures of Olivia in the dress," she orders her publicist. "You, get Bobbi Brown here to do Olivia's makeup and Sally Hershberger here to do Olivia's hair," she orders her assistant. "You two," she says pointing to the Twins, "Olivia wants diamonds, lots of diamonds. And you," she says, pointing at me, "three o'clock. Don't be late."

"Of course, Olivia, I'm here for you," I say. My sandals squish across the floor as I close the front door behind me.

The soothing sound of the sitar fills the large studio, which still emanates the faint smell of sweat mixed with incense from the 6:30 P.M. class. Stretching out on my yoga mat, I feel the lunacy of the day evaporate as I do my best to ground myself in the earth. Normally I like to hide out in the back corner, but Cricket insisted on a spot by the front because "Curtis Hanson and David O. Russell always practice near the altar," she tells me. This explains why Cricket's in full makeup, hair artfully tousled just so, looking ravishingly gorgeous in a white spaghetti-strapped unitard that offsets her milky skin.

The lights dim as S. D. Rail's angelic voice suddenly engulfs the room. I immediately feel the molecular structure of the atmosphere shift; S. D. exudes an irresistible sex appeal that causes intense jockeying for mat space from the female yogis. It could be the fact that he looks like Robert Redford in *Butch Cassidy and the Sundance Kid* and chants like a young Mick Jagger.

S. D. brings his hands together in prayer pose. "I'd like to set the intention of the class on something that has been on my mind, and that is love."

Great. Love. The last thing I need to focus on is how screwed (or sadly, not screwed) I am in the whole love department thanks to SMITH. I close my eyes and try to drop into this love, love, love. Suddenly I'm Dorothy in a terrifying tornado set a-spin by Olivia Cutter, the Tin Man; Adrienne Hunt, the Wicked Witch of the West; and SMITH, the Cowardly Lion. How do I get out of here? What's wrong with me? Why aren't I over SMITH?

"Find your way to downward dog. Everyone take a lion's breath, open your mouth wide, and let it all out. Aahhhhhhh," S. D. says sensually. "Really let it go."

I can't. I can't let it go. I don't want to let it go. S. D. doesn't know the torment that is Olivia Cutter. S. D. doesn't know the vast ocean of betrayal that is Adrienne Hunt. He doesn't know SMITH, the shit.

"Keep coming back to your intention of love, letting love resonate throughout your body," S. D. tells us again. I want to scream at him to shut up with all the love talk.

Nevertheless, after seven sun salutations and a vinyasa flow series, I have to admit I am starting to feel much more balanced. Or maybe I'm just too exhausted to care anymore. S. D. settles us on our backs.

"If everyone would please gather around Cricket here for a moment as she demonstrates wheel," S. D. requests.

He moves in to adjust her. I'm no yogi, but as far as I can tell, the pose is flawless, but S. D. is the pro. He straddles Cricket's legs as he places his hands underneath her sacrum, pushing her up into what seems to be his crotch. Yep, most certainly his crotch.

"Inner spiral those legs," S. D. instructs Cricket as he presses himself hard against her. Suddenly I'm not sure which school of yoga S. D. is practicing. I look to Cricket for a sign of discomfort, but all I notice is an unusual glow in her cheeks.

As soon as we hit the dressing room after savasana, I lean in to Cricket. "Oh my God, Cricket, I would have kneed S. D. in the balls. Sometimes these hot men think they can get away with anything. Are you okay?"

Cricket, who's changing out of her white unitard and rifling through her black Samsonite carry-on, doesn't seem to be paying any attention to me. I realize she is very simply ignoring me.

"Cricket, excuse me, you're not listening to me, and besides, what's with the suitcase?"

Why isn't she answering me?

"*Cricket!* What is going *on?*" I plead.

"I can't talk about this here, Lo," Cricket says, giving me that shut-up-*now* look.

All at once it comes flooding over me. How could I have been so dense? "Oh no, Cricket, don't do this, *do not* do this," I whisper. Of course. The raw food diet. The intention of love. The weird sexual demonstration. The fully packed suitcase. That glow.

"Talk to me," I demand as Cricket pulls me into the bathroom stall and locks the door behind us.

"Listen. Lo, I'm in love, okay? It's love," she insists in a hushed voice.

"Cricket, why didn't you tell us?" I implore, flustered. "Kate and I would have fully advised against this. You know about the blow jobs in the back room. He uses that rock star magnetism to his advantage."

"This is why I didn't tell you," Cricket sighs. "S. D. is so misunderstood. He's absolutely brilliant. He's teaching me about Buddhism, Hinduism, Sufism. He's a mystic. He's the most amazing lover. He's a tantric practitioner. And let me tell you," Cricket leans in to whisper in my ear, "it's the best sex of my life. He taught the workshop Sting studied at."

I collapse onto the toilet seat, picturing the inevitable heartbreak. "How did this happen?" I ask.

"He asked me to assist him at the Thai massage workshop. We would have these intense ten-hour days of study and then we'd follow it up by four-hour dinners at Rawvolution. He thinks I'm a gifted practitioner," Cricket explains.

"Listen, Cricket, SMITH told me I was a gifted actress when we first started, okay? This is what men do," I say.

"Come with us to Juliano's tonight for dinner. You'll see how fiery his inner spirit is," Cricket says, clearly a goner.

"Inner spirit," I ask, opening the bathroom stall. "What is that, S. D. speak?"

"Oh, I know, he's just infectious."

"That's what I'm afraid of." I look at my cell phone for the first time since the two-hour class began. "Thirty missed calls? Have you ever heard of such a thing?" I read a text message from Olivia's manager:

> Olivia and I want to profusely apologize on Thor's behalf. He is new to the family and is unaware it's inappropriate to pee on strangers. ;-) Naturally, my princess was oblivious to the whole thing. But I can assure you that her mortification was abundant after you left. Thanks not only for cleaning it up, but moreover for the dress. She is happy as a clam.

And crazier than Larry Wachowski. But at least she's happy.

My cell rings. "Hello," I answer softly, lest I get the Cell Phone Death Stare for using the forbidden gadget inside the studio.

"I've been trying to reach you for hours. Where have you been?" a shrill female voice barks.

Whatever happened to a friendly "hello"?

"Who is this?"

"It's Jennifer from Ken Sunshine's office. I need you to get over to Jake Jones's house *now*. The GM show's tomorrow. Why weren't you picking up your phone? It's Oscar Week! He's in the middle of his poker game, but he said he'd sit out a hand. You've got ten minutes with him."

Hold on. Jake's publicist canceled his fittings ten times in the last three weeks and *I'm* the asshole? Screw the intention of love. I hate this job. *Do it for Julian,* I tell myself. "How do I get there?"

I trudge up the steep stairs to Jake Jones's Topanga Canyon ranch-style house, a surprisingly funky place that feels like Jerry Garcia might have lived here in the 60s. Not quite the cold, sleek, Palm Springs modern or Mediterranean sprawl that seems to inflict young movie stars searching for a tasteful image. Though the fully loaded black Mercedes parked out front is entirely on par with what I would expect from a bimboy. My legs are already sore from the numerous vinyasas and my aching chataranga arms can barely balance the garment bags holding the four custom-tailored Julian Tennant suits that have been in my car collecting dust since Jake's publicist first canceled on me. I feel like Janis Joplin in Cricket's dark chocolate slouchy halter dress and her taupe Birkenstocks, but I didn't have time to go home and change, and I simply couldn't bear to put those pee-soaked sandals back on my feet. Julian would be absolutely horrified by this thrift-store schmatte and these appalling hippy sandals. On Cricket they look bohemian chic; on me, they look boho bag lady. However, I'm thinking it's a good thing I couldn't feel less sexy as I prepare to meet the actor about whom *In Touch* trumpets: "Why We're *Jonesing* for Hollywood's Hottest Hunk."

As I knock on the door, the screaming voice in the back of my head is wondering what the heck I'm doing here at eleven o'clock at night when I should be buried beneath my sheets with a Kiehl's soothing Algae masque on my face, watching my TiVo'd *Oprah*. Instead I brace myself for a live episode of *Entourage*. Typical actor late-night bullshit. Always having to cater to their selfish whims. I prepare myself for the retinue of young payrolled hangers-on from the old school 'hood gathered for their nightly poker game.

The door swings open. It's him. Jake Jones answering the door himself? Well, I guess eleven o'clock really isn't that late. I'm sure he's had a really busy day. It's not like I go to bed before one anyway. Who am I kidding? He's devastating. Absolutely, undeniably dangerous. Those big blue husky dog eyes, that goofy, crooked smile. Oh God. Oh no. I'm in trouble.

"Hi, I'm Jake. Are you Lola?" Oh my God, he's approachable. He's down-to-earth. This is not what I had in mind at all. He's gorgeously disheveled in that guy's guy way. He's wearing Hawaiian-print board shorts that cling just below his hipbones and an oversized navy blue long-john shirt. His blond shaggy hair is a mess. I almost reach over to smooth it down and question my integrity immediately. Is it so easy for me to fall off the wagon? Straight away I begin my sobriety mantra: 187 days. 187 days. 187 days. No actors. No actors. No actors. I realize I'm looking at the ground trying desperately to avoid his big blue eyes. Oh no, I haven't said a word.

"Um. I'm Lola. I have a suit. For you. Do you want to get undressed? I mean by yourself. I mean . . . you know what I mean." Oh Jesus. I've officially made an ass of myself. Somehow I don't think I'll have to worry about Jake Jones jumping my bones now. Problem solved.

Jake smiles reassuringly, as though receiving blithering idiots on his doorstep is all in a day's work. "I was just about to eat a burrito and I have an extra one. Are you hungry?" he asks, taking the garment bag out of my arms.

"Actually, I'm starving."

"Good. I'll heat 'em up," he says, heading inside and throwing the garment bag over his couch. "Do you want me to bring the burrito out there to you? I mean I could, but it's kinda cold out there," he adds as he finds me still frozen to his doormat.

"Sorry, I was distracted. It's kinda been a tough day."

"I'm sorry about that. Do you wanna talk about it?"

Do I wanna talk about it? What's wrong with this guy? He must have a stubby penis because this is not within the realm of any human interaction I've had with an actor in Los Angeles. Ever. Well, he asked for it.

"Well first off, I skipped my latte. I'm trying to get off coffee. But it was a big mistake, because then I ended up having to drink two espressos to counteract the shot of tequila I had at LAX because Julian—the man who designed your suit, you're going to love it—missed his plane and I have no idea if there's enough Xanax on the planet to get him on the next flight and the nutbag rock star we were going to dress for the Oscars just got thrown in jail on obscenity charges and then there was Miss I Only Speak In Third Person, and Thor the Amazing Leg-Peeing Dog . . ." The floodgates open as I stand at Jake Jones's threshold, still uncertain whether I'm ready to cross over. I go on and on, vomiting words uncontrollably.

"I think you could use a game of air hockey and a beer," Jake says when I gutter out at last, pulling me through the door and into his living room. As I follow him into the kitchen I'm amazed at how proud Martha Stewart would be: the coordinated couch and throw pillows, the cashmere throws, the Diptyque Figuir and Feuille De Lavande candles, the white orchids. Oh. Ohohoh. He's gay. Of course, he's gay. What a relief. I can climb right back on that wagon. As we pass the dining room, I notice the green felt poker table that still has the remnants of the game Jake must have just finished with his buddies: full ashtrays spilling over with stubbed-out cigars, empty Amstel and Heineken beer bottles, peanut shells. Okay . . . not gay. All right . . . you know . . . what's one game of air hockey and a beer?

"Chicken or beef," Jake asks, holding up the oil-stained paper bag from Baja Fresh.

"Actually I'm a veg . . . beef, I'll take the beef," I say, suddenly feeling unapologetically, ravenously carnivorous as I take a seat on a black leather stool at his marble kitchen countertop.

I inhale my burrito in record time. I didn't realize how desperate my body was for protein. "Oh boy, that steak is good," I say, looking up to find Jake has barely taken three bites of his chicken burrito and is peering at me curiously. Man, is he sexy. I reach for a paper napkin from the pile strewn on the counter. Just as I'm about to wipe my mouth, I read *"Sarah 818-555-9160—looking forward to that game of air hockey,"* followed by a big bubbly scribbled heart. I turn the napkin over to find the Whiskey Bar logo.

I dangle the napkin in front of Jake. "It's a good thing I didn't use this. Sarah's number could have been lost forever," I say. "Or is this your idea of a Rolodex?" pointing to the messy pile. Jake tosses the Whiskey Bar napkin into the trash.

"Rolodex? You're so last millennium."

"I'm a pen and paper kinda gal. Call me old-fashioned." I say. "That poor girl's waiting by the phone, you know."

"She'll get over it. Believe me, she's better off. She's getting her Master's in Nursing at UCLA. She'll meet a nice doctor."

Why can't I meet a nice doctor? Or a nurse, for God's sake. I'd take Ben Stiller in *Meet the Fockers*. "You know it's getting late—maybe you should try the suits on now," I say, suddenly completely uninterested in this meat-puppet.

Jake looks at me levelly. "How about a game of air hockey first?"

"I'll leave air hockey to the Sarahs."

"One game," he says, leaving his half-eaten burrito on the counter and hitching up his pants.

"Are you going to finish that?" I take the chicken burrito with me into his game room-slash-den.

Focus on the task at hand. Just get him into suit. Oh no, he has to get undressed to get into suit. Oh no. Uh-oh. Image of naked Jake Jones as his hand brushes over mine to hand me the red plastic pusher thingy I'm supposed to hit the puck into the goal with. Okay, focus on air hockey. Focus on scoring. No, not that kind of scoring, puck into goal, no not that kind of puck into goal.

Swoosh. Jake scores. "Man, you better pay attention," he teases.

"I gave you that one," I say as I stare into those eyes. I hold the stare as I put the puck back on the table and go for a goal. Score!

Jake smiles at me appraisingly. "Hey, not bad! I like a girl who's a straight shooter." Is he flirting with me? Forget it, mister.

"So how come your poker game broke up early?" I ask as he puts the puck back on the table.

"I kicked everyone out. I have an audition tomorrow," he says as he shoots.

"Right, you need your beauty rest," I say. "What's your audition for?"

He scores again on me and arches a triumphant eyebrow. "I'm screen-testing for *Hawkman*."

"Wow, good for you! My brother always felt Hawkman was the most underrated of superheroes. He *is* king of ornithology and de facto ruler of the sky."

"Hey, you're the first girl I've met who's ever *heard* of Hawkman. Well, Hawkman won't be underrated anymore if Jerry Bruckheimer has anything to say about it. The man is king of the blockbuster and de facto ruler of the summer," Jake says, blocking my shot.

"I hope Jerry stays true to the original mythology. I was always so inspired as a kid that Hawkman became a superhero after being abandoned as a baby. I mean, think of all the people with abandonment issues Jerry could inspire to overcome their childhood."

"Wow. That's deep. I was just thinking about how I'd look in spandex."

Um, me too. Bad Lola! Bad Lola! Stop it!

"They'll probably give it to Matt Damon anyway." Jake offers me a lopsided grin, but he actually looks a little . . . sad . . . and insecure. Oh *no,* I can't take it when actors get all vulnerable on me. Time to get down to business.

"I'm sorry, I'm keeping you up, this is a big deal for you. Let's get this fitting over with." I put the red hockey pusher on the table and get the garment bag from the other room.

"You're just a sore loser," Jake says, his voice suddenly husky as he walks toward me, hitching his shorts around those famous buns. I brace myself for the impact of my fall off the wagon. Uh-oh. "Lola." His electric fingers move toward my face. Oh boy, here it comes. "You have a piece of . . . uhhh . . . I think it's lettuce on the side of your face."

I can feel my cheeks flaming. "Oh, oh my gosh, oh . . . I'm, um, can I use your bathroom?"

I grab my purse from the kitchen counter and flee down the hall. I quickly lock the bathroom door and begin madly splashing my face, feverish with self-loathing and humiliation. I whip out my cell and resist the urge to call Dr. Gilmore, since she wants me to work on creating boundaries in our relationship. (Just because I called her on Sunday night at 11:00 P.M. Twice.) I sit down on the toilet seat and speed-dial Cricket, in desperate need of a sponsor. It goes straight to voice mail. At least Kate picks up right away.

"This better be good. I'm at the *Premiere* party and I just spotted Hugh Jackman without his agent," Kate answers.

"I need an intervention."

"Shouldn't you be calling Cricket for this?"

"Her phone's off. Guess what? She's sleeping with S. D."

"I knew it. No one would subject themself to raw food if it wasn't about sex. What's that echo? Where are you?" Kate asks.

"I'm in Jake Jones's bathroom and I'm about to fall off the wagon."

"Lo, so fall already. I mean it's been like six months since SMITH. You may as well join the nunnery at this point. Do it. It'll get you over him," Kate says.

"Wrong answer. You're supposed to tell me it will end in another heartbreak, that he's a player, that he's just another stupid actor. I know you think I'll be okay if I just get right back up on that horse"—I have to violently shake off the unbidden visual of Catherine the Great and the stallion in the harness—"but it just doesn't work that way with me. If I get involved with one more actor, you're going to have to visit me at Shady Acres."

"Lola, it's just sex. Don't overanalyze it."

"Kate! Can't you just channel someone else for a second, anyone else?"

"You should be talking to Cricket. But even she's too busy getting laid."

"I'm hanging up now."

Click.

I'm here for Julian, not for sex. Here to make something of myself, and help a friend. Here to conquer my Career Deficit Disorder and my Actorholism and do whatever it takes to get to Day 188. I resolve to say a polite good-bye and get home to my bed to dream about my husband, the non-actor. I'll find out from the publicist in the morning which suit Jake prefers.

I throw open the bathroom door to find Jake Jones standing before me, looking absolutely disarming in Julian's charcoal gray pin-striped three-button suit. He grabs my face and plants one hell of a kiss on my lips. *Definitely, undeniably, falling, spinning, twirling, jumping off that wagon.*

tuesday

149 hours, 13 minutes, 7 seconds until

the Oscar is handed out for Best Screenplay.

"did you sleep with him or not?" Kate yells as I use the battering ram of my large English Breakfast latte to push past the front door of her one-bedroom apartment in the El Royale on Rossmore, which is naturally a dollhouse-sized replica of Bryan Lourd's Benedict Canyon house. "Jesus, it's a simple question! What kind of moron are you?" I blanch until I realize that Kate's now hectoring a disembodied voice on her headset. "Can you get him on the phone now, or not? Just do it, Adam!" She shakes her head in disgust, whips off her headset, and tosses it onto a side table. She arches an eyebrow at me. "Well?"

"We slept together, but we didn't sleep-sleep together," I confess.

"Didn't you *want* to?"

"It's even worse; I really like him," I say, collapsing in a heap on the Christian Liaigre bone-colored sofa she had shipped from Paris. Bryan Lourd's decorator convinced her it was worth going into debt for. It *is* the very couch Matthew McConaughey rests his famous ass on when he visits his uber-agent. As always, Kate's apartment is freakishly *American Psycho* clean. And those damn Cartier picture frames B. L.'s decorator placed strategically around the apartment are still staring back at me with those freaky filler models that came with the frames—three years ago. Despite the fact that it's only 5:00 A.M., Kate has already finished rolling her European calls, watched the east coast feed of *Good Morning America,* and read *The New York Times, The Hollywood Reporter,* and *Variety* cover to cover.

"You're not supposed to *like* him, Lola, you were supposed to sleep with him to get you over SMITH."

"Jake isn't a blow-up sex doll, he's a human being," I protest.

A loud sigh gutters from Kate's lips. "No, he's an *actor,*" she says.

"Oh God, I know. You're right. Actors are the enemy. They're a national security threat. If I were Dick Cheney, I'd shoot every last one of 'em."

"Heather Graham playing a neurosurgeon would be more convincing than you are right now."

"It's just that I think this one's different, Kate. I mean, Jake's sensitive and approachable and he really listened to me and he didn't even try to pull off my La Perlas."

"So what, he's gay?"

"He's not gay. He's a *gentleman.*" Kate throws me a "yeah, right" look. "Okay, he's under strict orders from his Reiki master, who told him in order to fortify his career chi, he has to refrain from sex for at least twenty-four hours before a big audition. When Jake had sex the night before the *DaVinci Code II: DeCoded* audition, Ron Howard gave the part to Billy Crudup."

Kate caws in triumph. "Actor bullshit, Chapter One."

"Kate, it's *five* o'clock in the morning. I should be deep in REM but instead I'm standing here in one of Cricket's thrift store schmattes and her *Birkenstocks*. This is obviously a cry for help. Intervene! *Please.*"

Kate bends over to lace up her Nikes and grab her jump rope for her 5:30 A.M. ass-whooping "drop and give me fifty" Special Forces-inspired workout at Barry's Bootcamp.

"Okay! Okay! Let me focus," Kate says, sitting down next to me. "We'll get through this. I've gotta think. You know I'm not very good at this." Her ringing home phone saves her from channeling Dr. Phil. She clicks on the speakerphone of her cordless Panasonic.

"K-a-a-a-t-e!" Will Bailey shrieks like an eight-year-old girl on helium. "Do you hear that?!" he screams over a deafening roar. "That's the sound of *f-r-e-e-e-e-e-e-dom*! I'm standing on the tarmac with Tom Cruise. He's about to take me up in his World War II fighter plane."

"Tell Tom you want a part in *Mission: Impossible 4* while you've got him alone up there," Kate says. "Tell him—" she clicks off the speakerphone for a more private audience and throws a give-me-a-sec index finger in my direction.

While Kate talks to Will, I kick off Cricket's atrocious footwear, lie back on the couch, and flip on the east coast feed of *The Today Show*. Meredith Vieira's interviewing Deepak Chopra. You know, that guy everyone was into *before* they got into Kabbalah. And Transcendental Meditation a la David Lynch. And *The Secret*.

"Meredith, addiction is our society's biggest problem." Deepak's voice is smooth, silky, soothing, a bath in a chocolate fountain. He leans forward in his chair, magnetizing the talk show hostess toward him.

Their noses are almost touching. "No matter what the drug of choice is, alcohol, sex—" *Actors,* I think to myself "—addicts have to come to a place where they realize that the drawbacks of their habit outweigh the benefits."

"That's so true," Meredith says, breaking the traction beam of Deepak's gaze.

As they cut to commercials, I grab a script from the giant stack on Kate's coffee table and dig into my purse for a pen. I flip over the script and jot down "drawbacks" and "benefits." "Drawbacks": Being an Actorholic makes the dating pool in L.A. shrivel to the size of a Fendi baguette. As I go to jot it down in my "drawbacks" column, I hesitate. Is that a benefit? I mean, actors are the hottest breed of man ever. No. It's bad, bad, bad. Focus. Drawbacks of being an Actorholic: Well, you pay for the month of bliss where you feel like the sun rises and sets in your pants with the inevitable heartbreak that leads to many pints of Cherry Garcia and endless viewings of *Breakfast at Tiffany's.*

I hear the click of Kate disconnecting from her phone. She looks at her Rolex. "I have five minutes to intervene and save you."

Suddenly a totally strapping man in a navy "Home Jeeves" uniform bursts out of Kate's bedroom, grabs a fold-up scooter from the corner, and heads out the front door, giving Kate a smart salute as he exits. Kate grins and blows him a kiss.

"Who the hell was that?" I ask.

"One too many martinis at Zach Braff's house after *Premiere* magazine's party at The Skybar last night. So I called 'Home Jeeves.' They sent that guy to give me a ride home and then I gave him one."

"Well, I guess that's a heck of a lot better than a DUI and a Mel Gibson mug shot on The Smoking Gun." I don't know which is cuter: the adorable little scooters they stick in your trunk or the 'Home Jeeves' guys who slip the keys out of your hands.

"Look, I've got four minutes. Are you sure you're okay?"

"You know, I think so. I just saw the most amazing segment with Deepak Chopra, and he gave me this great idea for a list. He's so much more relatable than Dr. Phil. Why doesn't he have his own show?"

I swear I see the ghost of Thomas Edison switching on the lightbulb in Kate's brain as she dials her cell phone and heads for the front door, "Adam, we need to find out who represents Deepak Chopra. . . . No, I don't know how to spell it. I'm paying *you* to spell for me. . . . I want it on my desk by seven-thirty. Yes, a.m."

"I better get half of that commission," I yell after Kate as she shuts the door behind her.

I'm jolted out of a valerian root-induced sleep by my ringing Nokia. I wipe the drool from my mouth and sit up on Kate's couch. Damn, I missed the call. My anxiety was so piqued after that earful from Deepak that I just *had* to try the herbal tincture that Demi told me about when I ran into her and Ashton at Rabbi Eitan's birthday party. I mean, it's mandatory for a girl to balance her nervous system. Note to self: it totally knocks you out. Good when going through a breakup and the world is insufferable. Bad when having a work-related nervous breakdown and you have to function at highest potential.

What time is it? Damn it. It's noon! I'm supposed to pick up Julian at LAX in twenty minutes for our Olivia Cutter fitting at 2 P.M. Thank God he agreed to get on a plane after I told him Tom Ford booked a candlelit table for dinner at the Sunset Tower before the GM Show tonight. I grab my keys and bag and throw on Cricket's Birkenstocks. I'm just about to fly out the front door when I realize there's absolutely no way I can get home, change, and drive all the way to LAX in the next twenty minutes. And I *cannot* show up in this schmatte. Julian will go

Joan Crawford wire-hanger cuckoo if he sees me in *this*. After all, I'm part of his brand extension. I beeline for Kate's closet and start frantically rummaging through her uber-agent power gear: H&M khaki twill, not right; Lela Rose metallic tweed, definitely wrong; black Prada, Kate you traitor, should be burned; Burberry navy shift dress, will do.

I bolt to the sink and rip off Cricket's dress and furiously scrub under my arms with Kate's green tea hand soap. I splash my face, grab the bottle of Listerine, throw my hair in a ponytail, and spritz with her Must de Cartier. Fifteen minutes. Panic setting in big-time.

Underwear. Riffling through Kate's underwear drawer. Red lace and, um, crotchless; okay, gross. Hot pink satin and dental floss, wouldn't even cover Anastasia's Brazilian. Leopard and crotchless again; my God, does she not own one pair of plain, cotton panties? I turn my honorable gray cotton La Perlas inside out. I throw on the navy shift dress and sprint for my car. Eleven minutes. I floor the gas pedal.

I whip out some mascara at the stoplight at La Cienega and Rodeo (not Drive, *Road*—we're talking *Tar-jay* not Tiffany). If I weren't so late, I'd nip in and pick up a pair of Isaac Mizrahi driving moccasins for $13.99. So what if they're *faux* leather, they're *$13.99*.

My screen starts flashing INCOMING CALL.

"Hello?"

"Want a partner in misery? Candy Cummings is out on bail and up on indecency and assault charges," Christopher shouts over the phone line. "I just got a call from the record label who saw a rough cut of my video. The execs think it's brilliant, but it's a no-go from Cummings— her scumbag attorney thinks it'll damage her reputation in their upcoming court case. Like offering to share her blow with the bailiff didn't?"

"They're still paying you, right?" I ask.

"Yes."

"Okay, good. We'll talk about your career later. I have to deal with mine. I have call waiting."

Click.

"It's Katya." Julian's long-suffering assistant. What did he forget this time? His Hot Tools flat iron? His pink duck Hermès ascot? His lavender Tweezerman nose hair trimmer?

"Oh hi, Katya. Did Julian get off the plane already? I should be there any sec—I'm just looking for parking," I fib.

"Um, well, it depends on what you mean by 'get off the plane.'"

I get a familiar sinking feeling. "I'm not Kenneth Starr, Katya. Give it to me straight."

"I'm at Julian's apartment. He didn't get *on* the plane."

"He what?!" I say, practically poking my eyeball out with the curved mascara brush. "Put him on the phone."

"Well, that's the thing, he's comatose. There's a box of Tamiflu, a bottle of Ativan, some Imodium, and a half-eaten plate of grilled vegetables from Masa on the bedside table. I put a mirror under his nose so I know he's breathing. But I can't get him to open his eyes, or speak."

Okay, breathe. Inhale. Exhale. Inhale. Exhale. This is not the G8 Summit, for crying out loud. It's just the fricking Oscars. Holy crap. It's the fricking *Oscars*. Some jerk behind me in a yellow Porsche pounds his hand on the horn. I look up. Green light. I pull off to the side of the road and take a deep breath. "Katya, would you please put the phone up to his ear?" I ask. "Nick Lachey came out of the closet!" I scream at the top of my lungs.

"I kneeeeew it," Julian slurs, back to life.

"Julian, this really is not the time for you to pull a John Belushi on me. You can't do this to me again. You've got to get here!"

"I waaaant Tooomm Fooord to hooold meee in hiiiss arms and telllll meee everythiiing's goooing to be okaaay."

"Julian, I'd like Johnny Depp to have my babies, but the thing is, he already has two kids with Vanessa Paradis and he lives in France. You've got to pull it together and get on a goddamn plane. Have you forgotten that Olivia Cutter is our last chance for the Oscars? And P. S. the only penis that's ever going to get within five millimeters of Nick Lachey is his own."

Click.

I throw my head onto the steering wheel. I'd like to be comatose myself right now. Then I wouldn't have to face Olivia *alone*. Again.

I feel my blood sugar plunging. I look to my right and spot a Winchell's Donut Shop. I throw on my hazards and head over to the "Home of the Warm 'n Fresh Donut." As my hand hits the front door, I spot a HELP WANTED sign. LOOKING FOR FRIENDLY, ENTHUSIASTIC, RELI-ABLE EMPLOYEES. Okay. I'm friendly. I'm *totally* enthusiastic about donuts. And I'm completely reliable. I've never missed an episode of *America's Next Top Model*. Not even *one*. I continue reading. PRIOR EXPE-RIENCE NECESSARY. I have tons of experience with donuts. I mean, I've only been eating their jelly donuts since I was, like, five. Okay. Who am I kidding? If I can't get *someone* to wear Julian Tennant to the Oscars on Sunday, I'm not even qualified for a job at *Winchell's*. I have *got* to nail this meeting with Olivia.

I order the fourteen-donut dozen—too bad Krispy Kreme doesn't offer *that*. Halfway back to my car, I stop and stare down at the box. Adrienne's offering up python purses and God knows what else, and the best I can come up with are *donuts?* I wolf down a sprinkled sample to ease my anxiety. My phone beeps. I look down. One new voice mail. It's Olivia's manager, John.

"Olivia's had to clear her day for a little seven-year-old Make-A-Wish child named Sofia who idolizes her. Naturally my angel dropped everything and rushed to be by her side when she found out poor little Sofia's white blood cell count plummeted suddenly. Olivia's so selfless! She said, 'The Oscar dresses can wait.' We will re-schedule the fitting pending Sofia's condition. Please say a prayer."

I replay the message. Poor Sofia. Wait. Poor *me*. The Oscars are in five days. The dress *cannot* wait. Oh God, I'm the devil. A little seven-year-old girl is *dying* and I'm worried about some stupid dress! I should be sending a huge wave of thanks to Ganesh for removing Olivia from my day. Wait, did John say "dresses"—as in *plural?* Oh God.

My cell trills.

"Lola, I'm so happy you picked up," Cricket says frantically. "I need to borrow that Yoko Ono wig you wore last Halloween to Fiona Apple's Halloween party. You know, when you and Julian dressed up as John and Yoko. I need it right away. Kate got me an audition for *Found* tomorrow. It's this totally intense ensemble drama about Ninth Parish N'awlins residents who find evidence of extraterrestrial life after the floodwaters recede. The breakdown says they're looking for the next Sandra Oh to play the smart-talking, sexy, Sudoku-addicted receptionist at the police station!"

"Cricket, it's not a magic wig, you're still going to be a white girl wearing a bad black wig."

"Charlize Theron isn't a brown-eyed, 150-pound, lesbian serial killer—but she won an Oscar *playing* one. I'm a chameleon and I can convince them I'm Asian if I commit. S. D. says my energy is perfect for it. Can I please have the wig or would you rather drive me to the bus station and put me on the next Greyhound back to Ohio?"

"I'm not letting you go back to Ohio. I'm dying for a patty melt.

Meet me at the BH Hotel Coffee Shop in an hour. I'll treat you to a strawberry shake and a wig."

My five-inch Roger Vivier stiletto barely hits the salmon-colored concrete of the Crescent Drive side entrance path to the Beverly Hills Hotel when I'm accosted by a silicone-enhanced Amazonian PR tycoon. I've known since the womb that parking at the side entrance with the *real* Angelenos is the only way to go—not to mention saving twenty-five minutes and twenty-five bucks valeting with all those Hollywoodites *doing* lunch.

"How are you, sweetie?" the PR Queen Bee asks, leaving a gap of two inches between my cheek and her Restylaned lips as she looks over my shoulder for any sign of someone more important heading into the hotel. "Come this way, I want you to meet my client. I hear you haven't gotten anyone to wear Julian Tennant to the Oscars yet." Nice how bad news travels faster than on the AP Wire in Hollywood. "She's gonna be the Next Halle Berry," PR Queen Bee says, grabbing me by the arm and pulling me down the banana-leafed path.

Lord, not *another* "Next Halle Berry." Third one in two days. My cell phone is clogged with frantic messages from the PR purveyors of the *next* Naomi, Nicole, Cate, Hilary. I'd rather wear Cricket's Birkenstocks to Dani Jansen's Oscar Party than meet the next *Next* Halle Berry, whose sole credits to date include a nerve gas victim on *24* and one scream in *Scary Movie 8*.

"It's my favor to you to make up for deleting all those photos of Sienna at your birthday party last year at The Roosevelt," PR Queen Bee says. "She was posing with a Jimmy Choo bag for WireImage and I just couldn't let that happen in good conscience since Coach is my client," she says as she drags me onto the sunny Polo Lounge patio.

"Um, you did what?!" I say to the PR Queen Bee, but she's too busy buzzing from table to table in search of uber-pollen to answer me. I swear her head's going to spin off her body like Linda Blair in *The Exorcist* as she tries to figure out whose ass to kiss first. I go into instant auto-smile as she hands out air kisses galore. The first one goes to Michael Moore as he bites into fettucine alfredo. I'm surprised the maître d' sat the die-hard Democrat so close to Bill O'Reilly, who's gorging on steak tartare. I'd love to see M. M. pelt O'Reilly with one of those rosemary rolls. Daniel Radcliffe gets quadruple pecks from the PR Queen Bee. Shia LaBeouf only gets two.

Oh no. The PR Queen Bee is beelining for Charlotte Martin and Graydon Carter's table. It's not that I *still* blame her for checking herself into Promises. So what if she screwed up the course of my life forever by dropping out of my father's *Zorba the Greek* remake? Everyone's got that life-defining moment that alters their world forever, right? Like Rosa Parks on that bus, or Paris Hilton and that sex tape. But go over to Charlotte's table and say hi? I'd rather not. Even if she is with G. C. I struggle to twist free and make like my stilettos are Air Jordans, but PR Queen Bee has got a vise grip on my now practically blue fingers.

"Graydon, so excited for Sunday night. I mean, who cares about the Oscars? It's all about *your* party." I contemplate holding Graydon's ashtray under Queen PR Bee's mouth to catch all the drool pouring out of it. She's clearly trying to bump herself up from a 12:30 A.M. invite. Fat chance.

Graydon flashes the PR Queen Bee a requisite half-smile before turning to me. "Lola, tell your Pops best of luck on Sunday and not to show up unless he's got gold in his hands," he says. He turns to the actress across from him. "Of course you know Charlotte Martin?"

"Why, of course, it's so lovely to see you again, Lola," Charlotte purrs in her creamy Southern accent. She clasps her delicate hands in supplication across her "J'adore Dior" pink T-shirt, tossing that hair that has entire Web sites devoted to duplicating those big, loopy auburn tresses. She emerged fresh as a daisy from her "exhaustion" to claim the mantle as the latest America's Sweetheart, pulling down fifteen mil for her Doris Day redux in *Pillow Talk*. "Will your father *ever* forgive me for pulling out of that movie?"

"The Helmut Newton photo you sent him certainly didn't hurt."

"Good. It's still a dream of mine to work with your father. But will *you* ever forgive me? I personally didn't think you were *that* bad," Charlotte says, flashing me the smile that topped *Us Weekly's* "Luscious Lips We'd Most Love to Lock" survey. The saccharine taste floods my back molars.

Before I know it, I'm reaching across the pink tablecloth for Charlotte's half-drunk glass of Fiji water to wash down the Mack truck blocking my throat. "Yuck," I say, spraying *vodka* all over my blue and white floral camisole. I wonder if they taught Charlotte how to pass off her booze for Fiji in Promises? Graydon offers up his pink napkin so I can pad at my cami.

I flash Charlotte *my* most saccharine smile and say, "Living one day at a time, isn't that what they say in A—" but before I can get the other "A" out, the PR Queen Bee cuts me off.

"Okay, well, it was *super* to see both of you. Enjoy your salads and Graydon, can't wait for Sunday," she says as she yanks me away from the table.

"Who's Julian Tennant?" the Next Halle Berry asks the PR Queen Bee after she tells her, unbidden, that I'd be *thrilled* to give her a Julian Tennant masterpiece to wear to George Maloof's Oscar Party at Koi.

What? PR Queen Bee has *got* to be kidding me. As if Julian would ever let—

"I wanna wear Armani," the Next Halle Berry whines as she answers her ringing pink RAZR.

"Sorry, sweetie, I tried," PR Queen Bee winces before I can say a word. "Say hello to your divine mother for me." She whips out her BlackBerry and squeezes into the pink booth.

Okay, refrain from shoving the heel of my stiletto into her mouth. She's not Worthy of the damage to the rose Viviers. As if a thumbnail shot of the *Next* Halle Berry in *In Touch* with Nick Lachey's brother— what's-his-name, who cares if he won *Dancing with the D-List Stars*— was gonna catapult Julian into the *next* fashion stratosphere. Have fun at Koi in Armani, the Next Halle Berry. Yeah right, maybe Giorgio will loan you that dress—if there's an 8.0 earthquake and you're the only actress left alive.

"Well, enjoy the McCarthy salads and hope you have fun in Armani," I say, beaming with pride that I'm taking the Mahatma Gandhi high road. As I turn to leave, I spot—a what? Is that a *Choo?* It's a *Choo* for crying out loud. And it's shoved onto the PR Queen Bee's fat foot. Oh no, no, no, no, no.

"Nice shoes, *sweetie.* Oh wait, are those *Choos?*" I say, quickly prying them off her feet before she can react. Would Gandhi back me on this? "I'll just *delete* these . . . as my favor to you. I'm sure you've got an exquisite Coach pair in your trunk," I say as Queen PR Bee's face turns the same shade of pink as the hotel. I turn on my heels, drop the Choos into my purse, and head downstairs for my patty melt.

"The Polo Lounge should be re-named The Pariah Lounge. Here, I got you some Choos," I say, handing over the Queen PR Bee's sandals to Cricket. I sit down next to her at one of the twenty coveted pink wrought-iron bar stools downstairs at the Coffee Shop's classic curved pink Formica counter. What a relief to be down here where even Colin Farrell can take off his wraparound shades and eat his thirty-dollar burger in peace.

"Jimmy Choos? For me?" Cricket says, as she reaches over to hug me. "Um, eew, these are clammy," she says as she drops one back into my bag.

"We can sage them later. Trust me, it was totally good karma to liberate them."

"A patty melt and a strawberry shake, Lola?" Ruth, the veteran pink-clad waitress asks.

"Make it two please, Ruth."

"No, Ruth, I'll take a head of romaine and a whole tomato, sliced, please. Lola, I'm raw, remember," Cricket says as she pulls out raw goat cheese and a sprouted sunflower dressing from her hemp handbag.

"You were serious? The sex must be spectacular."

"I don't want to embarrass you, or me, or S. D., but last night I had to have him walk me through exactly how both my legs got behind my head and my hands got wrapped around his ankles."

"Ew, I'm trying to eat," I say, biting into the patty melt Ruth has slid into place. "Are you sure you don't want a fry?" I ask Cricket as she takes a bite of her measly plate of lettuce.

"How can you eat those death fries? The polyunsaturated fats from the oil in those cause aging, clotting, inflammation, and even cancer. Didn't you see *Super Size Me?* Seed and nut oils—" Cricket's fervent condemnation of my delicious fries is muted when my eyes fall upon a discarded *New York Times* Arts Section on the counter next to me. "Donatella vs. Miuccia! Dressing for Battle—A Look At The *Real* Oscar Race." The headline jumps off the page at me. Even *The New York Times* knows that what they're wearing is more important than who's winning. Then my eyes fall on the first paragraph: "*Adrienne Hunt is the lat-*

est *It Girl in the Hollywood Ambassador trend. She is the mastermind behind Prada's PR for the Oscars.*" I scan the article for Julian's name. Nothing. Nada. Zilch. A wave of panic rushes over me. I contemplate asking Ruth to hand me that giant knife they use to chop the Gary salad with, but decide against it. I'm certain my death would provide Adrienne *way* too much pleasure.

"Are you okay, 'cause you look pale," Cricket says. "Is this about Jake? Kate told me what happened last night and, so what, you kissed him, the important thing is you're not going to do it again." Cricket wraps me in another hug. I bury my nose in her hair and inhale her Aunt Vi's Aura Spray—God knows I could use a little aura enhancement.

"Look," I moan, flashing her the article. "The Oscars are in *five* days and *The New York Times* doesn't think we're even in the Oscar dress race. Cricket, I'm really worried that I'm not going to be able to pull this whole thing off for Julian. Even the *Next* Halle Berry wants to wear Armani."

"Lola, you can do this. You just have to commit to your career *completely* and *no more actors.* Visualize yourself doing it. Visualize Olivia walking down the Red Carpet in Julian's gown. Close your eyes," Cricket orders. "Lola? I mean it. Do what I say."

I close my eyes. I mean, look, I'm desperate.

"Olivia is floating down the Red Carpet looking like a luminous, gorgeous peacock," Cricket intones. "Cojo is asking Olivia what designer she's wearing and she tells him it's Julian Tennant. Cojo says 'Perfect. Perfect. Perfect. You get an A plus, plus plus. You go, girl—'"

My eyes fly open, the spell broken. "Cojo would never say 'you go, girl,'" I say.

"You're missing the point, Lola. Listen." Cricket leans into me as if she's got the cure for cancer or the secret to how Diana Ross has the dewy skin of a twelve-year-old. "You've got to *act as if*. Act *as if* and you *will* manifest it. Step into the role, Lola. This morning I totally visualized myself as that smart-talking, sexy, Sudoku-addicted receptionist at that police station in New Orleans. I'm going to walk into that audition tomorrow committed to being Asian and I'm going to get that part." Cricket fishes through my bag for my Yoko wig and puts it on. "How do I look?"

"Perfect—if you're auditioning for the *Sonny and Cher* biopic," I say.

"Are they making that movie? Do you think Kate can get me an audition? Hey, isn't that Brad Grey in the corner? I hear Paramount's casting *Groupies* right now. That girl from *Wedding Crashers* is in it and it's like *Almost Famous* but funnier. I saw Brad Grey with Jim Carrey at my yoga class. Maybe I should introduce myself?"

"Cricket, you know the Coffee Shop rules: no introductions, no pitching, no talking shop *please*. Let the man read his *Variety* in peace. If he wanted to be seen, he'd be out there with the pariahs on the patio."

As Cricket and I make our way down the path back to our cars, we pass the hotel bungalow Graydon's uber-team has transformed into the *VF* "war room." One of G. C.'s uber-assistants is wailing into a Bluetooth headset through the open door.

"Tell Candy Cummings she can send Graydon twenty more autographed Fender guitars. *We don't care*. After her drunken *applauding* episode during the 'In Memoriam' portion of last year's awards show, there's no way she's ever getting in. Plus she's a convict." And here I thought the Big House was more revitalizing these days than Canyon Ranch. Look at what it's done for Paris.

"Okay, so clearly there's no way *I'm* going to get in," Cricket says, crestfallen, as we peek into the banana-leaf wallpapered bungalow. One assistant, magnifying glass in hand, is inspecting the printing on the customized *VF* M&M's. Another ragged assistant takes a red Sharpie to the eight-foot-long event schedule taking up the entire living room wall. A third sorts extravagant gifts for G. C. by brand—purple Asprey boxes in one pile, blue Tiffany boxes in another, orange Hermès in another. Do you think Graydon would notice if I pinched one of those adorable orange boxes? Actually, I could take care of Christmas *and* Hanukkah shopping for the next ten years if I cleared out the place.

"Cricket, you'll be at the *VF* party next year," I say, giving her a squeeze as we reach my Prius.

"Remember, *act as if*. Step into the role," Cricket says, giving me one more hug before she walks up Crescent Drive to her car. Her determination's kinda catching. I *will* overcome my CDD. And my Actorholism. I *will* make something of myself. I *will* figure out my life. I *will* act *as if* I'm as successful as Oprah and as sober as Robert Downey, Jr. I *will* stay away from actors. And I *will* find myself a career. Damn it!

As I'm mid-visualization, I spot Maggie Gyllenhaal out of the corner of my eye making her way down the BH Hotel path. Thanks to Papa's direction, she's gotten the best reviews of her career in *Whispered Screams*. She owes him. I wonder if she's decided which designer she's wearing Oscar night to present. It's not like we're total strangers. I mean, I did meet her at the wrap party. So what if it was for like two seconds? Remember, act *as if*. What would Oprah do? Oh no. There's Charlotte Martin. I watch her sashay toward Maggie and the next thing I know the two are huddling in a corner. I can't do it. Oprah's a better woman than me. I jump into my Prius and dial Papa's martyr-slash-assistant.

"Abby, I need you. Can you get my father to ask Maggie Gyllenhaal to wear Julian Tennant to the Oscars?"

"Oh, sweetie, you know I'd do anything for you, but I really think you'd have better luck with that one than I would."

"Can't you just sneak her onto his call sheet? You know, just dial the number and then coach him on it while the phone's ringing?"

"Do I look like Phil Jackson to you? I'd be making millions coaching the Lakers if I were that good." I hear a struggle over the phone line.

"Darling, quick, what direction does the toilet in the master bath face?" Mom's voice, tinged with hysteria, comes over the phone line.

"What are you talking about, Mom? Put Abby back on the phone."

"I'm filling out a stone lion application form. I simply must have one of those hand-carved sculptures by Mr. Chung. There are only fifty available and Goldie Hawn told me the Wise One's already gotten a thousand applications. I desperately need to transform the wayward energy balance in this house so your father can get his Oscar on Sunday. I'm certain this house has atrocious feng shui. Why else didn't Papa win the DGA award last month?"

"So what if the Director's Guild Award went to Wes Anderson for *Bottle Rocket Relaunched*? It doesn't mean Papa's not going to win the Oscar," I say, although I'm feeling a twinge of doubt myself.

"Really? I Googled it. I have a better chance of getting ahead of Victoria Beckham on the wait list for a Vuitton leopard-print leather Steamer than your father does of winning that Oscar. Since 1949 the winners of the DGA and the Oscar have only differed six times," my mother says.

"Mom, this isn't Florida; a slab of stone isn't going to change the votes that have been in for the last week."

"Nonsense, darling. Streisand said that her stone lion created a complete metamorphosis for their house. Even her housekeeper's cooking improved."

"Mom, please, I can't focus on this right now. I just got a text from Dr. Gilmore. She's agreed to squeeze me in and I am *not* going to miss that appointment. And I have to rehearse my material for therapy. There's a lot to cover. But first I need to speak to Papa. Where is he?"

"He's with Agostino at the restaurant. Darling, just be sure to keep the toilet seat down in your bathroom. Otherwise all of your abundance will flow away. We must take every precaution we can this week."

"Mom, please, put Abby back—"

Click.

I deliberately avoid Melrose Avenue on my way to Ago, where Papa is a co-owner just so he'll have a kitchen that's his personal playpen. I can't afford a pit stop at James Perse or Maxfield to relieve the pretraumatic father stress. That measly salary Julian's paying me barely pays the rent. I make a left onto Melrose from La Cienega Boulevard and a quick right into the car-show-worthy parking lot. I suppress the strong urge to back out of the parking lot and nip into the Marc Jacobs boutique across the street. I know I'd feel safe and comforted surrounded by all those Stam bags.

The last time I asked my father for something, it was an autograph from Keanu Reeves. He looked at me coldly and said, "I'll think about it." That was when I was eleven. And no, he didn't get me the autograph. Did you have to ask?

I make my way through all the Zegna suits in the tightly packed dining room and toward the open kitchen. I weave past the bus boys cleaning off the typical half-eaten Hollywood dishes—a hundred dollars' worth of shaved white truffles over the squid ink pasta, with only two forkfuls missing—the sous chefs chopping Portobello mushrooms and broccolini, and the pastry chef whipping up my favorite tiramisu. My father is bent over a big bubbling pot, wearing a sauce-splattered apron. The co-owner and chef, Agostino, gives me a huge hug. I wish I could say the same for my father, who gives me a curt hello. Papa doesn't like to be disturbed when he's cooking. Who am I kidding? He doesn't like to be disturbed by me. Period. Maybe I should go back to Plan A and just have Abby do this for me.

Don't be such a wuss. I'm just asking for one tiny little favor. What's the worst he can do, yell at me in front of *all* of these people? Throw the pot of pureed Tuscan bean soup in my face? I turn to leave. No. I *have* to do this. Act *as if*. As if. As if.

"Um, Papa? I'm wonder—"

"Taste this," Papa says, sticking a wooden spoon full of steaming sauce in my face.

"Delicioso," I say, ignoring the searing flesh of my tongue. "It's absolute perfection. Don't add another thing."

My father tastes another spoonful himself, squinches his eyes in thought, then reaches for more rosemary and hot pepper flakes.

"When are you going to get yourself into a kitchen? A woman should know how to cook, Lola," Papa says.

"Give me a little credit. I finally perfected the microwave time for my Amy's Sante Fe enchilada bowl." Come on, Lola. *As if. As if.* "Anyway, um, so, I saw Maggie Gyllenhaal today."

"And?"

"And, um, well, it gave me this idea. I think it's a really good idea. A great idea!" My father stops stirring and is staring at me with flinty eyes. Okay, so now I'm thinking this was a really *bad* idea. "So, anyway, I think she would look really good in Julian Tennant—you know, for the Oscars. And it would be really great for me because she's presenting. And Papa, I've been working so hard, but I haven't had any luck yet.

And she would really be a coup for us—for me. Papa, would you please call her for me? And maybe just set up a meeting? You know how much she adores you. Please?"

"You want me to call an *actress* and ask her to do *me* a favor?"

"Um, well, yes, it would really help me and Papa, it's just a phone call. I'm asking for *one* phone call."

Silence.

"No." Papa turns back to his sauce and lowers the spoon into it once again. Class dismissed.

"Why?" My voice is about fifty octaves higher than I've ever heard it. I sound six years old.

"Because it's humiliating for me that my daughter is on her knees for these actors. It's like Ridley Scott's son busing tables at the Warner Bros. commissary. How do you think it makes me look? It makes me look like an idiot."

Don't cry. Don't cry. Do *not* let him see you cry.

"Right. Yeah. Well, enjoy that pasta," I say. If I weren't going directly to my appointment with Dr. Gilmore I'd have to stick my head straight into that wood-burning oven next to the bacon-rubbed grilled ribeye.

After fifty minutes of primordial sobbing, wrapped in Dr. Gilmore's pink-for-protection cashmere blanket, with her rose quartz resting on my chest for heart healing, I shred the last tissue in the now-empty Kleenex box on my lap. Dr. Gilmore sits across from me as usual in her leather armchair. She smoothes her Ann-Margret red ponytail, crosses one linen pant leg over another, and pulls out a ball of red string.

"I'm giving you some homework, my dear. I'd like you to take this red string and tie it to your doorknob and hold the other end really tight. Then I want you to cut the red string, which symbolizes the bloodline, while you visualize letting go of all of your expectations about your father. The more you can accept him for who he is—a very limited human being—the less pain you will be in. I also want you to take this," Dr. Gilmore says, reaching for the antique Chinese tea box that's large enough to hydrate all of China. She lifts off the peeling lid and plucks one rubber band out from the mother lode inside. She hands it to me. "Put this around your wrist. When you see Jake Jones tonight, or any other actor for that matter, I want you to snap yourself with my rubber band so that you're reminded of the cycle of pain you're perpetuating by choosing these actor-types."

"Doctor Gilmore, um, it's yellow and well, that's really not my color," I say. Dr. Gilmore arches one eyebrow expectantly, and I put the band around my wrist anyway. I'll tell people it's the symbol of some hot new religion that even Madonna isn't onto yet.

"Well, every time you look at the rubber band, you should also think about how those men aren't your color either," she says. "Lola, as you snap that rubber band, I want you to feel yourself taking your power back. It's important not to position ourselves as victims and to remember that we have a *choice*. I'm here to support you. Now let's sit for a moment in a visualization. What color is the pain?"

"Um, beige . . . well, more camel really," I say.

"Camel, interesting. Okay and what's the texture of the pain?"

"Lizard."

"Lizard?" Dr. Gilmore gives me a perplexed look.

"Sorry, it's just that I got totally distracted by your shoes. Are those Sergio Rossis? It's so hard to find the perfect camel pump. Can I ask you where you got those?"

"Lola, I'm concerned you're not taking our work here seriously."
Dr. Gilmore steeples her fingers and gives me a searching look.

"Doctor Gilmore, I take shoes *very* seriously."

As I turn the doorknob to leave Dr. Gilmore's waiting room, I stop my-self. I look over to the red string in my bag. Why not let go right here and now? I'm about to fish out the red yarn when the door swings open and nearly knocks me over.

"I'm so sorry," Therapy Guy says, nearly stepping on me with his worn-in running sneakers, wrapping his large hands around my shoul-ders to steady me. "You okay?" he asks. I don't think I noticed his sparkly green eyes before.

"Oh yeah; no, I'm sorry, I'm totally in the way here. I'm in one of those post-therapy dazes," I answer.

"Oh right, trying to figure out what your next move is," he says run-ning his fingers through his hair. "Well, the red string thing is excel-lent," he says, noticing the ball of yarn peeking out of my bag.

"I was kinda thinking of getting started on that doorknob," I say.

"The sooner the better," he laughs. "Here, I'll help you out," he says, pulling out the yarn and reaching into the pocket of his khakis and handing me a Swiss Army knife.

"I haven't seen one of these since I was kicked out of Girl Scouts," I say, popping out the scissors section. "Very practical."

"Yep. Everyone should have one. Dare I ask what you got kicked out for?" he asks, smiling.

"I re-designed the uniform," I say. "My troop wasn't quite ready for the avant-garde direction I was taking them in."

"I can only imagine," he says, laughing so heartily I can feel it in my toes. "All right, go for it," he says, holding the red string taut and nodding his dark curls toward the string. I hesitate. "Go ahead," he urges me on. I close my eyes and wonder why I don't feel embarrassed doing this with a total stranger. Okay, so we're Therapy Comrades. But when did we cross over into ritual? Okay, I take a deep breath and really visualize letting go. I open my eyes and cut the string and let out a sigh that's a little too loud. Again, oddly not even a tinge of embarrassment passes through me. This is so not normal. But he is. So maybe that means normal people stand in their therapists' hallways cutting red string together. I mean, I've always *wanted* to be normal.

"Good work," he says, handing me back the red ball of yarn as Dr. Gilmore opens her office door and Therapy Guy waves good-bye, vanishing into that room.

"Thanks," I call after him. And I mean it as I shove that ball of yarn back into my ridiculously heavy bag—because *I'm* feeling lighter already.

A hot shower and an outfit upgrade later and I valet the Prius at the corner of Hollywood and Vine where General Motors has erected a tent the size of the MGM Grand Casino for their annual "Ten" fashion show. I flash my credentials at the black T-shirt-clad security giant at the backstage door. I've never had a credential for anything and I feel momentarily validated. Maybe I'll hang the laminated piece of paper on my fridge so that I can remember this feeling every day. I make my way through the mass of photogs, stylists, makeup artists, publicists, managers, and talent (read *actors*) flitting about backstage. There's Djimon Hounsou smoking a cigarette. He's all alone. Maybe I should—*Snap*. Ow, that rubber band hurts! Ryan Gosling balancing three plates of food from catering. I wonder if he needs me to—*Snap. Snap.* Michael Vartan checking his voice mail. I wonder if he needs me to check his—*Snap. Snap. Snap.* Okay. Ow. I think I'm getting the hang of this.

I spot Kate standing with Will Bailey and head her way. No temptation to snap here; Kate's treated me to too many stories of Will's textbook tantrums. How he demanded Razzles in his trailer on his last shoot, then went postal when he claimed the gum stained his veneers. How his assistant has to buy him paper underpants when he goes on promo tours because he won't let his Calvins be laundered outside of L.A. And how his mother-slash-manager-slash-maid-slash-mega-pain-in-the-ass must always have an adjoining room when they travel.

I'm about to show Kate my new yellow accessory when, sure enough, I hear Will in full tantrum mode, blue velvet-clad arms jerking about madly.

"For fuck's sake, Kate, where the hell is Heath Ledger? That cheerleader from *Heroes*—B List. That guy from *Scrubs*—C List. Maria Menounos—I don't know what list she's on, but I'm nominated for a fucking *Academy Award,* Kate." Will jerks to and fro in front of the mirror as if he's got Tourette's while his entourage looks on: Kate, his publicist, his brother-slash-assistant, his cousin-slash-makeup artist, and his mother.

The effect of Will's rant is somewhat muffled by his mother's aquamarine sleeve, which she flings across his nose every time he's within eyesight of the mirror. No, it's not just a slanderous rumor on the pages of *Star* ("Nobody Nose The Trouble He's Smelled: The Five Faces of Will Bailey"). Will has a tormented relationship with his schnozz. I personally think it's a very *decent* nose. I mean, it may have gotten a *little* weird after the fifth nose job. I wonder if Ma Bailey's limb is cramping from holding it up in the air for so long.

"Heath had to pull out to host *SNL*," Kate says calmly, used to the requisite neurotic actor outburst. I'm tempted to take a swig of that valerian root tincture on her behalf.

Without unfastening his gaze from the mirror, Will semaphores a hand-to-mouth gesture in his brother's direction. The brother hand-rolls a cigarette lightning fast, which his mother deftly slips between Will's lips with one hand while simultaneously removing the other arm from in front of the offending nose. The creepy choreography reminds me of a puppet show Nanny No. 12 brought me to when I was nine. We both left crying.

"Why the fuck aren't *I* hosting *SNL, Kate?*" Will asks, turning away from the mirror.

"Because you said the show's gone to shit since Tina Fey left," Kate says with the patience of Job, and then some. "Will, remember when you were still on that sitcom opposite Adam Carolla and I brought you to this party? I was standing next to you when Jamie Foxx strutted down the runway in his white *Saturday Night Fever* suit with a bright yellow Hummer H3 rolling behind him. You swore that would be you someday. That someday is today." That's my girl, I cheer silently, resisting the urge to high-five Kate.

"But I look like Austin fucking Powers in this blue velvet suit, don't I, *Lola?*" Will says, turning to me.

I freeze; just can't stop staring at his nose. Is the left nostril starting to collapse just a little bit? Kate sends me a pleading look.

"Actually, Will, I think you look absolutely—" I'm cut off mid-sentence by a familiar voice.

"You're far more shagalicious than Austin, baby," Adrienne says, purring like Catwoman. Dear God, where did that devil woman come from? She presses up against Will's back, does a little shimmy, and runs a skeletal arm down his sleeve.

"Nice to see you, Adrienne," I say.

"And you too, darling. Isn't it a crazy, crazy night?" Adrienne beams at Will. "Such a gorgeous, lucky man. Miuccia is very much in demand. Did you know I'm also dressing Rebecca Romijn, Anne Hathaway, and Eric Bana tonight? Who else are you dressing here, Lola darling?"

I take a sacred pause to reflect that she is one evil, evil bitch. "We want Jake Jones to be the standout tonight, so he's doing Julian Tennant exclusively," I say levelly. "Hot new actor and hot new designer."

"Hot. Really, darling?" Adrienne says, smirking. "Didn't you see *The New York Times* Arts Section?" She blows a kiss at us, her blue-black bob swaying. "Well, I'm off. So much to do before the show. See you in a few, Will!"

As Adrienne scampers away, Will turns to me. "Be honest, Lola. How do I look?"

Like a roid-rage Smurf? Like Elvis after he's huffed a few liters of carbon monoxide? Kate's fixing me with another you've-got-to-come-through-for-me stare. I take a deep breath and beam at her hottest client.

"Shagelectable, Will," I say. "Jessicas Alba *and* Biel-would-fuck-you hot." Will's shoulders collapse from around his ears. "Listen, I've got to chase down Jake and get him ready. Good luck!" Kate mouths "thank you" as I scurry off.

"How'd the audition go?" I ask Jake Jones casually as he stands there practically buck naked. "I'm sure the only reason you haven't called me *all day* is because Bruckheimer loved you so much that he took you straight to get your Hawkman wings fit," I say, aiming for a light, carefree tone, and regret it almost immediately. I blame the Calvin Klein boxer briefs. And that twelve-pack. Man, Jake's adorable.

Those husky blue eyes widen innocently. "Was I supposed to call you? About the suit or something?"

Oh my God, did I imagine last night? No. He kissed me. He *definitely* kissed me. Great. He's just going to act like nothing happened. This is bad. This is *really* bad. Wait, maybe this is good. Yes, this is good. This means I'm safe. I'm *definitely* safe. It will go no further with Jake Jones. He struggles to pull his pants up. I reach over to help him. *Snap.* Well, it is my *job* to dress him. *Snap. Snap.*

"What's with the rubber band?" he says, reaching for my hand. "That looks like it hurts," he says, rubbing my wrist. *Snap. Snap.* "Ow. What'd you do that for?" he asks as the rubber band flicks his finger.

"Oh sorry," I say flustered. "It's this thing my therapist, I mean, you know, it's this exercise that, um, is supposed to, um . . ." I take a deep breath. "Look. I'm an Actorholic. And you're an actor. Okay? There it is. I said it. I'm 188 days sober. And then you kissed me last night and I almost fell off the wagon. But I didn't because *you* had to save up your chi. And so I'm supposed to flick this rubber band every time I have an impure actor thought so that I *don't* fall off that wagon. It's pathetic, I know. So let's just get that suit on you and get this thing over with so that I can get to day 189."

Jake looks around to make sure no one's within earshot, then leans forward and cups my ear. "I have ten years in OA," he whispers.

"O-what? I can't hear you," I yell over the blaring U2.

"Overeaters Anonymous." Jake moves in closer. "I was 350 pounds."

Mr. "We're Jonesing for Jake Jones's Buns" was 350 pounds? I'm shocked. I try to imagine Jake Jones in Kirstie Alley's pre-Jenny Craig body.

"I used to have to spray Bitter Apple in my mouth whenever I had a craving," Jakes says.

"The doggie spray?" I ask, horrified. Cricket had to use it that one time she was babysitting John Malkovich's Weimaraners and they wouldn't stop eating his loafers.

"The doggie spray," Jake confirms. "I carry this in my wallet because I still feel like I'm in that 350-pound body." He delicately unfolds a *Rolling Stone* cover of him in his skivvies, his twelve-pack oiled up and on offer. "It reminds me of how far I've come," he says, tearing up. "I'm telling you this from one addict to another. If my agent knew I told you, he'd make you sign a confidentiality agreement. All that was my old life, with my old name and fifteen months locked in my studio apartment in Tarzana with my Richard Simmons DVDs. It feels good to talk about it."

A guy who really knows how to work on himself. That's so inspiring. Jake is so vulnerable. So sensitive. Well, I mean, he has to make a living *somehow*. Oh no. *Snap, snap, snap.*

Jake fixes me with a meaningful stare. "So I really get where you're coming from. I've been there too. I really admire what you're doing. Can I have my assistant get you a club soda?" A club soda?

Before I can say a word, Jake's manager rushes up to us. "*Access Hollywood* wants a sound bite. Billy Bush is waiting."

"One day at a time," Jake mouths to me as his manager drags him away.

Oh. A *club soda*. Okay, great. The guy thinks I'm in frickin' *Alcoholics Anonymous*. I need a drink. I just poured my heart out and the guy didn't hear a word I said. Okay. Well. It's loud. It's very loud. The good news is, I'm still sober, and Jake's a pretty good guy. And so sweet with that caterpillar-into-a butterfly story. *Snap. Snap. Snap.* The sound of one hand snapping is interrupted by The Red Hot Chili Peppers blaring out of DJ AM's speakers. The crowd starts howling as Patrick Dempsey and Mandy Moore make their way onto the massive catwalk that's been transformed to look like the 405 freeway. No wonder the crowd's howling, you can see absolutely *everything* through Mandy's sheer Proenza

Schouler gown. A turquoise '53 Chevy Corvette follows them down the runway as faux snow sprays them. I try to run up to the crowd to get a better view, but my purple python thigh-high Alaïa boots aren't built for comfort or speed.

I've barely reached the front row when the audience starts cheering wildly as Jake Jones struts down the runway with a bright yellow Cadillac Escalade rolling behind him. He looks absolutely magnificent in that Julian Tennant charcoal, three-button, pin-striped suit. Yes! I lift my hand to high-five Eva Mendes in a vintage chain-mail tank-dress standing next to me. She indulges me with a slap worthy of Shaquille O'Neal sinking a free throw.

I'm floating to the bar to treat myself to a celebratory glass of champagne, proud that Oscar Week accomplishment number one can be checked off the list. And that I got Jake Jones dressed with my sobriety still intact. Only one more hour until day 189. I'm fantasizing about my next session with Dr. Gilmore. She's up to the part where she's saying how proud she is of me. That I'm well on my way to conquering my CDD *and* my Actorholism. Then I'm stopped dead in my tracks by the sight of SMITH. My stomach starts to churn. Suddenly I'm locking eyes with SMITH, the man who lobotomized my heart 188 days ago. *Snap. Snap. Snap. Snap. Snap.* The rubber band breaks. I didn't really need it anyway. Every cell in my body already aches. The pain with him is Pavlovian.

"Hey," SMITH says, flashing me *that* smile.

"Hey," I manage to get out. I may be sick all over his Gucci loafers.

"You look good," SMITH says coolly. I send a quick thank you to Ganesh for giving me the guts to wear this dress that's so ultra mini I thought it was a shirt when Julian gave it to me. I can feel SMITH's eyes like fingers running up and down all five threads of it. Let him see what he lost. And what he's never getting again. But then I feel my body responding despite myself, literally pulled to him. No! Okay, snapping's clearly not going to do it. Breathing might help. I take a deep breath but can't seem to find the air in the room. It was just here a minute ago.

SMITH leans over and whispers into my ear, "Breaking up with you was the mistake of my life." Now I'm gasping for that air. Did he really just say the words I've dreamt of hearing every second since he sent his assistant with that break-up note? *Snap. Snap. Snap. Snap. Snap.* The sound of the phantom rubber band is drowned by the little whispers in my head. Maybe he never stopped loving me. Maybe he's changed. Maybe we should talk. I'm about to throw my arms around him when I spot the blond bimbo in a skintight zebra-print dress scurrying to his side.

"Here's your drink, honey," she says, slipping a glass into SMITH's hand. She trains a vacant smile on me. "Oh, hello. And you are—?"

Oh, right. Stupid, stupid Lola. I don't need a rubber band, I need a tourniquet—around my brain. "I guess you still like those martinis dirty," I say and turn to leave. Just get me the hell out of here. Fast.

"Great seeing you, Lola," I hear SMITH say, but I don't bother to turn around. All I want is to get to that damn valet.

The valet line is a total cluster fuck. My heart is thumping like the speakers in Snoop Dogg's Lincoln Navigator.

"You look unwell." Of course it would have to be Adrienne Hunt standing right behind me in line, hip cocked. "Not to worry. Your boy did well enough tonight. Naturally, no one will remember your success here tonight in the morning," she says, blowing a shroud of smoke from the Gitane permanently resting on her lips. "And I hear you've got no one for the big night. Such a shame for Julian."

"And the very best to you too, Adrienne." I march up to one of the attendants and offer him five bucks to give me my keys. He cocks an eyebrow. I hand him another five. Good thing he doesn't ask for another one, 'cause I don't have it. But I'd pay my last dime to get away from Adrienne and SMITH and this whole Oscar Week mess. Keys in hand, I start walking down Hollywood Boulevard to find my car. Uh-oh. I feel a car slow down beside me. I try not to look. Oh my God, someone thinks I'm a hooker. I curse Ganesh after all for letting me wear this micro-dress with these five-inch thigh-high boots. I keep walking. A black Mercedes with tinted windows pulls up beside me. I pick up my pace and hear the window roll down. Shoot. Shoot. Shoot. It's probably a creepy agent prowling the GM party for fresh starlet roadkill.

"Hey, do you need a lift?" It's Jake Jones leaning out the window.

Do I ever. No. No, I don't. Not from him. Not from another actor. I will keep walking. I will walk straight into my 189th day. Only twenty-eight more minutes. Twenty-seven. Twenty-six. Don't even look at him. Just keep walking. *Snap. Snap. Snap,* I say to myself. Why did I break that damn rubber band? There's a filthy scrunchy languishing in a muddy puddle. I picture fishing it out and sliding it onto my wrist. So what if it squishes instead of snaps? It's better than getting into that car. Whatever it takes. Whatever it takes. Whatever it takes. I look back at Jake, back to the puddle, Jake, puddle, Jake, puddle. *Snap. Snap. Snap.*

The door handle clicks softly as I open it and slide inside.

wednesday

103 hours, 19 minutes, 23 seconds until
the Oscar for Best Makeup is handed out.*

AAAAAAAAAAAAAHHHHHHHHHHHHHHHHHHHH!!!!!!! I've just been pushed out of John Travolta's 707 at 35,000 feet. And the parachute's not opening. I'm free-falling toward the Hollywood sign, which I can barely make out through the cream chiffon of my Madame Gres goddess gown, which has flown up above my head. I'm plummeting toward a Britney Spears rock bottom. How'd I get here and *why* am I wearing Kate's crotchless leopard dental floss? Am I the new Queen of the Noonie Moonie?

"Yes, you are," a voice says into my ear. Oh no. I hope I'm not bald down there like all those other Moonies. I don't care what anyone says; bald is so *not* the new Brazilian. But wait, who the heck is that on my back? Is that God? I yank my skirt down from my face and crane my neck around, blinking away tears whipped up by the 600-mile-per-hour winds. I'd like to see what the rascal looks like, for crying out loud. Oh God indeed. It's *Jake Jones* riding tandem on my back. Great. So this is how it ends: I plummet to my death with an *actor* strapped to my back. At least I'm wearing couture. I'd always envisioned myself entering the Big Hereafter at the age of 100 (not looking a day over a Diane Sawyer sixty-five, of course) in my sleep, lulled by the turquoise waves of the Caribbean, with my soul mate, the non-actor, next to me.

I'm not ready to die—especially not like *this*. Maybe there's still time to save myself. I frantically pull at the cords on my harness. Nothing happens. What's wrong with the parachute?

"Relax, I'm going to save you," Jake Jones says calmly. Jesus, just because he's up for Hawkman doesn't mean he can really fly. These actors are so delusional and self-aggrandizing. Wait. That's not Jake Jones's voice. It's SMITH's. I can barely make SMITH out behind these goggles, which are doing nothing to keep my Great Lash from running all over my face with this eye-watering whiplash. "I'm going to save you," SMITH says again. No way, I'll save myself, thank you very much. I reach for the buckles on my harness to pry myself free of him. They won't budge. We start somersaulting; head over ass, ass over head, limbs flying everywhere and we're picking up speed.

I can barely make out the Kodak Theatre beneath me. Oh *no!* It's Oscar night. I've got to get down there. I frantically search the sea of stars for that peacock masterpiece. I don't see it. I can't find *anyone* wearing Julian Tennant. Is that—oh dear—oh no—it's Adrienne Hunt. She gives me one Prada-painted middle finger.

"Open the parachute!" I scream at SMITH. He doesn't answer. The ground's getting closer. Head over ass, ass over foot. Closer. Oh my God. This is it. There's the ground. *WHOOSH.* I'm suddenly floating. The parachute!

"You're going to be fine." Wait. That's not SMITH's voice. It's Dr. Gilmore's. She looks absolutely ravishing against the white clouds in white Chanel goggles and a white Chanel flight suit. Why wasn't I put on the short list for those? But wait, are those white Chanel *wings*?

"Don't go! Don't leave me!" I beg, but Dr. Gilmore's gone. Oh no. The parachute is collapsing on top of me. I can't see. Where's the ground? I'm shrouded in a ball of nylon and chiffon. And I'm spinning—faster and faster.

WHACK. My head ricochets on the hard earth. I'm certain every bone is broken. Suddenly I'm splayed out on a gurney. At least the paramedic pulled my dress down. The doors of the ambulance swing open. Is that— George Clooney? What's *he* doing here? He puts his hand on my forehead. That feels nice. He starts to speak, but it's gibberish. It's the wah-wah-wah of Ann Coulter. The wah-wah-wah turns to beeping. Loud beeping. *Beep. Beep. Beep.* The EKG machine. Oh my God. I'm flatlining. *Beeeeeeeeeeeep.*

I'm startled awake by the shrill beeping of a truck backing up on the street. It's so loud it feels like it's in my ear. As I crack an eye open, I'm accosted by bright white light. Is this Heaven? Or wait, is this the VIP penthouse suite at Chanel? As my vision clears, I spot my hankie of a dress, crumpled in a ball on the floor. And my python boots collapsed nearby. Oh, it was a dream. Man, I can't wait to bring that one to Dr. Gilmore. But wait—this isn't my room, and these aren't my Pratesis— I'd never put these flannel sheets on my bed. Where am I?

Oh God. Oh no. This really is rock bottom. There he is. Jake Jones—in bed next to me. Uh-oh. He's naked. I quickly check under the covers. Oh no. So am I. What've I done? And is that a life-sized poster of Jake Jones in his skivvies hanging next to the sixty-inch Fujitsu? Are those *Girls Gone Wild* DVDs lining his "bookshelves" sans a single book? How many of those videos did they actually make? Take me back to REM fast.

"Mr. Jones, Mr. Jones!" the housekeeper yells in a thick Filipino accent. Please don't let her come in here.

"Hamas, I'm sleeping. Come back later," Jake mumbles, throwing his king-sized pillow over his head.

"There are men here. They say it's important," she says, barging through the bedroom door.

I dive under the covers and try to make my body as flat as Fergie's abs. I peek one eye out from underneath the plaid flannels. Two burly men trail Hamas, carrying a great big box with a white sheet draped over it. Jake stirs awake. Jesus, is that a *cage*?

"Where do you want it?" one of the deliverymen asks.

"What is it?" Jake asks, bolting upright.

The two guys lower the gigantic cage to the floor, and the other deliveryman lifts the white cloth. "It's a hawk, man."

"Is that thing real?" Jake asks, pointing to that brown creature with the six-foot wingspan.

"Sure looks like it, man," one of the men says. They're both staring at me. Judging from my pillow, which is streaked with black mascara, I can only imagine what my face looks like. Bad, *very* bad, I'm guessing from the looks of the deliverymen and Hamas, who's likewise staring at me. I give them a meek half-wave as Hamas escorts them from the room, tactfully closing the door behind her.

There's a fearsome flapping of wings as the hawk resettles itself on its perch. Oh God. Even the hawk's staring at me with those piercing eyes. Why won't it stop glaring at me? I am so ashamed. The hawk makes a loud, wailing "klee-uk, klee-uk," sound from inside his enormous cage. Oh my gosh, is the hawk trying to communicate with me? I don't speak hawk. What's he trying to tell me? That *he* would have given me a good morning kiss? No. I know. He's saying that I should get out while I still can.

Okay, so I don't *really* know what the hawk says, but I do know what the hawk means. I have an unfortunate flashback to the time when SMITH got a part in a Bruckheimer movie. Bruckheimer sent SMITH a NASA spacesuit (somehow even Jerry knew he was good at going to the moon).

"Congratulations. I think *you're* the new Hawkman," I say to Jake.

"Is that what this means?" he says in shock. "No, no, it couldn't be. One of my buddies is messing with me." Sure, honey. Like your friends have a few spare grand to play a practical joke. So Jake doesn't exactly qualify as a Mensa member. He still looks adorable, his mouth gaping in surprise like a kid on Christmas morning. The sleek cell on his nightstand trills.

"Hello," Jake answers. "No, really? Who is this? *What?*" Jake says, lightning-bolting out of bed. "You had the hawk shipped from Panama?" Jake says. "It's Jerry! I got the part," he whispers, covering the receiver and jumping up and down on the bed, naked, his non-Mensa member in full salute. "Of *course* I can be at the studio in an hour to meet the Brazilian fight coordinators. . . . Stallone's chef from *Rambo V?* Yeah, I have a guesthouse he can move into right away. . . . Sure I'm available for an interview. Right now? Yeah, no problem." He covers the receiver again. "*People* magazine," he excitedly mouths to me. "Listen, thanks again for the hawk, Jerry. And for the part." He clicks off the phone. "I'm Hawkman, I'm Hawkman, I'm Hawkman," he begins chanting, running circles around his bed. Still naked. He stops at the foot of the bed and looks me square in the eye—for the first time this morning. I wait for the words every girl wants to hear the morning after sleeping with a guy you really like for the first time: "I think I'm falling in love with you"— followed immediately by, "So where are we going to breakfast?"

"They loved me! I knew they loved me. This is the greatest day of my life!" he crows. Oh. And I was just about to suggest Cora's for eggs in a hole.

This officially ranks in my all-time top five most shameful moments. It's right up there with the time my mother toasted my first period at a dinner party in front of Ashton freaking Kutcher. Jake heads for the bathroom. His phone rings.

"Can you grab it?" Jake says, his voice muffled by the bathroom door.

"Hello, residence of Mr. Jake Jones," I say, trying to sound like a Filipino housekeeper and not the Slut of the Week. "Yes, of course, I'll get him immediately." I cover the receiver with my palm.

"*People* magazine," I say as Jake strides out of the bathroom, a towel wrapped around his waist. I hand him the phone.

"Thanks, yeah, I mean, Hawkman, it's a dream come true," he says into the receiver. As Jake talks to the reporter, I slip out of bed and crawl around the floor in search of my clothes.

"I don't really like to discuss my personal life," Jake says. "Well, no, there's no special lady in my life right now. You know how it is, my career's my relationship. Yep, I'm single. *Totally* single."

I freeze, naked on the floor. Jake Jones's floor. I want to die. On second thought, I'd like to kill him and *then* myself. Did I mention that I'm not wearing *any* clothes? "No special lady" rings in my head. "*Totally* single." No, wait a minute. Oh duh. I bet he *has* to say that. His publicist probably sat him down and made him *promise* to say that. Okay, okay, okay. Maybe I'm overreacting.

"My type? I love all women, man. . . . Well, no, I'm so not into blondes. I'm from Texas. I don't really understand these L.A. ladies. I prefer 'em au natural. You know, sweet and simple. . . ."

I run through the list of me. *Blonde*. From *L.A. Sweet*. But definitely not simple. Okay, this is yucky. Totally and officially gross. No, I am *not* overreacting. No publicist taught him to say *that*. Kate was right. Jake's not a human being. He's *another* narcissistic, insincere, vapid *actor*. And this is *Typical Actor Bullshit*, Take 507. Boy, did he have me fooled with his whole caterpillar-into-a-butterfly act. It's more like caterpillar into an *asshole*.

Has he forgotten completely that I'm here—and *naked*? Not to mention, we had s-e-x. And not just sex. *Great* sex. Doesn't that count for anything? I curse myself for jumping headfirst off that wagon and onto an actor. It's all SMITH's fault. If he hadn't blindsided me at the GM show, I never would have fallen into Jake Jones's bed. Why do I always lose my footing with SMITH? He makes me feel like I'm walking a Cirque du Soleil tightrope in six-inch Lanvin stilettos.

Jake clicks off the phone and pumps his fist. "Yes! Awesome!" He heads back to the bathroom, then stops, as if he's hitting his mark. I can practically hear the gears turning in his head as he has an afterthought. That's me: the afterthought. Jake takes a dramatic pause, turns to face me, and in his best Hugh Grant says, "Last night was great. I'll call you." The bathroom door closes softly behind him. That's it? Yeah, that was about as heartfelt as Donald Rumsfeld.

Okay. I officially hate myself. I cashed in my actor sobriety chips and *this* is what I get. This is even worse than when Adrian Grenier took me to Baja Fresh and wanted to go dutch. Jake Jones makes A. G. look like Prince Charming. I've *got* to get back on that wagon. Day One and counting.

I grab my clutch, throw on my crumpled dress, and struggle to pull up my thigh-high boots as I make my way down the long hallway, bolting for the front door. It slams shut behind me. Wait. Oh no. My car. Where's my car? Oh God. I left it at the GM Show. It's like eighty miles from here to Hollywood and Vine. Okay. Deep breath. What am I going to do? I try to open Jake Jones's door—it's locked. Oh no.

I pull out my cell to call a cab. No service. Dang it. I hold the phone in the air and walk around Jake Jones's front yard in search of reception. Please have a bar. Can I get a bar for crying out loud? Nothing but a big fat *X* where the bar should be. What kind of an idiot lives in Topanga Canyon anyway? I'm crouching behind a pink azalea bush, searching for cell reception, when Jake's garage door opens. He pulls out in his black Mercedes. Please don't let him see me. I look like one of those people you see combing Venice beach with metal detectors. I haven't even brushed my teeth or taken a look at my face. I crouch down lower behind the azalea in utter mortification. Phew. He's gone. He didn't see me. I look down at my cell. One bar. Yes! I dial information. The call fails. Damn it. The front door swings open as I'm crawling around the lawn on all fours in search of reception.

"Lady, what are you doing?" Hamas hollers from the doorway.

"Oh hi, Hamas, oh my gosh," I pull myself up off the wet grass. "Hamas, I, um, well, I don't have my car. I mean, I left it—well, Jake, you know, he drove me—last night I needed a lift—and um, there he was—Jake in his black Mercedes—and well, the rubber band was broken by that point—and um, it was between Jake and a wet discarded scrunchy—and well, I chose Jake. . . ." Hamas is staring at me like I've gone Sally Field in *Sybil*. Maybe I have. "Hamas, look, I need to use the phone."

"My name's *Imas*."

"Oh, I'm sorry. Jake was calling you Hamas."

"Little secret, lady—he don't listen," Imas says, tucking her dark brown Lesley Stahl coif behind her ears, revealing small gold heart studs and smiling at me with sparkly brown eyes.

"Yeah, I noticed that."

"But he pay me. He don't pay you—so it's not worth it for you, nice lady—no?"

"No, Imas—not worth it—no."

"You come in. We have nice coffee together. You call your taxi."

"Just Say No," Imas says, pointing to the D.A.R.E. T-shirt she's wearing as I pour my heart out to her about my Actorholism. I take in her sage words and another bite of Jake's Weight Watchers Southwestern breakfast wrap that Imas heated up for me.

My ringing cell phone interrupts our heart-to-heart. *Now* I get service.

"I went onto WireImage at four a.m. and Jake Jones was *ravishing* at the GM Show. I'm so proud of you," Julian says. "I just got back from rescuing a cow from slaughter in upstate New York with PETA and I'm feeling *much* more grounded. I'm ready to get on that plane. I promise. I hope Olivia isn't mad at me that I wasn't at the fitting yesterday. Is she mad at me? Did she ask about me? What's that noise?"

"Wait. You're getting on a plane?"

"Yes and if the plane crashes, I'm leaving you *everything*. But don't change the subject. What's that noise?"

"It's Hamas—I mean, Imas—she's DustBusting the floor around my feet."

"What *are* you talking about? Who's Imas? Where are you?"

"Jake Jones's house."

Silence.

"Don't tell me. You saw SMITH and spiraled out of control and I wasn't there to save you from the depths of self-loathing. Don't deny it, I saw him on WireImage. Go ahead, tell me you hate me. Tell me I've ruined your life. Tell me it's all my fault and that you'll never forgive me."

"It's all your fault and I'll never forgive you."

"How can you say that to me? I've been your best friend since I saved you from those tapered acid-washed Guess jeans and leg warmers. Actually, I'm feeling very inspired by the eighties right now. I'm thinking Boy George may be my muse for my next collection. But listen. Katya booked me on the five o'clock American Airlines flight. I land at LAX at eight p.m. Pick me up and I'll take you to Giorgio's for your favorite langoustine pasta—my treat."

"My treat will be getting you here so that I don't have to do this whole Oscar Week thing alone anymore."

"I've got more incredible news. Did I ever tell you about my vet who takes care of Catherine Keener's bicoastal Chihuahua, who plays with Jack Black's German shepherd when she's in L.A.? Well, Jack's dog walker walks Willow Fox's publicist's puggle. And the dog walker is my manicurist's cousin. Long story short: Willow Fox is interested in wearing me to the Oscars!"

I can't believe it! "What? That girl from the *Fast Times at Ridgemont High* remake with Jared Leto? Julian, this is huge!"

"Well Willow Fox is going to be even *huger*—or at least her breasts are gonna be. You're not going to believe it. She's playing *Dolly Parton*. After Reese won the Oscar for *Walk the Line*, Universal smartened up and realized it was time to make—are you sitting down?— *Dollywood*! You need to meet Willow at the Soho House in an hour. Katya FedExed the dresses from my showroom to the Soho House concierge."

"An hour, Julian?! I can't. My car's—"

"Lola, need I remind you that we're talking about the Oscars? And you *know* the only person I worship as much as you is *Dolly*. You can't blow this meeting. If we dress Willow, maybe I can visit her on the set and meet Dolly. Then I can die a happy man. See you at eight to-night!"

Click.

"Imas, you are an absolute lifesaver driving me all the way here," I say as we pull up in front of the Soho House. "I don't know what I would have done without you. Are you sure you don't want to come in? I could get you a new pair of Seven Jeans. Maybe a massage? Or a *free* diamond pendant from Chopard. Maybe you can hawk it on eBay and get away from Jake Jones." Wait. Maybe *I* could hawk it on eBay and get the hell out of Hollyweird.

"You and I are friends now, Lola, no?"

"Yes, Imas, friends. Great friends." I lean over and give her a hug.

"So you remember what Imas tell you. Just say no," Imas says, tapping her T-shirt for emphasis. "Mr. Jones not good enough for you. He make me go to Costco for his fat-free SnackWells. Then he make me go to the beach to get salt water—he must have for highlights. Then I must pick up his dog at vet, buy cigars for poker night, then Mr. Jones make me go to Hustler on Sunset Boulevard to buy his custom-fit condoms—and fur handcuffs."

"He makes you do that? That's disgusting, Imas," I say. But why didn't he pull those out for me—am I not Worthy? I feel as cheap as a Chinatown Louis Vuitton knockoff.

"I can find you a better job, Imas," I say.

Imas chuckles. "Just find youself a better man. You got enough to worry about."

We watch as the Next Eva Longoria steps out of her Mini Cooper convertible and heads toward the Soho House. She's wearing a cream silk babydoll dress. Imas shakes her head mournfully. "She should not be wearing that ruching. She think it make her boobs look big but it just make her waist look big. These LA girls don't have no sense."

She's got that right. I give Imas another hug and try to tug down this shrunken dress that I'm quite certain Julian never intended to be worn in the bright light of day. These damn python boots have chaffed my thighs so much they look like Jenna Jameson's. I've tried to repair my face as best I can with only Imas's moisturizer, but I'm absolutely sick with myself *and* I'm about to walk into the Soho House—the same ultra-posh members-only British club Samantha Jones couldn't even get into when they leapt across the pond and opened in NYC. It's too bad the Soho House is only in L.A. during Oscar Week because it'd be bloody nice to be able to take a dip in their fresh saltwater pool all year long—though I could do without the $1,500 annual members fee. Fortunately, during Oscar Week, *everything* at the Soho House is *free*—no cash, checks, or credits cards necessary. The Naked Chef Jamie Oliver's brilliant lobster ravioli? On the house. Vera Wang lace negligees? Completely complimentary. Five-hundred-dollar mink eyelash extensions? Comp'd. Even the deejay lessons with Tony Okungbowa, Ellen's Ex, are gratis.

The Soho House is one of *twenty* "hospitality suites" set up in ritzy hotels, swank salons, and humongous Hollywood homes around town during Oscar Week. They exist only to pamper, pedicure, pluck, primp, prep and beautify, Botox, bedeck, and bejewel all the "-istas," "-tantes," and "-ites" readying themselves for Oscar. *Every* product and treatment under the sun, from $1,500 porcelain snap-on teeth that will give you Jennifer Hudson's smile, to an Oscar gold-toned made-to-measure Frette-padded Miracle Bra by Victoria's Secret couture designer is *free*—just as long as you give the nice photographers from *Us Weekly, People,* and

InStyle a Brite Smile care of Dr. Dorfman while posing with your brand spanking new $25,000 diamond-encrusted digital Nikon that fits into your sterling monogrammed Altoid box.

Spending too much time in the Land of the Free and the Home of the Swag can give any gal a severe case of the Gimmes. Think *Supermarket Sweep*—only custom red chevron Goyard monogrammed trunks instead of grocery carts. And poor publicists-slash-sherpas having to *return* fifty of the hundred pairs of $400 sunglasses their clients stuffed into the twenty pairs of mink-lined Ugg Boots because the RayBan rep begged them to.

Sheesh. These celebs don't know how good they've got it. When Diane Keaton was nominated for *Annie Hall,* all she got was a friggin' *Oscar.* I mean, she didn't get *Jack*—nope, not Nicholson, not even a *free* roll of LifeSavers. Heck, she drove *herself* to the Dorothy Chandler Pavilion in her VW and borrowed her brother's suit. Man, that must have sucked. Thank you David Yurman, thank you Jaguar, thank you Sony, for recognizing the needy ones—the stars who make ten million dollars a picture and just need more *free* stuff, even if their accountants do have to pony up the coin later to cover the taxes.

The uptight British door bitch confers with someone inside via headset and stares over her gold sunglasses at me like she's Steve Rubell and I'm Gary Coleman. There's nothing quite like a door bitch sizing up where you fall on the food chain to make you feel like a sad slab of mercury-ridden tuna from Hirozen. But with a get-up like this, I probably wouldn't let me in either.

"Julian Tennant's gowns are waiting for you on the second floor." The British bitch sends me inside with a magic wave of her Montblanc. I walk inside the ten-thousand-square-foot circular bachelor pad with a killer 360-degree view of the city. Inside it looks like James Bond's lair. A cute British waiter (bad teeth, natch) offers me a mimosa. Well it is *almost* noon, and it is predominantly orange juice. And I'm not sure Imas's Olay Daily Defense Moisturizer is going to be enough protection against all of theses Swagaholics Winona Rydering. And after my night, my morning, my life, I think I deserve a little chemically enhanced joy. Besides, I need to put on a happy face for Willow Fox. And we all know I'm not that good an actress.

"Wait, don't go," I say to the waiter as I grab another mimosa. "Cut me off after this one." I try and sneak a peak at who's brunching on the tented terrace beneath the ginormous Venetian glass chandelier. I can make out Kimora Lee Simmons's bling from all the way over here.

"Are you Lola Santisi? Are you finding everything you need? Would you like me to take you around?" a young fresh-faced PR pip-squeak runs up to me, knitting her eyebrows earnestly. She clearly only looks at the pictures on Page Six, because if she read the fine print she'd realize I'm not Worthy of even a *free* Tangerine Emergen-C packet. "My name's Anna. You're much prettier in person," she says. Okay, she's a keeper. This is a *much* better buzz than those mimosas.

"Thanks, Anna, you're so sweet. Are those J Brand jeans?" I ask. "Okay, Anna, here's the deal. I have a meeting with Willow Fox here and for reasons I can't go into at the moment, I look like I work for Heidi Fleiss, not Julian Tennant, the next Tom Ford. So, can you please help a sister out and get me those jeans in a size twenty-five and I need a top too, something, you know, anything? I'd take a Hanes wife beater."

"I'll grab you some James Perse, C&C, and Primp T-shirts. Oh and we have L.A.M.B. tees too." In five minutes flat she's back with an arm-load of airspun cotton.

"Thank you so much, Anna. I know you've given me so much already, but are those Swarovski crystals on those Adidas flip-flops?"

"There are six hundred hand-set crystals on them," Anna recites dutifully. "They retail for $280 at Fred Segal."

"Do you have those in a 7½ in navy?"

Anna leads me to the second floor, which is done up to look *exactly* like Barneys, only better because everything is *free*. There are more cute British waiters passing more mimosas and offering up minibagels with smoked salmon and scallion cream cheese, and peanut butter frozen bananas. It feels good to be out of that shred of chiffon and those boots, especially because I dig what these jeans are doing for my derrière. Hmmmm, maybe I should have held out for a pair of those leopard print Giuseppe Zanottis with the metallic gold trim instead of these striped Swarovski'd slides. Even the spa sandals I spot on Sarah Michelle Gellar as she ducks into the Bodacious Bling room are better than the Masai Barefoot Technology they're hawking at The House of Flaunt. They're supposed to feel like you're "walking barefoot on springy moss or a sandy beach," but honestly they just make you look like you have clubbed hooves.

Okay, okay, I'm not here to shop; I'm here to find Willow Fox and get her to wear Julian. Focus. Anna hands me Julian's garment bag and sends me upstairs to the spa floor to meet Willow Fox.

"I'm definitely booking you a placental facial for after you're done," Anna says, leaning in confidingly. "Meg Ryan just left after getting hers and her skin looks *so amazing* it *totally* took the attention off the lips. You look a little tired—like you could use a little pick-me-up."

"Good idea, you're a doll, Anna." I'm not sure when we stepped into the Cameron Diaz and Toni Collette roles for *In Her Shoes*, but I'm not knocking the *free* services. I wonder whose placenta they're using. Didn't I read that the stuff comes from sheep? Well, those baby lambs look pretty fresh-faced, don't they? Although aren't they a little . . . woolly? Maybe ignorance is bliss.

Wow, it's nicer up here than Chris McMillan's salon on Burton Way. Are those Relax The Back mechanical shiatsu therapy haircut chairs? It's like *Extreme Makeover: Oscar Edition* up here. We're not just talking mani-pedis, blow-outs, cellulite wraps, and extensions by the hair legend Danilo (who does Gwen Stefani *and* Miss Tyra Banks) and makeup by Sue Devitt *herself*. We're talking fanny facials (scary), glycolic bikini peels (scarier), *free* consults with Dr. Novak (Mom's cosmetic reupholsterer), and ThermaCool with Hollywood's Fairy Skin Mother.

I finally find Willow Fox in the "lunchtime face-lift" room, where Hollywood's Fairy Skin Mother herself is presiding. She's been so Botoxed, peeled, and pulled that I have to resist the urge to touch her to make sure she's not one of Madame Tussaud's. Willow's got enough wires coming out of her head for a remake of *The Bride of Frankenstein*. She's wrapped in a terrycloth robe and her dark hair is sprouting out of a towel like a Chia Pet. I can't get a good look at that face that moves millions of magazine covers.

"Who's there?" Willow Fox says from behind the two slices of cucumber resting on her eyes.

"Hi, I'm Lola Santisi. I have Julian Tennant's gowns to show you."

"I'll leave you two alone for a few minutes, but please be sure not to disrupt my wires," Hollywood's Fairy Skin Mother says, dialing the knobs on a console straight out of Starship Command. "Relax, Willow, I'll be back in ten," she says and closes the door behind her. I'm tempted to beg her to stay. I'd rather not be alone with an actress, especially one hooked up to all that voltage.

"I can come back when you're done, if that's better," I offer.

"No, let's look at the dresses now," Willow says, making no effort to remove the cucumber slices from her eyes.

"Are you sure you don't need to wait for your stylist—or your agent—or your manager—or your publicist?"

"Positive."

Whoah, no entourage? No hairdresser-slash-best friend? No mother? No numerology handler? Not even a *dog*? I unzip the garment bag and pull out a pale cascade of multiple organza ruffles.

"Ahem," I cough to try and get her attention. Willow gingerly turns her head in my direction, careful not to disturb Hollywood's Fairy Skin Mother's wires or the cucumber slices.

Oh-kay. I hold the dress out in front of me, fluffing the delicate ruffles.

"Oh, that's a stunning teal blue—I love the color," she says.

"Oh well, right, um, actually it's *white* organza."

"Oh, it must be the light in this room."

Or maybe those freaking cucumber slices.

Willow settles back into her recliner. "Could you describe it to me? I'm a very visual person."

Describe it to her? Would she ask Alexander McQueen to play auditory charades with his couture collection? She can't be serious.

"Go ahead," she says.

Oh-kay. "Well, um, the bodice is a plunging vee to the waist and the skirt is a waterfall of ruffles to the floor—oh and there's a black satin ribbon detail at the waist. It's very chic. Like a sexy Scarlett O'Hara."

"Oh, that won't work—the proportion's all wrong for my body. What's next?"

"Well really, I think if you could *see* it—maybe even try it on—you might feel differ—"

"No, I can see it in my mind."

What mind? Maybe I should ask Hollywood's Fairy Skin Mother to turn down the capacitive radio frequency on that machine; I think it's frying the trio of brain cells she's got in there. On second thought, maybe I should ask her to turn the frequency *up*. Maybe the electric shock will get to work on recircuiting her brain.

"I'm wai-ting," she sing-songs, exhaling heavily, like *I'm* the crazy one. Which at this point I'm thinking I may be.

"Okay, well, here's a black and rose-gold color-blocked gown. Julian's intricate draping and ingenious system of gathers and small seams nips and tucks the body in all the right places. It'll save you a trip to the plastic surgeon," I laugh but my joke falls on deaf ears.

"No, no, no, the fabric's way too shiny. I don't want to look like Shakira at the Grammys."

"Can I just peel *one* corner of that cucumber off your eye, because it's really not *that* shiny. It's silk brocade. It has the patina of an ancient wall hanging in Rome. It's really quite beautiful."

Willow lifts one itsy-bitsy millimeter of the edge of the cucumber up as though she's sipping tea with the Queen at Buckingham Palace—pinky cocked and all.

"Too shiny," she says matter-of-factly. "Next."

Okay, breathe. Inhale. Exhale. Inhale. Exhale. Darn, it's not working. Okay, how about a Sacred Pause. Shoot. Not working either. How about I walk over to that machine and turn the frequency all the way up myself? Or better yet, how about I rip those damn cucumbers off her eyes so she can actually *see* Julian's masterpieces? Okay, I promised Julian I wouldn't screw up this meeting.

"Right, well, this one you're really going to love. It's a billowy ballerina number. Julian hand-dyed the fabric himself and it's like a rainbow of degraded pinks—nude to fuchsia. The fuchsia just tinges the hem of the gown," I say.

"Okay, it's perfect. That's the one," Willow says, cucumbers firmly planted on her eyes. "Can you just measure the length and tell me how long it is?"

Perfect? I love the sound of perfect. So what if she hasn't *seen* the damn dress. Uh-oh, I don't have a tape measure. My lip gloss barely fit into that clutch. I lay the dress on the floor and carefully pace off beside it.

"It's four feet," I say.

"How many inches is that?"

"Forty-eight inches," I tell her. What, did she drop out of school in kindergarten?

"Tell Julian it needs to come up four inches."

"But if you lop off four inches, you'll completely lose the fuchsia that's on the hem," I point out. *The fuschia you haven't even seen,* I think.

"So what?"

"Well, um, that's what makes the whole dress, otherwise it's just a nude chiffon dress."

"I like nude. It feels very avant-garde to show up at the Oscars looking naked. Tell Julian he's a genius. Tell him it's my dream dress."

"Are you sure you don't want to *see* it?"

"You're incredibly descriptive."

"Okay, right, so you're gonna wear this dress—on Sunday—to the Oscars."

"It was love at first sight."

That's one way of looking at it.

I never thought I'd have a fond feeling toward a cucumber again—until Dora, the facialist, places two cooling slices over my eyes and slathers my face in placenta. I'm loving every minute of my Easy-Like-Sunday-Morning-on-an-Oscar Week-Wednesday moment because I just got Willow Fox to *commit* to wearing Julian to the Oscars. She may not be Natalie Portman, but she's no Tara Reid either. I, Lola Santisi, closed the deal! I like the way this whole *succeeding* thing feels. It's a real confidence booster. And with me on my way to licking my CDD, I plan on convincing Olivia she *has* to wear that peacock sensation on Sunday. I haven't figured out exactly how I'm going to do it, but I've been working on my material with Dora, who's already invited me over for Shabbat dinner after Oscar Week.

My phone trills. I contemplate not answering it; I'm extremely busy picturing my Isaac Mizrahi moment on the Red Carpet—"You're a Superstar!"—and my new complexion, which Dora promises will look like a newborn's bottom. But, oh shoot, what if it's Olivia Cutter's people?

"Quick, will you grab my phone, Dora, and hold it to my ear?" Now I sound like Mariah, but it can't be helped. Dora presses the phone in place.

"Hi Lola, it's Matt."

Matt Damon? Matt Dillon? Matthew Broderick? Matthew McConaughey? *Please* be Matthew McConaughey. What am I saying? No more actors. Let it be someone normal, someone in the real world—someone like—like Matt Lauer. Yes! Let it be Matt Lauer!

"Matt Wagner, Willow Fox's agent. I'm not sure what you put on her Corn Flakes, but she absolutely loves you. She can't stop raving about your vision."

Oh-kay. "Yes, well, Willow has an amazing eye for fresh talent," I say.

"So how much," he says.

"How much what?"

"For the dress."

"Oh! The dress is free. Of course, it's *free*."

"Yes, we know the dress is free. Willow Fox isn't," Matt says, his voice suddenly armored in pure Gordon Gekko in *Wall Street*. "Willow loves Julian. She also loves Ungaro, Etro, Moschino. And Escada. They offered us $100,000 this morning."

Oh man, I should have known Willow Fox was too good to be true. What's it going to take to get a freaking break? Those were cucumbers hanging off her face, not a Sotheby's sign. Like Willow really needs that money. Universal's only paying her two *million* for *Dollywood*. What happened to the days when celebs were just thankful they didn't have to go to Neiman's and pay retail? Now we're supposed to *pay* them—to wear a freaking dress? Matt Wagner can shove his auction up his ass. I have to think fast.

"Well, Matt, what I have to offer you is *the* hot new designer. Julian Tennant is going to launch Willow Fox into a whole new fashion stratosphere on that Red Carpet. That's going to mean so much more to her career in the long run than money right now. Let's get her on that style icon list with Gwyneth and Nicole. Then you'll be naming her price on the big screen."

"I'm naming her price *now*."

Click.

"Dora, can you get this placenta off—fast?" Or maybe I should have her shroud my whole body with it so I can crawl right back into the womb and stay there until this whole nightmare ends? Okay, calm down, let's do a Dr. Gilmore re-framing: at least I got to taste success—for like the first time *ever*. So what if it was for all of three and a half minutes, I liked it. Okay so this is a bad break, a *terrible* break, a *horrible* break, but I'm not going to let it be a career-ending break, damn it. I'm still going to get Olivia to wear that peacock gown to the Oscars on Sunday—if her people ever call me to reschedule that fitting. But what if they call me back wanting all of Bank of America?

The second I'm done with that placenta facial I decide to go back downstairs to the Stiletto Fetish Salon to pick up those Giuseppe Zanottis to lift my spirits. Stiletto therapy is foolproof, especially when they're *free*. I'm tucking the box under my arm when I spot PR Queen

Bee escorting the *Next* Halle Berry, her arms so full of swag she looks like a stock clerk at Tar-jay during the after-Christmas sale. I duck for cover behind the display of Benefit intense lip plumping masks and speed-dial Kate. Her assistant Adam picks up.

"Lola, Kate's on the other line with Brian Grazer."

"Tell her I'm getting a pedicure next to Naomi Watts and she's thinking of leaving CAA because they can't get her the Hillary Clinton role in *All the President's Women.*"

Kate jumps on the line faster than the Malo people can stuff cashmere sweats into Star Jones's Fendi Spy Bag. "Tell Naomi I can totally envision her in that little red suit. I'll put a call into Mike Nichols before the enamel dries on her toes," she says. "No, wait, just hand her your phone for me, please? I want to talk to her myself."

"Naomi's not here, I need you to pick me up from the Soho House—asap."

Kate lets out an exasperated sigh. "Where the hell is your car?"

"It's still on Hollywood and Highland."

Silence. A very judgmental silence.

"I slept with Jake Jones last night because I ran into SMITH at the GM Show," I blurt out. "Jake Jones is a total cad. He's another one of *them.* They can't be trusted. What am I saying, *I* can't be trusted with myself. I should have a Danger sign plastered to my forehead. There I was, in his bed, *naked,* and he tells *People* magazine there's no special lady in his life. I know I wasn't exactly in his *life*—or exactly a *lady*—but I sure as heck was in his *bed.* Did I mention that I was *naked*?"

"I don't care whether you were naked or packed into a full body Yamamoto cyborg suit. The part I'm worried about is that you're *surprised.* Where's the damn choir for this: He's an *actor,* Lola. I told you: It's okay to sleep with them, just don't fall for them. You know that."

"Well, Kate, I *asked* you to save me and you didn't, so here's your chance for a do-over. Please come pick me up. I feel sick. I feel used. I feel as bad as Burt Reynold's facelift. I should be in a coma right now I fell so hard off that wagon."

"Listen, I'm sorry, but I can't pick you up. I have therapy."

"Did I just hear you correctly," I say, rattling my head to try to adjust to the image of Kate on the couch.

"Not for *me*. For Will. He called this morning and wants me to go to therapy with him and his mother. She's still angry with me because she feels I didn't protect Will's *assets* in that *Vanity Fair* cover shoot—she thinks his package looked small next to Josh Hartnett's. Do you want me to send Adam to come get you?"

"No, it's okay. You should just tell the therapist that no one was going to notice Will next to Josh Hartnett. Hold on, I have a private call waiting and it could be Olivia Cutter's people."

"I'm calling for my chance to be forgiven." Oh my God. My palms instantly become the Pacific Ocean. It's SMITH. "Have dinner with me tonight."

I rear back so suddenly I nearly catapult myself into Zooey Deschanel. Thank God that heap of Missoni four-ply cashmere travel blankies and socks she's holding would break my fall. I decide on the safer option, to take a seat right where I am on the sisal carpet. Actually, I don't decide; my knees give out from under me. My voice seems to have caught a flight to Aix-en-Provence without me.

"Please," SMITH says.

He's always had a way of ripping the air right out of my lungs. I can't think straight right now, I have no oxygen. I shake the Giuseppe Zanottis out into the box and cup the satin shoe bag around my mouth. Inhale. Exhale. Inhale. Exhale.

"Are you okay?" I pull my head up from the shoe bag and look up. J-Lo's standing above me, pure hip-pop diva glam in a pair of micro-shorts and one of her signature huge floppy umbrella hats. She must have stopped by the AquaBar Hydration Station because she's positively radiant. I momentarily consider breaking it down for her. If anyone understands an *ex* drama, it's J-Lo.

"Don't mind me, I just found out they don't have these in my size," I say.

"I know the feeling. Last season when Donatella gave Kylie Minogue the last pair of gold-studded runway stilettos, I felt the same way," J-Lo says, strolling off toward the counter of Shu Uemura 14k gold eyelash curlers.

"Babe, are you still there?" Oh no, he cannot start calling me *that*. What makes him think he can swoop back in and start throwing *babe* around? No way. I am *not* falling for the babe bit.

"Hang on," I say to him, clicking back to Kate for emotional coaching—okay, so I'm desperate. "Please still be there."

"You got lucky, I got distracted reading 'Dlisted.' Did you know Teri Hatcher's a man?"

"Kate, forget that. SMITH is on the other line and he wants to see me tonight."

"If you're even contemplating it, you're beyond help. And FYI, it's Oscar Week. I'm not going to have time to check you into the Menninger Clinic when he decimates you all over again. Tell SMITH if he and Simon Cowell were the last men on the planet—you'd choose Simon."

"Okay, okay, got it. Let me tell him while it's fresh. Good luck in therapy with Will and his mom." I click back over.

"I, I, I—" I've only been waiting for 189 days to give SMITH a *Dirty Harry*-style revenge. I think about giving him the Simon Cowell line. But the thing is, Kate's never been in love. And now that my moment's arrived, I can't do it.

"I can't do it," cracks out of my throat.

"Don't say you can't. Say you don't want to. But I know you want to."

"Please—I can't. I have to go." *Click.*

The inch-deep sisal rug waffle marks on my ass have nothing on the gashes in my heart. But I did it. I didn't let SMITH back. I can act *as if* I have a spine. My phone beeps. One new text message.

Olivia's too emotionally drained from spending the day with her little Make-A-Wish child Sofia for a fitting. Please be at Olivia's house tomorrow at noon. John.

Great. That's just freaking great. That's the maraschino cherry on *my* emotionally draining day. I take my Giuseppe Zanottis and nearly trip over the De Beers people and the David Yurman people fighting over who can give Katherine Heigl more *free* loot as I storm out of the Soho House.

"Hollywood and Highland," I say to the cabbie as I climb inside.

He screws his head around and looks me in the eye. "You have cash, right? Tori Spelling just tried to tip me with bronzing powder when I picked her up from the House of Flaunt."

I drag my Buddha and Ganesh from my neglected home altar into my bathroom where I'm drawing a detoxifying soak. Some people like to bathe with rubber duckies—I prefer my Buddha and Ganesh, especially after this day. I wonder how many rock bottoms you have to hit before you become an official member of the Whitney Houston Less Than Zero Society. I thought I'd been hand-delivered my Platinum WHLTZS card when SMITH threw me in the garbage like the Viagra pen in the

Vegas Magazine goody bag. I figure I upped my status to an all-access Black Card by cashing in my sobriety chips to another no-good actor who declared himself "totally single" ten minutes after screwing me. And now SMITH wants to regift me? Fat chance.

I lie down in the tub and plunge my head under the steaming hot water. Can I get a rebirth please? I'd like a do-over. Here's how it'd look: I'd be Dorothy. I'd be wearing those ruby heels. I bet no one in Kansas speaks in third person or ever asked Dorothy to watch them shave their *crotch*. Of course she did have to deal with that whole Oz fiasco. But she got to go *home* in the end. The only home I know is Hollyweird. And that makes Oz look like a spa day at The Golden Door. So where do I get to go when I click my Louboutins? After Oscar Week I swear I'll click my heels and figure out what will make me feel like I've come home.

FLIGHT 29 FROM JFK REROUTED TO KANSAS, the American Airlines arrivals board flashes in front of me. Kansas? What? Oh no. Did I manifest the Kansas thing? Oh boy, this is going to be bad. *Really* bad. I speed-dial Julian.

"I'm a total wreck—I almost died on that flight from hell," he sobs into the phone. "They said the hydraulic system had failed. We were all sure we were going to crash. I was going to perish in flames right next to someone who was wearing Dockers. And reeking of Stetson cologne. I'd be under the covers right now, but the sandpaper they're passing off for sheets at this Days Inn at the airport in Wichita doesn't qualify for *any* thread count, let alone the Frette 600 thread count I'm accustomed to. Can you *imagine* what a black light would reveal?" I can picture Julian shuddering.

"Oh my God, Julian. I'm so sorry. Breathe. It's going to be okay.

You'll just get on the next flight out and you'll be here in a couple of hours and I'll be waiting. I'll take you straight to the Chateau. I got that poolside bungalow you love and Mohammad will make you a steamed artichoke. Then you can take a bubble bath, light a candle, and climb between the *Frette* sheets."

"Two words, Lola. *Emergency Landing*. If it weren't for the bottle of Soma I took before I got on the plane, I would have died of cardiac arrest when the pilot got on the intercom and told us to assume the crash test dummy position. The stewardess told us to stay calm with the same voice she used to tell us they were starting the *Mr. and Mrs. Smith Prequel*. How exactly was I supposed to remain calm? The woman across the aisle was wearing Kathy Ireland separates and *Aerosoles*. Listen closely, I am *never* stepping a John Lobb loafer on an airplane again. Not if Clive Owen *and* Eric Bana were going to take turns blowing me all the way to L.A."

I feel for Julian, but sometimes you have to just rip the Band-Aid right off. "I know this isn't the best time, but are you sitting down?"

"What would you suggest I sit on that's not going to give me Chlamydia—this hideous Flower Power bedspread? The pea-green, mildewed chair? Or the flea-infested brown shag carpet? God knows what's breeding in there."

"Go sit in the bathtub."

"Fine. Hang on." I hear muffled footsteps. "Okay, I'm here. But hurry up, the showerhead's dripping on me and the Soma's wearing off."

"Willow Fox wants $100,000 to wear your dress and Olivia Cutter canceled her final fitting *again*."

Silence.

"Now I wish the pilot had flown that plane straight into the Mississippi. I really thought we'd pull this off. I didn't think I'd end up losing my—" Julian says.

"What? Julian, say it again, I can't hear—"

I hear rustling, a crash, then Niagara Falls.

"Julian? Julian!"

"Oh, don't mind me. I was just trying to tie my orange crocodile belt around the showerhead so that I could hang myself from it. But they can't even get a showerhead right in this place. I ripped it straight out of the wall. Now there's brown water gushing all over my Hermès shirt, *and* my hair that I had Luigi flat-iron for the trip is ruined."

"Julian, we *will* pull this off, we have our meeting rescheduled with Olivia for tomorrow. I'm at the airport. Why don't I get on a plane and come and get you and I'll hold your hand all the way back to L.A.—and I'll bring enough Lunesta for the two of us."

"Lola, what about my never getting on a plane again do you not understand?"

"Julian, I can't do this without you. You've *got* to meet Olivia with me tomorrow, or we have no chance! Will you at least ask the concierge about a Greyhound schedule?"

"The concierge? I'm sorry, did you mean the scarecrow out front? Or the guy with no teeth by the soda machine? This is not the Four Seasons, princess. I'll be lucky if there's a tractor to run me over."

Click.

Is Mercury going to be in retrograde for the rest of my life? I start the long trek back to my car. But not before a quick stop at the Cinnabon in terminal six. I deserve to get *something* out of my visit to LAX—my third this week. I take a bite of the warm, gooey roll—it's totally worth every one of the gazillion grams of fat. Okay, so it's not the seared alba-core with crispy onions from Koi. But damn if it's not making me feel better.

I have a particularly mammoth, melty piece in my mouth when I feel a tap on my shoulder. I spin around to find myself face-to-face with

SMITH. I practically choke on the bun and reflexively spit it out of my mouth and into my napkin. Oh God, did I really just do that in front of him?

SMITH takes me by the shoulders. "Lola, are you okay? It's a good thing I learned the Heimlich for that part in Gore Verbinski's *Code Blue*."

"What are you doing here?" I sputter. From this moment forward I'm committing exclusively to Burbank and the Bob Hope Airport.

"We're shooting nights here on *Nothing to Declare*. I'm playing the commitment-phobic customs officer. Claire Danes is the kooky tourist who thinks it's only Kahlúa in her carry-on. Michael Mann is directing. We're on our dinner break. You should join me. I can see you're already onto dessert, but maybe we can work backward."

"I can'—" SMITH places his fingers over my mouth to stop me.

"I'm not taking no for an answer," he says, keeping his fingers on my lips much longer than is legal.

There go the knees again. And the stomach. And the heart—in the throat. If I'd known I was going to run into SMITH, I would have stopped at Rite Aid on the way and cleaned them out of rubber bands. Not to mention thrown on some lip gloss—and that little black YSL dress he adores—and my sickeningly tall Louboutins. Oh no, I look absolutely awful in these sweats. Maybe it's a good thing. Maybe it's divine intervention. Sacred Pause. Act *as if*, Lola. Act *as if* you were Kate.

I take his hand and remove it from my buzzing lips. I hold him by both wrists so that he doesn't try and stop me from what I need to say. "If you and Simon Cowell were the last two men on the planet, I'd choose Simon." I turn on my Uggs and with the conviction of Reese Witherspoon in *Election,* I walk away. I did it! Kate would be so proud. So would Dr. Gilmore. *I'm* proud.

"Simon Cowell? The guy from *American Idol*?" I hear him say, but I've already left him in a cloud of Fracas. Thank you Ganesh for making sure I spritzed after my bath. I will not turn around. I will not turn around. I will not turn around. I will walk straight into my future. Fifty-two more gates and I'm outta here. Fifty-one, fifty, forty-nine. I officially hate LAX. Don't look back. Do *not* look back. Focus on aching feet, not aching heart. Forty-eight, forty-seven, forty-six.

At gate forty-five I feel SMITH's hand on my shoulder. He's spinning me around and straight into his—uh-oh—*lips*. I think about pushing him away—for like a *millisecond*. Not that I'd have the strength. I've always been a melting Pinkberry green tea frozen yogurt in his arms. I'm sorry, Dr. Gilmore. I'm sorry, Kate. I'm sorry, Cricket. I'm sorry, Julian, Christopher, Mom, Papa. I'm sorry. SMITH's my first real love—who happens to be an actor. And I still love him. What if this is a sign? Maybe Aphrodite rerouted Julian's plane because SMITH and I are meant to be together, like Bogey and Bacall, Harry and Sally, Jay-Z and Beyoncé.

Suddenly there are flashes. No, not the stars-swirling-around-my-head kind. Although those are there too. The paparazzi kind.

thursday

82 hours, 3 minutes, 58 seconds until

the Oscar for Best Cinematography is handed out.

C hopin's *Nocturna* CD streams through the Bose speakers in my shower stall. Nanny No. 9 said it always helped her when she was having man issues, and I have enough of those to fill the Hollywood Bowl. I have to face an ugly truth: I'm still in love with SMITH. *No!* I will *not* let this happen. Better switch the soundtrack in my head to *South Pacific*. I'm lathering up my peppermint shampoo to wash *that* man right out of my hair. Suddenly a slender hand switches the curtain aside and turns off the spray. Oh God, I'm going to be Janet Leighed in *Psycho* and I never even got to kiss George Clooney.

A scream freezes in my throat. But it's not a butcher knife that passes before my eyes, along with my so-called life; it's a newspaper.

"How do you explain *this?*" Kate says, shaking Page Six at my face.

Oh no. The photo of SMITH and me kissing at LAX last night. It's *HUGE*. Norman Bates would have been a relief. "Which part of 'I don't have time to fly you to Pennsylvania and check you into the Menninger Clinic did you not understand?"

"Jesus, Kate!" I scream, "You scared the crap out of me! I'm going to be in post-traumatic shock for the entire day!"

"Well, join the shockfest. I was doing breakfast at the Chateau with James Cameron. We were going over the casting list for *Titanic 2: Love Floats* when I saw this." She rattles the offending photo at me again for emphasis.

"How can James Cameron do a sequel to *Titanic* when the ship sank and everyone *died*—including Jack?" I point out.

"Did you go to their funerals?" Kate glares at me. "I didn't think so. Now stop changing the subject. What happened to the Lola who was going to conquer Oscar Week and swear off actors forever? How could you do it?"

"It was a drive-by kissing. Like one of those freak L.A. accidents. It's not my fault. I gave SMITH the Simon Cowell line and everything. The whole thing happened faster than Kristin Cavallari's fifteen minutes."

"Who?"

"*Exactly*," I say.

Kate grabs a towel and wraps me in it, pushing me down next to her onto the ledge of the tub. "Lola, this is absolutely forbidden. You are *not* going back there with him. You're better than that. I need you to promise."

"I—I—" I contemplate promising with my fingers crossed behind my back to avoid incurring more of Kate's Tony Soprano wrath. But I can't lie—not to Kate. I take a deep breath. "Kate, you don't understand," I say, putting my head in my hands, not really understanding it myself. "I love SMITH. I just do. You've never been in this kind of relationship. All you're looking for is Mr. Right For Tonight."

"And you call *this* a relationship?" she says, shaking that damn Page Six picture in the steamy air yet again. I'm about to grab it out of her hands and flush it down the toilet. But I stop myself. The truth is I want to take a closer look at it once she's gone. "This is the guy who sent his freaking *assistant* to dump you. He doesn't even write his own dialogue when he's talking to you. Jesus, Lola, he annihilated you and I had to pick up the pieces. He doesn't get to have an All Access Pass to you again. Do you understand me? SMITH is *not* coming back in." Kate starts pacing around the bathroom, tossing her chocolate-covered mane, her olive skin dewy from the misty bathroom. "You're the perfect example of why I don't get involved. You're beyond losing your identity to these men; you've never been able to find it because you get so lost in them."

It stings because Kate's probably completely right. But aren't I just a little bit right too? "Love doesn't make a person weak, Kate. It's okay to have feelings. And it's okay to be vulnerable. It's not going to turn you into a Desperate Housewife like your mother."

"And it doesn't make me your father, Lola. My career is the most important thing to me. I'm not going to make the mistake your father did by pretending that I'm capable of love and then failing." A shadow creases her face, then just as suddenly, it's gone.

Silence and steam fill the bathroom. I listen to the drip-drop of the shower. The years of our friendship, all that Kate and I've experienced growing up together, plays like a slide show in my head. I feel a surge of affection for my old friend, tough guy act and all.

"It seems like the last time you actually *had* a feeling was for my brother—and we were *sixteen*."

"Yeah, and he went off to college and dumped my ass. I was

devastated," Kate says in a falsetto I never knew was in her range. "I decided then and there I'd never do that again."

"Whoa. Kate. Why didn't you ever tell me that Christopher ruined you for your whole adult life?"

"Jesus, Lola, don't be so dramatic," Kate says, snapping back to her usual tenor. "Those feelings were a waste of time then. And they're a waste of time now."

"Hey, Kate," I say softly. "Maybe you should waste some time now and then."

Kate rolls her eyes. "I give up. Don't say I didn't warn you." She fossicks around in her caramel tote and pulls out an envelope. "I guess you can open this. I was going to burn it, but go ahead. It came with those peonies by the front door, which I assume are from SMITH and which I refuse to bring in."

I tear open the envelope. Kate reads it over my shoulder: "You look so good next to me" he's written on the clipping from the *Post,* and he's scrawled a heart around our picture. "It's a good thing we're in the bathroom. I think I may be sick," Kate says.

"I think it's kinda sweet," I say.

"Yeah, if selfish and self-centered is sweet," Kate says. Her cell trills. "Thank God. My assistant to save me from one more emotional thought." She clicks on the speaker. "What is it, Adam?"

"Kevin Dillon's publicist called from Cedars to let you know that Kevin's just out of surgery."

"Messenger the Dennis Dugan script to him at the Steven Spielberg wing at Cedars and tell him Universal needs an answer by Monday," she orders.

"Shouldn't you send flowers or something too?" I ask.

"It's not like he had a kidney transplant; he had his appendix removed."

I throw Kate a look. "Fine. Adam, deal with the flowers. Who else?"

"Your sister called to see if you'd changed your mind about going to her rehearsal dinner tomorrow night."

"Tell her I can either *pay* for the rehearsal dinner or I can *go* to the rehearsal dinner—she can take her pick." I throw Kate another look. "Oh, okay. See if you can schedule a call with her for this afternoon and Adam, you know the order—clients, colleagues, family."

"Right. Will called. He has to go to St. Tropez Tanning at three p.m. so he wants you to pick up his cousin from the airport."

"*Another* cousin? Tell him to call *Nanny 911*. On second thought, Adam, you go."

"Will specifically said he wants you to go and he'd like you to bring her a box of red velvet Sprinkles cupcakes."

"Remind me how much ten percent of five million is." *Click.* Kate snaps her phone shut and gives me an aggrieved look.

"I gotta go. I've officially reached my emotional limit for the week."

"Oh, Kate, I love you." Kate rolls her eyes and squirms stiff-armed out of my hug. We walk to the front door, where my eyes stray to the ginormous bouquet of delicate pink peonies waiting just outside.

"Oh, go ahead," Kate says. "I know that if I throw them in the trash, you'll go fishing them out anyway." She hands me the super-sized vase of flowers from SMITH, but she could just as easily be referring to the men in my life. "I'll see you at the Gagosian gallery tonight." Gagosian's having a retrospective of Robert Graham's work and Cricket's one of his models. Anjelica Huston must be one secure wife, because Cricket—and all the other forty-nine models—posed *nude*. "Do you think if I buy one of Robert's sculptures Anjelica will sign with me?" Kate says as she walks toward her Porsche. "And tell SMITH I'll call *The Enquirer* and tell them he has a small dick if he hurts you again." I can't hear her say it as she starts the ignition of her Porsche, but I can read her lips as she pushes on her aviator sunglasses. "And I love you too."

My cell phone is ringing as I step back inside. It's my BGF. Please God let Julian be calling from LAX.

"The headline in *The Wichita Eagle* is 'MaryBeth Conroy Caught Cow Tipping Again,'" Julian moans. "I need *real* news. Read me Page Six verbatim."

I hide the paper behind my back, as if Julian could see it. "I think my neighbor's been stealing my *Post*," I say, panicked. The last thing I need is Julian on my case about SMITH.

"I'm counting on you to keep me connected to the world while I'm here. Can you believe room service put *mint jelly* on my *peanut butter* sandwich? It was the only thing on the menu that wasn't barbequed," Julian says. "Thank heavens that Billy Joe, the waiter, was absolutely delicious. We're talking Brad Pitt in *Thelma & Louise*. And I plan on playing Geena Davis's role."

"Is he gay?" I ask.

"I don't know, but I'll have plenty of time to find out while we're alone in his pickup truck. He's agreed to drive me to L.A."

"You're *driving* from Kansas? What does that take, like, a week? No way. We're supposed to meet Olivia *today*. I can't face her alone again. It's pure hell."

"Hell is where I'm going when I die in a plane crash. Billy Joe is driving me. Period. I'll be there Saturday latest."

"Saturday?! Julian, *you're* driving *me* crazy! The Oscars are in *three* days. I need you here *today* to make sure that Olivia Cutter wears you on the Red Carpet. I can *not* do it alone anymore."

"Yes, you can, Lola. You said she loves the gown. You said she's been petting it for the last two days. It's just a hair and makeup test—you'll be fine. Oh—and tell Olivia's hair and makeup people I'm envisioning a pale lip, a dusting of peacock blue eye shadow, and a Brigitte Bardot updo."

"Fine. Just get your ass here and don't get arrested on the way. I've got to get ready to meet Olivia—*alone*—*again*."

Click.

As I toss my towel back on the rack in the bathroom, I survey the evidence of my aborted shower: one leg shaved, hair washed but not conditioned, one elbow loofahed. No time for damage control. I sheathe my forearm in hot pink rubber bands—heaven forbid I should have another one break—throw on a pair of slouchy Marni menswear trousers, a white tank, and my Sonia Rykiel heels. Or should I call them *heals*—they just make me feel so much better about the world.

Fifteen minutes later, I turn up Sunset Plaza Drive to find a frenzied herd of paparazzi swarming Olivia's wrought-iron gate. I frantically scavenge my glove compartment for the Olivia Cutter Access Pass her assistant sent me: a laminated David LaChapelle photo of Olivia doing her best Marilyn Monroe with Thor by her side from his *LaChapelle Land* book. I hold it up for the security guard. As he waves me into "Olivia Land," I hightail it beyond her gate before one of these damn paparazzi now banging on my window jumps on my hood.

I march up the brick stairs to Olivia's house, throwing my shoulders back confidently, preparing to act *as if* Olivia will wear Julian Tennant to the Oscars. Before my finger hits the buzzer, her front door swings open.

"Come here often?" Adrienne Hunt has an unlit Gitane hanging from her red painted lips and a garment bag over her arm. "Still trying to peddle Julian? Poor thing, you *still* haven't found anyone to wear him to the Oscars. Such a shame. It seems like *everyone* wants to wear Miuccia!"

"Except for Olivia," I tell her. "She's already committed to wearing Julian." Act *as if*. Act *as if*.

"Has she now? Then, my dear, why did she just have me in for a fitting? And why do you look so scared?" Adrienne strokes the garment bag, then cocks her head sympathetically. "Although it *is* sad for Julian. Especially with his investor ready to pull out. I don't like you—and God only knows why he hired you—but Julian's got talent. I'd hate to see him go down Isaac Mizrahi-style."

"What are you talking about, Adrienne?"

"Oh, I'm sorry—he didn't tell you," Adrienne says with mock pity. "He probably didn't want to put so much pressure on your frail little shoulders."

"His investor wouldn't dream of pulling the plug."

Adrienne curls a slim talon around my wrist. "Not if he got all that Oscar press. It just takes that *one* right celebrity. That *one* person committed to wearing Julian Tennant down the Red Carpet. Which, unfortunately, he doesn't have—because of *you*."

She's totally bluffing. "You really are pathetic," I say, brushing by her. "Now, if you'll excuse me, I have an appointment with Olivia."

"Ask him yourself," I hear Adrienne say as I slam Olivia's door in her face. That Adrienne Cunt. She doesn't know what she's talking about.

Or does she? What if Julian's investor *is* going to pull out if I can't get *someone* to wear him on Sunday? Oh God, Julian, why didn't you tell me? Olivia Cutter is the *only* celebrity I've got—and I don't even *have* her.

I take a Sacred Pause and head into Olivia's robin's egg blue den with the weight of my BGF's life on my Chloe-clad shoulders.

"Ahhhhhhhhhhh!" Olivia shrieks at the top of her lungs. She ducks down behind her pale blue shabby chic couch in hysterics, throwing her arms protectively over her head. All I can see is her wraparound sunglasses with the mirrored lenses dwarfing her elfin face.

Thor runs over to me and growls, flashing me his canines. I'm tempted to growl back. That yappy little dog better not bite me—or pee on me again. Not on these Rykiels.

"Maria, go get her blankie," Olivia's assistant commands the housekeeper.

"What's the matter?" her publicist asks, handing her a tissue.

"Olivia—Olivia—Olivia—" Olivia tries to get something out, but she seems to be hyperventilating. She decides to return to screaming as a more effective means of communication. "Ahhhhhhhhhhhhhhh!" She's going to shatter her Lalique crystal fish collection if she doesn't stop.

"Here's her blankie," the housekeeper says, wrapping Olivia in a scrap of shredded blue fabric before returning to her dusting. She looks more bored than alarmed.

What the hell is going on? Her Dream Team has created a perfect circle around Olivia, who's still cowering behind her couch screaming bloody murder. I have a strange impulse to play duck, duck, goose with their heads. Instead I walk over to Olivia to give her the evil eye necklace my mother gave me. She obviously needs it more than me.

"Hello, Olivia. I have the most wonderful good luck charm for you! My own mother made one for my father for his Oscar, so of course I asked her for one so you can win *your*—"

Olivia's shrieks rise to a pitch higher than Sissy Spacek's in *Carrie* as I approach. She hurls the blankie over her head and starts scooting backward. Is she trying to get away from *me*?

"You can tell us, sweetie. What's the matter?" the Wonder Twins coo in unison.

At last Olivia stops screaming and takes a few gulps of air. "When

Olivia was eight, Olivia was attacked by a p-p-p-p-igeon," she stammers out.

A *pigeon?* Is there one roosting behind me? What the hell is going on?

"Honey, I'll kick any pigeon's ass who tries to come near you," John, her manager, says.

Olivia sticks an arm out from under the blankie, blindly grabs her publicist by the side of her head, and whispers frantically into her ear.

"*What* shirt, sweetie?" her publicist asks.

"L-l-l-ola's," Olivia shrieks.

My shirt? I love this airbrushed Chloe tank. It was the last one at Tracey Ross and I had to fight Debra Messing for it.

"Get it off! Get it off!" Olivia's Dream Team yells at me.

Before I can blink an eye, the Wonder Twins are running at me with duct tape. I look down at my shirt. No. It can't be. Can it? Then I realize this whole level-eleven meltdown has been about the tiny airbrushed *hummingbird* over my left boob. Olivia Cutter has a bird phobia? Before I can stop them, the twins are duct-taping my boob to cover the offending bird.

"Okay. It's safe now," the team coos to Olivia.

Olivia pokes one eye out from under the blankie and peeks around the corner of the sofa, then quickly retreats again. "Olivia knows it's still under there. Olivia wants you to take off that shirt and burn it!"

"Burn it!" Olivia's Dream Team shouts at me.

This must be how poor Goody Bishop felt during the Salem witch trials.

John pulls off his sky blue V-neck sweater and hands it to me. Ew. I thought it was illegal to wear one of those without anything on underneath. "Quick," he says. "Get that shirt off."

"Hurry," her agent begs.

"Faster," her publicist yells.

I sneak a peek at the label of the sweater before I put it on. Prada. *Of course.* Will that woman stop at nothing? I surreptitiously stuff my beloved tank into my bag and throw on the sweater. I want Olivia in Julian Tennant. I want it as bad as that new Balenciaga handbag—and world peace. But I'm *not* letting her burn this tank.

"The shirt's gone," her agent says, lifting the blankie off Olivia and pulling her up to her feet.

"I'm really sorry," I say to Olivia with a smile. "I totally get the phobia thing." Maybe I'll develop a new phobia and not be able to go near another actress for the rest of my life.

Streams of black mascara are pouring down Olivia's cheeks under her sunglasses, which she refuses to take off. Her publicist pats at the rivulets with a tissue. Olivia blows her nose and throws the tissue on the floor. She did *not* just throw her dirty snot rag on the floor. Did she? No. It must have slipped out of her hands, right?

"Maria," Olivia yells, gesturing to the Kleenex on the floor. Maria drops her dust rag and stonily fishes the Kleenex off the floor. Whoa. There's got to be some Housekeeper Protective Service I can report Olivia to.

"Um, so, I've brought Julian's fabulous pea—" I catch myself about to say the word *peacock.* Hopefully Olivia doesn't know that a peacock is a *bird.* The Cato Institute isn't exactly knocking on her door. "So maybe you'd like to try on Julian's *gown* now?" I quickly correct myself, walking over to the overcrowded racks of clothes. I shove the other dresses out of the way and hold up Julian's gorgeous gown to Olivia. "What do you say?"

"Olivia, let's get you in the dress," the Wonder Twins say, grabbing it out of my hands. Finally—a little freaking backup. Thank God they didn't use the P-word.

"Fine, but Olivia wants everyone to turn your backs," Olivia says as she steps behind one of the jam-packed racks of designer freebies. What's with this newfound modesty? We've all already seen this woman buck-naked. She was starkers on the cover of *Vanity Fair* for crying out loud. But why expect logic from Olivia Cutter? We all dutifully turn around.

"Where are the hair and makeup people?" I whisper to Olivia's assistant.

"Oh, John didn't tell you?"

"John didn't tell me what?"

"Olivia met Shirley MacLaine at Jason Schwartzman's house the other night and she sent her Kirlian aura analyst over. She told Olivia not to make a move without her. Shirley told Olivia she's the reason she won an Oscar for *Terms of Endearment*."

Puh-lease! A kindergartner could tell Olivia Cutter's aura is as dark as Marilyn Manson's eye makeup.

"Where's this Kirlian aura analyst?" I ask.

"Oh, she's upstairs, taking a photographic inventory of Olivia's closet to determine which pieces of clothes are darkening Olivia's aura," she says. Sure. Blame the clothes. "Maria, will you go get Anouska," Olivia's assistant commands.

Minutes later Anouska appears. If Paul Thomas Anderson were making this movie, he'd cast Lily Tomlin in her role. She has more crystals hanging off her than a Swarovski chandelier. And she does seem to have a certain white light around her—or maybe it's just those crystals reflecting off the white marble floor. That's either a super-absorbent waffle-weave hair towel around her head or a turban.

"Well?" Olivia says, stepping out from behind the rack of clothing in the peacock gown.

Anouska whips out her super sci-fi "Gas Discharge Visualization" Polaroid camera and starts snapping Olivia from every angle. As Anouska silently studies the Polaroids, I study Olivia. The dress looks different. Is that a new panel in the back? Hang on. What's going on in the front? Forget the gown being altered. *Olivia's* been altered. Her tiny titties aren't so tiny anymore. I couldn't tell underneath that Free City sweatshirt she was wearing, but now it's abundantly clear that Olivia's journey to Make-A-Wish was code for Make-A-C-Cup. I lit a candle for Olivia's poor little Make-A-Wish kid Sofia, for crying out loud. Did she really think I wouldn't notice? Hold on, her lips have had a little augmentation too. I wonder if she got fat injected from her ass. I've heard that it lasts longer than collagen.

"Olivia's waiting," Olivia huffs to Anouska.

Anouska looks up from her pile of Polaroids. "The dress is perfect," Anouska declares. Yes! I breathe a huge sigh of relief. "But it needs to be remade in purple for the Oscars. Purple is prosperity, it's power, it carries a vibration of peace. For Olivia, purple is perfect," Anouska pronounces. "You will lose the Oscar if you wear this blue dress."

Lose the Oscar? Because the dress is *blue?* But if she looks like freaking Barney, she's going to *win?* For the last time, people, the Oscar votes *are already in!* Oh God, I can hear Cojo calling her a Fruit of the Loom grape already. I can't let this happen.

"Purple's my favorite color," flies out of her publicist's mouth.

"Love it," John says.

"A purple peacock," the Wonder Twins coo.

Olivia arches a perfectly plucked eyebrow. Oh God. Oh no. They said the P-word. I throw my hands over my ears. Here comes the ear-splitting screaming.

Instead, "Oooooooooooooh," Olivia purrs. "Olivia *loves* the idea of being a purple peacock," Olivia says. Okay, she has *no* idea a peacock is a *bird*.

I try to inject some reality. "But peacocks aren't purple, they're blue. *Peacock blue*. It'd be like dying Thor purple."

Olivia takes a long pause. Oh my God. I've broken through. *Finally.*

"Maria, call Chateau Marmutt and tell them Olivia wants them to dye Thor purple. Thor should be powerful and prosperous and peaceful too." Oh no. What have I done?

"Are you sure? I mean, the blue sets off your eyes so amazingly," I say, desperate to save Julian's masterpiece. "And *I* find blue very powerful—and peaceful. The ocean's blue. You can't get much more peaceful than that, right?"

Olivia's blue eyes have taken on a decidedly flinty cast. "Anouska said purple. Olivia likes purple. Olivia likes prosperity, Olivia likes power, Olivia likes peace, Olivia likes peacocks, and Olivia wants to win the Oscar on Sunday. Do you want Olivia to lose the Oscar?"

"No, no, of course not," I reassure her. "But Julian had this fabric imported from Peru and it can't be dyed and the Oscars are in three days and I just don't think there's enough time to make a whole new dress."

Olivia stares at me imperiously. "Olivia wants you to re-make the dress in purple. If you can't, Olivia's sure Donatella or Giorgio or Miuccia will."

Donatella, Giorgio, and *Miuccia* certainly will *not*. Especially not *Miuccia*.

"That won't be necessary. Julian and I want you, Olivia, to be prosperous and powerful and peaceful." Because, honey, you've already got *pathological* down pat. "Julian will time travel back to ancient Persia to find the perfect purple for your dress, Olivia. He will work tirelessly for the next seventy-two hours to get you what you want." What? Where did that come from? Okay, so I've lost my puny purple mind with the rest of these people. It's contagious.

"Good. And this time, Olivia wants you to get the size right. Olivia's stylists had to alter the dress because it didn't fit," Olivia commands as she leaves the room. Right, and this time *you* make sure not to get *yourself* altered again. Thor trails behind Olivia. I actually feel sorry for him. He has no idea he's about to be dipped in a vat of purple dye.

"So you're wearing the dress to the Oscars," I call after her for clarification.

"Bring Olivia purple swatches," she yells from the hallway. "And Olivia wants you to bring Julian Tennant too."

"No problem," I muster, trying to sound reassuring despite the fact that every molecule in my body is awash with doubt and dread. I'd like to impale Olivia on her People's Choice award. And then I'd like somebody *else* to tell Julian he has to *remake* the entire gown in *purple*—by Sunday—which I just don't see how we can do. Even if Julian wasn't *driving* from Kansas. An even grimmer thought takes hold. What if Adrienne Hunt is *right*? What if his investor is going to pull the plug if I don't get someone into Julian Tennant for the Oscars? Oh God. Oh no. If we don't get this dress remade in purple, then Julian could lose everything—because of *me*. No! I have to save my BGF. I have to find a way to get that damn dress remade in purple. For that I need the razor-sharp focus of Anastasia when she's doing my Brazilian.

I rush out of Olivia's house, jump in my Prius, and speed-dial Julian's cell.

"All circuits are busy."

At the stoplight at LaCienega and Sunset my cell trills. "Julian!?"

"I have the most exciting news!" my mother says. "Master Chung agreed to install a stone lion after I agreed to get him an invite to the *Vanity Fair* party."

"Is there *anyone* on the planet who doesn't want to go to the *VF* party? Can you even *get* another invitation? Today's *Thursday*."

"I don't know, I'll just tell Christopher he can't come."

"You can't do that to Christopher," I say adamantly.

"Fine, then you can't come," she says.

"*What?*" I gasp.

"Listen darling, I think the promise of a stone lion has already changed this family's luck. Anjelica Huston's Armani dress is stuck in customs and now she has nothing to wear to the Oscars and she's presenting best costume design. I reminded her all about you and Julian. I hope this will make up for my not wearing him."

"Oh, Mom, you're amazing!" Make up for it? If Anjelica wears Julian on Sunday, my mother will have made up for doing the *opposite* of everything Dr. Spock recommends for raising well-adjusted children.

"Anjelica's holding on the other line. Can I conference her in?"

"You're keeping her *holding?!* Oh my gosh, yes!" I yell.

"Okay, you're conferenced in. I'm going to leave you two to talk," my mother says.

"Anjelica, hi, I'm so sorry about your Armani," I say, secretly ecstatic that customs has imprisoned the thing. If the iconic film goddess wears something of Julian's to the Oscars, then even if Adrienne Hunt *is* right, there's no way his investor would dream of pulling the plug.

"I just can't believe they won't release the gown, it's not as though Giorgio's smuggling WMDs in it," Anjelica says.

"I have some really gorgeous Julian Tennant gowns at my house. I'm certain you'd look absolutely stunning in all of them. And it'd be such an honor if you would wear something of Julian's. I'm almost home, I could grab the gowns and bring them straight over," I offer.

"Actually when your mother mentioned Julian, I pulled out the look book you sent me last month. There's a beautiful pale-blue silvery wrap gown with floating petals of beaded lace. I'd love to try on that one," Anjelica says.

"Oh," I say, feeling my stomach seize. Of course she wants the *one* gown out of the entire freaking collection that I *don't* have. Last time I saw it, it was back in Julian's New York showroom. "That's Julian's ode to Madame Butterfly. He sewed every petal on by hand. But I also have a dazzling champagne beaded sheath that would be extraordinary on you," I try to steer her in another direction. "I think it would photograph beautifully from every angle on the Red Carpet."

"That sounds lovely," Anjelica says. "But I was really hoping for the Madame Butterfly gown."

Damn it. "Let me just make a few phone calls. I'm certain I can track down the gown for you," I say, feeling completely *uncertain*.

"That would be wonderful. Perhaps you can bring it with you to Robert's show and I can try it on after dinner tonight."

"No problem."

"Great. Thanks, Lola, you're a real lifesaver."

Click.

The perfect purple fabric is going to have to wait. I've got to locate that Madame Butterfly gown for Anjelica ASAP. I send a pleading prayer to Ganesh to clear out all fashion *and* cell phone service obstacles before I try Julian again. Still no service. I speed-dial his assistant.

"Katya, hi. I've been trying to reach Julian for hours. Have you heard from him?" I ask nervously.

"Last time we spoke he was somewhere between Grand Rapids and the Grand Canyon and without cell phone service," Katya says. "I could barely make out what he said because he'd run out of Purell and refused to touch the pay phone. Then he ran out of change and I haven't heard from him since. Is there anything I can do to help?"

"Yeah, actually you can start by telling Julian he has to remake Olivia Cutter's peacock masterpiece in purple," I say.

"*What?!* Oh no. There's barely any time. And you know how Julian feels about purple!" Katya says.

"That's why I don't want to be the one to have to tell him," I say, my own panic rising. "Listen, we may have gotten a big break with Anjelica Huston. Her Armani is stuck in customs and I think I convinced her to wear Julian."

"Oh my God, Lola. That's amazing. How can I help?"

"Anjelica wants to try on that Madame Butterfly pale blue silvery wrap gown."

"Uh-oh," Katya sighs.

"What do you mean '*uh-oh.*'"

"Natasha Greer Smith's wearing that gown in a Japanese commercial she's filming right now for Isheido's Nightingale Droppings anti-aging cream," Katya says.

"Did you say *droppings*, as in—"

"Shit. Nightingale shit," Katya says. "Apparently it's been the geishas' secret to youthful skin for centuries."

"Katya, I'm talking about the *Oscars,* and you're talking about *bird shit.* Natasha Greer Smith *won* an Oscar last year. Why is she hawking bird crap in Japan?"

"I hear they're paying her two million bucks," Katya confides.

"Katya, I *need* that dress *tonight!*" I say, feeling my pulse quicken.

"Well, thankfully they're shooting in L.A. But they were supposed to finish shooting last week and they keep going over schedule," she says.

"Jesus, Katya, they're not filming *War and Peace.* I've *got* to get that dress. Where are they filming?"

"On the Universal lot," Katya says.

"I'm on my way," I say making a quick U-turn on Sunset Blvd. "Can you call the stylist and tell her we need that gown back *now* and make sure that they leave my name at the gate so that I can get onto the lot? And if you hear from Julian, get him to call me right away."

Click.

After three near *fatal* car collisions, one speeding ticket for going fifty in a thirty-five zone cutting up Franklin, and getting *flipped* the *finger* at least five times, the fierce, un*flapp*able, and focused Road Warrior of an hour ago is gone. *Fucked* on the freeway going 10 mph in bumper-to-bumper rush hour traffic is more like it. Is *everyone* driving to Universal?

My cell rings.

"Hi, Cricket," I say, shaking my fingers free from their white knuckled paralysis around the steering wheel.

"You don't sound so good," she says.

"I'm not. We've got a last-minute shot to dress Anjelica Huston for the Oscars but the gown she wants to try on after the Gagosian dinner is all the way in the valley and I could get to Tokyo faster."

"Lola, that's incredible! Anjelica might wear Julian to the Oscars!"

"Incredible would be if Scottie beamed me up to Stage Twelve," I say, feeling my back spasm from sitting like a ninety-year-old grandmother at the edge of my seat.

"Try and practice your Uijayi breath, it's very calming. Call me back after Universal."

"No, don't hang up. Talk me through this traffic. Where have you been, anyway? Don't tell me you and S. D. have been going for the tantric world record."

"I haven't even seen him since Monday night. Just because it's Oscar Week everyone wants a shaktipat of instant Zen, a Get Out of Karma Free card—*and* sculpted biceps."

"Not me—all I want is to get to Universal. How'd the audition for the New Orleans thing go? Are you the new Sandra Oh?" my voice cracks as my eyes lock on the speedometer as it drops to *zero*.

"That's a big Oh no." Cricket's voice cracks right back. "The wig was a total waste of time. They said they're—sing it with me, sister—'going in a different direction.' They're bagging the whole Asian angle and hiring this chick who's supposed to be the Next Halle Berry or something."

"Oh, Cricket, I'm so sorry," I say, though I don't know who I'm more sorry for—Cricket or me and this Road Trip Horror Film *I'm* currently starring in. "Does Kate have anything else lined up for you?"

"She got me an audition for *CSI: Tel Aviv.* I wish I still had that Star of David from Kabbalah."

"Remember when you made us call you Rachel?"

"Oh my God. I made you wear that red string that bled all over your cream crocheted dress when it rained. Listen, I want your approval on this Gucci dress I got for the Gagosian thing tonight. *Everyone* is supposed to be at Robert's retrospective tonight. Maybe Bruckheimer will even be there. I really hope posing in Robert's show is going to help me land my big break."

"Well, you did pose *nude,*" I say.

"You're coming, right?"

"If I ever get off the 101."

"You know the sun is in Libra right now—it's a very auspicious time for you. Anjelica's *definitely* going to wear the gown. I just know it."

Click.

Seventy-nine *un-auspicious* minutes later and the speedometer is still stuck at *0* mph but the temperature outside has risen from 75 degrees to an unbearably sticky 95 degrees (it's always so much hotter in the valley). And my blood pressure is probably 160 over 100. Not to mention that I can feel myself getting a urinary tract infection from holding my pee in for the last two hours and nineteen minutes.

That's it. I've got to get off this freeway. I fight my way over to the right lane and turn off the off ramp. I spot a Starbucks. I put my Rykiel to the metal, floor it across the street, and sprint to the women's bathroom. As I rush out of the front door I run straight into—Therapy Guy. What's he doing all the way in the valley? Does he *live* here? He's wearing a Harvard sweatshirt. Did he actually go to school *there*? He's got a copy of *Doctor Zhivago* tucked under his arm.

"Hi," Therapy Guy says.

"Hey," I say. "Have you gotten to the part where Julie Christie and Omar Sharif kiss?"

"It's the *novel,* not the *movie,*" Therapy Guy laughs. He's got a nice smile.

"Right." I smile back.

"I see you've moved on from the red string to a serious number of rubber bands?"

"What?" I say. He glances to my left arm, which is wrist to elbow in hot pink rubber bands. I'd forgotten all about them. "Oh, these, well, I had one break, and I can't risk that again."

"I know the feeling," he says, holding up his own—a single black rubber band on his right wrist.

"Here, have a spare," I say, taking a band off my wrist, and as I place it in the palm of his hand, I wonder what *this* guy needs a rubber band for—to stop himself from buying another Oxford from J. Crew? "It's nice to see you but I've really got to go."

"See ya," he says, "and hopefully I won't be needing this," he says, giving the pink band a final snap before walking into Starbucks.

"Yeah, you and me both," I say speeding to my car. My phone vibrates. One new text.

Don't tell me you don't like peonies anymore.
xo, ME

It's from SMITH. Oh no. I propel myself into the driver's seat and sit on my hands to keep myself from texting back. I'm definitely not texting him back. I will *not* tell him that "I don't like peonies, I *love* them. xo, me." No way. I look down at my phone. Then to my arm full of rubber bands. Back to my phone. Arm. Phone. Arm. Definitely not hitting "send."

MESSAGE SENT, my phone screen flashes.

Oh God. Why did I do that? I can*not* let SMITH distract me from getting to Universal and getting that gown. I put the pedal to the metal and make like Jeff Gordon the rest of the way.

I finally arrive at Stage Twelve, certain I'm on the verge of cardiac arrest, only to find a huge bodyguard blocking the entrance.

"Hi, this is where they're shooting the Natasha Greer Smith commercial, right?" I ask, craning my head to make eye contact.

"Who are you?"

"Oh, hi, I'm Lola Santisi and I'm supposed to be meeting the stylist, Daisy Adams, here."

"Sorry, it's a closed set," he says without blinking an eye.

"What do you mean *closed?* It can't be closed," I say, looking down at my watch with growing panic. "Daisy knows I'm coming. She was supposed to leave my name with you but since she didn't, could you go get her for me?" I ask.

"Sorry, ma'am, but I can't leave my post," he says unwaveringly. "A photographer from the *Star* tried to sneak in earlier when I went to the john."

"Listen, sir, I promise you that I don't want a photo. I work for the fashion designer who made the dress that Natasha Greer Smith is wearing and it's very important that I get it back. I just spent the last three hours in mind-numbing traffic to get here. *Please*. Just give me a break here."

He returns my desperation with a blank stare.

"*Please*," I plead, feeling the dam break. "Everything is riding on my getting that dress back! Anjelica Huston wants to wear it to the Oscars and if she wears it then my best friend—who's also my boss—won't lose his entire business," I say, unable to restrain the deluge. "And I'll have a career, which I need desperately, because if I fail again I really don't think I'll recover from it," I ramble. "Please, sir. I've got to get in there. I'll even leave you everything I own as collateral," I beg, pushing my black Chanel bag into his arms.

"I could get into a lot of trouble for this," he says, looking around.

"Please," I plead again, pulling off my jacket and starting to un-buckle my heels.

"Okay, okay, stop taking off your clothes," he finally says, holding open the door for me.

"Thank you," I say as I rush inside the sound stage.

"Isheido Nightingale Cream. Take 133," a bedraggled young assistant di-rector announces wearily. He's wearing a canary yellow rain slicker. That's weird. I look around the large sound stage. The entire crew is wearing bright yellow rain slickers. What's going on? I scan the crew for Daisy but don't see her anywhere. The AD clacks his clapboard in front of Natasha Greer Smith, who's standing in front of a giant green screen in Julian's pale blue, silvery gown. She looks like a sexy screen siren from Hollywood's golden age in Julian's gown, which is hugging her curvaceous figure like a second skin. It's too bad they'll only see how gorgeous she looks *in Japan*.

"Action!" the worn-out looking director yells from underneath the hood of his slicker. "And cue the rain." *Rain?* All of a sudden I'm pelted by torrential sheets of water. I squint through the golf-ball-sized BBs of rain at Natasha Greer Smith, who's getting completely drenched. Oh God. Oh no. Julian's gown. No! I watch in complete torment as his gorgeous couture gets sopping wet.

"Oh my gosh, Lola, you're soaked," Daisy says, rushing up beside me in Dior Wellington boots and a matching Dior rain slicker. She holds an umbrella over my head to shield me from the manufactured monsoon.

"What's going on, Daisy? Julian's gown is dripping wet."

"Natasha and the director decided to scrap the original commercial concept and do an ode to *Singing in the Rain*. I promise I'll have the dress dry-cleaned for you as soon as we wrap and it will be as good as new by tomorrow," Daisy says.

"Didn't Katya tell you that I need that dress *now?* Anjelica Huston wants to wear it to the Oscars and I'm supposed to meet her in—" I check my watch in horror "—an hour and forty-five minutes, all the way back in Beverly Hills."

"I'm so sorry, Lola. I don't think it's going to be much longer because they're running out of water," she says apologetically. "Why don't you go wait in the wardrobe trailer. You're going to get pneumonia standing in this rain." I'd gladly take pneumonia over not getting Anjelica the gown—and failing again.

"Okay, but come get me the minute you've wrapped," I say, squishing out the stage door.

"Here you go," Daisy says one nail-biting hour later, thrusting the soaked gown into my outstretched arms. "I'm really sorry."

I pluck the dress out of my palm and hold it out in front of me. I'm so screwed. I'm supposed to be at the Gagosian Gallery in *forty-five* minutes—with a dry dress in my arms. I Prefontaine the precious threads back to my car.

I'm inches away from flinging open my Prius door and hopping inside when my heel slides across the cement and my ankle buckles beneath me. As I'm plummeting to the ground, the headline playing on the marquee is: Save The Dress. If it touches this filthy, oil-stained pavement while it's wet, it will be ruined for good—and so will I.

I twist my body around in midair and propel the dress above me with all of my strength so that it doesn't hit the ground as I land with a thud on my side. I bolt upright onto my knees, my snapped stiletto now dangling from my ankle like a five-year-old's loose tooth. My arms are shaking as I reach heavenward for the priceless French lace tumbling through the air in slow motion and—by some celestial fashion miracle—into my arms. The gown did not so much as graze the ground. I could weep with joy—and pain—but there isn't time.

I place the dress safely in the passenger seat and skid down the five floors of the parking garage. I look over at the flooded dress in panic as my temperature rises. I flip on the AC. How the heck am I going to get this gown dry? And then I realize what my only option is: turn off the AC and blast the *heat*. So what if it's 90 degrees outside and will probably be 110 in my car and I may die of asphyxiation, I wave the dress in front of the vents. I pummel down the 101 steering with one hand and watch with relief as the speedometer makes it up to 45 mph. As I drive down the Cahuenga Exit and start winding like a mad woman through the side streets of Los Angeles, my bicep starts cramping. I don't think it's seen so much action since Neiman Marcus's Last Call Sale six months ago. And damn it, the dress is still wet.

———————

I think I hear a choir of angels when I finally see Beverly Hills in the distance. I floor it down Santa Monica Boulevard and turn onto Rodeo Drive. I'm about to turn off Rodeo when something catches my eye. I make a U-turn.

"Thank God you're still here this late," I say to Frederic Fekkai as I stagger into his salon on my broken heel.

"It's Oscar Week, honey," he says, with his trademark sloe-eyed grin. "You need," he pauses and looks me up and down, "*everything*. We could start with a blow-out."

"There's no time," I say, dashing for a hair dryer. "Frederic, do you mind if I use this?" I say, frantically waving the dress in front of the blasting hot air. "And do you have a steam iron by any chance?"

I skid up to the valet in front of the Gagosian Gallery with one minute to spare, grab the dress, and make a mad dash inside. I nearly trip over the flounce of the gown running through the door when it occurs to me that Anjelica may not want the gown shoved in her face at her husband's art show.

"Would you mind checking this dress," I say so rapid-fire to the gallery assistant standing in the entryway that I can actually see her Jonathan Antin tresses blow back.

"Are you an invited guest?" she asks, looking me up and down as though I live in a cardboard box on Hollywood and Vine. Which is exactly where Julian and I may end up living *together* if I don't succeed at getting someone to wear him down the Red Carpet. I furiously dig through my bag for the crumpled invitation.

"I know I'm terribly underdressed," I say, craning my neck to do a quick inventory of the room in the hopes of spotting Anjelica. What an understatement. My hair is plastered around my face from rain and sweat. My poor wrinkled Marnis are still damp. So is Olivia's manager's sky blue Prada V-neck that I'm *still wearing*. I don't have on a stitch of makeup and then I look down at my feet—at the pink paper pedicure slippers that I grabbed at Fekkai so that my ankle wouldn't end up as busted as my Rykiel.

"Here," the gallery assistant says as she hands me a claim check for Anjelica's dress.

Inside the cavernous gallery I spot Cricket and Kate standing together. Cricket waves me over.

"Where's Anjelica?" I gasp as I catapult toward them. Kate frowns as I practically collapse in her arms.

"You look terrible."

"Thanks for pointing that out," I say, scanning the immaculate crowd air-kissing one another in the 8,000-square-foot gallery Richard Meier designed. The only elements the parade of supernovas spent their day weathering were Chris McMillan's hair dryer, Bobbi Brown's makeup brush, and Dolce & Gabbana's zipper. "I came straight from Universal," I say, trying to catch my breath. "It's been the day from hell. Think trekking the Amazon Rain Forest *and* Sub-Saharan Africa in one day and you'll get the gist of what my day's been. But it's all worth it because Anjelica's going to wear Julian to the Oscars!"

"Lola, that's amazing news!" Kate says. "When did this happen?"

"It *will* happen just as soon as I find Anjelica," I say, scanning the crowd as I pull my two friends by their wrists. I'm momentarily distracted by the Robert Graham sculpture in front of me.

"Cricket, is that—"

"My clitoris? Yes." Cricket ducks her head, blushing proudly.

"You've got to show me how to get into that position," Kate says, gesturing to the bronze sculpture of Cricket on her head in the splits—*naked*. Guess all that yoga paid off.

"Whoa. I never thought I'd be so intimately acquainted with that part of your anatomy," I say, back to frantically surveying the Gagosian Gallery for Anjelica.

"Robert said I had a certain radiant energy," Cricket says. Well, I guess calling someone's noonie radiant is a compliment, isn't it?

"I mean, when Brett Ratner sees this, he'll *definitely* give you a part in *something*." I nod toward the notorious lothario director and Jessica Alba huddled in conversation in the corner by a seven-foot, anatomically precise bronze specimen of female perfection. Still no sign of Anjelica anywhere.

"Why do you think I went into debt on this Gucci dress?" Cricket says, pirouetting in the black column dress that makes her flawless ivory skin glow. "It's an investment in my future."

"Um, sweetie, your cervix is in bronze. It's not about the *dress*," Kate says.

"I *love* the dress," I say, feeling the kink in my neck already developing from the newfound degrees it's turning in my mad search. Where is she?

"Really? I think modeling in this show is going to give me a leg up on other actresses," Cricket says.

"You've definitely got the leg-up part down," Kate says as we take in an aqua-resin cast of Cricket arching in a half-moon yoga pose. "Sorry, ladies, gotta go. I see Sacha Baron Cohen standing alone. I'm going to go talk to him about Liv Tyler co-starring with him in the *Borat* sequel. Cricket, go work that radiant twat of yours. And Lola, good luck with Anjelica." Kate disappears into the crowd.

"Thank God Will's not here yet," I tell Cricket. "If he sees Kate talking to another actor, he'll go Glenn Close in *Fatal Attraction*."

"He'd probably boil her BlackBerry," Cricket agrees.

I finally spot the beauteous Anjelica and Robert talking to Larry Gagosian on the other side of the room "Listen, Cricket, do you mind if I abandon you? I really have to talk to Anjelica."

"Not at all. Good luck," Cricket says. "I know Anjelica's going to love the dress."

I hope Cricket's right. Please let her be right. Anjelica looks every bit the fashion and film goddess in a vintage Saint Laurent forties-shouldered black tuxedo skirt-suit and ruby lips. I envision the statuesque Oscar winner stepping onto the stage of the Kodak Theatre looking ravishing in Julian's Madame Butterfly gown. I elbow my way through the crowd, nearly knocking over the brothers Wilson, who are checking out Brooke Shields's bronze bust, fling myself at Anjelica's feet—and hope that she doesn't notice mine.

"Lola, hi," Anjelica says, giving me a squeeze.

"Hi, Anjelica," I say, trying to cover up my panting now that I'm finally here standing before her. "I've got the dress with me, so whenever you'd like to see it it's here for you. I already spoke with your assistant, who said that 11 a.m. tomorrow would work with your schedule for the fitting. So I've arranged to have the tailor at your house then. And then we'll have it dry cleaned after the tailor's worked his magic—" I stop mid-sentence, because Anjelica is giving me the strangest look.

"Lola sweetheart," she interrupts me. "I've actually been looking all over for you. My Armani dress cleared customs late today after all. I hope you didn't go to any trouble to get me Julian's gown," she says.

Any trouble? I think back on the last five hours of utter hell. "Oh, no, no trouble at all," I finally stammer in shock, staring into Anjelica's genuinely concerned dark brown eyes. I can't believe it. My body feels like it's hovering above me. Anjelica's not going to wear Julian's gown. After all of *that*.

"I'd love to wear Julian to Cannes in May," Anjelica offers, sensing my complete meltdown, despite the fact that I'm acting my *As if* off.

"That would be great," I say, wondering if Julian will even still be in business by then. "Well, Anjelica, I know you're going to look just beautiful on Sunday," I say, giving her a kiss on the cheek.

As Salman Rushdie slices between us to give Anjelica a hug hello, I spot Christopher on the other side of the room. I make a beeline for him.

"Christopher, I'm freaking out. Anjelica's not going to wear Julian's gown anymore. I've got to go. Will you tell Mom and Papa I wasn't feeling well?"

"I'm so sorry, sis," he says, giving me a tight hug. "Do you want me to come with you?"

"Not unless you have a loaded .45 and you're willing to shoot me," I say.

We're interrupted by a six-foot, golden-haired stunner who slinks up against him and places her pouty lips on his scruffy cheek.

"Hi, babe," Christopher says. "Francesca, this is my sister, Lola." Francesca smiles warmly from her vantage point eight inches above my head. "We met at Bungalow 8 after the Marc Jacobs show a few weeks ago," Christopher says. "Francesca was the prettiest girl in the show." The ensuing lip lock is my cue to depart.

"Love you," I say to Christopher, heading over to Kate to say good-bye.

"So who's that with Christopher?" she asks without missing a beat.

"Another one of his usuals. I give it two days. Why don't you go say hello?"

"I can't," Kate says, cutting her eyes in the direction of Will's mother. "If I wasn't stuck baby-sitting, *I'd* be closing the deal with the Bosnian Vince Vaughn. Instead Patrick Whitesell's got him cornered," Kate whispers. "This is a nightmare."

"Nightmare On Camden Street. Anjelica's Armani cleared customs," I say as Cricket grabs my arm.

"Oh God, Lola. I'm so sorry," Cricket says.

"Look, it would have been great if Anjelica had worn Julian, but don't worry: you've still got Olivia," Kate says bluntly. "That's all that matters."

"I don't exactly *have* Olivia yet, Kate," I point out, feeling myself spiraling deeper into the abyss. I look at my BAF's face, whose wattage is dimming in the shadow of my crisis. "Cricket, this is your night, let's not talk about me anymore." My voice comes out barely audible despite my best effort. "What did Brett say?"

Cricket shrugs. "He told me I looked even more radiant than my statue. He asked me for a headshot. And a private yoga lesson."

"Yuck," Kate says in disgust. "So, you gonna do it? Will it be Down Dog or 'Down, you dog'?"

Cricket grimaces. "Lola, are you sure you're going to be okay?"

"I think so," I lie. "But do you mind if I skip the dinner at Chow's?"

"Of course not," Cricket says. "Oh wait, I want you to meet Jeremiah," she says, placing her hand on the shoulder of a very handsome man walking by in a blindingly white tunic. "He's a spiritual guide. He's here to direct Kate Hudson and Goldie Hawn through Oscar Week so they stay centered in the sea of superficiality." She leans in to whisper in my ear, "He's taking me to Tom Ford's after dinner."

Where do I get my own superficial seaman?

"There's something very special about your friend," Jeremiah says to me.

"Yes. Yes, there is," I agree. Why, haven't you heard? She has a radiant twat. Wait, is that a—spare rib Cricket just grabbed from a passing tray? "Cricket, you're eating *spare ribs!*" I say to Miss Raw Vegan.

"Jeremiah says red meat brightens your inner light," she says, tearing into one like she's on Day 39 of *Survivor*. "I'll call you tomorrow,"

Cricket calls after me as I wave good-bye to her with one hand, grab a spare rib with the other, tear the dress from the closet, and head out the door. I could use some help in the inner light department myself right about now. Heck, if someone handed me a lightbulb and said it would brighten the situation—I'd swallow it.

I drive up Marmont Lane to my house. I can't wait to climb into bed. What idiot parked that Aston Martin in my spot? Who even drives an Aston Martin? Oh no. SMITH does. There he is. On my stoop. I am *not* equipped to handle this right now. Not after this day—and certainly not looking like *this*. I'll just keep driving. It's not like SMITH's gonna stand there all night, right? Oh God, how long has he been standing there? I park across the street to wait until he leaves, climb into the backseat, and close my eyes. I'm just so *tired*. Maybe if I fall asleep, I'll wake up and he'll be gone. There's a tap on my window.

"Lola, I can see you. Your windows aren't *that* tinted," SMITH says, opening my car door.

"Oh right, I was just getting my—"

"I was filming a very emotional love scene tonight," SMITH says. "Michael Mann was asking me to go deeper, to really dig in and find the sense memory of the time I was most loved. Claire Danes was giving me nothing compared to what you gave me. *You're* my sense memory. I need you. I want you to be my leading lady, Lola," he says, climbing into the backseat next to me.

friday

loud car door slam jerks me awake. Is that a seat belt . . . in my hair? What time is it and where am I? Oh God. I'm still in the backseat of my *car*—and it's not even 6 A.M. Is that—*Julian?* Getting out of the white Big Horn Ram pickup truck parked next to my mailbox? And who's the Brad Pitt twin in faded 50ls and a snug white tee sliding out from behind the steering wheel?

Uh-oh. SMITH's dead asleep next to me. I quickly look down. Phew. I'm wearing all of my clothes, for a refreshing change. My Cosabellas are staying put until I know he is too. I pry my forehead away from the seat belt and take another look out the window. Oh thank God—it *is* Julian. He made it. He's *here*. My BGF is *finally* here. He's *really* not in Kansas anymore.

Although he seems to have brought the wardrobe from there. My Julian, whose birthday suit was probably black Gucci, is now clad in a red gingham ascot, chocolate brown Stetson, and—it can't be—*overalls*. Instead of his John Lobb loafers, he's wearing John Deere work boots. The image of Julian dressed for a barn-raising and line dance produces so much cognitive dissonance that I have to blink twice to make sure I'm not hallucinating. But who cares? He's here, and now I don't have to do this Oscar Week nightmare *alone* anymore.

But first there's a major distraction to take care of. I don't know what'll happen if Julian sees SMITH in the backseat with me. The last time they met face-to-face, Julian told SMITH if he so much as breathed in my direction, Julian would strangle him with his Hermès ascot. Of course, SMITH has about four inches and fifty pounds on Julian, but I thought it was a sweet gesture.

Time for a preemptive strike. I ease the door open, step out, and close it behind me gingerly so I won't wake SMITH and blow my cover. Then a full-on sprint toward the truck where I throw my arms around my BGF's neck.

Julian stiff-arms me and looks me up and down. "Oh my God, what the hell happened to you? You look worse than Christiane Amanpour after six weeks in the caves of Afghanistan."

"This is what trying to get celebs to wear you on the Red Carpet looks like," I say, looking down at Olivia's manager's V-neck sweater that's been so drenched in sweat and rain it's now a shade of puddle brown but has shrunk to fit me. "I never thought I'd be so happy to see a man in a red gingham ascot," I say, taking in his *Brokeback Mountain* ensemble. I nuzzle into Julian's neck and let out a loud sigh.

"It's called *assimilation*. I'm lucky to be alive after that truck stop in Amarillo, Texas. All I did was ask that trucker if I could check the style number of his Levi's. He thought I was hitting on him. *Puh-lease*—he

looked like Grizzly Adams. The jeans just happened to be the perfect
boot cut. I thought even the chickens in the coop were going to kick my
homo ass—not to mention the starch in the salad bar at Denny's in
Flagstaff," Julian says, massaging his stomach. "Who ever heard of
Wonder Bread salad dressing?" Julian motions toward the Brad Pitt
lookalike reading a "Star Map." "Billy Joe was kind enough to provide
me with camouflage. B. J., get your pretty ass over here and meet my
Best Girl Forever. B. J., *this* is the Lola I've been talking about."

"For the last twenty-three hours on Route 66," B. J. says, offering
one large rough hand. "The pleasure's all mine, miss." And damn if he
doesn't tip his hat.

"Wow, you're a real cowboy, aren't you?" I say, somewhat dumbfounded at Julian's version of the Marlboro Man. "You, on the other
hand, Julian—the only thing *that* ascot has you passing for is Halloween
in the Castro."

"Lola, red is the new black—for the red states," Julian declares. Can
he be serious? Oh Lord, he's serious. "Besides, you're not one to talk.
You're murdering my image in that ensemble. Look at you," he says,
waving his arms madly at the cardboard texture of my pants and my
pink pedicure slippers. "What have you done? And tell me you slept in
your car because you sold your house to pay Willow Fox the hundred
grand she wants to wear my dress on Sunday."

"Julian, you know I don't *own* that house," I say, my own stomach
seizing as I remember that we've only got two days to pin down Olivia
to walk the Red Carpet on Sunday—in purple. "We need to talk."

"Ooh, this sounds serious," Julian says idly. His eyes have suddenly
gone blank.

"It *is* serious, Julian," I say.

I cup Julian's cheek and look at him searchingly. What's that behind
his eyes. Pain? Panic? I cut my eyes toward the Marlboro Man.

"B. J., why don't you go find a movie star?" Julian says with a defeated sigh. "Lola and I need a moment *alone.*"

"Found one!" B. J. yells as SMITH climbs out of the backseat of my car. He even *wakes up* looking like—well, a movie star. Oh God. Oh no. My stomach flips just looking at him. And Julian, well—he just flips— *period.*

"Ahhhhhhh!" Julian screams at the top of his lungs at the sight of SMITH, nearly catapulting himself into the bed of B. J.'s pickup truck. "What the hell are *you* doing here?" Julian sounds like he's just seen the ghost of Coco Chanel.

"Nice to see you too, Julian," SMITH says, reaching out his hand to shake Julian's, which stays firmly planted in the pocket of his—*overalls.* Julian fixes him with an icy stare, his mouth set in a grim line. "Nothing to say to an old friend? I think that's my cue to leave," SMITH says, giving me a kiss and one of *those* grins that always goes straight to my groin.

"Can I get a picture?" B. J. asks, fishing his camera phone out of his back pocket, flinging an arm around SMITH's shoulder, and snapping a photo before SMITH can reply. "I loved you in *Code Blue,* man. It was so awesome when you ricocheted off the Stratosphere in Vegas. You're, like, my *hero.*"

SMITH smiles serenely, with the noblesse oblige of the seven-figure hero who sips spirulina smoothies in his three-thousand-square-foot Gulf Stream trailer even as his stunt double rappels down the Stratosphere while spraying the thugs with gunfire, plunges the Porsche Boxter into the white-water rapids, or grabs the lone parachute from the bad guy's back as they tumble out of the flaming Cessna. "Thanks, man," SMITH says, giving B. J.'s hand a quick squeeze while deftly removing it from his person. "Appreciate it." B. J. stares down at his anointed hand in quiet awe. Touched by a *Code Blue* angel.

"*This* is what's wrong with America," Julian whispers, rolling his eyes.

"Julian, Dolly Parton is *your* hero, for crying out loud," I hiss back.

"I'm going to head over to the gym, Lola, I'll call you as soon as I'm done," SMITH says, walking toward his car.

For a second it looks as though Julian's going to go after him, but he quickly reconsiders. Instead, he turns his glare on me. "I think I need a Dramamine after watching him kiss you like that," he says. "We *are* going to talk about this." He storms off toward my house without a backward glance.

"Later," I yell after him. "We've got something a lot more important to discuss. You know, it's really hard to take you seriously in those *OshKosh B'Goshes*." Julian pointedly ignores me as he roots around for my Hide-away key under my potted bougainvillea.

"Take off those boots," I scream at Julian as he swings open my front door. The last thing I need is my floor to become a breeding ground for Mad Cow disease from those clodhoppers. "Come on in, B. J., make yourself at home," I call out behind me as we step inside.

Julian sits stoically on my living room sofa and wraps himself in my orange-for-vitality-and-shielding cashmere blanket. "B. J., can you go make me a nonfat soymilk latte?"

"This isn't the freaking *Coffee Bean*, Julian," I say. I reach into my purse, take out some cash, and hand it to Billy Joe. "B. J., would you mind going across the street to the Chateau? Ask for Mohammed. Get Julian his latte, order whatever you want, and tell Mohammed I want my usual. He makes an amazing artichoke eggs Benedict that's not on the menu."

B. J. looks at me like I'm talking Swahili.

"They make a mean burger too," I say.

"Extra foam," Julian calls after B. J. as he heads out my front door.

I turn back to my BGF as soon as we're alone. "Julian, we have to talk."

"Okay, so what's so serious that you're not even registering how divine that man is," Julian says.

"Julian, quit stalling." Now that the moment has arrived, I'm suddenly having a hard time finding the words. I take Julian by the hand.

"Okay, now you're freaking me out," Julian says.

"Why didn't you tell me that your investor's about to pull out?" I ask softly. If I'm quiet enough, maybe it will disappear. "How long have you been in the red, Julian? And I'm not talking about wearing it."

Silence.

"Julian, would you look at me?" I say. "What's going on? Talk to me, Julian."

Julian slowly removes his cowboy hat. His usually impeccably coiffed dark hair seems to be standing on end. I reach over to smooth it down. "Fine. Here it is. My dresses aren't selling," he says in a whisper. "I thought it would go away. That I'd wake up one morning and the fashion fairies would have fixed it. It's not going away. I'm about to go out of business." Julian stares at some unknown object out the window.

"But what about all the buyers you got after you won the CFDA award?"

"Look, I may be a hot designer within the industry. But nothing's moving at Neiman's or Saks because Tina in Tampa doesn't know who the hell I am. No one's going to buy me until they see my dresses on Charlize Theron at the Oscars or on Jennifer Garner in the latest *In-Style*." Julian drops his head and pinches the bridge of his nose tightly.

It feels like a punch in the gut. I don't know what's worse: that Julian is going under, or that Adrienne Hunt was right.

"I'm sorry I didn't tell you," he says remorsefully. "But Lola, what was I supposed to say, especially to you? That I'm a failure? That I'm about to lose everything if you don't get a big star into one of my gowns for the Oscars? I couldn't put that much pressure on you."

"That's *why* you should have told me!" I shout. "So that you could have gotten someone better than me."

"There's no one better than you," Julian says, finally turning toward me.

His hazel eyes are so hopeful, so desperate. Now I know *exactly* how Susan Sarandon felt in *Dead Man Walking*. I may as well be personally escorting Julian to the electric chair. *I'm* his only hope for salvation? My chest feels like Nancy Grace is pressing down with both Manolos firmly planted on my ribcage.

What I want to say: "Julian, I can barely save myself." What I do say, since I know full well that there's no getting out of it—I'm going to have to save *both* of us: "We can do this." Julian has dropped his head into his hands. I reach down and gently lift his chin up. "Julian, I mean it. We *can* do this. All I need right now is for you to come with me and do one last little pitch to Olivia. We've got her on the hook; we just need to reel her in. This is practically a done deal."

Julian's eyes are rimmed with red. "Lola, do you really think so?"

I take a deep breath. "I do. I already called Manolo and he said he has the *perfect* pair of stilettos—they have a purple peacock feather around the ankle. He's FedExing them today. Bulgari has the most divine amethyst, emerald, and ruby earrings. They're genius. And Shiseido makes the most gorgeous eye shadow. It's called 'Purple Haze.' I promise you: One day the Met's going to be archiving your gown. Anna Wintour will be showcasing it in the annual fundraiser. Maybe I can even get her to wear—"

"Lola, did you just say a *purple* peacock feather?" Julian's eyes narrow with suspicion. "And did I hear you say *amethyst* earrings? And *purple* eye shadow? Lola? My gown is *blue*. Peacock blue."

Screw the Sacred Pause. "Okay, Julian. Here's the thing. Olivia *loved* the dress. Olivia's Kirlian aura analyst *loved* the dress. It's just that, well, um, she—" Oh, just spit it out, Lola. "She just wants you to make it—in *purple*," I take a step toward the coffee table in case I need to duck for cover.

"*What?!* No! Never! That's like asking DaVinci to make the Mona Lisa *blond. Not happening*," Julian shrieks, propelling himself lengthwise onto the couch.

"Julian, what's not *happening* is your future in the annals of fashion history unless you make a new dress! We've got two days to save our ass. We've *got* to get Olivia in that dress."

Julian says nothing. He just pulls himself into a fetal curl and begins rocking back and forth like a patient at Shady Lanes.

Think, Lola. Think. You can do this. "Maybe the Mona Lisa would've had more fun as a blonde," I venture meekly.

Silence.

"Look, purple is prosperity, it's power, it's peace," I say.

Julian stops rocking. "Are you kidding me?" he says acidly.

"Okay, okay I know, it's what the freaking Kirlian aura analyst said. But eggplants are purple and you love the eggplant miso at Nobu. And oh—what about grape Bubblicious? That's your favorite," I say.

"Lola, we were *ten*. Plus it loses its flavor in two seconds and so will that dress if I'm forced to change it to *purple*."

"Julian, just try and wrap your head around purple. *Please*—with a seedless Concord grape on top. You're a true artist, but even artists have to make sacrifices sometimes for their art. Or for Olivia's ass. So get your act together and let's go fabric shopping."

Julian lets out a long, guttering sigh, then nods in resignation. "Lola, you just told me I have to bury my favorite gown. And I have no choice in the matter because otherwise I'm about to lose everything I've ever wanted. I need a moment to mourn, okay?"

"You've got exactly seven minutes to wallow while I jump in the shower and get ready and you get yourself out of those horrible over-alls. Then we're pounding the pavement until we find the perfect purple fabric."

"E-e-ew!" Julian shrieks for the gazillionth time today. This time we're in the middle of World of Textiles in—Chinatown. And the cause of said screeching? A piece of purple georgette. *"E-e-ew! Get it away from me,"* Julian screams.

"Are you *sure?* I don't think it's *that* bad," I say.

"Lola, Cojo would use that scrap to clean his gold Dior sneakers and then put Olivia Cutter straight on his worst-dressed list," he screams. Okay he's right. It's downright disgusting.

"Julian, this is the millionth fabric store we've been to in, like, the hundredth zip code. Are you sure you haven't seen *any* purple fabric you like in the entire state of California? There aren't that many places left," I say, gesturing to my list of fabric stores that's as tall as me—in *heels.* Can there truly be no decent purple fabric in all of L.A.? Does it not exist, or is it all sold out? Is that aura analyst seeing *everyone* in this town?

"Lola, we're in *Chinatown.* The dim sum might be good, but the fab-ric freaking *sucks.* And maybe if I actually *had* some food I could think straight. I'm going to pass out on that ream of revolting purple paisley polyester. You promised after Fiesta Fabric in *Agoura* you would feed me. That was three hours ago. I need an egg roll."

"Julian we only have two and a half hours before we have to meet Olivia. There's no time for eating. If we don't find the perfect purple fabric, we're not even going to be able to afford an egg roll because we'll both be out of jobs."

"Honey, we've searched every fabric store in this godforsaken city from Chenille Palace in Pass-a-dena to House of a Thousand *Terrifying* Fabrics in the *Death* Valley—and all I got was *this*," he says, waving his hive-covered hands in my face. "Even my fingers are rebelling. I *need* to e-a-t." He stands there flapping his splotchy hands like an exhausted toddler.

"Fine, Julian. We've got ten minutes for eating. Empress Pavilion is across the street. We'll get it to *go*." I grab his hand and pull him through traffic.

Julian literally digs in his heels as I pull open the front door. "Lola, this restaurant has a *"B"* in the window. We're not eating *here*," he says.

"Julian, the health department hands out Bs for misprints on the menu. And it's either this or a Slurpee and a hot dog from the 7-Eleven on the corner," I say, dragging him into the restaurant and shoving him into a booth. "Sit. Order yourself everything vegetarian on the menu but get it *to go,* Julian. I'll be right back. I have to use the ladies room."

I wash my hands in the stained sink—the health department probably gave them that "B" for this filthy bathroom—then spread the plethora of purple swatches on the Formica counter. Silk dupioni. No. Stretch gabardine. Gross. Crushed organza. Yuck. Eyelet cotton chiffon. Ick. Julian's totally right. *All* these swatches are totally *wrong,* and I have only a few hours before I'm forced to throw in the purple towel. This is a total nightmare.

My ringing cell disrupts my private pity party.

"Oh my God, oh my God, I didn't get the part in *CSI: Tel Aviv!*" Cricket trills, giggling. "And I even wore a Star of David!"

"Then why do you sound so *excited?*"

"The casting director thinks I might be a good fit for a small part in

a Jerry Bruckheimer *feature!* Kate's sending me in this afternoon! Jeremiah has a really strong feeling about it. He thinks it's the perfect part
for me!"

"Who?"

"The spiritual guide from last night. Remember? He dikshah'd me
this morning."

"Is that like another tantric sex thing?" I ask.

"No, it's like a shaktipat on steroids," Cricket says.

"Oh right. Now I really get it," I say. "What are you talking about?"

"It's a transfer of positive energy. It totally cleared out the space for
the Bruckheimer movie to come in."

"What does S. D. think of your filling your spiritual tank at another
pump?"

"Jeremiah understands me on a soul level that S. D. just wasn't tapping into," Cricket says. "Plus he teaches a Visualize Your Screenplay
into Being workshop that everybody goes to: Sam Raimi, Cameron
Crowe, Bryan Singer. He's the Robert McKee of spirituality. I'm going to
get that part, I just know it!"

"You really des—" The words die in my throat. Oh my God. There it
is. Right in front of my eyes. I can't believe it.

"Lola? Lola, what's wrong? Are you there?" Cricket's voice pleads
on the line.

"Cricket, I gotta go," I bark into the receiver. *Click.*

I practically sprint back into the dining room and grab Julian by the
arm. "Come on, get up! Come with me. I've got something to show
you," I say, dragging him to the bathroom door.

"Lola, what are you doing? I can't go in *there.* I may be an honorary
girl, but I cannot step foot into the ladies room."

I yank on his arm. "I want you to see something: the answer to all
our problems."

"I highly doubt the answer to all our problems resides in the ladies room of Empress Pavilion."

"Julian, stop talking!" After a quick peek inside to make sure there are no other occupants, I push Julian inside. "Look," I say.

"How come women always get the full-length mirrors?" Julian says, inspecting himself in it. "Ugh, I still have cowboy hat hair. I'm a *disaster.*"

"Julian, forget your hair. Just *look,*" I say, pointing at the grimy windows, which are framed by curtains. Purple curtains.

"Okay, I'm *looking.* Can I go back and check on our order now?"

"No, *LOOK,*" I scream at the top of my lungs. "There, see? Those curtains are perfect for Olivia's gown. The fabric is flawless. It's the *perfect* shade of purple—not too grape, not too violet. It's *Moulin Rouge* meets an impossibly chic Chinese *Odyssey.* It's—"

"Lola, I'm calling Doctor Gilmore and getting you on an antipsychotic. You're clearly having a delusional break."

"Julian, shut up and just take a closer look at the fabric," I say, pushing him toward the window.

He steps forward and gingerly reaches out toward the curtains, as though to pet a cornered jackal. "*Eew.* They reek of pork fried rice," he says, batting them away.

"We can have them dry-cleaned," I say.

He fingers the fabric, then gasps. When he turns around, he's practically smiling through tears. "Oh my God, Lola, you're right. You don't understand. They don't make fabric like this anymore. Look at the hand embroidery and the tulle edge detail," he says, grabbing my hand and placing it on the curtains so I can have my own Helen Keller wa-wa moment. "Feel how light and fluttery it is. It's like a meringue from Poilâne's bakery on Rue du Cherche Midi in Paris," Julian says. "Quick. Shove them in your purse."

"They're not going to fit into this bag. And we can't just *steal* their curtains."

"Yes we can. Empress Pavilion has *no* idea what they've got here," Julian says. I look at the curtains. Back to Julian. Curtains. Julian. Curtains. Julian.

"You mean, what they *had*," I say.

"Julian!" Olivia Cutter screams, running down her Tuscan yellow hallway. She screeches to a halt several yards away from him, suddenly flinging her rose gold snake braceleted arms around her mouth and nose. "Olivia wants to know if you're still contagious," Olivia says from behind her arms, refusing to shake his outstretched hand. "Are you all better? Did you get the flowers Olivia sent you?"

"I don't think I got the flowers. But I'm feeling completely recovered now that I'm seeing you," Julian says.

I can't help but notice the gorgeous spray of flowers on the credenza. A card peeks out from the calla lillies.

Fingers crossed for Best Dressed! Miuccia sends her love!
xoxo ADRIENNE

Oh nonononono. *NO.* Oh, it is *on.* It is K Fed-on-Britney's-bank-account on.

"Darling, how is it possible that you look even more gorgeous than the last time I saw you? Those lips—they're just so full and luscious," Julian croons to Olivia. "And that figure. Va-va-va-voom. Honey, you could turn a gay man straight." Nicely done.

"Oh Julian, that's what all the gay men tell Olivia—but none of them have turned for her," Olivia says. Is she actually batting her eyelashes? "Marcie!" Olivia yells. Her beleaguered assistant comes scurrying in with fear in her eyes. "Why didn't you send the violets to Julian? Olivia told you to get Julian flowers from Robert Isabell. Olivia's surrounded by assassins," she says into the air. Yeah, sure, you told her to send flowers. Note to self: try to get Marcie a new job too, as soon as you relocate Imas. But first things first, get Olivia into a freaking dress for the Oscars.

"We've scoured the planet for the perfect purple material for you, Olivia, and we've found it," I say, linking my arm through hers and leading her down the hall. There's no way Adrienne Hunt is getting Olivia. Period.

Julian sweeps his arm around Olivia's shoulder and together we whisk her toward the living room where the usual circus performance is in full effect. Olivia's manager, John, is surrounded by tabloids and making little hash marks on a pad of paper—is he counting to see if Olivia has more mentions than Jessica Simpson? Her agent is shouting into a Bluetooth headset and the Wonder Twin stylists are poring over racks of gowns.

"Olivia wants to introduce you all to the fabulous Julian Tennant, designer extraordinaire," Olivia says to her Dream Team, as though she's introducing the opening night of the Metropolitan Opera. She opens her arms to give Julian the stage. Julian steps forward as though he's Madame Butterfly in the flesh.

Olivia's agent actually hangs up her phone. "Designer extraordinaire," she says, shaking Julian's hand.

John actually puts down his *People* magazine. "Designer extraordinaire," he says, wrapping Julian's hand in his manicured mitt.

The Twins leave their post. "The fabulous Julian Tennant, designer extraordinaire," they say together, taking turns shaking Julian's hand.

No, did Julian just take a bow?

"When Lola told me Olivia wanted purple, I couldn't have agreed more," he says to his rapt audience. "I had this fabric that I'd been saving for years for the perfect occasion." Turning to Olivia to make her feel that his words are for her divine ears only, he adds, "You know, blue is so passé. And you're not going to believe where we found it—"

"—in a tiny temple outside of Shanghai Province," I interrupt. *Work with me, Julian*, I plead silently.

Julian gives me a baffled look. "It was hiding beneath the . . ." Julian hesitates.

"—three-thousand-year-old gold Buddha," I finish. "What do you think?" I say, spreading the curtains over her couch. Thank God we fumigated them by hanging them out the car window as we raced down Beverly Boulevard, after which I misted them with the Fracas I keep in my glove compartment for emergency use. "The texture is incredible. It will give the effect of cascading water. Suri, the Princess of Persia, asked Julian to make a dress from this material last year for her wedding." Okay. So there isn't a Persia anymore. But *Olivia* won't know that.

This time Julian knows his cue. "I wouldn't do it. She wasn't worthy of this material," he says confidingly.

"You, Olivia, will look *stunning* in it," I say.

"*Absolutely* stunning in it," Julian adds.

"Stunning," the agent pipes in.

"Stunning," the manager coos.

"Stunning," the Twins concur.

Look, it may be weird, but I'll take all the help I can get.

"Suri? Isn't that Tom Cruise's daughter's name? Olivia *loves* Tom. Olivia's loved Tom since she was twelve," Olivia says. Of course she does. Bet they chow down at Thetan barbecues and refuse to take their meds together.

"Suri means red rose," I say. At least that's what they said in *Us Weekly*. I figure it's as reliable a source as any.

Olivia circles the plush fabric, inspecting every inch. Thor runs into the room. His fur is now an electric Hendrix purple. The poor thing jumps up on the couch to nestle in the curtains, his purple fur so camouflaging that I can barely find him to swat him away. If he pees on it, so help me I will give him an all-expenses-paid trip to Chateau Marmutt for the euthanasia special. Julian quickly picks him up and starts kissing him everywhere.

"Oh Olivia, he should win best in show. He's just *perfect,*" Julian says. I hold my breath waiting for the Dream Team to chime in with *perfect,* but even they've got to draw the line somewhere. The dog is now *purple,* for crying out loud.

"Did the Kirlian aura analyst agree with Thor's shade?" I attempt a joke with Olivia's agent.

"We devoted the day yesterday to the consultation," the agent says with the tone of Larry King interviewing Osama bin Laden.

Right.

"Will she be approving the material we've brought?" I ask.

"She's working on Sandra Bullock's gown today," the Twins say in unison.

Thank goodness. Saved from the aura analyst. I don't know, maybe she's helped. Olivia has brought it down to a Level 5 on the craziness meter.

Olivia takes a deep breath and plucks Thor out of Julian's lap. *I* take a deep breath in anticipation of what's coming out of her mouth next. Too plum? Too grape? Too violet? Too *unprosperous?*

"Mommy wants to know what Thor-y Wor-y thinks," Olivia goo-goo ga-gas. "Does Thor-y like the pretty purple fabric that Julian brought Mommy back from Chile?" Whoa. I don't know what's creepier—that

Olivia thinks Shanghai is in *Chile* or that doggy-talk that takes Olivia's third-person baby-talk to a whole new level of dementia. Thor starts barking uncontrollably. On and on and on. Olivia drops the tiny dog on the floor and yells, "Olivia wants Thor to shut up now! Thor's embarrassing Mommy in front of her guests." Oh, *now* we're guests. "Why won't you stop barking? Purple was supposed to make you peaceful." I'm sure multiple dips in a vat of steaming dye were very calming. Okay, the craziness meter is fast approaching a Level 10—and rising.

I fluff the embroidered purple curtains out over the couch. I need to bring Olivia back down to a Level 5. Fast.

"This fabric makes me think of the color of the Carribean as the sun sets from the balcony of Oscar de la Renta's house in Punta Cana," I say. Okay, so maybe I shouldn't have mentioned *that* Oscar in trying to sell Julian for *the* Oscars. Better fix it. "Can't you just picture that glint of gold against that gorgeous purple? You, holding your Oscar."

Olivia cocks her head like the RCA dog, considering. "Olivia wants to see what the fabric looks like against Olivia's skin," she says, moving toward the mirror and getting into a Red Carpet-Worthy pose. Vamping in an over-the-shoulder stance, she sing-songs, "Olivia's *wa-iting.* Five. Four. Three. Two," she begins to count impetuously as the Twins scurry toward her with the material. I shudder to think what will happen if Olivia gets to *one*—but the Twins quickly twist the fabric into a toga around her body.

"No, it would be more like *this,*" Julian says, his fingers flying through a series of elaborate pleats. He grabs Thor's stray Vuitton leash from his doggie basket and wraps it around the makeshift dress. He makes Olivia Cutter look like a purple-clad Greek goddess in two seconds flat.

Olivia studies the fabric, running her fingers over the material and posing for the mirror.

"Olivia wants to know who the princess of Persia was marrying," she asks, turning to Julian and me.

"Who?" Julian and I say in unison.

"*Suri*, the princess of Persia. Olivia wants to know who she was marrying," she says again.

"Oh of course," I say. "She married a highly respected carpet dealer. You know, specializing in priceless kilim carpets," I say quickly.

"Ew. Olivia doesn't like that. Olivia doesn't like a carpet salesman," she says, hurriedly shedding the material as if it's a contaminated Martha Stewart synthetic rug from Kmart.

"That was just his day job," I continue smoothly. "He's also the Prince of Morocco. Otherwise known as the Prince William of the Middle East. You know how bored those royals get." Okay, so I got thrown off my game. But I'm back on. I'm like David Beckham taking on Zinedine Zidane—and Posh—single-handedly.

"He also happens to be a direct descendant of Mohammad," Julian adds. Goal! My striker's back in the game.

"Olivia loves boxing," Olivia says, moving back in toward the fabric. Who am I to give her a history lesson or sport tip when she's massaging the fabric like she's Nobu Matsuhisa and it's a Kobe cow? Suddenly she wraps herself in the fabric and closes her eyes. She kicks up her powder pink rhinestone Jimmy Choo stilettos and gets horizontal on the couch. Is she napping? Having a mini-stroke? Did the Thorazine just kick in? We all stand around her, surrounding her in silence. I wait for someone to say something. I look to Julian, to John, to the Twins, to her agent. Not a peep. Should we chant? Run for the defibrillating pads?

"Olivia wants you all to join hands around me," Sleeping Beauty finally announces. She opens her eyes and stares up at us all standing around her, slack-jawed. "Do it!" Olivia demands. We join hands like we're at the Log Cabin for an AA meeting, while Olivia closes her eyes again and goes back to caressing the fabric. Five minutes? Ten minutes? I don't know how much time has passed—I do know that my hands are getting clammy. Julian's got my left hand in a death grip, his nails digging into my palms. A chunky signet ring on the agent's hand is slowly excavating my right hand. I'm about to take a peek at my watch to see what the freaking time is when Olivia breaks her ritual, bolts upright, and announces triumphantly, "Olivia thinks it's fabulous. Olivia will be a purple peacock on the Red Carpet on Sunday. And Olivia will win the Oscar in your dress."

Julian and I nearly propel ourselves onto the couch and on top of Olivia.

"Olivia, you will be the most exquisite woman there," I say, my voice shaking. I don't know whether to laugh or cry or collapse in a heap on the floor. Thor could lick me, pee on me, and poop on me in all his purple glory and I'd be thrilled. Heck, I'm pretty sure purple's my favorite color. "You'll be more magnificent than Grace Kelly the day she became Queen," Julian adds. I look at Julian—our eyes fill up with tears.

"Olivia already knows that," Olivia says curtly, untangling herself from the fabric, getting up from the couch, and heading toward her bedroom. Guess magic fairy circle time is officially over. "Now Olivia wants you to get to work," she says, and closes the door behind her.

"She's wearing the dress?" Julian says in shock, turning first to Olivia's agent.

"You heard her, make the dress," her agent says.

"She's actually wearing the dress?" I say, turning to her manager in disbelief.

"That's what she said, make the dress," her manager says.

"She's wearing the dress?" we say, turning to the Twins.

"Yes! She's *wearing* the dress," the Dream Team yells at us in unison.

"Oh my God, Oh my God, Oh my God!" Julian and I scream together as we pilot my Prius down Sunset Blvd.

"I knew you could do it, Lola," Julian says.

"Oh my God, I did it. Well, I mean, with your help, Julian."

"*You* were the sundae. I was just the fairy on top," Julian says. "Of course, we still have to *make* the dress," Julian says. "But I have you to thank, Lola, for saving my scrawny little ass. And you know—Cannes is just around the corner."

"Oh God, Julian I'll just be thrilled to get through Sunday," I say.

"Oh God, Sunday! Today's *Friday!* How in hell will I ever get this dress done in time? I've got to do the cutting, the pleating, the trim, the—"

"And don't forget you have to make a showing at Ed Limato's tonight. Isn't your investor going to be there? Why's he in town, anyway?"

"Marty's starting a production company."

"Oh good. Just what we need. Another producer. Is there anyone from Yakima to Kennebunkport who doesn't want to *produce?*"

"And he wants to meet Olivia Cutter."

"Of course he does. 'Produce' is really code for put up the *cashola* to get cozy with all the hot Hollywood ass," I say. "Anyhow, you've got to stop by and play the hero—Marty'll be thrilled to hear that you've landed the hottest Oscar-nominated ass in town."

"I can't go to a party now! Lola, are you insane? I'm going to need every spare minute to do that dress." Julian starts a low moan, clutching his head between his hands as though he wants to twist it off.

"Julian, it's all about appearances. Marty needs to see that his star designer investment is part of the A-list scene. That you're calm, collected. We'll do a quick champagne toast to Olivia Cutter, fluff Marty up a bit, then off you go back to the Chateau to work on the gown. Your bungalow's already set up. I'll see what I can do to line you up some help."

"No, no one touches the dress except for me," Julian protests. "I cannot possibly allow anyone else to touch my master—"

"Okay, okay, got it. I'll have you in and out of Ed's in one hour, tops." I reach over and squeeze Julian's hand. "We can do this."

Julian exhales a stream of air through his nostrils. "Okay, one glass of champagne. At least Marty'll be kissing my ass, not kicking it, tonight when we tell him Olivia Cutter is going to be wearing my *purple* peacock tour de force," he says.

"What about Billy Joe?" I say as we pull up in front of the Chateau. "Is he back from Universal Studios?"

"If he is, I'm going to see if he's got one ride left in him," Julian says, puckering his lips to send me a kiss as he floats toward the hotel.

"Wait—Julian," I call after him. Stepping out of the car, I open the backseat door. "I almost forgot. Here, take these." I hand him the bouquet of calla lilies.

"What are these?" Julian asks, reading the card nestled in the flowers. "Are these from *Adrienne?*"

"I pilfered them from Olivia's house. What does Olivia need with *those* now that she's wearing *you?*" I say, giving Julian a hug. "Congratulations again."

"That Adrienne Cunt can cross her fingers—and her fangs," Julian says. "*We're* the ones getting Best Dressed at the Oscars—even if I have to give Cojo a kidney."

Skipping down the brick path to my house, I stop and do a little victory jig. I did it! I did it! I did it! I'm not going to have to apply for that job at Winchell's after all. Man, this whole *succeeding* thing is way better than *failing.* I'm going to call Dr. Gilmore. I cannot wait till my next session to tell her about my major triumph. She's going to be *so* proud. I'm proud. Career Deficit Disorder? Ha! Try Career Domination damn it.

I swing open my front door and bound inside. Wait, am I in the wrong house? I run back outside and check the address. I rush back inside. Whoa, whoa, whoa, whoa. I've been robbed. Well, not robbed-robbed—more like *redecorated*. My Spanish bungalow has been transformed into—a turquoise and white Mediterranean villa. It looks like something in—*Greece*. Oh my God. It looks *exactly* like—my hotel room—in *Santorini*. I bound to the window and press my nose up against the glass. Is that—white *sand* in my backyard? And a *volcano*? No. It can't be. Can it? I run through my French doors and out into my backyard. Oh my God. It's a—*backdrop*. And it looks *exactly* like the view from my balcony in Greece. I spin around.

SMITH walks out from my bedroom. Oh my God. Our first date in my hotel room in Santorini. That incredible dinner out on my terrace. SMITH did *this*. For *me*. He gives me *that* smile.

"What's going on?" I say, running toward him.

He hands me an envelope. It looks exactly like the one he sent to my hotel room in Santorini. I tear it open. "Take me back. And then let me join you for dinner," it says in SMITH's handwriting.

Take him back? My heart never let go.

"Do you like it, Lola? I had the chef flown in from our hotel in Santorini to make your favorite Greek meal," he says, turning toward the array of warm pita with tzatziki, fresh Greek salad with kalamata olives, dolmades, moussaka, grilled lamb and vegetable skewers.

"I love it! It's the most romantic thing anyone's ever done for me," I say, grabbing him and kissing him over and over.

"This time's going to be different," SMITH says, wrapping me in his arms. He pulls me toward the café table and the glowing candles. "Hungry?"

"Not for food. Not now. I always preferred the nights when we skipped the dinner part," I say, leading him down the hall.

"Here's looking at you, kid," he says. "It's you and me. Forever. I want *you* to be there next to me when the Academy gives me my life-time achievement award."

Who cares if he's lifting a line from Humphrey Bogart? SMITH's back.

"You'll be happy to know I'm on a plane on my way to Marin for my sister's rehearsal dinner—I'll get there just in time for dessert and the toasts—thanks to the guilt trip from you, Cricket, and Adam," Kate says over the crackling, popping in-flight phone.

"What time is it? Oh God, it's almost nine p.m." I catch a glimpse of my bedside clock. "I must've fallen asleep after SMITH left," I say as I unravel myself from my sheets and struggle awake.

"*SMITH?*" Kate says. Oh God. Oh no. How could I have let that slip? I totally blame that make-up sex.

"Yes. *SMITH,*" I say. Deep breath. And another. "I love him, Kate. And we're back together," I blurt out. I figure with Kate 35,000 feet in the air, this is the best time to tell her.

Silence.

"He had the set designer from *Pride and Prejudice* re-create our first date in my hotel room in Santorini in my *living room*. The woman won an *Oscar*. It was Hugh Grant-romantic-comedy *romantic*. Look, Kate . . ." I trail off miserably.

Silence. Oh my God, here it comes. If Kate's pausing this long, then it's going to be World War III.

"I just want you to be happy, Lola. And if SMITH makes you happy—" Kate gulps so audibly that it could be mistaken for engine trouble "—then mazel tov."

"Since when did you start speaking Yiddish?"

"Since two seconds ago, when you told me you were back together with him. I lost my grasp of the English language," Kate says. "Lola, I just don't want to see you getting your heart ripped out again."

"I know, Kate, but you've got to trust me on this one. How about we leave it at the part where English is your second language," I say.

Silence.

"Shalom," she says at last.

"What?" I say.

"It's the only other word I know in Hebrew," Kate says.

"Thank you, Kate," I say.

"But don't expect me to listen to all the gushy details about how it happened," Kate says. "Especially when I'm paying five dollars a minute for this shitty plane phone. The only details I want are from Ed's party tonight. Take a note pad if you have to."

Click.

"I'd like to propose a toast to Julian Tennant and Lola Santisi. Congratulations, kids, for getting Olivia Cutter. She's gonna make us all rich," Marty Glickman, Julian's investor, says. "Well, I'm already *rich*—richer than Mark Cuban," Glickman adds as we clink champagne flutes in Ed Limato's Coldwater Canyon foyer, which is currently crammed to the walls with A-listers. This house totally belongs in *Architectural Digest*— or on MTV's *Cribs*. It's entirely Versace-clad, from the tropical floral-print ashtrays to the tiger-print doggie bowls to the custom gold Medusa-print movie theater seats in his AMC-sized screening room. The silver-haired super agent is likewise decked out in Versace, with a bright yellow and black Versace shirt, unbuttoned, and billowy white silk pants. Ten percent is a *lot* more than I thought.

How'd Glickman even worm his way into Ed's party? His pre-Oscar uber-schmooze fest is almost as impossible to get into as *Vanity Fair*. Ed doesn't even invite some of his fellow agents—or even all the *clients*. Mom had to tell Ed that my father was looking for new representation to get Julian and me on the list.

"I was worried I was going to have to go Tony Montana on you, Julian," Glickman says as he gives Julian a little mock jab to the gut. Yeah, right, the only thing this five-foot-five New Yorker has ever wrestled with is the menu at Cipriani. *I* could take out Glickman—even in this Julian Tennant slithery sapphire sheath and these platform pumps. Though all that stiffened gel in his hair would do some damage to my fist.

"So when do I get to meet Olivia Cutter? I'm a huge fan," Glickman says, helping himself to a Beluga blini from a passing tray.

"I'm sure she'll be a huge fan of yours too, Marty," Julian says, tinking Marty's glass again. "The two of you will hit it off like Oprah and Gayle." Where does Julian come up with this crapola? Thank God Kate made me bring that notepad, I've *got* to write this down. "Excuse me, you two, gotta schmooze; we have a Best Dressed list to get on," Julian says, heading toward Cojo, who's paired off in the corner with Julianne Moore.

Oh wait. Oh no. Don't *go*. I can't believe Julian just left me alone with this smarm-monger. I study the enormous crystal chandelier looming above our heads—is it Versace too? I'm just wondering whether a 10.0 earthquake could send it selectively smashing onto Marty's head when Ed Limato himself nudges me out of the way.

"Excuse me, Lola," Ed says sweetly as he poses for a photo with Christopher Walken. Guess Ed, who waits barefoot by the front door with his personal photographer to greet his megawatt guests, doesn't think *I'm* Worthy of a photo.

I resign myself to the fate of the Unworthies: small talk with a "producer." "My wife wanted me to invest in contemporary art," Marty says, taking in the Jasper Johns above Ed's fireplace. "I took one look at that fourteen-million-dollar Damien Hirst tiger shark in a tank of formaldehyde and said no way to that schmuck at Sotheby's. The only fish I like are tuna," Glickman says, popping a Gruyère puff into his mouth.

"Well, at least your wife has better taste in clothes than she does in art." And men, I think to myself. Thank you, Aspeth Gardner *Glickman*, for demanding that your husband invest in Julian.

"My wife loves clothes the way Donald Trump loves his hair. The amount of money she was spending on Julian Tennant could rebuild New Orleans. I told her it'd be cheaper for me to buy the company—so I did," Glickman says. He washes his Gruyère puff down with a swig of Dom.

"Lucky for us," I say.

"Hey, Lola, do you think you could slip my script to your dad? It's like *Goodfellas* meets *Carlito's Way* meets *Reservoir Dogs*. Ed's trying to get me a meeting with Tarantino, but I loved *The Assassination*."

"Ed *Limato?*"

"Yeah Ed represents me," he says. Richard Gere, Denzel Washington, Mel Gibson, and *Marty Glickman?* Well, Marty's *money*. Ten percent of crap is still 10 percent. The world makes perfect sense now.

"You and my father would be perfect together, Marty," I say, but he's not listening to me, he's too distracted by Salma Hayek's ass, which is currently perched in front of Robert Rodriguez wrapped in a cranberry bias-cut Dolce & Gabbana.

"You'll have to excuse me, I'm going to introduce myself to Salma," he says, baring yellowed fangs in her direction. "I think Salma would be perfect for my movie. We need a Latina hottie to play the female lead."

Yes, I'm sure this Oscar-nominated actress will leap at the chance to play a cut-rate Elvira Hancock. "Good luck," I say, backing away. Why wouldn't one of the most gorgeous babes in Hollywood want to meet this leering hobbit?

At least they'll have one thing in common—their *height*.

I wind my way through Ed's crowded living room, admiring Courtney Love's slinky silver lamé Marchesa. Then make my way down Ed's palatial lawn toward the large magenta-tinted tent that's been erected over his tennis court. Ed's lawn is so perfectly manicured it looks like Jesse Metcalfe mows it daily.

I'm heading toward the tent when I find myself staring into some familiar husky blue eyes.

"Lola!" Jake Jones exclaims. "Wow, you look fantastic! I've been totally meaning to call you, but I've been working till like eleven every night. I just got done getting my wings fit." He flashes me one of his lopsided grins. "Listen, do you want to get out of here?"

"Yeah, actually I do want to get out of *here*," I say leaving him in the blur of my slithery sapphire sheath as I walk away.

I step inside the tent and head for the sumptuous Chaya-catered dinner. The buffet table is longer than the director's cut of *Apocalypse Now*. I get in line behind Javier Bardem. Is that Ed's *monogram* on Javier's—*cigarette*? Whoa. Graydon Carter must be *so* jealous he didn't think of *that*.

"Dark chocolate Oscar, Miss?" a Pam Anderson look-alike waitress says, pointing at the sterling tray of chocolate men engraved with the names of all of Ed's nominated clients. I've never been opposed to starting with dessert. I help myself to one, wondering who Ed got to make them, since the Academy positively forbids replicas of their sacred gold statues. Ed's really raising the party bar this year. I guess he has to, since Bryan Lourd started hosting a Friday night fete to compete with Ed, who was getting priceless pre-Oscar schmooze time with all of CAA's uber-clients. All the agents are running scared; the high anxiety level correlates exactly with the number of lobster satays and endive and avocado salads catered. Even the *real* Ari Gold, Endeavor's Ari Emanuel, is throwing a party tonight at his Pacific Palisades pad. And I hear he's giving away his client Paris Hilton.

I munch absentmindedly on Hayden Christensen's head—guess it's too much to hope that he'd absentmindedly munch on something of mine. Berating myself for this moment of emotional infidelity—after all, I'm all SMITH's, forever—I wander down to the pool house, where Julian's at the bar sipping a martini beneath the Andy Warhol portrait of Diana Ross.

"Where've you *been?*" I ask.

"Flirting with Theo," Julian says, pointing to the hottie behind the bar. "There's only so much sucking up I can do in an hour. Thank God you couldn't get B. J. in. It would have been like bringing chocolate to Godiva."

"Do you want a bite of Hayden Christensen's ass?" I say, holding up my chocolate man.

The cobalt crystals on my clutch start vibrating. I pull out my cell. One new text. It's from SMITH. Did he just overhear my dirty thought about Hayden Christensen?

Hoping to get off early and into your bed. Be waiting.
xo

Now the crystals on my clutch aren't the only thing vibrating. I quickly palm my cell before Julian can see.

"Why are you smiling like that?" Julian asks. "Are you medicated?"

"Oh, um—" I look down at my cell. Julian grabs it out of my hand and reads the text.

"That's it, I'm handcuffing you to the minibar in my room."

"Julian, I *love* him, Goddamn it," I say. "I just do."

"Fine," Julian says, exhaling loudly. "Don't say I didn't warn you. We simply don't have time to go into this now. Take me back to the Chateau so that I can sew—and *you*—I need another Dramamine just thinking about what *you're* going to be doing."

saturday

29 hours, 22 minutes, 17 seconds until

the Oscar for Best Actress is handed out.

ello?" I mumble groggily into my home phone, fighting off sleep. What time is it?

"Hi, Lola, it's John." Who?

"Oh, uh, hi—" I try to focus my eyes on my bedside clock. 7 A.M. *Geez-us.* My head just hit the pillow. When SMITH finally got in from shooting at 6 A.M. I couldn't find my way back to REM. Who am I kidding? I never made it to REM. I was too busy deciding between the pink satin nighty and the black lace negligee—though SMITH ripped my clothes off so quickly the second he walked through the door, he didn't fully appreciate my final choice of the pink satin.

"It's John, Olivia Cutter's manager," he repeats.

Oh no. No one phones at 7 A.M. the day before the Oscars with *good* news.

"Hi, John!" I bolt upright, trying to sound like I've already showered, had my latte, and a morning workout—which I guess I have if you count two mind-blowing trips to the moon. Which *totally* made up for the fact that SMITH couldn't get off work early last night.

"Get Julian. Get the dress. And get to Barneys. ASAP."

"*Barney's?* It's seven a.m. Isn't Barneys *closed?*"

"Not for Olivia Cutter."

"What's—"

Click.

What could Olivia Cutter possibly want with us at 7 A.M. the day before the Oscars—at *Barneys?* Maybe she changed her mind about the Shiseido "Purple Haze" eye shadow and needs the Vincent Longo counter? Maybe she's dropkicking the Bulgari amethyst, emerald, and ruby earrings for something less expected, like those Lanvin pearl and crystal earrings? Maybe that aura analyst nixed the custom purple peacock stilettos Manolo made and wants to assess which stilettos carry the best energetic vibrations? Oh God.

I bound out of bed and throw on the two closest articles of clothing by my feet on the floor: my wrinkled pink nighty—and the J Brand jeans that have been on my floor since I scored them at the Soho House Wednesday. I slide into an old pair of beaded moccasins. I think about leaving SMITH a note, but I hope to be back in bed before he's up.

I jump in my car and floor it around the corner to pick up Julian at the Chateau.

"Thank you for getting here so quickly," John says to us as a security guard unlocks the front door of Barneys and ushers us inside. "Follow me."

We trail behind John through the eerily empty store—just me and all the magical merchandise beckoning me to take them home. As we pass by the shu uemura counter, I can actually hear that limited-edition Tokyo lash box crying out my name. Wait. Forget the red lash box. Do you think that security guard will notice if I pilfer one of these Bottega bags?

If I could have one celeb superpower—besides charging *People* magazine four million dollars for the exclusive shot of me and my spawn so that I could feed the refugees in Darfur—I'd get them to open Barneys just for me. I mean, why shop with the rest of hoi polloi when you can have Barneys all to yourself? Okay, I'm not here to shop, I'm here to— I still have *no* idea exactly what we're doing here, at 7:23 A.M. the day before the Oscars. Why won't John tell us what we're doing *here?* I'm starting to get freaked out. Where's Olivia?

John finally leads us to Mecca, aka the shoe salon, where we find a solitary Olivia perched on one of the cushy tan leather settees surrounded by endless stacks of designer shoeboxes. Thor is frolicking merrily between the cardboard canyons. Hang on. I don't see that aura analyst—or the Wonder Twins—or Olivia's agent—or the publicist—or the assistant *anywhere*. Where is everyone? I'm officially freaked out.

Is that a lime green crocodile Manolo in Thor's mouth? That thing is like $1,500—and it totally clashes with his purple fur.

"Who's the Arnold Schwarzenegger on the cell in the corner by the Cesare Paciotti wedges?" Julian whispers. The man in the red tracksuit with the George Hamilton bake looks like he belongs on Muscle Beach.

"Security?" I whisper back.

"Oh my God! Give me that!" the bedraggled shoe salon manager shrieks as she pries the stiletto from Thor.

Olivia looks up from the Clergerie platform slides currently on her feet. "Thor's psychiatrist said Oscar Week has been very hard on Thor because Olivia has been so distracted with Olivia's nomination." She picks Thor up and holds him face-to-face. "If you don't start behaving better, Mommy's not going to take you to the Oscars tomorrow." Olivia covers Thor's ears. "John, you got Thor's seat next to Olivia at the Oscars, right?"

I can practically see the tension headache wrapping itself around John's head, a tight band around his Frederic Fekkai haircut. "Honey, you know the Academy has very strict policies against bringing pets to the ceremony," John says. He quickly adopts evasive action. "Why don't you try these on?" He holds out a pair of metallic T-straps.

Olivia doesn't take the bait. "Thor's not a *pet*, Thor is Olivia's *soul mate*," she says.

"But you're going to be sitting between Anthony Minghella and Meryl Streep," John pleads.

"Olivia wants to sit next to Thor. Doctor Fleischkopf!" she screams. Arnold Schwarzenegger's doppelganger rushes over. *Doctor?*

"Olivia, calm down. This isn't about Thor, we talked about that this morning," he says in a low, even tone with a—Long Island accent.

"Who is that?" I whisper to John.

"Olivia's psychoanalyst." He looks more like Mr. Universe than Doctor Freud.

"John wants Olivia to lose the Oscar," Olivia shrieks.

"Olivia, we all want you to win the Oscar tomorrow," Dr. Fleischkopf says calmly, taking Olivia's hand in his. "And we all came to Barneys very early this morning, because this is where you said you felt safest— surrounded by all these shoes." For once I know *exactly* how Olivia feels. Dr. Fleischkopf clears his throat. "Olivia had a terrible nightmare about her Oscar dress last night and I feel it's important for her to make peace with the dress before the awards tomorrow," he says. Whoa. Hang on. Olivia dragged us out of bed at the crack of dawn—the day before the Oscars—because she had a *bad dream?* "Olivia, please share your nightmare with all of us," Dr. Fleischkopf instructs.

John, the good doctor, Julian, and I sit on one of the tan sofas as Olivia takes a deep breath and begins, clutching Thor in her arms.

"Olivia was climbing out of Olivia's seat to collect Olivia's Oscar from George Clooney. The entire Kodak Theatre was on its feet cheering for Olivia as Olivia was making Olivia's way down the aisle. Just as Olivia was about to climb onstage to kiss her Oscar—and George Clooney—" she closes her eyes and shudders at the thought of what's coming next. "—the purple p-p-p-p-peacock—" she finally spits out "—ambushed Olivia from behind and started chasing Olivia through the aisles. That b-b-b-b-ird finally cornered Olivia between Tim Burton and Samuel Jackson and started pecking Olivia to death," she wails. "Tim and Sam tried to save Olivia but even they couldn't stop that b-b-b-b-ird." Olivia starts crying. "As the b-b-b-b-ird chased Olivia out of the theater, Olivia heard George Clooney tell Kate Winslet, that 'since Olivia obviously doesn't want this Oscar it's yours, Kate,'" she howls through her tears.

I turn to Julian to give him a can-you-believe-this-crap look. Is that—a tear trickling down his cheek? Maybe his eyes are just watering from sleep deprivation.

"Olivia, you poor, poor darling, come here," Julian says, taking her in his arms and hugging her. Olivia gives a final shuddering sigh and goes limp in his arms, all tuckered out.

"Olivia, your nightmare isn't about a peacock—or the dress. It's about your fear of losing the Oscar. You're projecting your fear onto the dress," Dr. Fleischkopf says.

"No gown of mine would ever hurt you," Julian says soothingly into her hair. "My purple peacock gown lives and breathes to make you, Olivia, gorgeous, gorgeous, gorgeous. Honey, George Clooney is going to slip you that Oscar—and his tongue."

"May I have the dress," Dr. Fleischkopf orders me. I wish there actually *were* a dress to give the doctor. I fish out the partially sewn panels from the skirt and hand them to him. "Olivia, sometimes fabric is just *fabric*," he says.

Julian gasps. "Fabric is *never* just fabric," he says. I cut him a sharp look and he hugs Olivia more tightly.

"Here, I want you to hold the fabric," Dr. Fleischkopf says, pushing the fabric at Olivia.

"No. Olivia *won't* touch that fabric," she says emphatically, shoving it away.

I'm way too tired and it's way too early for another Olivia tantrum. And if we're forced to spend another second here, Olivia Cutter won't have a dress to wear in twenty-eight hours and twenty-two minutes. Julian's *got* to get back to the Chateau and finish sewing. And I've got to get to Papa's Oscar abundance ritual.

I walk over to Olivia, escort her back to the tan settee, and take a seat beside her, the panels of fabric resting in my lap.

"You know, Olivia, I once had a nightmare that I couldn't get a pair of skinny jeans off. They were cutting off the blood to my legs, they were so tight. I had to crawl to the emergency room at Cedars because I couldn't walk or drive in those jeans. In the dream the ER doctor cut off the jeans with my legs still in them. When I woke up, I thought I'd never wear a skinny jean again until I realized it wasn't about the jeans, it was about my anxiety over spending my rent money on a pair of *jeans*."

Oh no. My skinny jean story isn't having its intended effect. Olivia's staring at the fabric in my lap with an odd glint in her eye—actually a *very scary* glint. She plucks out a panel of fabric, waves it in the air like it's a dirty Kleenex, and tosses the fabric on the ground. Julian jumps and yelps in tandem as the fabric hits the carpet. God knows how many dirty Chloe Paddington moccasins have stepped off Wilshire and traipsed all over this floor. That fabric is far too Worthy for a floor toss—even if it is the floor of *Barneys*.

"This isn't a dress!" she shrieks. "This is a bunch of crumpled fabric. Olivia wants to know what you're doing *here* when you've got so much work to do on Olivia's Oscar gown. Go, leave, shoo," she says, with a wave of her arm. We step over Thor, now chewing on the Plexiglas heel of a pink patent Pucci, and dash for the elevator.

"You never told me about that skinny jean nightmare. I'm your BGF, you're supposed to tell me *everything*, especially when high fashion and deep trauma are concerned," Julian says as we drive up Crescent Heights.

"It was fiction. I just wanted to get us the hell out of there so you could finish sewing."

"You're a much better actress than *Variety* gave you credit for," Julian says as we pull up to the Chateau.

"Julian, are you sure you don't need my help with the dress? I'd love an excuse to miss this abundance ritual."

"I told you, I want to sew *alone*," Julian says, doing his best Greta Garbo in *Grand Hotel*.

"Did you bring the Ganesh from Putaparti?" my mother asks, her embroidered chiffon Dries Van Noten sari—orange for opulence, centering, and *Oscar*—fluttering with the Malibu breeze. She's clutching handfuls of mini Ganeshes—party favors for Papa's Oscar abundance ritual.

"Hi, darling," Mom turns away from me to give a head-to-flawless-orange-Nina-Ricci-toe-clad Kate Capshaw a kiss. "Take one of these, love," she says, handing Steven Spielberg a vibrantly painted Ganesh—and one of the Govinda orange saris Mom had Abby order for those guests who failed to follow the strict orange dress code. "Put it on, darling," she instructs the director, who's dressed in his customary jeans and T-shirt. "*Now.*" Oh-kay. So my mother's *directing* Steven Spielberg.

"I brought the Ganesh, Mom. And I also brought SMITH," I say, holding his hand and my breath.

My mother's eyes dart to make sure her guests are out of earshot.

"Lola, Bruce Willis is here. Tom Brokaw is here. Maria Shriver is here," she says, pulling me by the collar of my orange tunic and whispering hysterically in my face. "We're at *Barbra Streisand's* house!" Mom halts as the orange rose petals that have been strewn around Babs's bamboo oceanfront deck flutter against our legs in a sudden gust of wind. "Get rid of him," she finishes in a whispered shriek.

"But Abby said I could bring a plus-one and—"

"Not *that* plus-one," Mom cuts me off. Even the lotus flower in her hair seems to be quivering with disgust.

"Blanca, you're going to have to get used to me," SMITH says to my mother. "I'm not going anywhere. I know I screwed up breaking up with Lola, but I'm back, and I'm going to make it up to all of you." I feel my entire body smile. I don't think SMITH's ever looked sexier than right here, right now in that ugly orange Oxford—standing up for me—to my mother.

Mom throws an orange diamond-ringed index finger in his face. "If you're really serious about my Lola, I'm going to have to call the Dalai

Lama *himself* to have him do a blue Buddha medicine healing ritual. That's how bad you fucked things up," she says.

"Richard Gere's been wanting me to meet the Dalai Lama ever since we presented 'Best Fall From a Helicopter' at the Stunt Awards to Vin Diesel," he says.

Very clever of SMITH to engage Mom in Zen and the art of Hollywood name-dropping. "You know, Richard and I dated," Mom says, oblivious that she's now squaring off against a fellow Zen master. One Richard Gere mention and she's completely forgotten about hating him.

"I'll have my assistant put in a call to Richard," SMITH says. Placing his large hand on Mom's shoulder, he adds, "that's how much your daughter means to me."

"I'll be the one to put in the call to Richard," Mom says territorially. "We'll get through this," she says, pulling SMITH into her arms.

"Now let's cover your face so Paulie doesn't see you," Mom says, handing him one of the orange saris.

"Hey!" Olivia Cutter's manager, John, says. Oh God. What's *he* doing here? "Do you know Kiefer?"

I'm surprised Olivia Cutter even *lets* John have other clients. I turn to Kiefer to ask him for the inside scoop on next week's episode of *24*, but he's already walking toward the Axe catered breakfast buffet.

"I didn't expect to see you here," John says, slapping SMITH on the back. "Good news, it looks like Olivia wants you to be her Danny Zuko in the *Grease* remake after all. Gotta tell you, man, she was really lobbying for someone else, but this morning she told me that it had to be you. Paramount's going to be sending you the offer Monday," he says, heading to meet Kiefer by the Jamba Juice bar.

"Can you believe it, Lola? I'm gonna get that part! I didn't think I had a shot at it. My agent said I was too old."

I'm a lousy actress, but I know a cue when I see one. "No way are you too old," I assure him. "But watch out—that Olivia Cutter is Satan."

"Yeah, I've heard that. But you're the one that I want, o, o, ooo, honey," SMITH starts singing, totally off key. He better get a voice coach pronto. "Here, help me get mummified," he says, handing me the Govinda orange sari. "*This* is love," SMITH adds as I wrap him up.

"I'd like everyone to join hands," Dr. Singh says over the crashing waves as a hundred of the *in* of my parents' inner circle gather underneath the Hermès orange chiffon tent that's been erected on the sand in front of Babs's house. Dr. Singh stands before a fifty-foot Buddha—did Marty Scorsese bring the prop from *Kundun?* I've positioned myself in the back of the throng, behind Christopher, the better to shield SMITH from Papa's X-ray vision. Dr. Singh is the lone white figure in the sea of orange-clad guests. Carbon Beach looks more like Christo's flagged Central Park—except most of *these* orange flags waving in the wind can get a movie green-lit faster than Renée Zellweger and Kenny Chesney can say annulment.

"Before we begin today, I must ask you all to turn off all means of communication with the outside world as we focus our energies inward and upward. Please turn off all cell phones, BlackBerrys, and other devices." A deafening cascade of trills, buzzes, and hums fills the air as the guests comply. "You too, Harvey." Dr. Singh nods at Harvey Weinstein, who guiltily powers down his iPhone. "And you," he says, looking meaningfully at Edward Norton.

On Dr. Singh's command, I grab Kate Hudson's henna-tattooed hand on one side and SMITH's hand on the other. I close my eyes and do a "please let my father be so occupied with heralding in his abundance that he doesn't notice SMITH" miniritual in my head. I wonder if Dr. Singh has a chant for *that?*

"We're here today to cast the negativity of Paulie's career into the ocean and to usher in a new chapter. We're fortunate to be here in Malibu—so close to Lakshmi, the Goddess of abundance, who resides in the ocean. Namaste to Babs—for making this possible," Dr. Singh says, clasping his hands in a prayer gesture and bowing to Barbra Streisand. Namaste to Babs for ditching the drab Donna Karan. She looks absolutely radiant against the ocean in those flowing orange Indian-inspired robes, although she's not holding anyone's hand. No one touches the mani. "Please close your eyes and repeat after me. Om and salutations to Lakshmi," Dr. Singh begins.

"Om and salutations to Lakshmi," we all repeat in unison. I crack an eye open and sneak a peek at SMITH. I can't believe it. His eyes are tightly shut and he actually seems to be very into the ritual. Except—oh no. He's taken the orange sari I wrapped him in and is now wearing it as a scarf. Papa's going to *freak* when he sees him. I will my hands not to get sweaty. But it's too late. One Papa thought and it's instantaneous. I hate that I'm making a clammy-handed impression on Kate Hudson. I look over to her. Thank God—she's so deep in meditation I bet she's not even in her body.

I gaze around the circle. My eyes are the only ones that are open. Except for Christopher's. He's between Jack Nicholson and Dustin Hoffman. He throws me a "how-the-hell-did-we-end-up-in-this-circus-act-of-a-family" look.

Dr. Singh tings a cymbal to bring the chanting to a close. "Each of you was handed a review when you joined the abundance circle. I will ask you to read them aloud one at a time and then cast the negative review into the ocean." Dr. Singh takes a long pause. "I want to prepare you. Some of these reviews are quite vicious. And I know for many of you here, this can trigger the deep trauma of your own negative reviews. But it is of the essence that we call up the obstacle so that we can release it and make space for Paulie's second Oscar. Please, Tom, I'd like to begin with you." Dr. Singh gestures to Tom Hanks, who's wearing a flowing orange sari and an orange do-rag over his head.

Tom grins sheepishly. "Sorry, folks, I didn't have time to do my hair," he announces.

He drops Rita's and Reese Witherspoon's hands and lifts *The New York Times* he's holding. Clearing his throat, he begins, " 'The Academy—' " he chokes over what's coming next " '—should take back Paulie Santisi's Oscar for *The Assassination*.' " He hesitates, looking up to the bright blue sky before carrying on. In a strained voice, he continues, " 'Paulie Santisi *assassinates* his own career with this—*bomb*.' " The sea of orange lets out an audible gasp.

"Let's get rid of this thing, huh, Paulie," Tom says supportively, walking to the water's edge and releasing the review into the pounding surf as the group cheers. Um, isn't that—*littering*? Tom and Rita just hosted the Global Green Rock the Earth Pre-Oscar party Thursday night with Larry David. Someone call the Malibu police.

"Go ahead, Sean," Dr. Singh says.

" 'More than merely another bad movie,' " Sean Penn says, blanching, " 'casting his daughter in the most pivotal role is the most depressing development yet in Santisi's career.' " I freeze as *everyone* turns to look at me—and SMITH. I contemplate casting *myself* into the ocean. What was I thinking coming *here*—unmedicated—and with him.

"Jesus Christ, what the fuck is he doing at *my* abundance ritual," my father yells. Thank God Uncle J's got him by the arm, because it looks like he might throw a haymaker. "First he ruins *my* movie, now he wants to ruin *my* abundance ritual?"

"Papa, please," I shriek from across the circle. "SMITH's here for *me*," I say, through the tears welling in my eyes.

"*Bullshit*. He's here *now* because he wants to ride on the coattails of *my* good Oscar press for *Whispered Screams*. Need I remind you that he dumped you because of *these* reviews," Papa says, tearing the negative reviews out of his guests' hands and waving them in my face. "I can't take one more second of this." Papa charges straight into the Pacific and flings the crumpled reviews into the waves. "Okay, Doctor Singh, let's get to the part where I win this damn Oscar," he says, rejoining the somber circle.

Dr. Singh sighs deeply. Clearly the path to enlightenment isn't writ on the sand of Carbon Beach. "I'd like everyone to re-join hands," he says.

"I'm sorry," I mouth to SMITH, taking his hand.

"Me too," he whispers, giving my hand a tight squeeze.

"I'm going to lead us in a mantra. Om and salutations to Paulie Santisi, who is infinite in his brilliance. Together now. Om and salutations to he who manifests every kind of abundance—*especially* in the Oscar race. Om victory, victory, victory. Om, Oscar, Oscar, Oscar."

"Om—" I try and chant with the group, but I just *can't*—not for Papa.

There's a loud noise overhead. We all crane our necks toward the sky. There's a plane towing an orange banner that reads OM AND VICTORY TO PAULIE SANTISI. Then an explosion of fireworks goes off over the water that rivals the show at Ron Meyer's yearly Fourth of July party, followed by orange smoke bombs. Even in daylight, they're magnificent. Then the finale: dyed orange doves released in a rain of orange rice toward the cloudless Malibu sky. I wonder what the budget on this thing is?

"Abby, what'd they do? Hire the art director from *Memoirs of a Geisha*?" I whisper to my father's assistant, who's standing behind me.

"Christopher did it," she whispers back. "A surprise for your father."

Why? I want to ask. But I already know the answer. So Papa will notice us. I scan the circle for Christopher. I don't see him anywhere. And neither does Papa. He never does. I finally spot Christopher—walking down the beach alone—with a sea full of orange litter on the horizon behind him.

"I'm on my way to Diane and Barry's Oscar brunch," Kate says into my cell as Christopher and I drive down PCH in his 1960 forest green Land Cruiser. "Meet me there."

"What? I thought you were in Marin," I say.

"I was, but Will's mother got food poisoning at Ed Limato's party last night. Serves her right, bringing Will to another agency's party. So I had to jump on the six a.m. out of Oakland to take Will to the Film *Independent*'s Spirit Awards," Kate says. "So can you meet me there in ten?"

"Sorry, I'm not driving. Christopher's giving me a ride because SMITH had to go to a *GQ* cover shoot," I say. "And if I have to go to one more Oscar Week party, I think I may have a psychotic break. I'm not getting out of my sweats for the rest of my life once this week is over."

"Let me put this differently: I'm not on the list and I really need you to get me in," Kate says.

"Hold on, let me ask Christopher," I say.

"No, no, don't do that," Kate says quickly.

"Why not?"

"Because I don't want him to think I'm a desperate, schmoozy agent," Kate says.

"Well, that's exactly what you are," I say. "Besides, since when did you start caring what he thinks?"

"Just get me in. I'll see you there in ten," Kate says.

Click.

"Remind me *again* why you're forcing me to come *here* when I could be in recovery from this morning with my hypnotherapist," Christopher groans as we pull up to Diane von Furstenberg and Barry Diller's Cold-water Canyon gate for their pre-Oscar "picnic" lunch for their BFF, Graydon Carter—and a hundred other megawatts.

"Is it so wrong to want some quality time with my brother?" I ask.

"Oh, I forgot, a morning spent at some bullshit Oscar ritual for our father followed by *this* party is our family's idea of quality time to-gether."

"Well, we are supposed to be here supporting Papa, Christopher."

"Because he's *so* supportive of us," Christopher says sarcastically.

"Fine, I'm coming clean. Kate can't get in without us."

"Over here!" Kate yells. She's stepping out of her 911. She looks fantastic, dressed in a pair of linen shorts and multicolored canvas mules that show off her killer legs. Even Christopher drops his sulky pout to give her an appraising look. "I got you a swag bag from the Spirit Awards," Kate says, handing me the canvas tote.

"Thanks," I say, sneaking a peek inside the bag. A coupon for a free Netflix membership, an IFC leather monogrammed iPod holder, and a lifetime supply of Pop Secret microwave popcorn. Oh well, I was kind of hoping for something Swarovski'd. But it *is* the Film *Independent*'s Spirit Awards, after all, in a tent on the beach in Santa Monica. Where Priuses are preferable to limos, Levi's are preferable to Versace, John C. Reilly is preferable to John Travolta, Roscoe's House of Chicken n' Waffles is preferable to Wolfgang Puck, and *real* acting is preferable to special effects. Independent Spirit means Nicolas Cage deferred his twenty-million-dollar salary because the entire budget of the movie was a tenth of that and changed costumes in his car rather than his usual two-thousand-square-foot Airstream. So what if you have to take the next Michael Bay movie to pay for the private jet and the family ranch in Montana? Independent means these actors revert to being *human*—at least for the twenty-day shoot.

I quickly toss the Spirit Awards bag into the backseat before the valet pulls away.

"Nothing for me, Kate? I did drive Lola here," Christopher says. "Good to see you again. She told me you were in Marin," he says, giving Kate a kiss hello on the cheek.

"I had to fly back for Will. He gave out Best Male Lead to Topher Grace," Kate says. "He was so good as that bowling lane operator with cerebral palsy who won Beyoncé's heart in *7–10 Split*. And it did get me out of the church walk-through followed by manis and pedis and lunch with my sister and mother and five disgustingly beaming bridesmaids before the wedding tonight."

"Well, I'm glad you're here," I say, giving Kate a hug.

"Me too, Kate. You look fantastic. How were the awards?" Christopher asks as we head toward the house.

"It should be illegal to force young Hollywood to wake up before noon and be photographed in broad daylight. Half of them were so hung over they looked like they'd just walked off the set of *Night of the Living Dead 3D*," Kate says. "And Lindsay I-Plead-Exhaustion Lohan showed up in the same dress she wore last night on Leno."

"Oscar Week should be illegal. It's totally hazardous to my health," I say.

"At least they serve alcohol at the Spirits. I think I'm going to have to have a double Jack and Coke before the Oscars tomorrow," Christopher says as we make our way toward the security at the door. "Don't let the fact that the two men guarding the threshold look like they just stepped off the catwalk for Hugo Boss fool you. B. D. probably hired them from the Mossad."

"Lola and Christopher Santisi with our guest Kate Woods," I say to the large blond man guarding the door, clipboard in hand and headset in ear. He eyeballs the list and, with a nod, ushers us through the enormous front door.

"Drink this," I say to Christopher, handing him a Mojito from a passing tray. Kate and I each grab a drink too, as we wind our way through the ultra-chic Marrakesh-meets-Madison Avenue living room and out into the vast backyard. The von Dillers' lawn makes Ed Limato's seem no bigger than Mary-Kate Olsen's bicep. A *picnic* at D.V. F. and B. D.'s is code for sitting at teak tables and lounging on Mansour rugs and antique Persian pillows scattered across the grass while devouring Cuban sandwiches, paella, Philly cheesesteaks, and mango and jicama salad—all while wearing $700 designer jeans and Tortoise shades. I slip on my black Jackie-O sunglasses. Man, that sun is bright. God wouldn't dare let it rain on the von Diller's outdoor fête.

The guest list is as international as the food, a fusion of east (Harvey Weinstein, Diane Sawyer and Mike Nichols, Barbara Walters) meets west (Steve Carell, the Pinkett-Smiths, Naomi Watts)—and a preview of all those Graydon has deemed Worthy to attend his party tomorrow night—in better clothes and more bling.

We swerve past B. D. talking to Carolina and Reinaldo Herrera and Alfonso Cuarón by the mosaic tiled pool. As Carolina crouches down to admire B. D.'s beloved Jack Russell, I can't help but admire her electric blue croc mini-Kelly.

"Does she swim?" I overhear C. H. ask B. D. as she pets the pooch.

"She loathes the water," B. D. says. "She's a Manhattan dog."

"Let's put in the requisite face-time for Papa and get out of here," Christopher whispers in my ear.

As I bite into my gooey grilled corn, I spot Charlotte Martin devouring Superman's face. Watch out, Brandon Routh, that woman is kryptonite. Then I spot the only thing deadlier than kryptonite—Adrienne

Hunt. With her usual Gitane dangling from her red-painted lips and head-to-toe black Prada, she's triple-fisting Mojitos like she's a professional waitress at the SkyBar. She wedges herself between Charlotte and Brandon on a Persian pillow. As Adrienne leans in to whisper in Charlotte's ear, she catches me staring at her. Then with a thorny smile she mouths, "Olivia sends her love."

I throw her a Death Ray.

"I'm so sorry I missed the abundance ritual this morning," I overhear D.V. F say. "Paulie, come say hello to Felicity and Bill." D.V. F drags my father across the lawn to the Huffman-Macys as Mom saunters over to Richard Johnson—because my mother would *never* miss an opportunity for a mention in Page Six.

"I've got to get out of here," I say to Christopher and Kate.

"Just wait one sec," Kate says. Her eyes are locked and loaded on two men deep in conversation nearby: Jerry Bruckheimer in all black and Bryan Lourd in a seersucker suit. As she makes her beeline, Jerry's face goes stony in the traditional Celebrity Deflector Shield maneuver, indicating that it is unacceptable for this peasant to assume an audience with the king. Kate ignores the semaphore and walks up to Bryan with a warm smile. I grab Christopher's hand and pull him into eavesdropping range.

"Congratulations, Bryan," I overhear Kate say as she shakes her idol's hand. "I heard you signed God at your party last night."

"Well, he was in need of new representation," Bryan says. Bruckheimer lowers his deflector shield and gives her an appraising look.

"Jerry, this is Kate—"

"Hi, Jerry, Kate Woods," Kate says, cutting Bryan off and confidently giving Jerry her hand.

"Lola, when do you think—" Christopher begins.

"Shhhh," I cut him off. "I'm *trying to hear.*"

"So Jerry, I hear you're considering Mischa Barton for the lead in *Days of Thunder II* opposite Orlando Bloom. I think it's a *big* mistake. Mischa's—"

"My *client*," Bryan cuts Kate off.

Kate turns to Bruckheimer. "America loves you because you're always casting the new girl in town." Kate ticks off the flamethrowers Jerry's created. "Jennifer Beals in *Flashdance*, Nicole Kidman in *Days of Thunder*, Liv Tyler in *Armageddon*. It's like William Goldman said, 'If Fox had cast Steve McQueen in *Butch Cassidy and the Sundance Kid*, Robert Redford might have remained just *another* California blond'." Jerry is gaping at her; who is this in-your-face punk with the chocolate hair and major attitude? "Jerry, Cricket Curtis—who I sent in for a small part in the pit crew—is your next Nicole Kidman."

"Let me take a look at her tape and I'll be the judge of whether she's the next *anything*," Bruckheimer says.

If Kate smells a kiss-off, she just shrugs it off. "I knew you'd say that, Jerry. I called your assistant, Jill, and persuaded her to put the tape in your Ferrari. You can watch it on the way to your four o'clock haircut."

Jerry arches his eyebrows appreciatively. "You've got balls, I'll give you that," he says. "How did you get Jill to put the tape in my car? And how do you know my schedule?"

Kate favors him with a Cheshire grin. "Trade secret," she says, whipping out a Montblanc from her tiger-print pochette. "For the contract signing," she says, handing it to J. B. "I have a feeling we'll be doing a lot of business together."

Jerry spreads his hands in mock defeat. "Just let me look at the tape first. Kate, nice meeting you." He squints at Bryan. "Better watch this girl, Bryan, she's going to be trouble." He walks off to fling an arm around Kate Beckinsale.

"You reminded me of the young me back there," Bryan says. "I'm not saying I wasn't impressed. But Mischa's getting that part. And if you ever run down one of my clients again, I will end you," he says, turning on his driving mocs.

"You don't want to end me, Bryan," Kate says. "You want to hire me."

I wrap Kate in a huge hug as she rejoins Christopher and me. "What's that for?" Kate asks.

"I'm just really proud of you—the way you went to the mat for Cricket," I say.

"Were you quoting *Adventures in the Screen Trade?*" Christopher asks.

"I bet you don't remember, but you gave me your copy of that book on the set of *Bradley Berry* in Texas," Kate says.

"My *signed* copy," Christopher says. "I remember."

Is Kate blushing?

"If I recall, you gave me something too, remember?" Oh my God, Christopher's flirting with her.

"I remember," Kate says, and now she's *definitely* blushing.

My cell phone trills.

"Hi, Julian. How are you?"

"Oh, other than completely *paralyzed* from my shoulders to my fingertips?"

"What? I think you said you're paralyzed. But I can't really hear you. Can you put the receiver closer to your mouth?"

"If I didn't resemble Daniel Day-Lewis in *My Left Foot* on his worst day, then maybe," Julian barks. "*Owwwwwww.*" I have to hold the phone away from my ear. That shrill shrieking sounds like a dying cat.

"Oh no. Julian?"

"Uh—*owwwwwww*," he yelps.

"Thank God you're on speed dial. I pressed your number with my—my nose."

"Where's Billy Joe?"

"Disneyla—*owwwwwww*. Get over here. *Hurry*," Julian begs.

Click.

Shoot, shoot, shoot, shoot, shoot.

"Christopher, I need to borrow your car. Julian's having an emergency. Kate, do you think you can give Christopher a ride home? I gotta go," I say.

"Yeah, sure," Kate says. "Anything I can do to help?"

"No, but I'll call you later to explain," I say, giving Kate and Christopher quick pecks good-bye. "Tell your sister congrats for me," I shout as I rush out of the backyard.

On my way out, I catch a glimpse of D. V. F pulling my father back and forth across the lawn like a leashed Rottweiler. Too bad I can't add a muzzle to the ensemble.

"Julian!?" I shout, flinging open the door to his poolside bungalow at the Chateau. I follow the trail of "*Owwwwwwww*'s" to find him. "Oh my God, Julian!"

He's flat on his back in the middle of the walk-in closet—I wish my *house* was *this* big—and howling like a dying animal. Like a dying purple *peacock*, to be exact. The two-foot-long train of Olivia's purple peacock gown is splayed across his body—only his head is peeking out from the plume of purple feathers. I rush to his side.

"What the hell happened?" I ask.

"Except for that bizarre Barneys episode, I've been sewing those feathers—" Julian points his nose like a springer spaniel toward the plume of purple feathers "—nonstop by *hand since last night,*" he moans. "And now I can't move my—my—*owwww*—hands—or arms. They've gone into complete spasm!"

Oh God. Oh no. Inhale. Exhale. Inhale. Exhale.

"Has this ever happened to you before?" I ask.

"Noooooooooooooooooo."

"Why didn't you call me earlier? How could you let this happen?" Julian says nothing, just lies there whimpering.

I reach over to touch his hand.

"OWWWWWWWWWWWWWWWWW!"

"Julian, I haven't even touched your hand yet," I say.

"It hurts just thinking about you touching it."

I whip out my cell and start dialing.

"Who are you calling?" Julian groans.

"911," I pant, trying not to hyperventilate.

"Hang up!" Julian shrieks. "The only thing I hate more than planes are *hospitals.*"

I look at Julian. Down at my cell. Julian. Cell. Julian. Cell. I hear a female voice ask, "What's your emergency?" Um, that my BGF is *paralyzed.* That *no one* is going to be wearing Julian Tennant on the freaking Red Carpet—*tomorrow.* Wait. Unless EMTs are trained in CPR, spinal cord injury assessment, and lace tatting appliqué . . .

"Hang up," Julian begs.

I click off my cell.

"Fine. No hospitals. But I'm calling my mother's acupuncturist, Doctor Lee. He's a genius—when Scott Caan accidentally shot Steven Soderbergh in the ass on the set of *Ocean's Seventeen,* Steven didn't even have to shut down filming."

"I hope he's a better dresser than her healer, Gonzalo."

I glare at Julian.

"Lola, his jeans were *tapered*."

"Julian, you are in no position to get sniffy about fashion choices at the moment."

"I hate the freaking color purple! Can you get me the bottle of Vicodin? It's in the bathroom."

I run to the bathroom and dial Dr. Lee. Voice mail. Shoot! I leave a message begging him to come to the Chateau and fix Julian. Then I kneel down next to him and pop the Vicodin into his mouth.

"Now would you please get me onto the bed? I've been lying on the floor of this closet for hours."

"Fine," I say. "Whoever thought I'd have to drag you out of a closet?" I heave him onto the bed.

"Can you fix the pillow?" Julian says, shifting his head around on the crisp white pillowcase. "And can you get me another Vicodin?"

"Forget the Vicodin, Julian. I don't have time to be your maid. This is bad. This is *really* bad," I say, pacing around the bed. "We only have *twelve* hours to finish the dress."

"It's over, Lola. There's no way we can pull this off." Julian closes his eyes and releases a tremulous sigh.

"Shhhh, Julian, it is *not* over. I have an idea." I frantically start dialing.

"Imas? Hi, it's Lola," I say.

"*Imas?*! You're calling *Imas?*!" Julian screeches.

"Shhhhhhh," I say to Julian. "Oh sorry—not you, Imas. Didn't you tell me that you made that skirt you were wearing when we first met, Imas?" I ask.

"Yes," Imas says. "I just finish making my niece's prom dress. She said she want pink strapless like Hilary Duff wear to MTV Movie Awards."

"Ooh, pink strapless. What length? Never mind. Imas, I *need* you.

Do you think you can slip away from Jake and meet me at the Chateau Marmont? I have a very good paying job for you. Bring your thimble."

"Mr. Jones say he no be home till late tonight. I can be there in half an hour."

"Thank you, Imas. *Thank you,*" I say, exhaling deeply. "Oh, and didn't you say you were friends with Olivia Cutter's housekeeper, Maria?"

"Yes, we know each other from the CHNSG meetings," Imas says.

"The what?"

"The Celebrity Housekeepers and Nannies Support Group."

"Do you know if Maria sews?" I ask.

"Maria love to sew too," Imas says.

"Imas, will you tell her that if she can get away, I'd like to hire her to do some sewing too."

"I call Maria and be over soon," Imas says.

Click.

"Have you lost your mind?" Julian screams. "You might as well let me swallow that whole damn bottle of Vicodin now because my life is O-V-E-R. What makes you think *Imas* can finish sewing Olivia's gown? Do you think John Galliano would let *Imas* lay a thread on one of his *couture* gowns?"

"Do you have any better ideas?"

"Jake Jones's housekeeper? Olivia Cutter's housekeeper?" Julian yells. "Why don't you just call up every housekeeper you feel has been mistreated in this whole freaking city?"

"Look, Julian, Imas is going to come through for us. Trust me. *Please,*" I say, dialing the hotel concierge. "I'm going to need at least three sewing machines sent to bungalow two. And can you have room service send over half a dozen croque monsieurs with French fries— and what do you want?" I say to Julian.

"A bottle of Patron *To-kill-ya*—put me out of my misery."

In less than an hour I've turned Julian's bungalow from the setting for the cast read-through for *Rebel Without a Cause* into the West Coast edition of *Project Runway*. I'd like to think I've created a far superior ambiance for *my* team: three abused housekeepers turned couture seamstresses.

Stevie Wonder's "Superstition" is punctuated by the clacking and purring of the Bernina sewing machines. The Fig Illume candles are pouring a soft light over the room. And an adorable waiter-slash-wannabe-actor has just cleared away the empty croque monsieur plates and deposited cappuccinos and chocolate soufflés. It's almost as though we're back in Paris with Monsieur Lagerfeld himself. Imas is bent over the corseted bodice, hand-stitching the intricate darts. Maria is carefully cutting the fabric for the delicate shoulder strap. Isabella, a third housekeeper, is changing out the silk thread on her machine, readying it for the hem of the front panel. And I'm spread out on the floor trying to find the perfect placement for the remaining peacock feathers that need to be stitched onto the two-foot-long train.

"Lola, can I talk to you for a minute?" Dr. Lee asks, walking out of the bedroom where he's been needling Julian.

"What's wrong with him?" I ask.

"His hands' peripheral nerves have been compressed and traumatized," Dr. Lee says. "He has a severe case of carpal tunnel. He'll be fine, but he should rest his hands for at least three weeks and under no circumstance can he continue to sew." Dr. Lee glances at his watch. "I have to run—I have to needle Mira Sorvino's dogs, but I'll call to check on Julian this evening." He folds up his acupuncture table and lets himself out.

Julian butts the bedroom door open with his head and whisks into the room. He's still wrapped in the hotel's terrycloth robe, his hands hanging like two limp rags at his side. He leans into Imas's lap to in-spect her progress, "No, Imas, more like this," he says, gesturing with his big toe toward the bodice and then looking to Imas for some sign of understanding. When she stares at him blankly, he moves his nose toward a stitch and makes a sweeping motion with his head.

"Oh, now I see," Imas says, going back to work.

"Gorgeous—yes! Yes! Yes!" Julian says, punctuating each yes with a staccato jump above Imas's head. Then he swings around to Isabella with the enthusiasm of Michael Tilson Thomas conducting an orches-tra. "Isabella, put another stitch right *there,*" he says, lunging his leg over her shoulder and placing his toe on the needle of the sewing machine.

"Julian, Doctor Lee said it's very important for you to rest," I say. "How about a hot bath with your favorite lavender bath salts?"

"No," Julian says, resuming his pacing around the women. "No, no, Maria. More like *this,*" he says, canting a toe in her lap.

"Okay, look, Julian, leave them *alone.* It's impossible to work with you waving your toes at them every second," I say, dragging Julian into the bedroom. "We've been over what you want a *gazillion* times. The gown is going to look like Yves Saint Laurent stitched it himself." I push Julian onto the bed and close the door tight behind him. Let him open it now without hands.

I think I may need LASIK eye surgery after five hours *straight* of tacking these purple peacock feathers onto this train. But it's been worth it. Ju-lian's masterpiece is coming together just the way he planned it. A total triumph. And best of all, Julian doesn't even know it yet. He *finally* agreed to take that Ambien. He'll be passed out on the bed for at least another few hours.

I look at the three women devotedly sewing away. A surge of appreciation moves through me. I don't know how the heck I'm going to repay these remarkable women. What I do know is that it's got to be *a lot*.

"Imas, Maria, Isabella—you guys are amazing. Wherever did you learn to sew like this?"

"We sew every week at our Celebrity Housekeeper and Nanny Support Group meetings," Imas answers. "Every week we work on pieces of our quilt."

"Quilt? What quilt?" I ask.

"The Abuse Quilt," Imas says. "Our CHNSG Therapist say it very healing to express ourselves artistically." She rummages around in her canvas tote and fishes out an eight-by-eight square. "See, this is Mr. Jones making me drain the mayo out of his Nate 'n Al's coleslaw and replace it with fat free mayonnaise."

The detail is astonishing, a Cloisters tapestry updated to twenty-first-century Hollywood. Imas must have used five different colors of thread alone to pick out the distressed denim on Jake Jones's Diesel jeans.

"Imas, I've never seen anything so intricate. You are just amazingly talented," I gush. "How many squares do you have?"

"We got, like, a hundred squares."

Maria digs around in her bag and produces her square. A screeching Olivia Cutter clutching a yapping Thor stands over a sad-faced Maria, who cowers on the floor on her hands and knees picking up piles of dirty Kleenex beneath the twenty-foot by twenty-foot David LaChapelle photographs of Olivia in Marilyn Monroe-esque poses that wallpapers her entire bedroom.

Imas nods at the remaining seamstress. "Isabella, show Lola yours too." I gasp when I see her square, which depicts a grim Isabella filling a garbage bag with condom wrappers, back issues of *Playboy,* and ripped thong underpants. I shudder to think who her boss is.

Suddenly, I know exactly how to repay these women. "Ladies, can I borrow these squares for a little bit? I need to make a phone call."

I catch a glimpse of the clock. It's eight o'clock. I'm supposed to meet SMITH to go to Jeffrey Katzenberg's "Night Before" party benefiting the Motion Picture & Television Fund at the Beverly Hills Hotel pool in *twenty* minutes. The last thing I need to do right now is go to *another* Oscar Week party. But I promised him I'd go.

"Imas, will you be okay if I run out for *two* hours?" I ask.

"How long Julian sleep with that pill?" Imas asks.

"At least another four hours," I say.

"We got it under control. But you, careful out there," she says, and bends over the purple bodice once more.

"You look stunning," SMITH says from my doorway. "I'm not only the sexiest man in the hemisphere, I'm also the luckiest," he says, laughing as he kisses me.

"We could skip the party," I say. I really don't want to go. So what if the Domestic Goddess herself, Nigella Lawson, is whipping up her delicious lobster thermador, they're auctioning off a country house on Mars, *and* Radiohead is performing? I barely had the energy to throw on this cream Julian Tennant ruched bustier and pencil trousers. And I'm having phantom aches in my feet just thinking about putting on those gold five-inch stilettos. I'd much rather climb into bed with SMITH. "You still owe me for not coming over until six a.m. I'm *exhausted*," I say, pleading my case.

"Yeah, me too. It was a brutal night of shooting," he says. "But I told my agent we'd meet him there. He said it'd be good for me to log some face time with the Paramount execs. And I paid $25,000 apiece for our tickets." Gee-*zus*. Is it too late to trade in those tickets so that I can put a down payment on a house? "I promise to show you just how much I appreciate you coming with me when we get home," SMITH says.

I slip on my stilettos, totter out to his Aston Martin, and toss my vintage cream coat into the backseat.

We wind our way down Sunset Boulevard. I look over at SMITH. And I'm certain with every cell of my being that if some agent crashed his Porsche into us en route to a signing meeting with the Next Chris Rock, I would die happy—because I'm with him. Okay, so I can't quite see a baby seat in the Aston Martin. Does Chanel make baby seats? But in five years when I'm ready for a baby, SMITH'll be ready for a Volvo. Okay, maybe not a Volvo, but he might go for a Range Rover.

The light at Sunset and Beverly Drive has obviously turned green because the BMW behind us starts honking its horn. SMITH doesn't stop kissing me.

"Forget about that jerk," he whispers. "I believe in long, slow, deep, soft, wet kisses that last three days," he says. Who cares that he's quoting Kevin Costner in *Bull Durham?* It still goes straight to my basal ganglia.

We pull up to the BH Hotel valet line and join the flock of Aston Martins, limos, Mercedes, and Bentleys.

"Thank you," I say to the valet as he swings open my door. I take SMITH's hand in mine as we walk toward the front door of the hotel. "Oh wait—my coat," I say. It's always nipple-alert cold by the pool. As he stops to chat with Philip Seymour Hoffman, I rush back to the car and grab my coat from the backseat. Is that? . . . No. Oh my God. *No.* My stomach sinks to my toes. Everything starts spinning. Inhale. Exhale. Inhale. Exhale. Maybe if I close my eyes, the spinning will stop. I open my eyes and try to focus them on SMITH.

"Hey you," I try and say, but no sound comes out. I climb out of the car.

"Are you okay, miss?" the valet asks.

I grip his shoulder to steady myself. My eyes are still trying to focus on SMITH.

"Hey you," I whisper.

"Miss?" the valet says.

I clutch my coat in my hand. I look at SMITH. Then down at my coat. SMITH. Coat. SMITH. The coat slips through my fingers and falls onto the cement.

"Miss, you dropped your coat," the valet says, placing it back in my hand.

"Thanks," I manage as I lock eyes with SMITH. He smiles *that* smile that would normally go straight to my groin. This time it stops right at my throat, which is so tight that I can barely breathe.

"C'mon," he mouths as he turns toward the door.

"Hey you!" I shriek, finding my voice. SMITH spins around. So does *everyone* else making their way inside. They all stare at me. Jennifer Connelly and Paul Bettany. Ellen DeGeneres and Portia de Rossi. Robert Redford. Jodie Foster. All of them. But my eyes stay trained on SMITH.

He flashes me *that* smile again. And this time it goes straight to my fist, which pulses with the desire to beat his face in. They were all right. All of them. Dr. Gilmore, Kate, Cricket, Julian, Mom—even Papa. And I was so *wrong*. And so dumb. And so used. What a fool.

"*Come here!*" I scream at the top of my lungs.

SMITH nervously scans the front of the hotel to see what the damage is—who *exactly* is bearing witness to my lunacy? He waves to Michael Douglas in a desperate attempt to smooth out the look of things, then saunters toward me.

"How do you explain *this*?" I yell, pushing my coat into his face.

"Your coat?" he says, confused.

"The *purple dog hair,*" I choke over the words, "that is all over my cream coat because your backseat is plastered in it."

"Oh, that . . . well . . . that's from . . . um . . . the wig I had to wear for my scene last night," he says.

"Stop lying! *I'm* the reason Olivia Cutter's dog is purple, you ass-hole!" I scream, trying to catch my breath and what's left of my sanity—and *dignity.* "You weren't shooting late. That's where you were last night, isn't it? You were with *Olivia.* Tell me the truth. *Now.* No more lies," I say, fighting back tears.

"Lola, you don't understand. I really want that Danny Zuko part in *Grease,*" SMITH says weakly.

It feels like I've been socked in the stomach. I lose the fight with my tears.

"Did you screw her?" I ask, but I already know the answer. I can feel it in my gut like I'm pregnant with it. He just looks down at his loafers. "Oh God. You climbed into *my* bed after you were with *her.*"

I look into SMITH's eyes. I mean really *look.* And for the very first time I see him for what he *really* is: a big fat fucking *phony.* He's just *another* narcissistic, vapid, idiot *actor.*

"I loved you! Despite what everyone said, I believed you. And you're a fake, you're a fucking fake. Come to think of it, you and Olivia de-serve each other. You don't deserve *me.*" As I say it, I realize that I actu-ally mean it. *SMITH does not deserve me.* I, Lola Santisi, deserve *better.* I take a good, long look at him for what I know will be the last time. "You don't deserve me," I repeat quietly through my tears as I run up the stairs to the lobby of the hotel and straight into—my father.

I look up at Papa with geysers coming out of my eyes. He must have witnessed the whole debacle, along with all of the other guests going into the party. All of them hearing me screaming like I'd just been sprung from the loony bin. I brace myself for the inevitable impact of a Storm Force 10 fit from Papa. Here it comes—my father to tell me how much I'm disgracing him. How stupid I am and how right he was. And it hurts because it's true. If the hotel pool wasn't covered, I'd grab the rocks hanging around Catherine Zeta-Jones's neck, tie them around my ankles, and leap right in.

Before I can formulate another self-loathing thought, my father wraps his arms around me and hugs me—*really* hugs me. And I don't think he's ever hugged me like this before. And he's doing it in the middle of the Beverly Hills Hotel, with all of Hollywood watching. He isn't paying attention to any of it, all of it's just melting away. I know there's nothing here for him except me in his arms.

oscar sunday

---

s the sun rises over the Chateau, I throw open the plastic lid of the trash can on the street in front of my house. Deep cleansing breath. One. Two. On *three* I hurl in the vase full of peonies from SMITH. I watch as the vase shatters and the pale pink petals fall apart. I feel the glass breaking in my bones. And I want to feel it. *This* time no matter how much it hurts, I won't be scavenging for the broken pieces in the garbage. I'm ready to let him go. I, Lola Santisi, with tear-stained cheeks and one hell of a hangover of the heart, am giving SMITH up—*for good*. It's time to put myself back together. It's Oscar Day.

Look, I was born on an Oscar Sunday and today, twenty-six years later, on another Oscar Sunday, I will be reborn. No more pity parties for one. SMITH may have annihilated my heart, but I'm not letting him destroy my will. Today I begin my quest for substance. For finding a man who doesn't need a director and a script to have meaningful dialogue. A *real* man. Not someone who plays a man.

I'm going to finish what I started and I'm going to *succeed.* So what if Olivia Cutter screwed him. *She* is going to walk the Red Carpet in Julian's peacock masterpiece and get on every goddamn Best Dressed Oscar list there is. Period. Exclamation point.

As I walk into my bedroom the television set is exactly as I left it— blaring through the night to drown out the self-loathing voices in my sleepless head. I scavenge for the remote to turn off Mary Hart's disgustingly cheery voice. Does that woman *ever* have a down day?

"From dazzling dresses to million-dollar diamonds, *Entertainment Tonight* will have all your Red Carpet coverage live from the Kodak Theatre. Who will Cojo name Best Dressed this year? Tune in today to find out. If it's happening at the Oscars, it's happening on *Entertainment Tonight,*" Mary Hart exclaims on the commercial.

I hit the power button on the remote and look over to my unmade bed. Screw it. I climb in and pull the covers over my head. Just as I'm dreaming up all the ways I'd like to violently torture SMITH *and* Olivia Cutter, I hear my front doorknob jiggling, then footsteps.

"If you're here to rob and kill me, I'm in the bedroom," I yell from underneath the covers.

"Lola," I hear Kate call out from the hall. The way she says my name ignites tears—lots of them. I've never heard Kate use that tone: *pity.* I poke an eye out from beneath the sheets.

"You heard," I manage to get out.

Kate lies down on the bed next to me and wraps her arms around me. "Sweetie, *all* of Hollywood was at that party last night. I think the guys in the mail room heard," she says gently.

"Well, if you're here to gloat about being right about SMITH and tell me that you're not picking up the pieces again, I'm already aware," I say.

"I wish I wasn't right, Lola. But I'm *always* going to be here to pick up your pieces," Kate says, which is enough to send me into full body sobs. If my BFF minds that my tears are staining her violet silk camisole, she doesn't say so.

"Thank you, Kate," I blubber.

"Of course, you couldn't wait till *after* the Oscars to do this," Kate says jokingly, stroking my hair. "We came straight from the airport."

"*We?*"

"Christopher and me. He came with me to my sister's wedding after Barry and Diane's."

I bolt upright. And stare at Kate.

"Don't look at me like that. You're the one who left Christopher carless. And—" Kate pauses. "I think I'm ready to do feelings," she says, smiling. "Okay, I know, *I* want to shoot me for saying that."

"Wait—you . . . and Christopher? Oh my God, Kate. You've always been like my sister, but now it's going to be *official*," I say, throwing my arms around my BFF and hugging her tightly.

"Jesus, Lola," Kate says, untwining my arms from around her torso. "My sister was the one getting married, *not* me. But we did have mind-blowing sex. He—"

"He's my *brother*," I cut Kate off. "Please spare me all the gory details," I say, falling back onto my pillow with a sigh. "Where *is* Christopher?"

"Getting us lattes."

"Kate."

"Yeah," she says putting her head on the pillow next to mine.

"Thanks for being here."

"We're gonna get through this, Lola," Kate says, squeezing my hand. "And I am so calling *The Enquirer* and telling them SMITH has a dick the size of a peanut."

"I'm really happy about you and Christopher."

"Me too," she says. "You know, Lola, it isn't just sex this time. I really do lo—" We both freeze as we hear a loud rumble in the living room.

Julian's voice booms. "Cricket, can you push my bangs back and give me another sip of that latte?"

"Julian, I can't hold your coffee, your banana chocolate chip muffin, your Nano, your cell phone, your sunglasses, your jacket, your lip balm, *and* push your bangs back," I hear Cricket say wearily.

"Here, I can push your bangs back for you," I hear my brother say.

"I've been waiting my entire life for you to say that to me, Christopher," Julian coos.

"This is me throwing my arms around you," Julian says, as they walk through my bedroom door. His paralyzed hands hang like weary tulips by his sides. Cricket drops Julian's sunrise accessories on the floor and climbs into bed on my other side. She hugs me so tight I think I may have punctured a lung.

"SMITH's an asshole. Olivia's an asshole. They're perfect for each other," Christopher says, handing me a latte and plopping down on the end of the bed where he wraps one hand around my leg—and the other around Kate's. She gives him a melting smile.

"I've thought about it and that woman is *not* wearing my gown," Julian announces. "I don't care if I have to eat SpaghettiOs for the rest of my life."

"Julian, I've thought about it too. She's *wearing* the gown. Period," I say. "We've worked too hard for this. But I'm pretty sure I won't mind if you leave a couple of extra pins in it."

"I'll get Imas on that. Maybe we can puncture her new implants," Julian says.

Kate glances at her watch. "Sorry, Lola, but I've got to go. I have to meet Will at his house to prep him for his Red Carpet interviews. I swear if I'm not there to help him choose which hair gel to use, what pair of underwear to put on, and to trim his nose hair, he's going to go ballistic. Cricket's going to stay here with you, and Christopher's going to drive Julian to Olivia's house. I'll come back as soon as I can," Kate says, clearly having already worked out the nursing schedule at the Lola Santisi Hospital for Decimated Hearts.

"Christopher doesn't have to drive Julian. I'm going to that fitting," I say.

"You're what?" they gasp in unison, springing up from their respective posts.

"If I could throw my arms up in the air in protest, I would," Julian says. "You are *not* facing that demon woman again after what she did."

"Yes. I am. I have to do this. I have to finish this job," I say. As I say it, I'm shocked that I actually mean it, that the commitment in my voice matches the commitment in my actor-broken heart.

"Are you out of your mind?" Kate says.

"Julian can handle it," Cricket says.

"No he can't," I say. "How can he do a fitting without his hands? Plus, knowing that woman, she won't wear the dress because she'll think Julian's carpal tunnel is contagious."

"I resent that. I can totally handle that bitch," Julian says. "Are you *sure* about this?"

"Yes."

They all look at me skeptically.

"I *need* to do this. I'm going to that fitting. *Okay?!*"

"Okay," Julian says. "But we better get a soothing algae face mask on you *pronto* because your eyes look like you've gone ten rounds with Mike Tyson."

I've been staring at the same sentence in *Us Weekly* for the last three hours straight in Olivia Cutter's den, waiting for her to appear. I shift uneasily on the cushions. My skin's crawling, wondering, did SMITH and Olivia do it on this couch too? Julian throws his leg over my knee to stop my foot from nervously tapping. I'm about to catapult out the door when Olivia Cutter steps a pink marabou slipper into the room, followed by an illegally short leopard-print robe and a headful of curlers.

"Olivia's wearing Prada," she announces. "You may go now."

"You're *what?*" I say. I feel my mental and emotional well-being cracking along with her Juicy Fruit chewing gum. I try to steady myself on my Louboutins as sweat pools on my lower back.

"You heard Olivia. Or are your ears as broken as Julian's hands are? Olivia's wearing *Prada.*"

I'm hovering somewhere above my body. I wrestle to pull myself back down to earth. I can't breathe. Inhale. Exhale. Inhale. Exhale. Where did all the freaking oxygen go and *why* did I wear these four-inch red slingbacks? If I were wearing flats I wouldn't have as far to topple down. I struggle to catch my breath and my balance.

I can't believe this is really happening. This is it. *No one* is wearing Julian Tennant on the Oscar Red Carpet. I look over to Julian, who's practically crumpling into the fetal position on the sofa. John, Olivia's agent, her publicist, and her assistant are all staring stone-faced at the white marble floor. Maria stops her dusting and turns to me with tearful eyes. I gaze at Julian's purple peacock masterpiece hanging limply from the garment rack. Oh God. I've failed Julian. I've failed myself.

Again. I've even failed Maria, Imas, and Isabella. That freaking Adrienne Cunt.

"Don't you want to at least *try on* the gown? Julian may have permanently *paralyzed* his hands sewing it for you," I say in a last-ditch effort to save my BGF's career—and my own.

Olivia props a freshly manicured hand on her cocked hip and lets out an irritated sigh. "Why? Olivia doesn't want to be a purple peacock. Olivia hates *b-b-b-irds.* Olivia wants to be a periwinkle *Prada* princess. The psychic Olivia met at the W retreat yesterday told Olivia that Olivia's going to win the Oscar in *Prada.*"

Her words reverberate in my ears. I think back on all the humiliating ways I degraded myself sucking up to that she-devil—kowtowing to every schizoid whim. And now she's not wearing Julian's gown to the Oscars? Oh *no.* Olivia Cutter can have SMITH, but I'm taking my self-respect back, Goddamn it. As Olivia turns on her marabou slippers to leave, I stop her.

"Wait a second, Olivia."

"What?" she asks, clearly annoyed.

I take a deep breath and plant both feet firmly on the floor. "You know what Lola thinks of Olivia? Lola thinks that Olivia is an abusive, spoiled, bratty, classless, ungrateful bitch."

Olivia's Dream Team lets out audible gasps. Oh *puh-lease.* They should all be applauding. They all wish they could tell Olivia what they *really* think of her.

"Lola thinks that Olivia is despicable for lying about Make-A-Wish to get a boob job."

"Lola—" Julian tries to stop me.

"No, Julian. Lola's not done telling Olivia what Lola thinks of Olivia," I say. "Lola thinks Olivia can shove Olivia's Kirlian aura analyst and Olivia's psychoanalyst and the psychic from the W retreat and

Olivia's annoying, yappy purple dog up Olivia's flabby flat ass because—newsflash, sweetie—the Oscar votes have been in for weeks and not even resurrecting Saint Anthony himself to perform one of his miracles is going to change them. And Lola thinks that Olivia doesn't deserve to wear Julian Tennant." I grab the purple peacock gown off the rack and yank Julian off the couch. Lola needs to get the hell out of this insane asylum for good.

"Olivia doesn't understand. Olivia wants to know why Lola's speaking like that." I hear Olivia say to her Dream Team as I slam her front door shut behind us.

"Julian, I'm so sorry. I—" I look at my BGF slumped across from me on his bed at the Chateau and into his tear-filled, hopeless hazel eyes. "I'm so sorry," is all I can say. My BGF's livelihood, his dream, the only thing he's meant to do, is coming to a crashing halt.

The hotel room phone rings.

"Unless it's Brad Pitt leaving Angelina for me, tell them I'm dead," Julian croaks.

"Hello," I say, picking up the phone.

"Hi, Lola, it's Marty."

I throw my hand over the receiver. "It's Marty," I whisper to Julian.

"Hang up," Julian says, bolting upright.

"We have to tell him, Julian."

"No we don't, we can lie and let him figure it out when he's back in New York—and I'm dead," Julian pleads.

"I'm sorry, Julian," I say. "Let's just get it over with." I press the phone to my ear. "Hi, Marty. How's the—"

"Forget the chit-chat," Marty snaps. "How'd the fitting go with Olivia Cutter and when do I get to meet her?"

Gulp.

"Look, Marty. I have some . . ." I struggle to get the words out, ". . . bad news."

"Spit it out, Lola," he barks at me.

"Olivia Cutter's not wearing Julian. She's wearing Prada," I blurt out.

I've never heard such a deafening silence.

"I'm sorry, I think the phone line is breaking up—or did you just say that Olivia Cutter isn't wearing Julian's gown," Marty bellows at me.

Silence.

"Is that what you said?"

"Yes," I mumble in defeat.

"Olivia Cutter is wearing *Prada* and you've got no one else wearing Julian on the Oscar Red Carpet?"

Silence.

"Um, right," I finally say.

"No one is wearing Julian Tennant on the Oscar Red Carpet? Is that what you're telling me—that *NO ONE* is wearing him?" Every one of Marty's words feels like a right hook to the face.

Silence.

I can practically see the frost forming on the receiver.

"Oh-kay . . . the party is O-V-E-R, kids." *Knockout.* I double over in despair. "We're done, effective now. I'll notify New York to close the offices. We'll fire all the people, and sell the furniture and fixtures for whatever we can get. Tell Julian he can keep his name, but that's all he can keep," Marty says.

"Oh God. No! Marty, please don't do this. You *can't* do this. Julian's so talented. He's going to be bigger than Karl Lagerfeld. You have to give him another chance. He deserves another chance, Marty. Please!" I beg.

"There are no second chances in the *real* world, kid. Marty Glickman is out of the fashion business. I would have been better off investing in that formaldehyde shark," Marty says. "And tell Julian he's moving to the Holiday Inn *today*. I'm not footing his bills at the Chateau anymore."

Click.

The receiver slips through my fingers and thuds onto the azure carpet. Julian looks at me searchingly, tears brimming in his eyes. I can't seem to find the right words. What am I supposed to tell my BGF who just lost everything because of *me?* I don't have to say a word. It's written on every pore of my face. I collapse onto the bed next to Julian.

"Draw the shades," Julian says, curling into the fetal position.

"What?" I say, lifting my head up from my hands where I've buried it.

"I prefer to die in darkness. And drugged. Bring me the bottle of Vicodin."

"No, Julian. Marty may have pulled out, but your career isn't over. This isn't it for you, Julian. You're so talented. I'll find you a new investor. I'll ask Papa for the money. I'll sell everything I own. Julian, this isn't it for you. This isn't the way it's supposed to be," I say.

"But this is the way it *is*," Julian says. "Lola, my life is over. I want to be alone. No plus-ones at my funeral."

"Julian, it's *not* over for you. I know it feels that way right now, but it's *not* over."

"Lola, when are you going to realize that Happy Hollywood Endings only happen in the movies?" he says. "To the rest of the world, Hollywood is just a smoggy, ugly town in California? If I wasn't so afraid to fly, I could at least die with dignity in New York and not as a Hollywood cliché in the Chateau. Please just let me be alone."

"Julian?" I say pleadingly.

"Please."

"I'm so sorry, Julian."

278 | Amanda Goldberg and Ruthanna Khalighi Hopper

"I know."

"Okay, I'm leaving. But I'm taking all the sharp objects in the room with me."

The second I walk through my front door, I swaddle myself in my orange-for-shielding cashmere blanket. As I pull it up to my chin, I realize there couldn't possibly be anything left to shield me *from*. Okay, maybe that Taepodong-2 missile Kim Jong Il has aimed at California. But somehow I don't think this blanket's going to do the trick when Hollywood goes up in smoke.

I toss the blanket off and reach for my phone to call Dr. Gilmore for an emergency session. I stop myself. What's the point? She's only going to tell me what I already know: that I'm a frickin' fool. And a big fat failure. I have nothing to show for this week of utter hell except a shattered heart and unemployment. And a best friend who's losing everything because of *me*. And three overworked housekeepers who I can't afford to pay. *And* I was supposed to be at my parent's house half an hour ago to start getting Red Carpet Ready. Why bother? So that I can watch Olivia Cutter accept her Best Actress Oscar in *Prada?* Fat chance.

My cell trills for the trillionth time. No doubt it's Mom *again*, wondering where the heck I am. I can feel the guilt growing with each ring.

I drag myself to my closet. I've been so consumed with dressing everyone else this week I have *no* idea what the hell I'm going to wear. I rifle through all of my dresses. None of them are right. I flop down on my bed. A purple peacock feather poking out from the garment bag I hurled onto the floor catches my eye. I stare at the iridescent purple feather. I bound off the bed and unzip the bag. Will it even fit? I shimmy into Julian's Met-Worthy gown and beeline for my full-length mirror in the bathroom. So what if it's a little short and a little tight? It's the most beautiful dress I've ever seen. Julian's gown was made for the Oscar Red Carpet, for crying out loud. And it's gonna walk down it. Even if it *is* just on *me*.

"Darling, you look terrible," Mom gasps, looking *Vogue*-cover Worthy thanks to Francois Nars *himself* in the middle of her vast crema marfil marble bathroom where I imagine she's been since dawn, readying herself for the Oscars. "I told Francois *everything*," she says, inspecting her blood red lips and smoky eyes in the mirror. "After Francois is done with your face, no one will know about the hell you've been through with SMITH and Olivia Cutter. Remember, darling, looking fabulous is the best revenge. Isn't that right, Francois?"

"*Absolutement,* Blanca! Screw killing them with kindness, kill them with great makeup," the star makeup maestro says in his très adorable French accent.

"I'm going to go light *another* abundance candle and do a final prosperity chant before I slip into Karl's gown. Francois, darling, make sure you rub your divine Body Glow all over Lola, it's magic," she says, grabbing the bottle of Rose Dom Perignon off the counter and striding out of the room.

"I'm thinking Ursula Andress in *Dr. No*," Francois says, staring at me intently with perfectly plucked brows, rubbing his perfectly groomed goatee with a perfectly manicured hand.

Thirty-eight minutes later—and three tubes of concealer, a bottle of oil-free foundation, a sprinkling of bronzing powder, a generous dusting of "Orgasm" blush, infinite individual lashes, a tub of black liquid liner, a trillion coats of mascara, multiple applications of Francois's "Barbarella" lipstick, and—

"*Voilà,*" Francois says as he spins me around in the makeup chair in front of Mom's three-way mirror. "Deadly," Francois pronounces.

As I stare deep into my Paris runway-ready eyes, all I can see is a frickin' *failure*. All the makeup on the planet couldn't possibly camouflage *that*. I think about Julian alone in his bungalow at the Chateau with the shades drawn and tears well in my eyes.

"No! Don't cry," Francois shrieks as he makes a mad dash for the Kleenex and strategically holds two tissues under my eyes to prevent the tears from staining my dewy cheeks.

"I'm sorry, Francois," I say, leaning my head back to try and keep the tears from surging out. "It's just that, I don't think I can do this."

"Nonsense. You're going to put on Julian's to-die-for gown and you're going to strut down that Red Carpet like Giselle."

"Like anyone is going to notice *me*," I sigh. "I just can't believe Olivia Cutter is wearing *Prada*."

"Lola, you've *grown up* in Hollywood, don't you know by now how *crazy* these actresses are? I'm sure Olivia's been through a dozen hair and makeup people in the last hour. The Twins called me last night to see if I was available but then Olivia turned around and fired them."

"She fired the Wonder Twins? Why?" I ask, vaguely recalling their absence from that total nightmare at Olivia's house this morning.

"Olivia saw Keira Knightley at some party last night wearing the same Matthew Willliamson crystal and feather brooch she was wearing and freaked. She barricaded herself in the bathroom for half of the night and called the Twins from the bathroom at midnight and fired them."

"Oh my God," I say, feeling a surge of empathy for them. "That Olivia Cutter is the Devil."

"Sweetie, it's *Oscar Week*—that's *nothing*. Charlotte Martin fired *her* stylist when she found out that both she and Olivia Cutter were wearing Prada to the Oscars because Charlotte refuses to wear the same designer as *any* other actress. She called the Twins at four a.m. in hysterics and *hired* them."

"Charlotte Martin was wearing *Prada* too? Jesus, is there anyone that Adrienne Cunt *isn't* dressing?" I say. "So which designer did Charlotte end up—" I stop myself. The Red Carpet starts in *three* hours and I'm certain Charlotte Martin has found some other designer's supremely fabulous frock to don by *now*. But what if she *hasn't*?

I bolt for my cell and speed dial the Twins. Voice mail. Shit. Shit. Shit. The Red Carpet is in *three hours* for crying out loud—what was I thinking? I know exactly what I'm thinking: if there's even a .0000000000000000000000000000000001 percent chance that Charlotte Martin could walk the Oscar Red Carpet in Julian Tennant, I'm going to make it happen.

Okay, think, Lola. *Think.* Ohohohohoh. Bingo baby. When Queen PR Bee dragged me over to Charlotte and Graydon Carter's table at the Polo Lounge the other day, Charlotte mentioned that she was staying at the BH Hotel. I'll just call the hotel and ask for—*uh oh.* Chances that she's staying under her own name: *zero.* Dang it.

Wait. *Ruth.* She's only been making me strawberry shakes and patty melts at the BH Hotel Coffee Shop since the womb. Surely if anyone can pull a few strings for me, it's *Ruth.* A quick call to Ruth and . . .

"Hello," a weary female voice answers in Charlotte Martin's hotel suite.

"Hi, this is Lola Santisi and I was wondering—"

"Lola?" one of the Twins says quizzically.

"Listen, I'm with Francois Nars and he told me about the whole Olivia Cutter nightmare—I'm sorry, by the way. But congratulations, because he also told me about Charlotte Martin—which is why I'm calling. I'm sure she's already dressed, but just in case Charlotte still doesn't have a gown, I thought I'd call because—"

She cuts me off. "How fast can you get to the BH Hotel?"

"Ten minutes tops."

"Bungalow 9."

Click.

Oh my God. Oh my God.

I throw on the purple peacock gown, give Francois a huge hug, and rush out of the bathroom. "Tell my mother I'll meet her at the Oscars," I yell out as I take the stairs two-by-two.

"No, no, no, no, no," Charlotte Martin fumes in her pink hotel bathrobe as she flicks through the rack of Julian Tennant gowns I've brought, a Marlboro Light in one hand and her quote unquote Evian *water* in the other. What would the world think if they knew America's Sweetheart smokes like a freight train and drinks like a blowfish? I think I can actually see the smoke coming out of her drop-dead Harry Winston 60-karat diamonded ears. "Someone *do* something," she yells as Laura Mercier, in the flesh, tries to gloss Charlotte's lips, currently in full pout, and hair guru Oribe removes the curlers around Charlotte's auburn tresses. Silence fills the room because there is nothing left *to do*. Charlotte's looked at every last gown. And rejected them *all*. I glance at the clock on the coffee table. Oh my God. It's 2 P.M. The Red Carpet starts in an *hour*.

"Won't you at least try this one on?" I say, pulling out Julian's brilliant garnet off-the-shoulder knee-length tiered ombré hand-beaded gown.

"Honey, that may be good enough for Olivia Cutter, but *Charlotte Martin's* in a whole other stratosphere," she says to me as she takes a long drag off her cigarette and hands her empty glass of *water* to a harried assistant to refill. As she storms across the room, looking devastatingly gorgeous even in half a head of curlers and that bathrobe—I realize she's right. Charlotte Martin is indeed in a whole other stratosphere. Charlotte makes Olivia look like a sad Steve Madden knockoff of America's Sweetheart. But doesn't Charlotte know that smoking is as over as Ben Affleck and leggings?

I can't let Charlotte parade out of here on those long legs in another designer. She's *got* to walk out of here in Julian.

"*This* is an extraordinary gown," I say, pulling out an emerald green slithery silk gown with illicitly high slits that I never bothered showing to Olivia. She couldn't have pulled it off. "The body-hugging cut and plunging neckline would be magnificent on you. It would accentuate your gorgeous long legs," I say.

"That color's all wrong. No. NO. *No*. Absolutely *NOT*," she says. "Hurry, people. Make something happen. What about 'I need to be on the Red Carpet in half an hour' do you people not understand," she screeches.

"When we met with Susan from Vera Wang, you said you loved this gown. How about trying it on again," one of the Twins says desperately, pulling out a magnificent lemon chiffon hourglass halter gown.

"I'm an actress. A damn good actress. I was acting. As in *make-believe*," she scolds. "It's awful. Dreadful. Get it out of my sight," she says, leaving an aura of smoke above her head as she waves her fifth consecutive cigarette in emphasis. I think I can actually feel that cigarette smoke killing me. Concentrate, Lola. *Concentrate.* I fan through Julian's dresses again.

"Charlotte, we've got to go. If we don't leave *now*, they're going to be rolling *up* the Red Carpet when we get there," her publicist says, frantically.

"Are you sure you don't want to rethink this one?" The Wonder Twins beat me to the couture, pulling out a stunning red beaded strapless dress. *No!* I try to send them a telepathic message but it translates as a useless glare.

Charlotte lets out a loud sigh. "All right. Which Italian is that?"

"Valentino."

Silence.

"Fine. Put me in it. I'll settle. God! I hate to settle! Why should I have to settle for anything."

Oh God. Oh no. The skies parted over Oscar Week and gave me another chance and I missed it. I force myself up off the couch and whip around to collect Julian's gowns. As I reach for the front door of the bungalow to let myself out, I look over my shoulder to say good-bye.

"Wait a minute."

It takes me a minute to realize Charlotte's talking to me.

"What's that?" Charlotte says, looking at me like I'm the pineapple-print ottoman in the corner that she's noticing for the first time. "I want to wear *that*."

"What?" I say in shock.

"That dress. I want to wear *that* dress," she says, pointing at me.

I look down at the plume of cascading peacock feathers. Of *course*. Why hadn't I thought of it sooner?

"Oh, right. Yes," I say, flinging the gowns in my arms onto the floor. "Help me out of this, ladies," I say as the Wonder Twins descend. I snatch up a hotel towel as I hand the gown to Charlotte Martin. "It is Julian Tennant's finest work." The Wonder Twins scurry over to her. She throws off the red Valentino and gracefully steps one gazelle leg into the peacock gown and then the other. The Twins zip and fluff and Charlotte Martin takes a step toward the mirror. I look around the room to see if my gasp was perceivable. I can't believe it. It is an immaculate fit. She is absolutely angelic in this gown.

"I've never seen anything so exquisite in my life," I say, standing before Charlotte Martin in this skimpy hotel towel with enough goose bumps covering my skin that I could wear *them* to the Oscars.

"Neither have I. It's *perfect*," Charlotte says, gazing at herself in the mirror. "Okay, let's go, people," she shouts, breaking the reverie. "*Move,*" she barks like General Schwarzkopf in the flesh. I run over to the rack and quickly throw on the garnet ombre beaded tulle dress *both* Olivia Cutter *and* Charlotte Martin rejected and hightail into Charlotte's awaiting limo.

"Shit!" Charlotte screams as the billboards on Hollywood Boulevard whiz past the limo as we speed toward the Kodak Theatre. Charlotte's scream causes me to squirt Krazy Glue all over my hand. I'd been using it to glue two peacock feathers onto her silver strappy Blahniks in an effort to recreate the shoes Manolo made especially for Olivia Cutter.

"What's wrong?" her publicist asks tensely.

"My toes. They're the wrong color for this dress. I can't have *red* toes with *this* gown," she fumes. "Shit. Shit. Shit. Shit. Shit. My toes *cannot* be seen like this." Even her flawless mask of makeup doesn't disguise the ugly twist of her face as she yells at the top of her lungs.

Laura Mercier's assistant flings open her makeup bag and starts frantically rummaging through it. "Here," she says after she dips a cotton pad in nail polish remover. "I'll take the right foot. You take the left," she says, handing me the readied cotton pad. Why *me*? Can't someone *else* do this?

"I'm not finished with these Blahni—"

"We'll finish these," one of the Twins cuts me off, plucking Charlotte's stilettos out of my lap.

"Close your eyes," Laura Mercier commands Charlotte, so that the makeup maven can touch up Charlotte's perfect purple lids as Oribe sprays her upswept auburn locks. I look around the crowded limo. I guess I'm the only one left for toenail duty since Charlotte's assistant is busy trying to cram the maximum number of Marlboro Lights into Charlotte's Tic Tac-sized Judith Leiber and her publicist is screaming into her cell, preparing the Red Carpet for Charlotte's arrival. But all is forgiven. Charlotte Martin is *absolutely* exquisite. I've gotten Julian Tennant to the Oscars. I've *succeeded.* I'll breathe in the toxic fumes of this Hawaiian Orchid nail polish—and her secondhand smoke—and I'll like it.

My spell is abruptly broken by Charlotte's roar.

"Oh no! This jewelry's *all* wrong with this dress," she shrieks, holding out her immaculately sculpted, sapphire and diamond bangled limbs like they're draped in cubic zirconias from Claire's. "I look like Ice Cube with all this bling when this dress is calling for Audrey Hepburn. What else do we have? I need something simple," she orders as she rips off the million-dollar bracelets and flings them at the Twins.

"That's the only jewelry we have. Remember? We went to Harry Winston and you chose what you wanted," one Twin answers meekly.

"You're telling me that there are no other jewelry options? Is that what you're *telling* me?" she shrieks.

"Yes," the Wonder Twins say together.

"What's that," Charlotte says, pointing to one of the Twin's hands. She's sporting a simple brilliant-cut diamond on her left ring finger.

"It's my engagement ring," the Twin says sheepishly. "It was my grandmother's ring."

"Give it to me," Charlotte orders.

Oh my God. I have to pull my jaw off the floor as the Twin twists off her engagement ring and places it on Charlotte's finger.

"Perfect," Charlotte announces. "Here it comes, people," Charlotte bellows as the Kodak Theatre comes into view.

The limo slows down as we approach the first security checkpoint. The car windows may be tinted pitch black, but they're far from soundproof. From a block away, we've been hearing the deafening roar of the swarms of screaming fans camped on bleachers for days for a glimpse of their favorite celeb. Hundreds of photogs and camera crews from around the globe are waiting anxiously, their telephoto lenses locked and loaded, on the mile-long Red Carpet. This is it. The Oscars. The biggest night of the year for Hollywood. I quickly put the final coat of Hawaiian Orchid polish on Charlotte's pinky toe and carefully slip on her strappy stiletto.

"Huh, Huh, Huh." Charlotte makes a sound from her diaphragm like she's a cadet readying to do a ropes course, followed by a deep, resonating "Yeahhhhhhhhhhh," and another staccato, "Huh! Yes, people. Let's do this," she says as the limo door flies open in front of the Kodak Theatre. Charlotte Martin morphs before my eyes into that twenty-million-dollar princess, stepping majestically out of the car in Julian Tennant's magnum opus and raising her arm to the fans in her role as America's Box Office Royalty. She steps a picture-perfect peacock-feathered Manolo onto . . .

The Oscar Red Carpet . . .

There are more explosions around Charlotte Martin than on the Fourth of July. She's smack dab in the middle of a major flashbulb storm. And she is *working* it—giving those photogs her front side, her backside, spinning and twirling the dazzling plume of cascading peacock feathers, slinging one slender thigh forward, arching her bronzed back, pursing those luscious lips—everything she's got she's giving them. It's the Charlotte Martin Show. And the hungry photogs and shrieking fans are lapping it up; begging for "just one more shot" as America's Sweetheart inches her way down the Oscar Red Carpet, waving and smiling like it's just another Sunday church picnic with her immediate family.

I can see more stars from here than I would from the Hubble Space Telescope. The frantic lensmen don't know whose name to scream first. The booming cacophony of megawatt names—"Brad and Angie! Look over here! Orlando! Reese! Johnny! Just one more! Tom and Katie! Tobey! Leo! Julia! Over here! George! Sienna! Jude!"—makes my head spin. Jennifer Aniston does her golden girl for the cameras in a jet black Givenchy sheath, Nicole Kidman gives them statuesque Aussie queen in a silver YSL strapless hourglass gown, Kate Hudson epitomizes earth mother goddess in flowing silver Stella McCartney chiffon, but my eyes stay trained on—Charlotte Martin. Not even Jake Gyllenhaal draws my attention away from her.

Oh my God, this is really happening. Charlotte Martin, the megastar to end all mega-stars, is actually *wearing* Julian's purple peacock masterpiece on the Oscar Red Carpet. And I can't stop staring, soaking up my triumph.

Charlotte glides over the Red Carpet, promenading down the press line while blowing air kisses to her squealing fans. Joan Rivers grabs her around the arm and pulls her toward her camera crew. Oh my God. This is it. Joan Rivers is about to decide our fate. I have a vivid flashback to Joan asking if Bjork was drunk when she put on that "chicken costume." I stand here on the Red Carpet praying that Joan Rivers doesn't have a thing against birds. Will she give us the Golden Hanger or the wire hanger?

"You're *stunning*. This divine peacock number makes the other ladies here look like a bunch of turkeys," Joan Rivers announces in her signature brusque voice. *Yes!* "Charlotte, who are you wearing?"

"Julian Tennant!" Charlotte gushes as I pinch myself. "He's a miracle worker! Put that name on your fashion guru list, Joan. You're going to be seeing a *lot* of him."

Oh my God, this is *really* happening. My hands are shaking as I rustle through my python clutch for my cell to speed-dial Julian.

"Julian, turn on the TV," I scream into the phone over the roar of paparazzi yelling, "Charlotte, here, look here! Charlotte over here!"

"Why are you torturing me like this?" Julian murmurs. "Are you trying to kill me for real?"

"Julian, just turn on channel 2 *now!*"

"Fine. Hold on." I hear a fumble and a crash. Is Julian operating the remote with his feet?

"Let me look at you," Cojo says, spinning Charlotte around in front of the *Entertainment Tonight* cameras.

"*AAAAAAAAAHHHHHHHHHH!*" Julian shrieks. "Is that— Is that—" he hyperventilates.

"Charlotte Martin in your purple peacock gown," I shriek.

"Oh my God, Lola. How'd this happen? Oh my God. Oh my God," Julian yelps breathlessly.

"Julian, just shut up and listen to Cojo."

"My darling, you're the most perfect peacock I've ever seen. Julian Tennant is a *genius!*" Cojo gushes. "When I die, I'm telling God I want to come back as this gown. It is *superb*. Where has this talent been hiding?"

"Julian, are you listening to this? Are you hearing what I'm hearing?"

"Shhhhhhh! I'm busy listening to Cojo tell me I'm a genius! I'm here, Cojo—this talent's been hiding at the Chateau," Julian howls.

"Quick, Julian, turn on E!," I say as Charlotte saunters down the press line, stopping to twirl the gown in front of Isaac Mizrahi's cameras.

"Honey, what is this fabulousness you're wearing?" Isaac leans into the gown as if to inspect the brushwork of a Cezanne at the Musée d'Orsay.

"I'm wearing my favorite new designer. Julian Tennant. He is magnificent. He's the next Karl Lagerfeld," Charlotte raves.

"Who gives a crap who wins at the Oscars? You're my best-dressed winner." Isaac beams, turning to his cameras to shake his head in awe at Julian's work of art. Then, turning back to the dress, he presses his index finger to his lips and with a sigh he adds, "Radiant. Just radiant. This designer is marvelous." Turning back to the camera, Isaac intones, "I've got my eye on you, Julian Tennant."

"Oh and I've got my eye on you, Isaac," Julian yelps. I can hear the springs in Julian's bed at the Chateau squeaking as he jumps up and down on them. "Isaac said Charlotte was his best-dressed winner! Isaac said Charlotte was his best-dressed winner!" Julian sings gleefully. I catch myself about to start jumping up and down with joy on the Red Carpet. "How'd this happen?"

"By the skin of my Julian Tennant ombre beaded gown, that's how," I say.

"You did it, Lola. You did it! You did it! You did it! You got me on that Red Carpet with Karl, Donatella, Oscar, Giorgio, Stella, Marc, Galliano, McQueen. Look out, world, I have arrived! I'm one of the big boys, thanks to you. You've made me a fashion icon!" Julian screams. "Okay, okay, I'm getting ahead of myself." He brings it down a notch. "But you put me on the fashion icon *road*—or should I say *Red Carpet*."

"Julian, get out that tux. You and I are going to be drinking bottles of Dom at Patrick Whitesell's after-party."

"Oh my God, Lola, maybe you can convince Graydon to let me into VF with you now that I'm a fashion star," Julian shrieks.

I spot my family in the sea of Oscar madness, about to enter the theater. "Julian, don't push your luck. I got you to the Oscars. My job is done."

"Lola?" Julian says so softly I can barely hear him through the cacophony of the Red Carpet.

"Yeah?"

"Thank you."

There's nothing to say. The silence between us says everything. What a feat. What a week. I hold the phone up above my head so that Julian can be here with me to taste the delirium of this Oscar frenzy. We did it. I did it.

"Can you hear that?" I say.

"Can I hear it? I think I've lost my hearing *and* the use of my hands."

"It's a rare Prada pratfall," catches my ear. I spin around to see Olivia Cutter in periwinkle Prada, her face crumpling as she speeds away from Joan Rivers. Olivia races up to her manager John to grab Thor out of his arms.

"Julian, quick, turn Joan Rivers back on. I've got to go."
Click.

"The girl looks like Boy George put his eye shadow on a potato sack; it's terrible, terrible, terrible!" clucks Joan Rivers. "Who let the poor girl go out looking like that?"

"Adrienne Hunt," volunteers one of the Wonder Twins standing a few feet away.

"Well, I say we Hunt her down and kill her for dressing Olivia Cutter in that utter disaster."

Where the heck *is* Adrienne? I hope she's watching Joan Rivers. *Please* be watching Joan Rivers. *Please.* I grab one of the Wonder Twins' arms. "I haven't seen Adrienne Hunt, have you?" I ask, trying to sound nonchalant.

"You haven't heard?" she whispers.

"Heard *what?!*" I'm desperate for the dish.

She pulls me inches from her face. "Madonna threw Miuccia a dinner at her house last night and—"

"Wait. Adrienne told me Madonna was in London and that she's staying at her house while she's out of town," I interrupt, recalling Adrienne gloating at Heathrow about staying in Madge's mansion.

"Don't be silly. Adrienne's staying at the Hyatt," she says. "And she should enjoy it while she's there, because it's much more comfortable than the four-by-four cell where she's going."

"*What?*"

"Miuccia spotted one of Trudie Styler's friends last night at Madonna's party wearing a one-of-a-kind Prada sample. When Miuccia asked her where she'd gotten it, she confessed that she bought the dress on eBay." The Twin pauses for emphasis and then cups her hand around my ear. "Apparently Adrienne's been spending hundreds of Prada dollars FedExing Miuccia's one-of-a-kind samples to her sister in Wales, then pocketing *thousands* from her sister selling them for her on eBay," the Twin confides.

"Oh my God," I gasp in shock. Stealing my quilted baby doll bag design in Paris is one thing, but stealing from Miuccia freaking Prada? Adrienne is way more diabolical than even I gave her credit for. I think back on the endless hours I spent praying, meditating, begging Ganesh for Adrienne's demise and now that the moment's arrived, it's even better than I imagined. Game. Set. Match. *Me.*

The Oscars . . .

As the glitterati scurry into their seats in the Kodak Theatre, I look over from my third row center spot between Mom and Christopher to my father, who lets go of his death clamp on Mom's hand so that he can stand up and give Meryl Streep a hug. The amount of sweat collecting in Papa's collar could fill the Bel Air Hotel pond. I'm worried he may ruin M. S.'s makeup as the side of his sweaty face grazes her porcelain cheek. Why isn't Mom budging? I'm stunned she's not taking this opportunity to propel herself into M. S.'s lap and turn her good side to the Laura Ziskin-produced camera close-up. There are three things about my mother at this moment that I've never witnessed before in my twenty-six years as her daughter. One: She doesn't seem to care that we're surrounded by a sea of super-uber's; not a single air kiss has issued from her lips. Two: She hasn't spoken for approximately seven and a half minutes *straight*. Three: She's green. Between her shocking pink ruffled satin Chanel gown and the green tone of her skin, she could double as camouflage at the Beverly Hills Hotel. Then I get it: Mom's afraid Papa won't win. Not because it would look bad for her. But because it would hurt him. And she loves him.

"Are you okay?" I lean in to whisper to Mom, who barely shakes her head yes in response. The lights begin to dim in the theater. My mother catapults her hand around my leg like a vise grip.

"I've never seen so many gorgeous women in so many gorgeous gowns tonight," Ellen DeGeneres says as she takes the stage, which seems to get my mother and father momentarily out of their zombie state. "I knew I couldn't compete, so I just threw this old thing on," she says. "No, not you, Peter O'Toole, this tux."

My laughter is cut short by a glimpse of Olivia stroking Thor's purple fur two rows down. Guess John must have snuck the yappy beast in. I have an unfortunate flash of her stroking SMITH—or worse—him stroking *her*. A wave of nausea moves through me.

George Clooney steps onstage to present the award for Best Actress. I'm so distracted by just how damn dashing he is that I actually forget where I am. I've sworn off actors forever, but maybe I could relegate him to the director category? Or the producer category? I'd march straight to Barneys after the Awards to return that Bottega Veneta tiger snake Amarillo bag I begged, borrowed, and stole to get, to get *him* out of the actor category. He's so supremely stunning, it actually deters me from the moment at hand—that he's about to settle Olivia Cutter's fate. George begins to read the list of nominees.

"Catherine Zeta-Jones, for her role as a plucky Wal-Mart worker slash single mom who leads an employee revolt in *Silent Smiley Sunday* . . ."

As George ticks off the other nominees, I don't even hear what he's saying; I'm too busy praying. Please God, do not let that woman, that witch, that wacko win an Oscar. *Please.* I close my eyes as he opens the envelope.

"And the Oscar goes to—" I take a deep breath. "Catherine Zeta-Jones for *Silent Smiley Sunday*," he announces. Yes!

I jump out of my seat to start the standing ovation and catch myself before I let out an audible cheer. Of *course* Catherine Zeta-Jones would triumph at the Oscars, for *Pete's sake.* Just as I'm fully reveling in Olivia's loss I catch a glimpse of her running down the aisle and out of the theater in that *disaster* of a Prada potato sack, with Thor scurrying behind. Suddenly my day just got *a lot* better.

Renée Zellweger is striding toward the microphone in a skin-tight sapphire strapless Carolina Herrera to present the award for Best Actor. I scan the theater for Kate. There she is, flanking Will Bailey on one side, Mama Bailey on his other. As the lights dim in the theater and a scene of Best Actor nominee Joaquin Phoenix lights up the screen above R. Z.'s head, Kate whispers something in Will's ear as Mama Bailey smoothes his hair. When the scene comes to an end, all the cameras in the house focus on Joaquin Phoenix where he sits beaming intensity from the second row. R. Z. squints her eyes and purses her painted lips as she moves onto the next nominee.

"And *Will Bailey* for his portrayal of Raul Sanchez in *The Day Before Today Is Yesterday*," she says as a clip of Will's performance as the gay Mexican philosopher who's murdered by homophobic bandits is projected onto the screen. As Will falls to the ground in his death scene, the lights come back up in the theater and the cameras swing to Will, grinning in his Prada tuxedo from the third row. All eyes are fixed on R. Z. center stage as she lifts the envelope.

"And the Oscar goes to . . . Will Bailey for *The Day Before Today Is Yesterday!*" R. Z. yells, as the theater erupts in applause. Will and Kate jump out of their seats and embrace. As Will bounds over his mother to make his way toward the stage, Mama Bailey clutches the back of Will's tuxedo jacket and ricochets him back into her arms for a kiss. Will takes the stairs toward the podium in twos. When he finally reaches R. Z., he gives her a huge, sloppy kiss on the lips and grabs the Oscar out of her hands.

"I'm stunned. I'm just—um—stunned. Mom, this is for you," Will says, waving the Little Gold Man in the air. He turns to walk away. What? That's *it*? What about Kate? No! Just as R. Z. threads her naked arm through his to walk offstage, Will turns back to the microphone. "Oh, and I'd like to thank my incredible agent, Kate Woods, who's been by my side since the beginning." Thank *God*. I turn to Kate. As her tears fall onto the sky blue chiffon bodice of her Marc Jacobs gown, I realize this is the first time I've seen my best friend cry since we were sixteen in that bathroom in Texas.

"Because the show is green—" Ellen DeGeneres resumes her post at the dais, snapping me back to the moment at hand "—the Academy wants me to recycle some of my older jokes."

The theater roars with laughter. Save for Mom—stone silent next to me—and Papa—who is now sporting his own shade of Grey Poupon. He hasn't moved his white knuckles from my mother's thigh for the last two hours. And now here it comes. Papa's fate. The train of Julia Roberts's champagne Gianfranco Ferre peeks out from her position backstage where she awaits her cue to stride those long legs onto the stage and announce who will take home the Best Director Oscar.

This is it. Julia Roberts takes her place center stage, dwarfing Ellen DeGeneres by a good three feet. A drip of sweat trickles down Papa's cheek. I consider passing him Christopher's flask, but stop myself when I realize there's a camera now recording his every move. I hope the hundreds of millions of viewers don't recognize a Xanax haze when they see one.

Julia Roberts clears her golden throat. "And the Oscar goes to—my favorite director. I'm still waiting to get to work with you—" Okay, J. R., get on with it. This is not about *you* for crying out loud. "—*Paulie Santisi* for *Whispered Screams!*" Julia Roberts announces with that huge, gleaming smile.

"Oh my God," I yelp, jumping out of my seat. Papa remains planted in his seat in shock as the entire Kodak Theatre roars to their feet. My mother immediately comes back to life, pulling him up and wrapping her arms around him, covering his face in kisses. Finally he smiles— something I haven't seen him do in, oh—*ever*. The mustard tone of his skin melts back to olive. Tom Hanks reaches out to him from the row in front of us as Papa makes his way down the aisle. He looks unsteady on his feet as he climbs the stairs to accept his award. I'm caught off guard by the surge of emotion plowing through me. It's a feeling I never imagined I'd have for my father—genuine happiness.

"God, it feels really good to be back," Papa says, clutching that Oscar by its throat. The crowd claps as Papa shakes his head in disbelief. "I'd like to thank my wife Blanca, who's been on this rocky road with me for thirty-five years and is still here and as beautiful as the day we met. My kids, Christopher and Lola, I love you."

I look to Christopher sitting next to me stoically and wonder if he's thinking what I am—that it takes a stage for our father to tell us he loves us. I take my brother's hand and I squeeze it hard.

"Ow, that hurts," he whispers, looking at me.

"I'm sorry," I say, looking back at him, as a tear rolls down my cheek.

In the limo on the way to Morton's for the *VF* party, I can't help but think how *wrong* Julian was. Happy Hollywood Endings totally happen in *real* life. At least in Hollywood.

vanity fair redux

---

2 hours, 30 minutes, 19 seconds since
the Oscar for Best Director was handed out.

C*UT TO*: Two-and-a-half hours, a flute of champagne, and at least one of Uncle J's scotch and waters later. The bobby pins in this chignon are causing pinpoint hemorrhages in my scalp. I'm drunk. I'm queasy from that In-N-Out cheeseburger—and the sight of SMITH's tongue so far down Olivia Cutter's throat that he could give her an appendectomy. *And* I just found my father in the bathroom stall of Morton's at the *VF* Party with his shimmering gold Oscar clutched tightly in one hand and *Charlotte Martin*'s Mystic Tanned, purple-peacock-sheathed ass in the other.

I've got to get out of here. I've got to find Kate. The bathroom door slams behind me. As I try to steady myself on these stilettos, it hits me like a ton of Oscars to the head.

I guess Happy Hollywood Endings don't even happen *in* Hollywood.

On second thought, it's *so* Hollywood—isn't it? America's Sweetheart diddling my dad in the purple peacock gown Julian paralyzed his hands making with fabric from the ladies' *bathroom* at Empress Pavilion in Chinatown for Olivia Cutter who's now shtupping my no-longer BOYFRIEND. If I pitched my story to Stacey Snider at DreamWorks, she'd tell me it was over the top. My answer: *of course* it is.

Thank heavens, there's Kate rushing through the crowd toward me. But her face is drained of all color and her blue eyes look gray. Her dark chocolate hair flies wildly around her head. Her Marc Jacobs chiffon dress hangs limply, a feat on such a perfectly sculpted figure. She isn't teetering on *Girl, Interrupted*. She's full throttle. This is only the third time in the eleven years she's been my best friend that I've witnessed her G. I. Jane steely exterior crack. I grab her shoulders to steady her.

"You first," I say.

"My life is over," she exclaims. "Will Bailey just *fired* me."

"I just caught my father doing *Charlotte Martin* in the bathroom." We stand there staring at each other in silence and shock, wearing the weight of this whole wretched week on our couture-clad shoulders.

"Did you hear me?" Kate says stunned.

"Did you hear *me?*" I say, equally stunned. "Jesus, I'm sorry," I say. "Are you okay?"

"Are *you?*"

"Yes," I finally say. "I'm okay." I may be drunk and queasy, but I *am* okay. Papa's *never* going to change. But I have. And for the first time in my life, I feel something toward my father that I've never felt before: acceptance—for who and what he is. "I'm okay," I say again.

"I'm glad you're okay: I'm not. Will told me that now that he has an Oscar, he wants to go to the next level. He said I'd always see him as the guy who works at zpizza, but that Ed Limato sees him as a *movie star*," Kate says.

"Oh my God. Will just thanked you on national television, for crying out loud," I say in disbelief.

"Don't remind me. I'll never get to CAA now."

"Screw Will Bailey and his *mommy*. You don't need Will Bailey to get to CAA." Kate looks unsure, a look I'm not used to seeing her wear. But as the words come out of me, I become *more* sure. Just like Kate doesn't need Will Bailey to get to CAA, I don't need Papa or some Idiot Actor Boyfriend to get to—well, wherever it is I'm going. "Kate, Will Bailey doesn't deserve you. And you *will* find the *next* Will Bailey," I say, and I can tell that somewhere deep down, my best friend knows I'm right. And deep down I know that I'm going to be *okay*. I'm going to be better than okay. I survived Oscar Week *and* my whole Hollyweird Life thus far. And I'm still standing on these four-inch Louboutins. "And you did just close that five-million deal for Will at Sony, so you still get to keep that commission, right?"

"Actually, I got Sony up to seven-point-five."

"That's my girl. Come here," I say, wrapping Kate in a hug. "Kate, Will *is* an *actor,* what'd you expect?" I say with a poker face.

"Your father *is* a director. What did you expect?"

"More."

"I know," Kate says, hugging me right back. "Forget actors. From now on, I'm working exclusively with writers, directors, and *animals,*" she says, back to being Kate.

"Come on, let's get Christopher and get outta here," I say.

"Kate, darling, you'll have to excuse us," my mother says, hands fluttering in excitement as she joins our huddle. "Come, Lola, *Bernard Arnault* wants to meet *you!*" she says, grabbing me by the arm and dragging me toward the fashion world's Bill Gates, a dapper, gray-haired man in an immaculately tailored tux. I quickly try to calculate the number of Louis Vuitton, Christian Dior, Marc Jacobs, Fendi bags, gowns, shoes, sunglasses that were sold to make him the seventh richest man in the world. I have to stop myself before I go into a fashion seizure and grand mal myself at his Vuitton tux shoes.

"I'll get Christopher and the car," Kate yells after us.

Mom plants me in front of the Chairman of Louis Vuitton Moët Hennessy. "Bernard, here she is. The woman who put Charlotte Martin in Julian Tennant tonight. I'll leave you two to talk," she says, disappearing into the crush of well-wishers.

"Congratulations, Lola. Your mother tells me you're responsible for Julian Tennant's success on the Red Carpet tonight," Bernard says.

"Well, I can't take all the credit; Julian did design the most beautiful gown I've ever seen," I say.

"I'd like to buy the company," he says.

I stare at him in disbelief. Bernard Arnault can't be *serious*. Can he? He doesn't seem like a man who jokes about *fashion*. I stare searchingly into his eyes. Oh my God, he's stone cold serious. The chairman of freaking LVMH wants to *buy* Julian's company!

"I've had my eye on Julian's career since his first show and I always believed he had the potential to be as big as Marc Jacobs," Bernard says. "Tonight you proved me right. I'm going to be in town until Wednesday. I'd like to sit down with Marty Glickman. Is that something you can arrange?"

"Well, I could—but Marty no longer owns Julian Tennant."

"Oh. When did that happen?"

"Just this morning," I say. And I can't help smiling like the cat who ate Marty Glickman.

"Who should I talk to about making this deal?"

Deep cleansing breath. Act *as if*. NO! Make that, act *as am*. "Julian," I say. "And me. The Chateau tomorrow. One o'clock?"

"I look forward to it," he says.

"See you then," I say, as Bernard Arnault walks over to hug Uma Thurman.

Take that, Marty Glickman. And *that,* Adrienne Hunt. And *that,* Olivia Cutter. *LVMH* is going to *buy* Julian Tennant. My BGF is going to be even bigger than Marc Jacobs.

I turn around and spot Mom way across the room, chatting with Katie Couric. She turns and looks at me and raises her hand to give me the thumbs-up. I blow her a kiss, feeling a sudden wave of love for my mother, who in her own way does her best for all of us. She throws me back a kiss. And as I see my father traversing across the room with that Oscar in one hand and his other stretched out to Mom, I know that in their own way they make as much sense as Lucy and Desi—or anything else in Hollywood. And I know that I will never, ever tell her what I saw in the bathroom stall tonight.

I bolt outside to tell Kate and Christopher the mind-blowing news. I *have* to say it out loud to my best friend and big brother so that I'm certain I'm not dreaming—which I'm scared I may be. I spot Christopher talking to—Cricket, who's jumping up and down. What's she doing *here*—and why is she jumping up and down like a springer spaniel? Where's Kate? Oh there she is, talking to—*Bryan Lourd.* Maybe I *am* dreaming. I rush over to Cricket and Christopher.

"I got the part! I got the part!" Cricket shrieks.

"Slow down. What part? And could you stop jumping up and down like that?"

"Oh sorry," she says, planting her Jimmy Choos on the pavement. "I'm the *Next* Nicole Kidman. Jerry Bruckheimer just hired me to star opposite Orlando Bloom in *Days of Thunder 2!*" she screams.

"Oh my God!" I yelp, grabbing Cricket. I can't resist the urge to jump up and down myself. Our pogo-ing is interrupted by a familiar voice.

"Hi, Cricket, Bryan Lourd," he says, slicing his hand between Cricket and me to introduce himself to my BAF. "Congratulations on the Bruckheimer picture," he says, shaking Cricket's hand.

"Thanks," Cricket says.

"I'd like you to come up to our office tomorrow so that I can introduce you to everyone at CAA," he says.

"I really appreciate the offer, Bryan, but I already have the world's greatest agent. She's smart, she's devoted, she's loyal, she's—"

"I know. That's why I just hired Kate," Bryan cuts Cricket off.

"You *what?*" Cricket, Christopher, and I gasp in unison.

"You heard the man. I'm moving to CAA," Kate interjects, materializing at Bryan's shoulder, beaming brighter than the Big Dipper.

"Kate and I have another project we want to talk to you about, too, Cricket," Bryan says. "Paramount has decided to dump Olivia Cutter and go with unknowns for the remake of *Grease,* and we think you'd be just perfect. Cricket, Kate, I'll call you tomorrow," Bryan says, turning to leave, "And Kate? Better send over a box of Montblancs. We have a lot of signing to do. Maybe you'll have some ideas for the next Danny Zuko. We're drop-kicking Olivia's choice."

Kate, Cricket, and I do a major group pogo the second Bryan's back is turned. Of course, I'm absolutely thrilled that my BFF and BAF are getting exactly what they deserved. But how delicious that SMITH is too? As I jump up and down on my Louboutins I can't help singing: *You're NOT the one that they want, oh-hoo-hoo, honey.*

Suddenly that familiar, grating British accent catches my ear. I turn and spot the source of *that* voice—one Adrienne Hunt—in head-to-toe black Prada, Gitane in mouth, out on bail I suspect, standing right where she belongs—*behind* the red velvet rope.

"Check *again.* Adrienne Hunt. H-U-N-T. Graydon put me on the list *personally.*"

"I'm sorry, miss, but your name's been crossed off the list." *Ouch.* I guess news in Hollywood travels faster than on CNN.com. Before I can fully digest what a bitch karma really is I hear—

"Lola." I spin around. It's SMITH.

"Lola," someone calls out from the other direction. I turn around. It's Jake Jones.

I look away and spot George Clooney. He smiles. Is he smiling at *me?* Oh God. Oh no. He's smiling at me. I look over to SMITH, then to Jake Jones, then back to George Clooney. SMITH. Jake Jones. George Clooney. SMITH. Jake Jones. George Clooney. *Screw that.* I'm JUMP-ING, LEAPING, HOPPING, DIVING, THROWING myself back on that actor sobriety wagon—*for good.* My name is Lola Santisi and I'm a *recovered* Actorholic. Day One and counting. I take a final look at SMITH, Jake Jones, and George Clooney and then I start running—no, *sprinting*—in the other direction.

"AAAAAAAAAAAAHHHHHHHH!" My four-inch Louboutin stilettos slip on the sidewalk and I go flying headfirst into Charlotte Martin puking into a planted palm.

"Let's see, party with Leo, Jude, Orlando, and Owen at Patrick White-sell's super uber after-after party at some fab mansion in the Hollywood Hills *or* hang out in the emergency room at Cedars," Julian says, striding into the crowded, fluorescent-lit waiting room in his Gucci tux where Kate, Christopher, and Cricket have been dutifully by my side for the past forty-five minutes.

"Julian, I'm so sorry," I say, wincing as Christopher adjusts the bag of ice pressed to my swollen ankle.

"Shut up. *Bernard Arnault* wants to buy my company because *you* got Charlotte Martin to wear my purple peacock gown to the Oscars.

You have a get-out-of-Julian-jail pass for life. Besides, I work for you. You're the CEO of Julian Tennant now," he says. "And I know three women who will be absolutely perfect as the head seamstresses for Maison Julian!"

"If you want Imas, Maria, and Isabella, you're going to have to fight Larry Gagosian for them," I say. "Thanks to me, he's going to be mounting an exhibition at his gallery of that Abuse Quilt I was telling you about. Half of Hollywood is in it! Larry's using the title I suggested for the show: 'A-List is for Assholes.'"

"I have a feeling Jake Jones and Olivia Cutter won't be lining up to see it," says Cricket.

"Nor will SMITH." I smile. "Turns out Isabella was his housekeeper."

"We've got a lot to celebrate," Julian says. "Christopher, would you mind doing the honors?" He hands over the bottle of Cristal tucked under his arm.

"I'd like to propose a toast," I say, raising my plastic cup full of champagne in the air. "To all of us for surviving Oscar Week. None of it would mean anything without you. To my BGF, who's going to be bigger than Marc Jacobs; to my BFF, the CAA super agent; to my BAF, the *Next* Nicole Kidman; and to my big brother Christopher, whose Burning Man documentary will be nominated for an Academy Award next year—once he finishes it: I love you guys."

"We love you," they echo back.

Christopher leans over and kisses Kate. Not even her ringing cell—or is that her BlackBerry—stops her from kissing him back.

"Lola Santisi," a nurse calls out.

I limp off my chair and follow her back to a stark, tiny room where I hobble onto the cold exam table. Sitting under the supremely unflattering fluorescent lights, I'm reminded just how much I hate hospitals. But as I sit here all alone looking at my busted ankle and my broken Louboutin in my hand, I realize how *un*broken I am. For the first time in my whole Hollyweird Life. I like it. I have *arrived*. I'm not sure *this* is exactly where I want to arrive *to*—but it's a start. And I'm switching to flats for a while.

There's a knock on the door.

"Come in," I say.

The door swings open and in walks . . . Therapy Guy. What's he doing here? And why's he wearing a white coat? I squint at the nametag. Dr. Levin? Dr. Levin is—Therapy Guy?! Yes, that's right. Sitting outside Dr. Gilmore's office all along was a *real live doctor*. Not someone who plays a doctor, not someone who went to Lee Strasberg: someone who went to an actual medical school. I smile into those kind eyes and he smiles right back.

"Wow, you look nice," Dr. Levin says, eyeing my Julian Tennant gown. "Any particular occasion?"

The End

acknowledgments

thank you to our dream team: Leonard Golderg, our mentor, for reading the hundredth draft as though it was the first, and shepherding us from the very beginning with your wisdom, wit, and ability to see clearly what we couldn't; Deborah Schneider, our uber agent, for being our greatest champion from the moment our manuscript landed on your desk and making our dream of becoming bona fide authors a reality; Jennifer Weis, our editor, for seeing our highest potential and then guiding us toward it; Betsy Rapoport, our teacher, for your remarkable lessons in writing—and life.

To our family: Anna and Larry Halprin, for your inspiration; Jahan Khalighi, for being a constant reminder of what really matters; Richard and John Mirisch, for always believing in your little cis; Toni and David Yarnell for your humor, love, and encouragement.

To Philip Raskind: I love you—even when I'm writing.

To our behind the scenes saviors: Michael Lynton, for getting us started; David Unger, for fortuitously introducing us to a couple of twinheads that fateful Oscar Week night; Edwin Chapman, Stefanie Lindskog, John Murphy, Hilary Rubin, Steve Troha, and the rest of our supreme team at St. Martin's, helmed by the incomparable Sally Richardson, for your excitement and support; Cathy Gleason, Julie Johnson, and Jaime Toporovich for your impeccable back-up.

For sharing your stories and counsel: Marisa Gallagher, Samantha Gregor, Nancy Himmel, Marisa Leichtling, Corwin Moore, Mally Roncal, and Debi Sokol-Treiman.

For honoring us with your sublime vision and friendship: McG.

For gracing us with your visionary style: Liz Goldwyn.

For your remarkable artistry: Richard Choi and Byron Williams.

For being one menchy Queen PR Bee: Sandi Mendelson.

To our emotional, spiritual, and creative triage team during the writing of this book. Thank you for putting up with us. Without you we couldn't have made it through: China Chow, Maxwell Federbush, Abby Feldman, Chelsea Gilmore, Stephen Hanks, Amy Pakter, Angela McNally Schell, and Emily Wagner. We can have dinner now and talk about you.